House Rules

Nan A. Talese
Doubleday
New York   London   Toronto   Sydney   Auckland

House Rules

Heather Lewis

PUBLISHED BY NAN A. TALESE
an imprint of Doubleday, a division of
Bantam Doubleday Dell Publishing Group, Inc.
1540 Broadway, New York, New York 10036

DOUBLEDAY is a trademark of Doubleday,
a division of Bantam Doubleday Dell
Publishing Group, Inc.

Library of Congress Cataloging-in-Publication Data

Lewis, Heather.
    House rules / Heather Lewis. — 1st ed.
        p.   cm.
        1. Teenage girls—Fiction.   I. Title.
    PS3562.E9453H68   1994
    813'.54—dc20   93-25614
                                             CIP

Book design by Claire Naylon Vaccaro

ISBN 0-385-47210-2

To

Constance

Jones,

for

every

single

day

And

to

Allan

Gurganus,

my

first

trustee

Acknowledgments

For a long time I've looked forward to thanking the people who helped me make this book. First, Meredith Carr, for having and instilling faith, and for seeing things through with me as well as seeing through things.

I'd also like to thank my close friends and close readers Mark Ameen, James Baker, Bree Burns, and Elizabeth Ilgenfritz. I'm indebted to Jerry Mundis for practical guidance and to Amanda Urban for editorial advice. And for early and continued encouragement, I want to thank Peggy Montgomery, Karen Rinaldi, Kathy Bonomi, Maria Epes, Betsy Wilcox, Linsey Abrams, Jane Cooper, Joan Larkin, and Grace Paley.

I'm extremely grateful to my agent, Malaga Baldi, for her belief in the book. And I'm thankful to Nan A. Talese and my editor, Jesse Cohen, for taking such good care of me.

Always remember, never forget,

damage is the house from which

we place our bet. The cause of

your suffering is the source of

your pride. Endure life on earth

without thickening your hide.

—*Mark Ameen,*

"Monologue of a Dying Beast"

one

1

I guess you'd say it started when I got kicked out of school.

It's not like I did anything so especially wrong. We had a party, some boys in the dorm. I got caught on the staircase literally holding the bag. There wasn't much in it, just a little bit of pot. I don't even like pot. I don't like boys for that matter either, at least not in the way that makes dorm proctors nervous.

I figured I got what was coming to me. Felt lucky it wasn't something the dean wanted to bring the police into. My parents, they blamed the school. Said the administration was making me an example. But of course when I called, I told them I'd only tried pot that once, just dumb bad luck. They believed me. Believing me makes life easier for them and this gives me a reason to keep on lying.

My lies on the phone that night were minor. At least at the time I thought they were. I said I had things worked out, had covered the options and picked the best one. Since it was so near midwinter vacation, I told them, it'd be hard to get me into another school. This was nearly true. I told them Silas had already agreed to put me up for a while, let me work for him at the stable. I figured this was true too, just not yet.

My mom, she agreed with all this, said it sounded like the

best solution. My dad, he was on the other extension wanting me home. My mom and me, we ignored him, pretended he wasn't talking at all. I pretended he wasn't even there.

So, I hung up thinking I'd taken care of it all. It wasn't until I made the next call and the phone kept ringing that it occurred to me Silas might not be around. It took me a minute to remember he'd be in Florida now, along with everybody else. I'd been so caught up, I'd forgotten about Florida—the horse world's yearly migration south. By now Jacksonville'd be finished and they'd've moved on to Ocala. Unless I wanted to wind up at home, I'd need a way to get down there.

It didn't take me too long to think of Liza Pierson. She still owed me money for some hash. Liza neglected her debts more from absentmindedness than lack of funds. She's one of those big-hearted Connecticut girls who wear wraparound skirts. She'd been friendly from the start and this made it easier to put my hand out.

She greeted my knock with the phone tucked under her elbow and the receiver still live against her ear. She motioned me in and finished her call quickly. Liza has good manners and she exercises them without discernment. "Lee, my God," she said, "I'm so sorry about what's happened."

She effused sympathy and I basked. Recognizing the shallowness behind my overnight celebrity didn't keep me from enjoying it. At the end of her commiseration she offered help.

"Well, I could really use that money," I began.

"Of course. How much was it anyway?"

The opportunity presented itself. I ran numbers in my head weighing how much I could add on and still feel fair. I came up with a figure, then just blurted out, "Could you get me a plane ticket instead?"

She put down her checkbook. "I don't know. I guess so. Where do you want to go?"

"Florida. They want me to leave here sort of quickly and my parents are away. I'm going to stay with relatives." The explanation was unnecessary. I recited it more for practice.

Liza looked uncertain, but willing. "I guess I should call my travel agent," she said.

"Maybe you should just call the airline." I didn't want too many records trailing me. I needed at least a head start.

"I've never done it that way."

"It's easy, you want me to . . ."

"No, I can do it. Just let me get my wits together."

Liza always took forever to gather her wits. I ached to grab her wallet, extract her credit card, and get on the phone. The same ache as when a dealer plays with you, makes you socialize when all you want is your stuff. I offered what help I could without pushing. Finally she secured my flight to Gainesville, the closest airport to Ocala. "You pick up your ticket when you check your bags," she said. "Hey, how on earth are you going to get to the airport?"

I hadn't really thought that far. We were a long way from Kennedy. I considered asking for more help, but didn't. Better to spread the favors around. "Oh I'm sure there's one of those airport limos pretty close by."

She tried to place it.

"You know the ones painted orange or green with all the doors?"

She faked recognition and forced this sad little grin that reminded me I liked her. "Guess this is it," I said, pasting on my own smile.

"Wait, you'll need this for the airport. Just mail it back." She handed me her credit card. I stood astonished. I'd completely forgotten I had to pay for the ticket. Hadn't realized how far I'd asked her to trust me. I thanked her four times and even threw my arms around her. But I still left her room wondering whether

I'd honor her trust. I could do a lot of damage with that card and it'd take a long time for anyone to notice. I tried to believe I'd surprise myself. Even vowed to write an envelope before I left so I could mail the card from the airport. I never quite could understand why things like this were so difficult for me, when for other people they seemed commonplace.

I sold most of my belongings. People bought out of curiosity and charity more than want or need. Their motives didn't matter though—the $435 did.

The next morning I left early, before I'd attract any more attention. A taxi took me to the limo drop and before I knew it, I was ensconced in the back-row seat of an orange-and-blue car with twelve doors.

I sat there sort of dreaming, but my body stayed rigid. My mind slipped around, wouldn't let anything hold its attention. Drawing pictures in the window's fog made me particularly restless, so instead I worked up a string of what ifs about Silas. I think I'd needed to be in motion before I could let myself know how big I'd gambled.

It wasn't that Silas wouldn't take me in; he would. He'd been doing that since I was eight, but always temporarily. A few weeks, maybe a month or two, that's how long I'd last before giving in to my father's pull. And then there was always Jeannie's push. She's Silas's wife and she wants me around about as much as my mother does.

Boarding school'd solved it, but here I'd gone and fucked that up, and in less than six months. Silas, he'd been the knee-jerk fix, but I knew I'd have to come up with something better or else be home by Easter.

When his phone kept ringing and I remembered Florida, right then I started thinking about Tory. I knew she'd be down there, and knowing it kept me moving. Right now, it kept my leg moving, twitching in a way I couldn't easily stop, and so when I saw the signs for Kennedy, I finally gave up trying.

As we funneled into the stream of cars and taxis and buses anxious for departure, I could almost manage to believe this was my anxiousness, too—an ordinary kind, having nothing to do with my fear that all the little things Tory'd said to me might still add up to nothing. That the only thing between us was my crush and going down there'd prove it to me.

Bumping up curbside, I forgot all this. Almost did. The worry stayed in my legs, keeping them twitchy and hard to control. Still, I hauled my bags, quite a few of them, into the Delta terminal and plunked them down at the end of the check-in line. Standing there seemed easier than walking and I began looking forward to being free of the garment bag, boot bag, duffel bags. It seemed once I accomplished this, everything would get better. I'd started measuring comfort by small degrees and walking unencumbered ranked high on that scale.

When my turn in line came, I half-dragged, half-kicked my things to the counter and then hoisted them onto the stainless steel platform. The sound scraped my gums, reminded me of veterinary examining tables and frightened animals. I hugged my tongue to my teeth and pressed the garment bag against my chest; looked to the woman behind the counter for some sort of help. She so embodied the ideal of airline personnel I feared I might've invented her, especially when I saw the red-white-and-blue name tag that said Cheryl Dallas.

"Good morning," she said. "How may I help you?"

I gave her my flight number and Liza's name, which I had to repeat since I mumbled it so bad the first go-round. I didn't think anyone would believe my name was Liza, but Cheryl

Dallas did. Her perfectly groomed fingernails entered my alias into the computer while my unlacquered but clean ones fidgeted on the counter. I picked up a pamphlet describing flight insurance, something I thought maybe I should consider.

"Here we are, Miss Pierson, first-class passage to Gainesville. Would you like an aisle or a window?"

I couldn't believe Liza'd booked me into first class. I wondered if it was force of habit or because she'd made the reservation so late. I was glad I hadn't known beforehand. I felt guilty enough already. She'd only owed me about sixty bucks. I promised myself I'd mail her credit card back as soon as I got to Ocala, as soon as all this airline stuff was over.

Cheryl Dallas still waited for my answer, but I'd forgotten the question. "Miss Pierson?" she said. "Aisle or window?"

I chose an aisle; easy escape is always important to me. Nonsmoking was a clear choice too—it had already become very hard to breathe. I handed over the credit card. It wasn't Liza's American Express, thank god, but her less assuming Visa. Even Liza wasn't going to send me off with an unlimited credit line.

When Cheryl Dallas handed me the bill and the pen, I shifted my garment bag; acted like it weighed a million pounds. I hadn't practiced the signature. Usually the first time you write it's the best anyway; after that you start thinking. I sort of hunched over, made like I had trouble holding the paper, all this to add to my authenticity, to the authenticity of the signature. I dashed it off as I'd seen Liza do so many times. Having a visual of her in action could only help. Still, as I handed it back I watched closely for any sign that Cheryl Dallas was reaching for the little red button under the counter.

Instead she gave me my boarding pass with a smile. "Enjoy your flight," she said. She sounded like she meant it.

When I got to the gate the last few people were boarding. I followed them through the carpeted tunnel and onto the plane. Since it was a breakfast flight, the stewardesses were big on champagne. They practically poured you a glass as you stepped on board—at least once they saw you weren't headed back to coach.

I figured it'd be best if I didn't look anxious to get drunk, so I declined. I took it as a good sign they offered, though. See, I'm fifteen and nobody really questions it if I claim to be eighteen. Sometimes, though, I get trouble on planes. Twenty-one's a lot harder for me to pull off and I knew if I gave them reason, they'd start asking. Then it'd already be over. I found my seat quietly, fastened my seat belt, and began wishing for a Bloody Mary.

My neighbor soon arrived, a gray-suited top-drawer type whose neck spilled over a shirt collar so crisply starched I expected it to draw blood. He settled into the window seat with friendly apologies for disrupting me. I gauged his potential as an ally for procuring drinks and since he reminded me of fathers of boarding school friends, I rated him high.

As soon as he took his seat, he threw his newspaper down beside his briefcase and turned my way.

"Fred Waters," he said, extending his hand.

I introduced myself, stealing a glance at his briefcase. The F.W. monogram stared back, but didn't prove anything.

"You know, I have a daughter about your age. Headed down to visit her at college. She's a senior at the university. You a senior?"

I looked for the wink in his eye, but didn't see it yet. "Nope, still a junior," I said.

"One more year of fun then."

I smiled and nodded.

He asked me about my major, what college I went to, all

that kind of thing. Luckily he was the type who took what you said and ran with it awhile. I didn't have to fill in too many details and so I got through takeoff without any fumbles.

As soon as the no-smoking sign chimed off, the stewardess came by asking about drinks.

"What're you having?" my neighbor asked.

"I'd like a Bloody Mary." I said it to him, more to shore up our alliance than to avoid the stewardess.

"Two Bloody Marys," he said, holding up fingers.

She mixed the drinks and he handed me mine.

I thanked him and then took a long swallow. The alcohol took no detours. It went right for the main wires and started unplugging. I hadn't really slept in a couple of days and was now real aware of it. My body dropped further into the seat. I hoped old Fred wasn't talking to me, because I sure couldn't hear him. Soon enough, though, I felt his hand on my knee, a light little shake. I turned toward him.

"I said, would you like to change seats?"

"What?" I asked.

"Would you like the window seat? I was just thinking how my daughter always likes the window seat and that maybe you would like my seat."

I sat there for a minute weighing how important it was to him, how important he was to me. "Oh yeah, that'd be real nice," I said. "Thanks."

He put up our tables and then did a lot of awkward shuffling. Shoved the armrest up so I could "just slide right over." He didn't put the armrest back and I was pretty sure I wasn't supposed to either, especially when he sat right about where it would've gone. My body wired up from touching his. I looked out the window while I finished my drink. Fred ordered another round.

The second round came on the heels of the breakfast trays.

The stewardess had covered our tables and laps with these over-sized cloth napkins. That left us pretty well draped and Fred's hand slipped onto my thigh. I started to eat, but the first bite left me knowing I didn't feel so good, whether about the events of the last few days or the last few minutes I wasn't too sure.

Fred noticed. "You young girls worry way too much about your weight," he observed. He was putting it away himself, quite an expert at eating with one hand. "You should relax and enjoy more." He punctuated this statement by squeezing my thigh.

"No, it's not that. I already ate."

He looked unconvinced, but let it drop. I sucked down that second drink. He kept up and ordered again. By the end of the third drink, I'd hit an absent state of calm. Began not to care where his hand was. Began holding up my end of the bargain. I reclined my seat so that it was even with his and decided he really thought I was twenty-one or two.

His hand slid up further, stroked between my legs. He'd stopped talking now. Our fourth round of drinks sat untouched on the trays. I felt sure I'd gag on the thickness if I tried to drink mine. I looked directly at Fred for maybe the first time. He still looked crisp, that sharp collar so tight against his neck I was choking for him. His eyes were closed and he looked so peaceful that when he took my hand and pressed it against his crotch I was surprised how much his grip hurt, how relieved I was when he let go.

He returned his hand to my lap and unbuttoned my pants. Wasted no time getting in my underwear. I kept looking at him. Knew he wouldn't open his eyes now. His fingers lost any pretense of tenderness and just rammed in. I shifted in my seat trying to find some comfort. His other hand rubbed mine up and down his prick. I looked around us. If anyone was noticing they sure weren't acknowledging it.

I closed my eyes. Played ostrich like Fred. But even with them closed I kept picturing his neck. That collar slicing it. The blood hovering in beads before rolling across the stiff white cloth. It doesn't leave a trace until it drops to his shoulder, begins forming a sticky puddle there. In my mind, we both ignore this. Ignore it so well that when he turns toward me with his face contorted, I think it's from coming, then realize the movement's slit his throat.

His hand lurched then. The sharpness in my belly grabbed me back. He dropped my hand; pushed it away from his lap. I opened my eyes; saw him heading for the restroom. I buttoned my pants, slid out from under the trays, all that linen. I crossed the cabin. Locked myself in the other restroom, leaned back against the door and pushed my pants down. I wanted that orgasm as fast as it could happen. Without it I'd always be sitting in that seat with his hand up my cunt.

I brought myself off in a way that made me weak-kneed. I told myself that's the alcohol. I peed, then buttoned my pants, washed my face. All the time avoided the mirror. On the way back to my seat I got a vodka. The stewardess handed me a glass with ice and the small bottle and I wondered if it would've been this easy without my neighbor. But then there's no point pretending this was about getting drinks and getting drunk and then letting him.

The thing is this stuff follows me around and once it starts I can't move till it's over. The drinks make it easier, not the other way around, though I'd like it better if you thought I just know how things work and so work them.

I got back to our seats before he did. Our trays had been cleared, the linen was gone. I sat down and poured my drink. Left the tray up. I didn't need to, though. When he came back, he couldn't look at me. Had decided his newspaper was what he'd wanted all along. I decided he really had a daughter my age. He was too familiar not to. I sat there and sipped my drink. Enjoyed his discomfort. His loosened collar. That he read the same page until we landed. My drink nursed me until then. And walking off the plane, I could convince myself I had the upper hand, even if it was on his dick. After all, who made who run?

2

Once I collected my bags, I found a pay phone. I'd planned to call Silas but then I realized that'd mean trying to get a number for the showgrounds and then waiting while somebody tracked him down and then, too, right off he'd be fussing and worrying and that'd get Jeannie's back up.

I figured the simplest thing was to try K.C. She was about my best friend when it came to horse-show kids. Or really I guess she was my only friend. We'd found each other by default. Since we were the only kids traveling without parents the rest of the kids got warned off us, and so with them keeping their distance we were left to each other.

The arrangement suited us fine, at least that's what we told each other. Mostly it did, though the years of slights had made K.C. more flamboyant than she might otherwise have been. That's how I saw it, anyway. Drugs, sex—she didn't do anything the other kids weren't doing, not really, it was just she refused to be polite about it, refused to hide it. And, for that, the old guard came down hard.

For these people everything depended upon not seeing what went on in front of their faces. They doled K.C. great dollops of hate. Served her a kind of specialized scorn usually reserved for the new money people unfortunate enough to have more money than the old money people. One thing you could never say about K.C. was that her money was new. It might be fast, or not spent properly, but it was antique. Actually I suspected some of what K.C. got had more to do with just how old and plentiful her money was. Even if she'd behaved, the most she could ever have hoped for was a cautious, courteous envy. As it was, she'd given cause to let go a venom sucked back for decades and always spewed behind her back. They'd never completely ice her out. Might've been easier if they did but instead they tightly smiled to her face and kept her on the invitation list.

As her second, I only caught sidestream shrapnel. I'd learned at boarding school that while I might be shunned, I'd be spared a certain degree of scrutiny proportionate to my parents' wealth, or lack of it. Everyone—the teachers, the students—they all assumed I was on scholarship, something that'd kill my mother after how determined she'd been to pay, or at least have people think she did. See, she longed for me to fit in with this old money set and while I could fake it a bit I could never hold off exposure for too long. It was like I'd been genetically encoded with a warning that tipped people. They'd maybe circle in for a look, but they'd always veer off.

Not K.C., though. She'd stuck around. I knew she'd be at the Ramada same as last year. It was the only motel anywhere near the showgrounds, so everyone stayed there. By Tampa there'd be a choice—the Holiday Inn if you felt flush or another Ramada if you didn't. But for now, regardless of funds, everyone was stuck together.

I got the number and dialed the desk. The only thing left to worry about now was whether she'd be there. It was Tuesday so the show hadn't started yet. Odds were she'd be holed up in her room—sleeping by day and carousing by night. As long as she hadn't unplugged the phone, everything'd be okay. I figured I'd have to let it ring, but she startled me by picking up right away. "Lee, honey," she said, "hold on a minute, I just walked in the door." I heard her set the receiver down, something else clunk to the floor. "What're you doing here? I thought you weren't going to make it."

I explained my situation and asked her to pick me up.

"Sure, honey. You just sit tight." She paused a second, then added, "God I'm glad you got yourself down. It's been a real drag so far."

The wait for K.C. would be long, so I found a pinball machine. I'd gotten through an hour and a half on a dollar's worth of quarters when she breezed through the door, finding me surrounded by my luggage and engaged in my first and only tilt.

"Good score, honey." She clamped an arm around my neck for a hug, then grabbed the nearest bag. "Let's get out of here," she said, already halfway to the door.

We stowed my stuff in the back of her maroon Porsche 924. She always described the color and model choice as understated. It'd been her sixteenth birthday present and I knew she'd wanted something flashier. That was three or four years ago now and so the car wasn't new anymore; didn't merit comment. Still, I loved riding in it and had to temper my enthusiasm or risk appearing wide-eyed. I had to do that a lot around K.C. It's a different perspective, I guess. I mean, I'm used to seeing quantities of drugs and all, but being weighed on a scale, not spread across a glass-top coffee table for public consumption.

First time I went to a party with her I had a lot of etiquette to learn. The excess scared me. Made me both nervous and envious. I wondered if I'd be less attached to drugs if I knew the supply was easy and endless. I feared they'd only hold me more. Watching K.C. gave credence to my fears, though I wasn't sure I could call her an addict.

"You want to go by the showgrounds, or the motel first?" K.C. asked as we motored along Route 441.

"The showgrounds, I guess. I've got to find Silas before I'll know where I'm staying."

"Guess it's a good idea. I haven't been over there myself yet. I imagine Richard would prefer I made an appearance."

Richard was the best and most expensive trainer around—for riders that is, not horses. It followed that he trained all the richest kids. Some were rich and talented, and some like K.C. were just rich. Richard gave the parents what they wanted, the illusion of propriety. And since K.C. tampered with the illusion, Richard humiliated her on a regular basis. He ridiculed her at opportune moments—those times when he had an audience, not just of students but of their parents too. K.C.'s part was to silently take it. Not talking back was the price she paid to remain his student; in exchange he let her continue her escapades, meaning he didn't report to her parents.

"Silas know you're coming?" K.C. asked.

She dropped the question so skillfully I scrambled for my answer, then delivered it too fast. "Course," I said, and decided it was a good time to look out the window.

I sensed her skepticism, but she didn't pursue the subject. Instead she said, "Carl and his bunch are here."

I knew she was fishing, trolling for why I'd really come down. See, Tory works for Carl Rusker. She does all his riding, while he does all the buying and selling to just about everyone. He's the best horse trader around. Best trainer, too, though you'd get more of an argument there. No one argues his results, though, that's the sure thing.

Just about every horse on the circuit had passed through Carl. He'd find them at auctions or little shows, even in people's backyards. Then he'd put Tory on them to get them smoothed out. And then he'd sell them. For ten or, these days, even a hundred times what he'd paid. Sometimes he'd sell to a trainer, who'd then sell to a client. But more often he'd sell direct to the client, Richard's or anyone else's. And a few horses he'd sell to keep. That meant an individual or a syndicate would buy the horse and then pay its way. Carl would handle the rest—stable the horse, take care of the training, and most of all keep the horse winning. He made mountains at this. Had a big operation going. His sister Linda runs the barn. The two of them and Tory are like heads of state in a country that can't give up its kings and queens.

So anyway, when K.C. mentioned Carl I knew she was really heading after Tory. Last summer I'd let on to K.C. about Tory, what I felt for her I mean. K.C. egged me on; saw flirting where I couldn't and then was frustrated when I didn't follow through on the openings she pointed out. Like a lot of other people, K.C. forgets I'm younger and so not as smooth about stuff like that, not as practiced.

"They been down all along?" I asked, doing my own angling.

"Nope. They skipped Jacksonville."

My relief surprised me. Now we'd got to Tory I didn't want to have missed anything.

K.C. went on for a while about how shitty Jacksonville had been, what a bitch Richard was. I voiced sympathy, then steered her back to Carl.

"Well," she said, "latest gossip has it they got here Saturday night, before the rest of us could even leave Jacksonville. Nothing wrong with that, of course, but Gus Taylor was the first one here Sunday morning."

Already I could see where this might be headed. Gus worked for the Cheslers, one of the oldest, primmest families in horsedom. Believe me, I knew. Silas had been friendly with them forever, would act as a second for Gus when needed. Because of this I'd ridden for them a lot over the years, for Mrs. Chesler that is. Mr. Chesler stays on the fringes. He even took her name instead of the other way around. Did this because her father'd had no son. The Missus, that's what Gus calls her, she'd had no children at all and so was always looking for surrogates. I was fast becoming the missing daughter and didn't much like it. Gus's son Reb already acted as a kind of heir. I didn't want the inheritance he'd ended up with—a lifetime of good manners and good behavior in exchange for her patronage.

The Cheslers' way was on the way out, already gone really. They were the last family to stable their own horses, employ a trainer and rider—Gus and Reb respectively—and show horses they'd bred or bought themselves. Things didn't work that way anymore. Now, the trainers stabled the horses and most thought of the owners as clients or customers. They sure didn't see themselves as employees. Richard, for one, acted more like the owners worked for him and since a lot of his owners were kids whose parents had bought them a string, they didn't exactly complain. Nobody bred horses anymore and the ones they bought, their trainers found for them, found through Carl. He'd become the most important link in the chain.

Mrs. Chesler had always disliked Carl but in the last few years dislike had become hatred. She'd never say so exactly. What she said, and said over and over, was she didn't approve of his "methods." I figured it was partly that and partly that Carl didn't kowtow to her. Richard, the other trainers, they at least gave her that. So anyway, I could see if Gus and Linda'd in any way butted heads it would've turned difficult.

"So what happened?" I asked.

"Well, the way I heard it, Gus pulled the Cheslers' trailer into the parking field—they've got an even bigger rig this year. Must hold a dozen horses and that's only half the string. Reb apparently was just a little way behind him with their second truck. So old Gus starts across the field, you know, to get to the tents and unload. Before he knows it, the truck's nearly turned over from bouncing on these great big ruts. Huge ones running clear across the parking field every which way you can imagine. So he gets out of the cab, cursing and spitting. Can you see it?

"And all of a sudden Linda's there. Supposedly with something of her own to take care of, but most people think just watching out. She offers to help Gus. Winds up driving the truck across for him—you know how she is with trailers. Anyway, after she's helped him unload the horses, even fed and watered them for him, she apologizes. Says they all had a little game of chicken the night before and the field was wet. That she guesses they made quite a mess. I mean, can you picture it?

"Of course, Gus is so old-fashioned, and taken with her besides, he probably just nodded and said thank you ma'am. But Reb, he's not quite the same way as his father. He saw most of it as he was pulling in. And he sure didn't let Linda drive his rig across. He's still furious. So's Mrs. Chesler. And just about everyone else. But like always she's the only one who made a formal complaint. And like always, the Horse Show Federation did nothing because no one else would say a word about it. Can't afford to sever those precious ties with Carl—the fucking federation most of all.

"I'll tell you, though, I wish I'd seen it. Not just the aftermath, but that chicken fight. I can't imagine any one of those three giving in to the other. And I don't guess they did. I hear there's paint streaks up and down the sides of their cars." She paused for a while, her admiration an extra passenger sitting between us. "You think all those stories about them are true? More and more I do."

There were plenty of stories, no question. And Linda took center stage in most of them. People who'd never have the gumption to say hello to her had no trouble repeating the worst behind her back. And every story seemed to end with someone wondering whether she wasn't getting too good with needles.

I didn't know for myself, but I believed people weren't fair to her. All the trainers were drugging horses. Richard's barn probably went through enough reserpine to keep the company in business and nobody talked about him. I'd picked up some of my slant from Silas. He remembered when Linda's veterinary skills were wondered at in a different way, when she was still young enough to be a kind of prodigy. So from Silas I'd developed a respect for her that matched Gus Taylor's. I kept these opinions to myself. Knew I'd find no ready audience for them.

K.C. still bounded on about Carl. He had her hooked nearly as bad as Tory had me.

"Course, now he's here, he's all anyone talks about," she said. "You think he'd ever look at me?"

Her voice had turned almost dreamy and when she paused she looked so eager for my answer.

"He already has," I said. We'd drifted so far into our own skulls we'd quit stopping things from coming out our mouths.

"Really?"

"K.C., you know he has, but think what you're in for. Remember what happened to Joyce?"

"I can't help it if she'd never heard of birth control. What'd she think? He'd divorce his wife?"

"All I'm saying is run it past the first act and picture where you'll be."

"Honey, the first act is all that interests me. Do you know that man actually has muscles? Believe you me, that is a rarity around here. Of course you don't have my problems. Hell, it's the girls who've got the muscles."

K.C. kept up her prattle about this person and that person. I tried to follow but realized she'd lost me several mile markers back. I noticed a ripple in my chest. It spread down my arms, fluttery, nettlesome. The closer we got to Ocala, the smaller my body felt, too small for my insides. Then the car felt too small. I longed to walk around, pace actually. The Bloody Marys had long since gone, leaving me cranky. By the time we exited off 441, I wished we were back starting from the airport again. I began to doubt Silas in an odd sort of way—worried he wouldn't recognize me.

When we got to the showgrounds, we had to park pretty far from the tents. I waited while K.C. changed her shoes. She didn't want to cross the field in heels. The ruts were there—as deep and sweeping as reported. Neither of us mentioned them, though, not even when we walked across them. It almost seemed they'd quieted us.

As we came closer to the tents, I asked K.C. where Silas's stalls were. She pointed to the furthest reaches of what we called the horse hotels—yard after square yard of green-and-white-striped canvas covering slatted wood stalls. An encampment broken down and re-created on a weekly basis for months at a stretch.

Even though it seemed like everyone got pretty much the same accommodations, you could see the hierarchy, if you knew where to look. Mostly the conveniences gave it away—who was nearest the show rings and the water supply, who rated an extra stall or two for storage. You'd find an eye turned from bribes and creative commerce. Protection could even be bought. Not actual muscle necessarily, but a kind of extra assurance that what went on under your little nook of the big top would be free from too much prying by the Horse Show Federation.

Silas didn't exactly rate preferential treatment. Well, not anymore. I feel funny saying it, but he was sort of seen as washed up. Once you get put in that category nobody talks about your accomplishments. And if you do, it makes people shuffle their feet and remember prior engagements. In his day, though, Silas did it all. Trained riders, trained horses, bought and sold them. And he won. All the time he won.

But now, same as Mrs. Chesler, Silas found his way of doing things didn't really exist anymore. These days "doing it all" marked you as either a small-timer or an old-timer, or in Silas's case both. If you wanted to be big-time, you had to play Carl and Richard's way, and you had to play with jumpers. Silas and Mrs. Chesler had always shown hunters and only hunters because that's what horse shows used to be about. Hunters meant manners and style and four-foot fences, all of which suited Mrs. Chesler just fine. For Silas it'd just been the way to go, the way you made money. Back then jumpers served more as a spectacle; were too rough and tumble for most people. See, with the jumpers, manners don't count, looks don't count, all that matters is how fast you can get around a course without knocking the fences down—fences five and a half or maybe six feet tall. You can see how it'd be more exciting, how it'd catch on, and that's pretty much what happened.

A small group of promoters had sold some corporate sponsors on show jumping. Said it was destined to become a spectator sport for the masses. The way they told it, it had all the necessary ingredients to keep America watching—danger, suspense, pomp. A kind of horse showing your average Joe could understand since all that mattered was whether you could jump the height and how fast. What could be simpler?

But there was more. Show jumping offered a soapy dimension pro football could never deliver—other people's money on display in huge quantities, real-life dramas acted out on a weekly basis. One promoter in particular was fond of stressing that the royalty factor alone could bring in a whole new market share.

Most of the interest came from company P.R. men who saw buying a few horses as a cheap way to generate an Old World image. Executives would have a new tidbit to drop during friendly conversations with clients and investors. Horse shows provided a new social arena—one that offered an especially pleasant and impressive backdrop to deal making. And, of course, a few captains of industry were horsey through and through, and anxious to make their friends share their interest.

I'd come into horse showing when all this was getting under way—right at the end of Silas's heyday and Mrs. Chesler's reign as grande dame. I was a chubby eight-year-old who rode Silas's ponies and did what she was told. The hunters were still the bread and butter, the place to make money whether you were a rider, trainer, or trader. A handful of riders went every year to the Olympic trials, and fewer still to ride jumpers at the games themselves. There were a few jumper classes at every show, but there was a real suspicion about them then. A belief that forcing horses to jump fences that high was unnatural, had no true sporting purpose. And back then most everyone believed jumper classes ruined riders, destroyed their softness. Made them cruel, even.

When I turned ten, I had a growing spurt that left me rangy and uncoordinated. Silas waited it out with me, kept giving me rides, and by twelve I got my balance back. Right then, when I was riding my first hunters for him and for Mrs. Chesler, everything that'd been shifting slowly for years, shifted fast. The jumper classes took center stage, bumping the hunter classes to outlying rings. Then Richard got into jumpers and that made it almost respectable. Took Carl to make jumpers the main event, though—Carl and Tory. Was another reason Mrs. Chesler hated him, and Tory and Linda too. When the jumpers became the big ticket and the hunters took the backseat, so did Mrs. Chesler, and Silas too. They're about the only ones left who don't have some kind of jumper thing going somehow.

The federation invented a bunch of different divisions—open jumpers, intermediates. Richard came up with the idea of junior jumpers—a scaled-down version for the under-eighteen set. It works for him because his kids need that many more horses and so he collects that much more in commissions. He still makes plenty off the hunters, though. All his kids ride junior hunters and they show in equitation classes, too—ones that judge the rider's form, not the horse's. His older clients, the ones over eighteen, they ride what's called amateur owner hunters.

Silas claims the junior and amateur classes make it too easy because the fences are lower than in the working hunters and the green hunters. I think he says this because I turned pro at thirteen, by accident, when he got me onto a horse for someone. A last-minute thing at some show and, anyway, I got paid for it. The federation watched that sort of thing way more back then and so that one slipup put an end to my amateur days—my junior days and equitation days, too, for that matter. I've been riding working hunters and green hunters ever since. I like it mostly, especially I like the young ones—the green hunters. I think I'd like the jumpers better but I can't even try them. Not and ride for Mrs. Chesler. She still believes all that stuff about the jumper classes wrecking the riders and horses. To hear her tell it, they've wrecked horse showing, and I guess for her they have. The deal is, if you ride for her you don't ride jumpers, not if you want to keep riding for her.

The position I'm in, I have to pay attention to Mrs. Chesler's rules. See, as Silas winds down, more and more of my rides come from the Cheslers' string. Mostly I ride their green horses, weed them out. Reb rides all the important ones. This last year, though, when a green one showed promise they kept me on him instead of moving him to Reb. And Gus, lately he took every chance he got to tell me how I should stay in the hunters, that the Cheslers would always see I had a solid place there, had slated me to take over for Reb one day. I respected what he said, knew enough to be flattered by it, but it wasn't what I wanted. I felt too hemmed; had right from the start, I guess. If Richard provided the illusion of propriety, the Cheslers offered the genuine article.

I'd hung on so far because Silas talked about getting into the jumpers, making a whole new go of it until he was back on top again. I'd conned myself pretty good about this. Could pretend my future'd be with Silas, riding his jumpers. I believed it by ignoring the way this kind of talk always came late in a night full of drinking. Last year I could still convince myself it could happen. This year I wasn't so sure.

I felt disloyal for thinking this on my way to Silas's stalls. Began rehearsing my speech instead. I admit to knowing a little how to pull a person's strings, but I try not to do it unless it's something important and there's no other way.

I saw Silas before he saw me. He sat on a hay bale smoking a cigarette. I hadn't seen him since the end of August when I left for school. He looked older and drawn and I wondered if he'd really changed in these last months. I'd seen him almost every day for so many years that maybe I'd never noticed any change in him before. Had been going all along on how he'd looked when I first met him. Maybe only now was I seeing who he'd become. In any case, he looked tired. His belly pushed against his shirt so it'd come untucked on one side. His old green corduroys looked out of place despite the cold, and his rubber boots were cracked and caked.

I was shy to look at his face, afraid he'd see me, but he wasn't looking. He was totally involved in smoking that cigarette. So much so, I expected he'd been drinking a little. His red hair, which I always pictured blazing, was mostly gray and copper, his face more flushed than ruddy. He turned toward me and I looked straight into his eyes. Thank god they were just as always—pale, pale blue and welcoming.

"Lee? Shouldn't you be up there in the snow and sleet bent over some book?"

"Not anymore." I tried to sound cheerful but could tell I didn't from the way his face changed.

"What's happened, kiddo? You're not looking so good."

I spilled out the whole story with none of the humor I'd planned. "So I came down here, Silas," I finished. "I don't know why. Guess you just seemed the safest place to go."

He made a space beside him on the hay bale. Put his arm around me when I sat down. "We'll figure something out. You got a place to stay? Just me and Jeannie come down. You want, I can sleep out here on the cot and you can stay with her at the motel."

"No, I'm staying with K.C.," I said. He looked about to say something, but I cut him off. "Really, it's fine. I won't get into anything I can't handle."

I watched him weighing whether or not to challenge me. He said, "Jeannie be back in a bit. We're going to knock off, go over to that bar. Remember from last year? You come on with us."

"Okay, but I've got to find K.C." I steadied my voice, I was sounding a little panicky. "Just need to tell her what I'm up to is all. You know where they've put Richard?"

"Right where you'd expect." He pointed me to the first row of stalls, the one closest to the show rings. Richard had the whole left side, apparently. I guessed that meant Carl had the other side.

Before I took off, I hugged Silas too long and too tightly, then felt him watch me go. I wondered how hard Jeannie's foot would come down this time. How long a grace period she'd give me before she began working to get me gone.

3

I found K.C. sitting on a tack trunk outside Richard's stalls.

"You check in?" I asked, sitting down beside her.

"Turns out he's gone back to the hotel already, so I missed my chance to kiss ass. How about you, things okay with Silas?"

"Yeah, everything's fine. Could I stay with you, though? Just for a couple of nights? Silas couldn't get a room on such short notice is all."

"Sure, it'll be fun, like school or something."

She'd agreed so fast it didn't give me enough time to adjust and then she was already asking was I ready to go and I was telling her yeah, but I just had to tell Silas and then I'd meet her back at the car.

I purposely went around the long way so I could pass by Carl's stalls. There was no one there, except a skinny kid dozing on a trunk. He had white-blond hair falling to his shoulders and the palest pink skin. I passed close enough he stirred, opened his eyes for a moment. Long enough for me to see they were red. I'd never seen red eyes before and so I kept staring even after he'd dropped off again, only stopped when I had to, to keep walking.

Rounding the corner I saw Tory's car pulled right up beside

the tent where, of course, you weren't supposed to park. Just like K.C. said, the black Mustang had streaks of white paint down the side of it and red ones on top of the white ones. Made it look like the car had this big gaping wound. I walked around it. The passenger's side was untouched. Walked around again, then just stood there gawking.

"Kind of stupid, huh? Now I've got to get a new paint job."

At the sound of her voice, my entire body stiffened. Mostly I noticed my thighs tightening, my skin heating.

"Yeah," I said. "I mean, no," realizing I'd just agreed she was stupid.

While I fumbled to answer this first question she was on to the next.

"Silas decide to call the big guns in? I'd heard you weren't coming down."

She pushed me more off base with this. See, no matter how many times she proved it to me, I still didn't quite think she knew who I was. My confusion left no time to think, so I lapsed into the truth. "I kind of surprised him."

"Surprised me, too. But hell, you did that all last year. Guess somebody's got to keep me honest."

Now nothing came out of my mouth, not even boneheaded stuff, just nothing.

"Well, I'm out of here," she said, tossing her bag into the backseat. "Hey, who's he putting you up on?"

"Oh, I don't know."

"Not giving anything away, huh? Okay by me. You want a ride back or anything?"

"No, no thanks," I said, trying to figure a way to take her up on the offer.

"Well, see you around the saloons, Cowboy."

I stood dumbly while she pulled her car out and cut across

the field. Eventually I started walking again. By the time I got to Silas my head had cleared some, still I wrote down where and when to meet him and Jeannie.

When I finally got to K.C.'s car, she wasn't real happy. "How long you expect me to wait around?" she asked as I got in.

I apologized and then stayed so quiet that when we hit the motel parking lot she said, "No sense getting sore, because I'm not staying sore."

We carted my stuff into her room. I felt really tired now and said so, made that the reason for my silence. She tossed a vial from her purse. I put it on the table by the bed, felt too jittery to start on it.

We took turns in the shower. K.C. got herself up pretty fancy, talking all the while about some party Richard was throwing at the home of a local bigwig. I lay on my bed watching TV while she gabbed, glad I had a built-in excuse for not tagging along. K.C. always likes me to tag along.

We sure looked the odd couple leaving, her in her black cocktail dress, hair out to here, me in the same jeans and boots, different shirt, an old suede jacket of hers I could tell might become a permanent loan. She dropped me at the Landlocked, the bar the serious drinkers liked.

I pulled the door open—one of those medieval-looking wood things you always think's going to be heavier than it is. Once inside, I spotted Silas and Jeannie right off. Jeannie looked pretty much the same, though it seemed she had even more angles to her. She carried the same cautious distraction in her eyes, watching for the other foot all the time, trying to see where it'd come from. She smoked a cigarette as long and thin as her fingers.

I made my way across to them and took a seat. Silas motioned for the waitress and I ordered a vodka on the rocks. She never blinked, just took the order down. Soon as she moved away, Silas said, "Kills me how you can always do that. Since you were ten you've been able to do that."

"Yeah. Guess as I get older, it's not so impressive. Besides, you think they card anyone, especially when we're in town?" He looked a little hurt and I felt bad for having taken his fun away. After all, he'd been saying this same thing since I was ten.

Jeannie said, "So it's good to have you down, Lee. Wasn't going to feel right not having you with us." Her fingers shook a little, making the smoke tremble.

I nodded to her. If she was starting out this nice, it meant she'd already won whatever fight they'd had over me—what to do with me, that is. I could guess what'd be coming next, if not the exact form it'd take.

"Silas tell you our plans already?" she continued.

"Nope, we hadn't got that far," I said.

Now Silas was the one looking edgy. "Let's have a drink first, talk business later," he suggested.

So they drank their drinks. And when my drink came, I drank mine. Nobody talked. Finally Silas said, "Here's the thing, kiddo. We're only here for these first two weeks, and the shoe-string's short. Not going on to Tampa. I brought two horses—a new one to show off, Charlie to sell. Counting on selling Charlie to get us home. Probably shouldn't have come this year, but it's a hard thing to give up. I've asked around for you. The Cheslers'll give you as many as you'll take. They understand the situation and offered to pay a little extra. I didn't ask, mind you, they offered. I want you on Charlie but, thing is, I can't pay you, can't even offer much of the purse. Be more of a favor. Hell, I want you on both the horses, but the same thing goes. We'll take you back north with us, no problem there."

I looked back and forth between them. Silas tugged at his

shirt collar and complained of the heat. Jeannie, other hand, looked at ease, no shake in her hand lighting that next cigarette. I didn't know what to say. I'd expected more time. If they weren't going to Tampa it meant figuring things out this week. I didn't have enough to go on and with Jeannie right there I sure wasn't going to ask what'd happen once we got north. Didn't matter, though. I knew the answer—I'd land back home. Only question was how soon it'd happen and looking at Jeannie I knew it'd be fast.

I'd stayed quiet too long, so I said, "It's okay, it's fine. I took my shot, you know?"

I watched myself reassure him. He looked no easier. We went through the motions of ordering another round. Jeannie clearly wanted to go, but she wasn't going to go by herself and I knew Silas wouldn't leave until I mentioned it. He'd feel he owed me at least getting good and drunk and so I guessed I owed it back to him. All the while, though, I fingered the money in my pocket. If I needed to buy a ticket back I wondered if I could swing going to Tampa on my own. I found Liza's credit card tucked among the bills and felt safer for it.

We finished two more rounds. Silas insisted on one more when I mentioned getting some sleep. Jeannie looked pained, but at the same time relieved. Her discomfort was at least finite now. When we finally got up to leave I didn't bother haggling the bill. I knew Silas wanted to pay, but I winced a little as he put the money down.

I crossed the room in a blur, more drunk than I'd realized. At the door I ran right into someone coming in, felt a pleasant prickle down my arms, magnified, I was sure, by the drinks.

"Hold on there, Cowboy."

I looked up and found myself face to face with Tory. Just behind her stood Linda and Carl Rusker. "Sorry," I mumbled, but she didn't let go right away. At least I imagined she didn't.

"No offense taken," she said. I heard Carl's low chuckle. Linda simply watched. Then the three of them moved past us. I couldn't help looking back. Looked until Silas took my arm and helped me out of there.

4

Silas dropped me at K.C.'s room. Said he'd pick me up in the morning. His eyes were full of apology, but he didn't say anything else. What was he supposed to say with Jeannie sitting between us? She said goodnight; gave me the signal to move on.

The ride back had sobered me. I walked to the room quite steadily, turned my key, and pushed the door open. As soon as I did, I heard unmistakable sounds and began to turn tail. K.C.'s voice called across the darkness. "Oh, Lee, wait. I'm sorry. I never expected you back so soon. Look, we'll get right out of here."

I closed the door behind me and began walking to the motel bar. Once there, I took a stool and downed three vodkas before I remembered I'd be paying for them. I borrowed a cigarette from the bartender to slow myself down. Began wondering if maybe coming down here'd been a big mistake. It sure wasn't like I pictured, which was I'm not sure what, except maybe it was something like when I was ten and Silas could fix everything—get me little-kid drunk, the kind where you feel happy and safe and can't see tomorrow.

He used to make my being drunk the reason he couldn't

send me home. The one he'd tell himself anyway, and the one he told me. I've still no idea what he told my parents, but whatever it was I'd get to stay with him and Jeannie awhile. It got so they kept the spare room made up for me, let me leave some things there. Worked okay back then, for a couple of years it did. But then I'd hear them fighting about it. Jeannie telling him she'd had enough, was time to send me home, and then the next day, maybe the day after, that's what would happen.

These days I couldn't get that kind of drunk anymore. My fifth drink at the motel bar did a pretty good job of it, though. I liquefied. Went to that place where I could go beyond thinking and concentrate on how I felt—literally how my body felt. You know, when things like lifting your hand become fascinating.

I paid up and walked back to the room. Figured I'd given K.C. and whoever more than enough time. I kind of hoped she'd be there. Knew, of course, she wouldn't. From outside the door, I could see she'd left the light on. Still, I sort of ducked when I opened it.

When I looked up, I found her bed made. Well, she'd pulled the spread up, which was as much as she ever made a bed. I stood in the doorway for a while. Clutched the doorknob for balance, finding it necessary to give all other attention to breathing.

My head kept dropping forward, which apparently obstructed my windpipe. I concentrated on holding it up, but when I did it slipped back too far, which hurt. Finally a car's headlights came up behind me, pushed me the rest of the way through the door.

I realized pretty quickly that I couldn't manage unpacking. I did get one of my jackets hung in the bathroom and turned the hot water on. I wanted to try to steam some wrinkles out before the morning. Then I dumped my boots onto the floor. They hadn't been cleaned since the end of the summer. I sort of rubbed a sponge over them. That only streaked the dirt. They'd have to wait too.

I lay down and didn't wake up until several hours later. All the lights were on and the water was still running. I hated waking up like this. It was already four o'clock. Silas would be by in an hour or so. I should've felt lucky to wake up before he showed, but all I wanted was for it to be a couple of hours earlier so I could start over, go to sleep right.

I opened the bathroom door. My coat hung limp and damp on the shower rod. I turned off the water, hoped it would have time to dry. I didn't exactly need an hour to dress but I figured I might as well. Get some unpacking done in the process. I hesitated on this last point though, not sure how much I should presume. I didn't want K.C. to think I was making myself at home. I figured she'd just tell me to stay, but maybe after last night she'd realize it'd be more convenient not to have a room-mate.

Silas drove up and honked exactly at five. I grabbed a bag with my jeans and sneakers and a garment bag with my still damp jacket. It's impossible to travel light in this business.

Silas gave me a quizzical look as I climbed into the pickup. I'd looked myself over and thought I passed, so I wondered what he saw. I wasn't going to ask, but then I knew he'd tell me and since there wasn't much road between here and the show-grounds he'd tell me soon.

"You up to anything, Lee? You're looking skinny."

"Nothing fun, if that's what you mean."

Truth was I'd noticed my pants getting looser during the trouble at school and I sure hadn't had any time to put weight back since then. I guessed I looked pretty scrawny, especially in my riding breeches. When those things bagged on you, most people began to wonder.

Silas kept glancing back and forth from me to the road. He kept that up until we pulled into the parking field. It was still pretty empty. In the half-light those tire tracks crossing the field looked like gashes and I couldn't keep from staring.

We got some coffee and headed back to the stalls, Silas carrying an extra cup for Jeannie. We passed Linda Rusker lunging one of their horses. Silas said the reason her help stayed so loyal was she always showed up as early as they did. Most of them got a ride over with her at four. I wondered how she kept going when she stayed out so late, especially since I'd always heard she stayed clear of all the speed going around. Usually people went through a lot of that just to keep moving.

I stopped by the Cheslers' stalls while Silas went on ahead. Dropping by this early made a good impression, especially if you came off bright-eyed. Reb Taylor wouldn't be there yet, but his father, Gus, would be. Gus liked me and that had helped me keep getting work from the Cheslers. He would tell them how polite I was, or that I was the kind who showed up early "with sense in my head." That was how the Cheslers distinguished between the good and the bad—the addicts and the clean riders —the good ones had "sense in their heads," the bad ones had "lost all sense." For them, "on drugs" was a phrase that always had a question mark behind it no matter where it came in a sentence.

For years I'd given them my best manners, my best smiles. My profile was low enough, discreet you might say. I wondered what Silas had said to them about me showing up, how he'd explained things. He'd forgotten to fill me in. I worried for a minute about word getting back to them about my being kicked out of school and all. Chances were it wouldn't or that even if it did, they'd find a way not to actually hear it. People like the Cheslers would let you coast a lot of miles with only manners and good riding fueling you.

When I hit their stalls, I found Gus braiding a mane. He was so tall he didn't need the stool he was standing on, actually stooped a little because of it. He called hello. We shook hands and started conversing about what a beautiful day it was. After a bit of that, he gave me the rundown. I'd be riding most of the green hunters. Plenty of them this year, so they were all glad I'd made it. Some real good prospects, too, like the one he was braiding. "A real looker," didn't I think?

I made sure I looked before I agreed. You always wanted to make it clear you had a basis for your agreement, but you always agreed. I chatted some more, asked after Reb and, of course, "the family," meaning the Cheslers, not the Taylors. Gus and Reb were all that was left of the Taylors. The Cheslers were "the same as ever" and Reb was "riding well."

Once I'd finished chatting with Gus, I left him to finish his mane. He'd told me I had ten horses for the day. Six in the regular green division, four in the green conformation class. I'd get upwards of ten dollars a hop, because that's what I usually worked for and Silas had said they were giving me a little extra. I'd find out how much extra when they handed me the check. With the Cheslers you never spoke openly about specific amounts, always "a little more" or "not quite as much." I could also count on the purses. The Missus never kept them, but each time you went through the same ritual—handed them over so she could make a point of handing them back. At least I wouldn't have to deal with her right off. She never appeared until later in the week, liked to wait until things got going.

Any case, it seemed I'd make out okay with money for a while. I know when you add it up it seems pretty good—$100 a day or more. But you got to figure in all those down days— travel days, days when you're working but not getting paid because there're no classes. Then you got to figure what comes out of it—your overhead. Dry cleaning alone would swallow two to three rides a week and when you added motels and food you just about paid your keep. Not much left over for play.

I hadn't talked to K.C. yet about paying her something toward the room. It was like with the Cheslers, she'd never want you to chip in, but she might get touchy if you didn't offer. K.C. was real sensitive about being used, but then she was real generous too—they seem to go together sometimes. I wondered whether she'd make it over to the show today or just stay holed up with whoever she was with last night. I hoped they'd been able to go to his room. I sure didn't want her having to pay for a second room on my conscience. Staying with her wasn't really going to work out for long. I had to start looking for another option.

Taking the long way back to Silas's stalls, I passed Linda bringing in her horse. She made no move to say hello, but she looked me up and down. I felt like she expected an apology for something and I squirmed as if I owed one. I didn't want to drop my eyes, I felt like that would lead to trouble. Still, it wasn't much longer before I did.

I believed everyone anywhere near us was staring. Of course, there wasn't really anyone close by at all. Didn't stop me from tripping over a stone, though. I was still trying so hard not to vary my pace, I couldn't make my feet work right. I pictured Linda smiling at my awkwardness, but when I stole a quick glance back, she wasn't even looking my way.

I was so intently watching everything but where I was going I walked right into Ted Bergan. "Steady there," he said.

He'd caught my elbow and didn't let go.

"Sorry," I said and tried jerking away.

He held fast. "Should really look where you're headed," he said, "not be watching her."

He pulled me in closer, said, "What is it you'd be wanting with her anyway?"

He sucked his teeth. I could taste tobacco on him, not smoke but fresh tobacco and liking how he smelled confused me to where I relaxed and kind of leaned against him. Partly it was to get my balance so when he let go it left me tripping again and he was laughing and I didn't like it; didn't like him and didn't want to be near him feeling so out of kilter and with everything he did making me more so.

Ted had worked for Carl for years until Tory replaced him. Now he was left picking up rides where he could find them; had no steady string of his own. It'd made him ugly. I mean, he'd probably been ugly before, but I didn't go back that far. He and Tory played out one of those supposedly friendly rivalries, at least he did. He was always pressing her, or so it seemed to me. Like with a lot of things, I figured I knew only a small part and so made up the rest to suit myself.

Finally getting back, I found Silas and Jeannie drinking second cups of coffee. "You got anything for me to do?" I asked.

"Nope," Silas said. "Why don't you get some breakfast?" He shoved his hand in his pocket but before he could offer me money, I started away.

"Hey, hey wait," he called, but I pretended not to hear. Last thing I needed was Jeannie calling me a charity case, especially since I knew she'd already started. I wasn't hungry anyway and even if I had been I had enough dough for that. Silas could really make me feel like a kid sometimes.

I went for another coffee. It'd gotten to be about half past six already, so people were starting to really show up and they all seemed to be on line at the concession stand. The boy who worked for Carl had a place pretty far up the line. He motioned me to join him. "What're you having?" he asked.

Now I was close up to him I saw his eyes weren't red—the irises weren't, I mean. It was the whites all bloodied red around gray eyes. Seeing this slowed me. "Just some coffee," I said, trying to catch up again.

"You and most everybody else. Guess it was a big night all around this town."

"Guess so," I offered.

"You're Lee, right?"

I nodded. "How'd you know?"

"Oh, I hear them talking about you. I'm Tim."

I nodded again, wondering how to ask him who'd been talking and what they'd been saying without coming off like a jerk. I knew he must mean Carl and them, but I couldn't imagine they'd be talking about me. I had a hard time imagining anyone talking about me, even people I knew did and not so nicely.

We were creeping up the line and finally he was buying about a dozen coffees and asking me to walk back with him. I agreed, but didn't know what scared me more—seeing Linda again or running into Tory. Least their stalls were near Richard's, so I could always flee to K.C.

Tim set the box of coffees down on a tack trunk and handed me one. I worked at tearing the little triangle on the plastic top, then almost dumped the whole thing when Tory came out from under the tent. "I never can seem to do that right," she said, sitting down beside the coffee box.

"I don't usually do it at all," I said, taking off the top. I looked to Tim for help, but he just picked up the box and took it into the tent.

"Have a seat," she said.

I sat down beside her and started shredding the plastic top. She pretended not to notice, or maybe didn't.

"So, when you going to start kicking our butts in the jumpers?" she asked.

"Not anytime soon, I don't think."

"How much longer you going to keep me waiting?"

"What?"

"I've been waiting on you."

"You serious?"

"Shit, yeah. Make it interesting again. You're good. You act like maybe you didn't know."

"It's the Cheslers pick the horses. I just go along for the ride."

"Yeah, well, that's the whole thing, isn't it? Even that tight-ass Richard can't teach that." She put one foot on the trunk and rested her cup on her knee.

"I can always see when someone's got it," she continued. "Right off I can see it. Course, so can the Cheslers, Carl.

"You ever look at who rides and who doesn't? Who's good and who isn't? Look sometime. Look how few ever let the animal run things. Even with a bad horse, you got to let him, you got to at least once, else you never know what he has to give you. But everyone holds on so tight. Doesn't work, all that fighting. We all know who's stronger. But you give a little, especially to a bad horse, let him see you trust him a bit, sometimes he'll trust you back. That happens, you got it made. He'll go for you like he won't go for nobody else."

She drank some coffee and when I didn't say anything, she said, "Shit, I'm going on. And all about something you already know." She considered me a moment, studied my eyes. "Well, least you know it here." She thumped my chest. I still felt her hand after she'd taken it away, gone on talking. Noticed it so much I lost the next few things she said.

When I caught up, she was saying, "Not that many of us. And so many of the other kind."

I stayed tongue-tied. Let her pauses hang and felt foolish for it. She bewildered me. Not anything she said, but that she'd singled me out some way. I believed I'd sit beside her on that trunk until she realized she'd confused me with someone else. But instead we finished our coffee and it was me who got up first, said, "Gus'll be waiting on me if I don't get going."

"I hear that," she said and pushed herself off the trunk. "Course, I haven't been anyplace on time yet."

I smiled at her. "See you later, then."

"You can count on that."

I headed over to the hunter ring. I hadn't really needed to get back to Gus yet, I'd needed to get away from her. Her attention had been so focused, it'd started that rippling in my chest, that too big for my body feeling. Not quite the same, though. This time it had no disquiet to it, up until she touched me, anyway.

No one else was at the ring when I got there. I found the course plans for the green hunter classes tacked to a wooden bulletin board splintered from too many rain days. I tried to study the course, looked back and forth between a brand clean paper full of marks and the fences in the ring. Nothing registered.

I'd never gone off course, but it was one of those things you always feared. Gave you a real bad rep. Tory'd do it and laugh about it. Not often, of course, but it'd happened more than a few times I could remember. And when it had, people'd started buzzing. Asking was she using again. The drugs came close to finishing her once, but that was pretty long ago. Meantime she'd become someone who could get away with things. I wondered what that'd be like since I was all the time getting caught. Seemed like not caring one way or the other might be the thing that made you immune, maybe made you safe.

I finally finished learning the course for my first class and by then it really was time to find Gus. The green classes were always pretty sizable affairs, so they liked to get them started on time. I headed back toward the Cheslers' stalls, meeting Gus halfway there. He was leading four horses, one wearing my saddle. I guessed Silas must've somehow brought it down with him and then given it to Gus.

I realized I was only half dressed, that my jacket and hat were still in Silas's truck. I told Gus and started off after them, but he stopped me. "I sent one of the boys for them. He'll be along directly. Let's get you on this one first."

He tugged the lead in his left hand, while the other three horses trailed to his right like a little caravan. I took the lead from him and slipped the halter off. He asked if I wanted help, but I waved him away. All of a sudden I couldn't wait to get on this horse. He was large, but kind of delicate; almost black but with a white star on his forehead. Once on him, I headed for the little schooling area next to the ring. It was starting to fill up a bit as I began working the horse.

Over my shoulder I saw Gus handing his charges to one of the Cheslers' boys, who was really a freckle-faced man at least ten years older than me. He stood there looking bored, surrounded by horses—Gus's three and two he'd brought himself. Over his arm, he carried my jacket; my hat was propped way back on his head. The Cheslers liked to bring as many horses as possible up to the ring at the same time. Gus said it reminded the guy at the in-gate who was who, which helped get the horses where they wanted them in the order, and that helped them get the judges' notice.

Believe me, they didn't need to play these games. One word from Gus could rearrange the entire roster for a class. He certainly didn't need to be pointing to half a dozen horses, but the Cheslers were set in their ways. They liked demonstrations.

I began to relax a little, trotting this horse around the

schooling ring. After he'd had enough of that, I eased him into a slow canter, then changed direction to see if he knew his lead changes yet. He switched his lead leg so easily I knew Reb'd spent some time on him. Reb picked horses more by how they went than by how they jumped. Said they could grow into better jumpers, but that if they didn't have a nice smooth way of going they'd never learn it, never be hunters. I'd picked up a bit of his eye and appreciation this way. Watching a gawky horse could even set me fidgeting sometimes.

This one put me right at ease. I liked it best when I could blend in with a horse, settle into his gait. Like Tory said, just let him run things. When that happened, nothing else mattered except being along for the ride.

Right now, though, I had to navigate around a pretty cramped area and get us over some fences. I saw an opening to a little vertical, caught Gus's eye and he nodded to go ahead and take it. As we loped down to it, I reined him in a bit so he'd shorten his stride some. You wanted always to check in, let them know they weren't alone. With a young horse especially, you needed to give this sort of reassurance often.

He took the fence easily enough, but gave a little twist with his hindquarters, the kind you usually feel a horse do when he has some real height to reckon with. I checked my own balance a little, wanted to make sure I wasn't contributing to his tic before I tried to fix it. We turned around and I looked for a chance to come back over it. Gus had sort of set up camp beside the vertical, so people were giving us a wide berth. It always helped to have Gus on the ground for you.

The second time over the fence, I didn't feel the twist. I hoped it'd been a fluke. Probably. Gus usually gave you a good horse first and the best of the bunch pretty soon after, while you were warmed up, but still eager. After that, he'd give you the trouble ones. Your hardest one would come right smack in the middle. Then they'd start getting easier again, so you finished up with about the second best of the lot.

I'd deciphered the pattern, knew it had to do partly with when he thought I'd be at my best, but more with how he figured judges. He said they almost always picked the winner early on. Then they'd relax awhile—a good time to squeeze your bad ones by so they'd get their practice, but not get noticed.

You didn't want a judge paying too much attention to a misbehaving horse, especially one you thought might turn around. If you weren't careful, horses could get pegged for life. The judge probably wouldn't even remember why, but he'd never like him, never pin him. Then word would get around to other judges.

So Gus would slip the trouble ones in during the lull and then when he gauged it over, he'd start with the good ones again. He maybe carried all this strategizing too far. He sure drove those poor in-gate guys crazy, always making them switch the order. But he got results. Wasn't unusual to see Chesler horses come up one, two, three, and four in the same class. I'd ridden the top four places for them many times in the green classes and Reb'd done the same with the working hunters.

Gus made a circular motion with his finger telling me to give this first horse a little more time while the class got under way. Through the rising dust, I saw Tory headed our way. Linda was leading her on a gigantic horse, a chestnut without a spot of white on him. He'd sweated himself into a lather and great gobs of foam hung from his mouth.

Linda had a chain lead wrapped tight around his nose. She held to it with both hands. The horse skittered and danced along the gravel walkway scattering pedestrians to safer ground. Tory simply tugged the horse's mane, patted his neck, kept her other hand loose on the reins. They continued down the pathway, leaving foam and lather in their wake.

Carl'd do this sometimes. Find a high-strung jumper prospect and set him loose in the hunters to cut his teeth. He'd have Tory take a horse around a hunter course knocking every single thing down. The theory was that letting them bang themselves up taught them respect for the fences. I'd seen her do it in jumper classes, too. But not very often. Sometimes if there was no way to salvage a class, if the horse had blown it early on and really pissed her off, she'd let him crack his knuckles. Get him set to a fence and then drop him right at takeoff.

It was dangerous doing that kind of schooling with fences close to six feet tall. I'd seen her, the horse, and the whole damn fence go down together. Didn't faze her much, though. She'd get up, dust herself off. Course, with what I'd heard about Carl's training methods I'd expect her to be used to this sort of thing. Still, I liked to think it ran counter to her nature, from the things she'd said that morning. I had to remind myself I didn't know her, had no idea who she really was.

"Better get one or two more in," Gus called across the ring. I put myself back in gear, but out the corner of my eye I watched Tory work the latest lunatic. Everyone else watched, too, and there were some near collisions among us rubberneckers. I took my last two fences and was glad to be done. Gus took the reins and led us through the ruckus. We parked under a tree. He took out his towel, buffed the horse first and then my boots. He passed up my hat, my jacket, and then a slew of cardboard numbers stacked one on top the other. Careful to keep their order, I tied each one around my waist.

By now, Carl and Linda had taken Gus's position by the vertical. Tory still jogged the horse around the ring, kept her distance from the other horses as best she could. At Carl's signal she moved him into a canter. He tossed his head as far as the martingale would let him. She soothed him with her hands. I watched her lips move, knew she was talking to him nonstop. With real wing-dings that helps more than just about anything else.

The ring had cleared out considerably, with people gathering along the sides to watch. It wasn't unusual for Carl to wind up with an audience, though he never acknowledged it. And watching him, you'd believe he was truly oblivious. He waved Tory to the vertical and she dropped the horse back to a trot. Made him keep the trot all the way to the fence. Even at that gait he was over it with plenty of room to spare. Then as soon as he landed, he went batty, took her for a ride around most of the ring before she reeled him back in.

They kept him at this, back and forth, back and forth, until he landed quietly. I watched her cooing to him, stroking his neck. While Linda and Carl raised the fence, she made him do lead changes down one side of the ring, one after the other on a straight line. She was even better at breaking a horse to this than Reb. If you had a horse who'd change on a dime, you'd shave fractions in the jumper ring. They clocked those classes down to the tenth of a second. She'd run a horse flat out if she had to, but more she'd go for turns, cut impossible angles, and still get the horse off the ground. That was why they trained so much this way, getting the horse to jump the most height from the slowest gait. I'd seen her get a horse up and over a five and a half foot spread fence from a near standstill. Not only won classes for her, got the crowd going, too.

"We're up next," Gus said.

As he led us to the in-gate, I ran through the course a couple of times. I realized I hadn't watched anyone go, had never even bothered to walk off the distances between fences. I'd get to see just the horse ahead of me.

"Only thing you need watch for is that last line," Gus said, giving us one more dust with the towel. "Comes up short at four strides, long at three. This one here, he can probably do it in three. He'll look better if he doesn't get all jammed up under that last fence. You use your judgment, though."

Gus had this way of leaving it up to you in the event of an emergency only. In this real gentle way he'd say "do it my way unless you get out there and find it's a kamikaze move." I watched the horse in the ring come down over the second to last fence. The rider held him back, played it safe. I guessed no one had done it in three strides, yet. Gus was right, of course. You couldn't make the last fence look good unless you took the stride out, and the judges would remember who tried it first.

Once inside the ring, I made the required courteous circle. Let the horse look around a little without being too obvious. We came out of the circle at a nice even pace. I let it build a little to the first fence. The course was simple. Down one side, up diagonal, then down that last line. We handled the whole beginning part fine, landing nice and easy from the last fence in the diagonal line. As we came around the turn to the last two fences, I let him lengthen his stride. I hoped it was gradual enough. The last thing I wanted was to look like I was chasing him to make the last line in three strides. That was the thing about the hunters, no matter what you were trying to pull, you had to make it look polite.

I egged him on subtly and we came out of the turn at quite a clip. I felt him get edgy then. Now it was my turn to start cooing. He composed himself a little but I had to keep the leg on him or lose the pace and that kept him jittery. I found a nice middle of the road spot to the first fence, didn't want him coming off the ground too far from that one or we might not make up the distance. We hit that first fence well and, as he landed, I gave him some room. No other way but to feed him some rein, keep up the leg, and hope he'd stay put together. He sensed what was up and so I kept talking to him, talked him all the way off the ground in three and could tell he'd made it look good. Another polite circle and then out of there.

On my way back past the bull pen, Tory rode up alongside me, came so close our stirrups clinked together. "Shrewd move, Cowboy." Then she actually tipped her hat—the lucky battered one she always wore. She took off before I could answer or her horse could get nasty. I flicked a splotch of foam from my breeches, a souvenir from his constant drooling.

I made my way to Gus. He was full of praise, told me to make sure I paced myself. Said all the stuff he always said to keep me pumped up and confident. I switched onto the next horse. We went on this way for most of the morning. I made sure I watched Tory go. For her purposes, she managed to squeeze five strides into the last line. She had that horse crawling down to and over the final fence. They took the top two rails with them. The ground crew who reset the fences always had a joke going with Tory. She'd come out of the ring wearing this "aw shucks, sorry boys" grin. Somehow she'd convinced each one he had a chance with her. This gave her a lot of mileage.

Our horses placed first, third, and fourth in that class. Gus was happy, though I knew he wanted that second spot, too. It was funny how the Cheslers never took anything below fourth, like they'd somehow made it clear only the first four slots interested them—the ones that paid points.

After this first class, I could knock off for a while and get some food. I ran across K.C. at the concession stand. Soon as we had our food she pulled me aside. We found a table under the tent by the grand prix ring. Not many people there, but K.C.

surveyed the ones that were. Having determined she was safe, she began with apologies.

"Lee, I'm so completely mortified, can you forgive me? It's just I was at that horribly boring party and Bill Hammond asked me to dance. He was, believe you me, the only thing of interest there. Do you know, he suggested we go up to one of the bedrooms in the house? Can you imagine? Well, I didn't fancy getting walked in on. Bill, however, seemed to hope this would occur. Oh, I admit, it was somewhat tempting. And the way he was pressed against me on the dance floor, I wasn't sure I could wait. I hate it when the act itself is anticlimactic. But rest assured, with him it wasn't."

She finally took a breath, though not a long one. I was further entertained with tales of technique and proportions. Bill was big, but not too big if I knew what she meant. She would try so very hard not to get carried away again, they would use his room from now on. Once I heard this and knew my lodgings were secure, at least for the moment, I paid less attention. Began noticing the activity in the ring, then saw Tory working that same leviathan in the schooling area nearby. I figured she must be acclimating him. I doubted they'd be putting him into a jumper ring anytime soon, but you never knew.

K.C. continued bravely on, was sure I must've felt the entire foundation of the Ramada quiver not long after she'd left our room. Bill'd become even more ardent after the interruption. He had, after all, been the one who wanted to be walked in on. Maybe she'd set it up to happen, subconsciously of course. She'd ask her shrink the next time she was in Manhattan.

I kept nodding and she kept talking. Way over on the opposite side of the ring I saw Linda Rusker leading Huey. As they passed by, people nearly genuflected. Huey was a celebrity. The undisputed number one horse in show jumping.

Carl'd bought him off the track. A two-year-old who acted like one, or so the stories go. Carl started him off as a conformation hunter. He looked the part all right—a big round bay with a perfect gait and a wide, handsome face. But he acted like a jerk. He could move well, won all the under-saddle classes when he behaved, but he jumped funny and when he landed he'd take the bit in his teeth and run, bucking his way around the turns.

That was when Ted still rode for Carl and Tory was a kid nobody'd noticed. She'd turn up at shows and grab whatever horses needed a rider at the last minute. They call it catch riding —what Ted's stuck doing now. Anyway, Carl'd pretty much given up on Huey by that summer. He put Tory on him at this big show in Connecticut mostly as a favor. She needed the money and was hanging around Linda. It was just a throwaway.

Tory surprised everyone by turning Huey around, making him behave. She didn't fight with him the way Ted had. Instead, she let him play until he got bored with it and they wound up doing real well together. Huey'd never win the hunter classes, not with the funny way he jumped, but people began to watch him. And people began to watch Tory, Carl most of all. He kept her on Huey the rest of the summer. Left her alone to do what she wanted with him.

And he gave her more rides on trouble horses and then so did other people. It sort of became her specialty. Carl could see where things were headed and wanted to remind people he had a claim on Tory. He started using her more and more and edging Ted out. And people fell in; started coming to him first to ask if she was available.

By the end of the summer Huey'd done about all he could as a hunter. Carl'd never admit it, but Tory's the one who first thought of trying him in the jumpers. The way I heard it, Carl had to be convinced, thought Huey was just too damn fat. Tory pushed it, though, and so did Linda, and finally Carl gave in; let them try. Once he saw it would work, he made it happen.

For years now, they'd kept Huey at the top of the grand prix circuit. Huey and Tory made each other's career. They were inseparable in people's minds. And it wouldn't be much of a stretch to say they were what got those corporate sponsors to shell out. Show jumping owed them a lot, but in that peculiar way things work, they somehow wound up owing back even more.

K.C. had paused, noticing my lack of attention. She must've followed my eyes. "Got your mind on your girlfriend?" she asked.

I smiled in spite of myself. "I don't know. Maybe."

"She looks at you more than Carl ever looked at me," K.C. said, picking up the sandwich she'd been ignoring.

I choked on mine, said, "You saying that because I warned you off Carl?"

"God you're naive sometimes, and blind to boot. Either that or you've been playing dumb this whole time."

I pressed her but she wouldn't say anything else, claimed she wanted to watch the class. Tory was schooling Huey now and soon they went into the ring. The announcer, taking his job seriously for this early in the week, read off a string of accomplishments. Then, without seeming to exert themselves, Tory and Huey made their way round the course without so much as ticking a rail—a warm-up exercise.

A polite smattering of applause followed them out of the ring. Knowing it was too early in the week for drama, K.C. and I made our way across the riser. I couldn't shake what she'd said about Tory but I didn't want to ask her any more about it. Was too afraid she'd take it back and I wanted to believe her even if it made me more a fool than doubting her.

I finished out the day well for both the Cheslers and Silas. Silas's horses both placed in the working hunters—fourth and fifth. Reb beat us out of the best slots but then it always played that way.

When I went around to see Gus before leaving, he gave me an envelope. I could tell it contained cash by the way it crinkled. All day long he'd been sticking the purse checks into my pocket. Apparently word of my dilemma had trickled down. I had to remember to ask Silas what he'd told them. I sure needed to know before going one on one with Mrs. Chesler. She'd never ask about it directly of course, but not knowing the cover story put me at a disadvantage.

I felt so out of synch I feared I could slip over into full-fledged paranoia. I worried I'd been too vacant with Gus, mooning over Tory while he tried to work with me. He probably attributed any strangeness to my "trouble." I was glad Mrs. Chesler wouldn't arrive until later in the week. I needed a little time to get my manners up to snuff.

Walking back to Silas's stalls I counted the money Gus had given me. $150 for ten horses. They'd given me quite a raise.

5

When I caught up with Silas, he told me they'd already found a buyer for Charlie and were taking him to dinner. He said the interest was due to my piloting and tried to get me to come along. He thanked me too much, which made it easier to beg off, and he didn't push because by then Jeannie was standing beside him. The two of them were headed back to the motel. I didn't want to leave yet. Told them I'd catch a ride with K.C.

Halfway to Richard's stalls I realized she probably would've left already. I was taking the long way round, a habit by now. This time when I came up on Carl's stalls, I found Linda's car backed up to the tent with the trunk open.

Her white Camaro had paint streaks down the driver's side —red and black scratches that matched the white and red ones on Tory's car. Gave me a pretty good idea what the side of Carl's Thunderbird looked like.

While I stood there gaping, Tim's bony arm shot out from under the tent, a big red plastic tackle box in hand. Then it jerked back inside when Linda yelled. "How many times I got to say the same thing to you? You don't ever touch that box. Understand me?"

She waited for his answer but it didn't come. I heard him put the box down, though. Could smell his fear above the hay and dust and leather.

"Hey Lin, how about Tim goes and brings my car for me?"

It was Tory's voice. I hadn't sensed her there.

"Go on then" was all Linda said. Then I heard Tory throw keys and Tim catch them. He sped past me and across the field, face frozen forward.

"He's only trying to help you, you know?" Tory said.

"Can't keep a goddamn thing in his head."

"He's trying so fucking hard to please you, he can't hope to."

They were quiet for a minute, then started laughing. Linda followed Tory out of the tent. She carried a black metal box, Tory the red plastic one. Tory dropped hers into the trunk of Linda's car. Saw me as she did.

"Hey, Cowboy. What you up to?"

She said it friendly, but I felt I'd been caught spying. Linda's behavior did nothing to dissuade me. She stood silently beside Tory for a long moment before slamming her box into the trunk.

"You waiting around here, Tore?" she asked, looking at me.

"Just waiting on my car."

"Well, I'm not. Give Tim a ride back."

"Yesum." She said it without a trace of a smile, which only made it harder for me not to laugh. I bit my cheek to keep still.

Linda closed the trunk very slowly and carefully. The way her mouth quivered, I would've said her feelings were hurt, but that seemed impossible. She went around and opened the door, leaned on the roof a minute before getting in. "I'll see you back there, then."

Tim drove up as Linda pulled away. He looked dismayed to the point of physical pain. Kept pushing his hair out of his face as if that would change the picture somehow.

"She that mad?" he asked.

"Yep, but not at you," she said, opening the door. "Move over, I'm taking you back. Part of my penance."

He smiled and she pushed him. He got his spindly legs tangled in the gearshift and parking break. She grabbed him by the ankles and tumbled him until his head was somewhere under the glove box. And in the midst of all this she looked up at me standing dumbly and grinning madly.

"You need a ride too, Cowboy?" she asked.

I nodded, grinning wider.

"In the back, Red-eye," she said, squeezing Tim through the tiny space between her seats.

I walked around and opened the passenger door, sank into her car pretending I had a part in their play. I went limp to conceal my wooden limbs, their anxious shaking. Looked, but found neither of them noticed me. They were still tickling and pushing each other.

I reached a hand out to join in, but Tory's was fast on my wrist stopping me, fending me off. They both targeted me now —his fingers clumsy and gentle, hers fierce and sure. He fell away soon, collapsed to his laughter. She kept on, but less manic now and when what she was doing went from tickling to touching, I was willing Tim to disappear entirely.

At last she held both my wrists, was leaning over me. I wondered if I looked as startled as she did. Tim's laughter still bounced through the car, but ours had stopped. She brought her face very close to mine and I tasted a smokiness on her breath; opened my mouth to it. But right then she let go; sat up and leaned back in her seat. I stayed crumpled in mine, gulping air. Was still breathing this way when she turned the key and we started across the field. Tim's head popped between the seats and she lay her hand along his cheek, tugged his hair, and I wanted so badly to be the one she was touching.

When we got to the Ramada, Tory drove around back and let Tim out. "Soften her up for me, okay, Red-eye?"

"Oh sure," he said.

We watched until the door closed behind him, then I said, "He doesn't mind you calling him that?"

"What?" she asked, then realizing she said, "Oh, yeah, you see, we tried to warn him."

"Huh?" I asked, not catching on.

"When he first came to work for us he had this bad habit. You don't know about this?"

"No."

"I guess there's no reason you would. Can't keep track of what people say about us anymore. Tim, he used to hold a horse by putting the reins around his neck. We kept telling him to quit it. That it was okay with the farm nags he grew up with but not with these hotheaded things we got. So one day one of them bolts and he gets dragged. You know, you get strangled like that, your eyes bleed. Sometimes they come back, but been long enough now I don't think his are going to."

I didn't say anything. Kept seeing Tim getting pulled in the dirt. She let me stay quiet for a little while then said, "Where to?"

I directed her to the other side where K.C.'s room was. She pulled up in front and parked. I looked around for K.C.'s car, but before I could really scope it out Tory said, "Guess I best go face the music."

She grinned sort of sadly, then relaxed her face. Around her eyes were tan lines left from squinting. She pushed her hair back, the dark curls catching in her fingers. Then she reached across and opened the door for me, a gesture right from the movies, or so it seemed to me.

I stepped out of the car, then leaned back in. Had nothing to say. She rescued me.

"You going out tonight?"

"Guess so," I said.

"We'll be back at the Landlocked, if you come by."

"All right."

I shut the car door. Wandered slowly to the room, until I realized she was waiting for me. I quickened my step, heard her pull away as I turned my key in the lock.

The room was empty, exactly as I'd left it that morning. I took a shower and only when I went looking for my jeans did I realize I'd left them and my sneakers back at the show-grounds along with my riding gear. Didn't matter really, the stuff wouldn't be going anywhere, but I worried what else I might forget if I kept on this way.

K.C. came in as I was dressing. "Where you been all afternoon?" she asked as I flopped into a chair, started pulling my cowboy boots on.

"Riding."

"Oh yeah, who you been riding?"

I groaned and she smiled, then began in leaps and bounds to tell some story about Richard being mean to her. Her clothing came off in a pile by the bureau, her shower was barely a semicolon in the nonstop ramble of her words. I listened as well as I could. She was soon in the chair next to mine, touching up her nail polish and snorting coke. I took a little from her vial, hoping to gain I'm not exactly sure what from it.

"What you planning on doing tonight?" I asked when she'd finished her story. I'd asked with too much investment. I could tell by her mischievous expression.

"Well, I can see you've got plans. Any new developments in the emerging romance? You really ought to keep me apprised."

I didn't say anything.

"Come on now, don't hold back on me. I hate being the last to know. Besides, I tell you everything. Could put an imbalance between us you keep this up."

"I just wondered if maybe you'd want to go to the Land-locked?"

"That tired old watering hole? I'd have to have incentive."

I weighed embarrassment against need. I didn't guess I was up to walking into that place alone. Could see myself sitting alone at some dark corner table waiting for Tory to show and then being too shy to approach her. If K.C. was with me she'd make me follow through and I could hide behind her if things didn't work out. "Well, Tory said they're going to be there."

"Well, that changes things considerably. Let me just give Bill a call and tell him our plans have changed."

My face fell. Bill Hammond had been trained from birth to treat people like Tory as hired help. People like me, too, I guess. I didn't much enjoy the idea of him turning the whole thing into a dirty joke.

K.C. saw my grimace. "Honey, just what am I supposed to do while you two go off and make eyes at one another? I can't exactly sit on a barstool waiting."

She was right, of course. I began counting carpet fibers.

"Now don't be like that. I'll keep him in line."

She made the phone call and we were in motion. Wardrobe choice was a sticky point. She wanted to dress down, but not too far. I settled on my other pair of jeans, K.C.'s white polo shirt, and my boots.

Bill came by and took us to dinner first. We sat through stories of his family's latest acquisitions. His prospects in the amateur owner hunters and how it was about time he tried his hand at the jumpers. Maybe he should ask my advice, he said, what with me being a "professional"—the word came out dripping. He didn't actually ask, though, leaving me free to bury myself in the lobster shell of my surf and turf.

When he finally excused himself, K.C. started laughing out loud. "I never actually talked to him, okay? I never said I did, did I?"

I shook my head, but was laughing mostly from my own anxiety. She made a circle with her thumb and forefinger and stuck her finger through it. "That's all I ever said about him, let's remember that for the record." She broke up again, barely putting herself back together when she spotted him coming across the room.

She ordered another round of drinks when he asked for the check. She and I belted them down in tandem, while Bill sipped his and looked amused. When he sent the check back with his credit card, K.C. excused us. She wanted to snort coke in the bathroom. I was shaky enough already, but couldn't quite turn it down. I tried my best to act patient while we waited for the valet parking and then waited for Bill to inspect his car.

Once in the car, I hid in the back; sunk as far as I could into the upholstery until the familiar smell of leather calmed me. Up front, Bill quieted and I saw K.C.'s hand between his legs. I heard her undo his zipper and then her head ducked into his lap. He looked back at me in the rearview mirror. And I surprised myself by holding his gaze. Believed I was getting something over on him until I remembered he liked to be watched and then I wasn't sure who was embarrassing who. He kept looking back and forth between me and the road. When his eyes closed altogether, I dropped mine to K.C., stared transfixed while she sucked him off.

She left him displayed. Pretended to be caught up in the moment, but her wink to me belied it. He got flustered, unable to take his hands off the wheel just then. His penis flopped back and forth on his chinos. I made a point of looking at it. Knew this was for me, how she meant to keep him in line. At the first opportunity he hitched himself up in the seat and put it away, zipping with an awkward flourish. I tried, but couldn't feel any of K.C.'s triumph.

When the three of us finally stumbled into the Landlocked, K.C. was still the only one at ease. Bill was flushed to the tips of his ears and couldn't look at me. He didn't have to worry, I still couldn't gloat. K.C. took charge and found us a table. I perused the room. Found Tory, Linda, and Carl at a corner table. I couldn't tell whether Tory'd seen us come in.

"What does it take to get a drink in here?" K.C. said almost as soon as we were seated. "Bill, be a dear and go on up to the bar, would you?"

He nearly leapt to his feet, but as he did I saw Tory getting up, so I said I'd go.

K.C. nearly knocked Bill back in his chair, taking no chances he hadn't heard me. "Yes, it's really better if Lee goes," she was saying as I began my purposeful walk to the bar. Half-way there I realized I hadn't even asked them what they wanted, then remembered it didn't matter. I tried not to watch Tory, tried so hard that when I got to the bar I wasn't sure whether maybe she'd been on her way to the bathroom or something. Just as this thought began to panic me, I felt her behind me. She pressed against me, using the crowd for cover.

"What're you having?" she asked and I felt her hand on me.

"Vodka," I answered as she pushed us through the people. She didn't let up until I was pressed against the bar. I had to put my foot on the rail to keep my balance while she squeezed in, half beside me, half behind me. She rested one arm on my shoulder, put her other hand on my thigh. Without missing a beat she ordered a bourbon and a vodka.

"Neat?" she asked, sliding her hand between my legs.

I nodded, completely unable to speak and sure my face showed everything. While the bartender made the drinks, Tory worked her hand back and forth. She didn't look at me and when I looked at her, her face betrayed nothing, had no trace of the playfulness she'd shown that afternoon. I almost thought she was mad at me, tried to tell by what she was doing with her hand. I'd dropped my foot off the rail by now, moved my legs further apart to make it easier for her. I had quite a grip on the edge of the bar.

The bartender brought our drinks and just before Tory raised her hand to take hers she pulled my fly so the buttons popped open. It was then she smiled, held her glass up to toast me while I fumbled with my pants. I felt a certain solidarity with Bill just then. We drank to whatever her toast was and she ordered another round, pointed the bartender back to their table. I followed her across the room, nearly clutching her shirt-tail.

Once there, she pulled an extra chair up and made the introductions—well, not really. What she said was, "You all know Lee, right?"

Carl nodded. "How're you doing there?" His hand came roundhouse-style and I shook it hard, smiling vigorously.

Linda didn't acknowledge my arrival and no one acknowledged her lack of acknowledgment. She said to Tory, "We've still got business, darling."

"I know it," Tory said, finishing the drink she'd left on the table and looking across for ours.

Carl waited till she looked at him, then started talking. "How'd Huey feel today?" he asked.

"Okay, I guess. Still feels like something's grabbing him, though." She stabbed her empty glass with a swizzle stick.

"You think he needs the week off?"

"No, I expect he's just stiff from traveling."

"You get him in a tub tonight," Carl said to Linda.

"Tim's doing that now," she said and looked about to say more, but she lit a cigarette instead and Carl turned back to Tory, said, "What's your take on that chestnut thing?"

Tory kept jamming the stick into her glass. "We might be wasting our time with that one, though he could jump the moon if he wanted."

"Real pain in the ass to travel with," Linda put in. "I had to leave an empty slot beside him in the truck and we don't have the space for that."

She and Carl started arguing about whether to buy a bigger truck. It was an old argument apparently. Tory kept at her glass with the stick, searched the room for the drinks. The more they acted like I wasn't there, the more I felt like maybe I shouldn't be and so I started my own fidgeting under the table, got my leg twitching a mile a minute. I became so involved in this motion I jumped when Tory put her hand on me to quiet it. Soon after, she tossed her stick on the table and said to Carl, "You need me anymore, Boss, or can I be excused?"

Both he and Linda looked surprised, but it was Linda who spoke.

"I thought you were going to stick around and drink with us awhile?"

"Shoot. Haven't you been listening to this man? I got a full day ahead."

"Full night you mean," Carl said and made a little clucking sound in my direction.

Tory shoved her chair back. "Rest it, Carl. It'll feel better." Then she turned to me, "You want a ride back or you going to stay?"

"I'll go with you," I said. I knew what she was doing by asking, but imagining staying and drinking with Carl and Linda, that had me on my feet before she was.

Carl laughed, not malicious so much as bested. "Look out for her, would you, Lee? She's got funny judgment."

I had no answer for him.

"What time, Tore?" Linda asked, filling the gap I'd left. She seemed off base, like Carl'd taken her part and played it different than she would have.

"Guess seven-thirty'd be time enough," Tory answered, the bite gone from her voice now. The alliances had shifted while I'd watched but I hadn't picked up and still couldn't. They were all practiced at this gaming table and I'd only just pulled my chair up.

They picked now to deliver our drinks. Tory drained hers before I could decide to pick mine up, then she'd decided for me. Had said her goodbyes and was tugging at my belt loop and then she'd pushed me in front of her, had her hand on my ass, and I could tell this was for Carl and not for me so I put my eyes on the door and concentrated on getting us out of there.

Once in the parking lot, she took the lead, making a line for her car. I trailed close behind, unable to find it in the dark. When we got to it, she came around to the passenger side with me and unlocked the door. I caught hold of her hand, let it go an instant later. She walked back around and got in before I did. I hesitated for an instant, enough time to see Silas and Jeannie getting out of their truck.

6

Neither of us spoke as we drove out of the parking lot. She still carried whatever Carl'd provoked. I didn't know her well enough to offer anything, so I wasn't going to try. She culled the longest roach from a collection in the ashtray and handed it to me. I pressed the cigarette lighter on the dash.

She laughed. "Never had that thing hooked up. Should be some matches somewhere, though."

I searched the dash for them, feeling stupid, like I should already know this sort of thing. When I finally found a lighter, I shook it hard before trying it. Was embarrassed by how relieved I was it worked. I had to pull pretty hard on the roach to get it lit. It tasted more like hash and tobacco than pot. I'd hoped she wasn't real into pot, it'd always been too rough around the edges for me.

I passed the joint to her and like she had ESP or something she said, "Remember when you could still get pot good as this? Well, almost."

I didn't. "Before my time," I said. "It's always seemed funny to me."

"You got a late start, then." She sounded surprised and I realized her confusion. I sure wasn't going to clear it up for her, though. Not now anyway. I figured if she knew how green I was, she'd back off. I hadn't set out to deceive her, just thought she knew my age and didn't care.

She took another hit, then passed the joint back. "I need to go by the tent and check on something, you mind?"

"Nope," I said, realizing I'd never thought where we were headed otherwise. I had sort of placed us back at her room.

"You going to let that thing smoke away?" She gave my shoulder a shove and I passed the joint back, never having taken my hit. After she took it I let my hand fall to her thigh. I tried to be casual about this, while she seemed genuinely at ease. She held the joint to her lips with one hand, the other loosely gripped the wheel. I felt her leg flex and then slack under my hand, remembered her hand at the bar. I couldn't get mine to do that. Actually, I couldn't make it do anything but sit there sweating.

She gave the joint back. Said, "Finish it." I nearly burned my lips trying to, then pitched the stub out the window. As we drew nearer the showgrounds she downshifted. She left her hand on the gearshift awhile then reached up and brushed my cheek. She didn't say anything, but I felt her looking at me. I couldn't look back. Knew if I met her eyes she'd know everything; know I knew nothing.

She put her hand on top of mine. Stroked it a few times, then eased it to the inside of her thigh. She had to downshift again to turn into the parking field. I felt her muscle working under my hand and squeezed at it. Then we hit the ruts, began bouncing up and down. "Damn us," she muttered, laughing low and quiet.

She turned back onto the dirt pathway and soon we were parked next to their stalls. I'd never been back to the show-grounds this late before. The sound of her door opening split the darkness.

"Come on," she next to whispered.

I skittered in the shadows, kept close to her. She ducked us under the tent flap and I comforted to the familiar sounds of horses shifting and chewing, the smell of bran mash and oats.

Her business took us to the little makeshift tackroom. She knelt in front of a trunk, began to rummage through it. I thought to put the light on, then thought better. She knew where the switch was.

As my eyes adjusted, shapes became objects—feed sacks, other trunks, a cot. Tory had her arms plunged elbow-deep into the trunk. She pulled things out, tossing them in a heap beside her. First came a stack of blankets and coolers, next some bridles, an old pair of boots. Finally she found what she was after, whatever it was too small for me to see.

I'd waited near the doorway this whole time and stayed there until she motioned for me. She was still on her knees, so I crouched beside her, saw a pill bottle in her hand. She ran her fingers along my jaw, pressed them to my lips. I slacked my mouth, let her put a tablet on my tongue. I flipped it back and down, hoped it wouldn't catch. She passed a pint bottle and I swallowed some bourbon. Then, not sure what was choking me, I swallowed more.

"All right?" she asked.

I nodded and gave her back the bottle. She washed her own pill down, then closed the trunk, put the bottle on top. We crouched there a moment longer and she kissed me. I bristled, disappointed because somehow I'd thought I would kiss her first. She began to pull away, not sure where I was. I clutched her clumsily, wanted only to keep her near but began straightaway to hide my inexperience in force.

I heard the bottle tip and fall as I pressed her back against the trunk. My hands looked large and desperate on her. She pushed against my shoulders, tried to lock her arms. I had the leverage, though, and pressed her down. Then we were on the ground and brawling. Our legs tangled in the blankets and bridles she'd left there. I kicked to get myself free. She was still caught in the blanket, so it was easy to hold her there.

I got on top of her and shoved my hand into her jeans, my tongue in her mouth. She fell off fighting. I shoved further into her jeans, pushed her underwear down. She put her hand under my shirt, but I yanked it away. Held her hair to keep her from me. She understood this better than me. Stopped moving before I knew I wanted her to. I tugged her pants down, got my hand between her legs, but she didn't open them. I was beginning to understand.

Holding her still, I ran my hand along her thigh, then pushed against her legs until she opened them. I tucked my hand underneath her and as I did, my fingers found this smooth ridge of skin. When I traced its path, she stiffened. I felt mean, but still didn't stop myself. The scar ran down the back of her thigh, but there was another branch to it, one that came round along the inside all the way to her groin. There it turned further in before it ended, hidden in the tangle of her hair.

I tried to press past it, but had gotten caught up. My hand turned tender and my mouth softened against hers. I kissed her neck and shoulders, her belly. Began to take myself down into her but she drew my face up and said, "Come on now, darling. That's long since healed."

Her saying this just made me softer, helpless really. She had to show me what she wanted, had to put my hand back between her legs. I fucked her how she told me and she met my hand at every drive. The feel of this led me to fuck her very hard and I couldn't escape how much I liked it.

Some time passed before I sensed her stillness. She'd shored up inside herself, leaving me alone to decide when she'd had enough. I left off her now that it felt unkind. Eased my hand from inside her and made my best attempt at love. I brought her off and all, but it took me no closer to her. She stayed lost in some place I couldn't get to.

I wanted to get up, but the darkness was all over me. The dark of her eyes, her hair. Thick knots tangled in my hand. I pushed it away from her face, but still I couldn't see her. Then all at once she turned, pressed her body into mine, and held me. I imagined my tears were hers, though I'd choked them off before they started. Didn't matter, she knew I wanted comfort, rubbed her hand in circles on my back, then did the same thing underneath my shirt.

I hid my face, afraid her tenderness would truly start me crying. Soon enough, though, she tucked her other hand inside my jeans. They were loose enough she didn't need to unbutton them, but she did anyway. I felt the gritty flannel of the blanket under me, her fingers on me, on my crotch. She held me tightly there, butted her palm against me. For a while she didn't move her hand, just kept it still until I began to rub against her. She watched my face so keenly I had to close my eyes. When I did, her hand went in me, her tongue into my mouth.

I opened my legs as she pressed harder. Now she held my hips down, wouldn't let me move. And when I thought I'd die if I had to keep still any longer, she pulled her hand out so slowly. Let her fingers unfold against me. I grasped at her, coming so quickly I startled her. She slid her hand back inside me and held it there quiet, held me, and I closed my legs around her.

We stayed that way a long time, but then that too big feeling started restless in my chest, in my cunt too and in between. Her head was resting on my stomach, but I didn't think she felt what was going on inside there. The horse in the stall next to us rustled for the first time I'd noticed. When he stamped his foot a second time I used it as an excuse. Shifted myself off her hand. Her head was pretty much in my crotch, now. She kissed my thighs, but I pulled her up before she could start anything more.

"Got anyplace we can go?" she asked.

"Maybe," I said, pulling on my pants.

She started for the door, buttoning her pants and shirt on the way. Only when she tripped on a bridle did she go back, open the trunk, and start to pitch things back in. We had to sit on the trunk to close it. She found the bourbon, took a swig, and handed it to me. I took one too, and promptly started coughing. She pounded me on the back and then was laughing. Said, "We got to toughen you up, Cowboy."

7

I didn't remember about her scar until we were driving back. I wanted to ask about it, but was afraid she'd retreat and I didn't want to push her away again. Be alone so soon afterwards. Besides, her quiet seemed peaceful. She drove easily, occasionally sipping from the pint, returning it to her lap. I'd given up on the bourbon after my coughing fit.

"So where to?" she asked as we stopped at a light near the motel.

I explained that K.C. likely wasn't in. She said that was good since Linda probably was by now. This was the first she'd mentioned of them sharing a room. I suppose I'd guessed it earlier, but I'd still had hopes. My hopes can blind me to the obvious even better than my doubts. I've decided this makes me an optimist.

Tory turned into the motel parking lot and drove straight for K.C.'s room. I was surprised she didn't need me to remind her where it was. Of course I was still having trouble believing this whole evening wasn't some elaborate mistake she'd made.

Soon enough we were parked in front of the room. She tossed what was left of the pint into the glove box and we got out. Through the curtains, you could see the lights were on. I figured this was K.C.'s way of telling us the coast was clear. I figured wrong. When we went in, we found her stretched on her bed dozing, the TV on with no sound.

As we turned to leave, she stirred. "Oh Lee, honey, sorry. I tried to wait up. Can you imagine? Bill said he wasn't in the mood." Then she saw Tory and said, "We're not handling this very well, are we?"

I said, "It's okay, K.C. Go back to sleep." I wanted Tory and me to get out before my embarrassment started showing.

In the parking lot, Tory started laughing. "How about we get ourselves a drink?"

I felt stupid because I didn't want to. I was just so tired. Lying down with her would've been fine but the idea of sitting in the motel bar, trying to talk, this seemed too hard. I wanted us to have someplace to go and said so. She nodded, but we weren't going to find it. Instead she sort of hugged me and the kissing tasted mostly like bourbon.

After, Tory got back in her car. Left me fumbling with my key. I couldn't get the door to the room open until she started the engine and the headlights went on, helping me find the lock. Once inside, I heard the car pull away. K.C. held her tongue a moment longer, then was wide awake with "was she good" questions.

"Jesus, K.C. That's so gross."

"Yeah, well, was she?"

I grinned and nodded because it was what she expected.

She hugged her pillow expectantly, ready for the all-out pajama party lowdown. "Where'd you two go anyway? I was sure I'd be walking in on you this time."

"We went back to the tents." I felt my smile disappearing as I remembered the tackroom, how I'd been with her.

K.C.'s excitement dwindled too. "Why'd you go there?" she asked, more puzzled than judging.

"She had to get something." I turned off the TV and went into the bathroom, closed the door behind me, and ran the water so she wouldn't try to talk to me. Then I sat on the toilet and tried to pee, something I'd needed to do quite badly just a little while ago, but now couldn't. I kept watching myself hammering her, couldn't shake how eerie it felt when I realized she'd left me. No matter how many times I told myself I'd done what she wanted me to, I still felt spooky for getting so caught up in it, for not knowing precisely when she checked out.

Maybe I was making too much of it. I mean, she seemed okay about it, okay about me. I concentrated on peeing, finally managed it. Then got up and brushed my teeth. My soberness after all that liquor surprised and irritated me. I stalled in the bathroom as long as possible, even used K.C.'s tweezers on my eyebrows. Eventually, though, I ran out of things to do.

When I came back into the room, K.C. looked at me funny, but didn't say anything more. She switched the light off as soon as I got in my bed.

"Sorry," I said.

"It's all right. You'll feel better tomorrow."

I guessed I didn't have too long left before tomorrow. I began worrying about everything to come, then stopped myself. I turned my back to K.C., put my hand between my legs and held on tight, there. Tried to touch myself the way Tory had. Couldn't get it quite right—that way you never can. Still, remembering her put that same prickly largeness in my chest, and I made myself come without a sound.

Didn't seem like more than twenty minutes before Silas's horn sounded. I wasn't sure, though. Not of how many times he'd honked, whether I'd slept, anything. I was adding up too many nights awake. Good thing I'd left so much of my stuff over to the showgrounds. I pulled on dirty breeches, a clean shirt, yanked on socks and boots, that same suede jacket. I swigged some of K.C.'s mouthwash, then swallowed it to see if it'd take the edge off a shakiness that'd stayed with me.

As soon as I got in the truck I could feel Silas weighing how fatherly to get. I found a brush in his glove box and ran it through my hair, hoped to show I still had some concern for appearances. It didn't stall him much.

"You know I'm not a meddler, right?"

I nodded. This was a bad beginning. I stared straight ahead and hoped he wasn't going to get too personal.

He coughed and then continued. "And you know I think people been too harsh on Tory Markham, but she's had real trouble, Lee. Lately you're acting like you forget that."

He kept looking for me to say something and I kept not saying it, so he kept going.

"Maybe you don't remember it, but I know you heard all those stories. You can't pretend to me you didn't."

We'd stopped at a light and so he was looking at me steady. I knew what he was talking about. I don't think anyone really knows exactly what happened. But everyone remembered how she stayed away afterwards. And they still talk about how she looked when she came back. They said she never looked right, never the same since. People seemed to like saying those kinds of things about her.

Whatever it was happened not too long after she got Huey going. This made it before my time and so all I had to go on were stories. They'd gone home for a layover and Tory didn't come back with them, not for a long while she didn't. That much was fact but the rest gets fuzzy.

At first no one knew what to make of her not coming back. They speculated about a riding accident or that she couldn't take the pressure of keeping Huey on top. Then talk started she was pregnant. Over time more details leaked out until the story got pared down to two versions—one blaming Ted and one blaming Linda. No one blamed Carl.

The plot stayed pretty much the same except Ted and Linda played different roles. The one account had Ted walking in on Linda and Tory and then bashing Tory around. The other had Linda as the one walking in and doing the hitting—most people liked this last version best, the men especially did. I'd always subscribed to the first one, though lately I'd found myself pretending there'd never been anything between Linda and Tory. Knowing differently didn't seem to slow me on this at all.

Didn't matter which way people told the story, Carl always got cast as the rescuer, the one who saved Tory from getting hurt worse. However it really happened, Ted didn't work for Carl after that. And Tory, she started in with drugs. Got so far in, it showed—things like going off course and making scenes. I remembered some of that.

Silas had stayed quiet for a bit, now he said, "She nearly killed herself, Lee. She nearly got herself killed."

I scraped my fingernail on the stubby armrest; tried to figure which way he meant this—the drugs or what'd come before them or both. And all this time I tried get her scar back to a more convenient place in my brain, but instead it stayed front and center.

When the light changed, Silas was slow off the mark. Took a car horn behind us to egg him along. But then he was back to driving and talking.

"I don't know if she's in trouble now. Don't know if or how much, but it doesn't matter. To these people she'll always be exactly as much trouble as at her worst. No amount of winning going to change that, nothing she does. You get too mixed up with her and all of them and you'll be in their trouble too. But you won't have Carl's weight behind you. You understanding me?"

I nodded again, this time sullenly. It wasn't at him, it was this picture still in my head but he didn't know, so he said, "Lookit, it's not like I want to be telling you this. You know I don't. But the last thing the Cheslers need to hear is you've got yourself mixed up with drugs. And if too many people start talking, and not just about that, what you expect the Cheslers'll do? They already wonder if you aren't looking too hard at the jumpers, now you start hanging around with that crowd? Don't push too hard, Lee. People like that, they can't take being pushed."

He'd said everything and most of all he'd said what he hadn't spelled out. By this I don't so much mean my being with Tory as where she'd take me—where she and I might end up. And what scared me wasn't so much what Silas said or didn't say, it was that I already knew none of it would stop me. That instead it pulled me.

This wasn't a rebellious thing, more reckless. And though it may seem so, I'm not reckless by nature. It's more I get a certain way in and then can't turn back. It's usually not a decision. I don't think of it that way, but then I don't usually have someone sitting beside me telling me the consequences before the damage is done, or at least done for good. People could make something out of my spending one night with her, but not much.

We stayed quiet for the rest of the ride over. I braced against the dash as we bounced over the ruts to a parking place about as far across the field as you could get. When Silas turned off the motor, I feared more sternness, but instead he turned sad. He opened the door but didn't get out.

"Lee, come on. It's just a few more days and we'll be heading home. Why you want to get mixed up in something now?"

I realized then he thought I could do all that damage in a couple days. I mean, I'd been thinking long range. But then maybe he was, too. I sure wasn't going to tip him; wouldn't say I wasn't going back with him, but I could tell he'd guessed it. Maybe only just now, or maybe that was what his whole speech had been about.

"Lee?" he said again because I'd been quiet so long and still stayed that way. He turned up the juice now, said, "It'll be okay, kiddo. Be like it used to be. That room's still fixed the same way. We'll get you into school. You'll stay as long as you want."

See this last part, this was the trouble—"as long as you want." The miles between Florida and New York could keep me from acting foolish. But Silas lived not more than twenty minutes from my parents. Not far enough for me to turn myself around once I headed back there.

And Silas wouldn't stop me. He'd never once blocked the way to my going home. It was why I could stay with him at all, except lately it'd started working against me, working me against him. See, he only knew the most general outline of things. Thought my father'd started in when I was ten. I'd never set him straight on this. Never explained it hadn't started then, it'd only changed. Become something I needed breaks from.

I couldn't see a way to explain this and keep it in outlines. I feared if he knew specifics he'd either look at me the way Jeannie did, or the way Jeannie already thought he did. Where Silas felt sorry for me about my father, to Jeannie it meant I knew how to do things and might do them with Silas. Maybe this was my fear, too. Or that Silas would finally see it, see through me, and then that's what he'd want from me.

I knew this didn't make sense, that Silas would never look at me that way, but still I kept worrying it. This last year or so especially, with the way things kept happening. Things like that guy on the plane. A lot of that. But Silas—I got confused each time I went too far thinking about it, confused and sleepy until the only thing I knew was things couldn't stay the way they'd been for very much longer.

"Just be careful. Okay, Lee?" This was what he finally said. And when he touched my cheek so he could get me to look at him, I jerked away because of what I felt and where—it let me fear him and wish him stronger with me but still not pushing and I couldn't see how anyone would ever strike that balance.

I stayed in the truck while he started over to the tents. I saw him walk past Linda's car, which was parked about where it'd been yesterday afternoon. I wanted to see Tim stick his blond head out of the tent and invite me in for coffee. He meant comfort to me now. Instead I saw Tory turn into the field, and way earlier than usual.

She backed her car in beside Linda's. Caught me watching her even before she got out. I snapped my head away, expected she'd ignore me. Automatically I believed she'd lost last night to some amnesia. Even when she started walking straight for me, I convinced myself she was headed for a point behind me. Finally she was standing right there, was knocking on the window. I hurried to roll it down.

"You dreaming?" she asked.

I tugged at my collar so I'd have room to speak. "You're here early," I said. It was all I'd thought of.

"Couldn't sleep," she answered, opening the door.

I slid over to give her room. She pulled herself up and in by grabbing my arm. My leg began quivering soon as she touched me. She couldn't help but notice.

"You nervous of me, Lee?"

"No, just cold," I lied.

She rubbed my leg like to warm it, but was soon just rubbing. Before long I quit looking to see if anyone was watching us. She coaxed me to scoot down more and slipped her hand into my breeches. She was sort of bent across me, so I put my hand on her back, tried to brace against her. I kept slipping, though, so I tucked my thumb through her belt loop and used her hip to push myself further back and down.

My butt was on the edge of the seat now. She'd been roaming around inside my pants about as far as the stretchy fabric would let her, which was pretty far. Her touching lulled me. She tugged my pants, yanked them down so I felt them bunching around my boot tops. Next thing I knew she'd shoved her hand up in me and I mean most of it. I folded over her as kind of a reflex, but that made it hurt worse so I leaned back again, held tight to her. Kept myself, just, from grabbing her arm, making her stop.

I tried to make more room but my legs might as well have been tied together. As it was I'd stretched my pants just short of tearing. She got her whole hand in anyway, that part she did slow and careful. Then she really gave it to me.

I clutched the seat with one hand, her shoulder with the other. Shoved myself forward until my knees buckled. The vinyl was cold and sweaty against my skin, something I concentrated on before pushing myself the rest of the way off the seat. When I did that, her hand was left supporting a lot of my weight. This got her in further so her strokes hurt more, but in a way I liked better. The pain of someone up inside you, not trying to get there. I liked this more and more for a while, wanted to see how far she'd go. How far I'd go. But then, very soon, she'd gone too far and I was sure I'd lose everything if I couldn't stop her.

I felt myself closing my legs around her hand and this blocked my breathing. I pulled her arm. She held completely still, but didn't take her hand out. I pulled again, sort of panicky.

"Hold on now," she said. "Lee, you got to calm down."

Her using my name made me listen. I felt her other hand smoothing my leg. Realized then how rigid my body'd gotten.

She kept stroking my leg, whispering to me, but I couldn't let go. It seemed forever till I quieted. Then she began easing her hand out. That seemed to take forever too, especially since I'd become more embarrassed than frightened.

After, she helped put me back together. My underwear was about the most serious casualty, pretty well gone. She shoved it in her jacket pocket, said, "I'm so sorry, baby. You all right?"

I nodded, horrified because she wasn't going to pretend it hadn't happened.

"You've never done that, have you?"

I shook my head. Began digging my fingernails into my arm. Did it underneath where she couldn't see.

"Jesus, you should've told me. After last night, I thought it was what you'd want . . . or that . . . Shit, when you moved like that I thought you wanted me to."

"I did," I said, about as defensive as I could get.

"Okay, okay."

I was looking down, saw her hands fidgeting. She'd go to touch me, then pull back. I looked at my own hand still clenched to my arm. Pulled it away and saw crescents of blood. I wondered how we were going to get out of this.

She started to speak a couple of times, then said, "It's just, you scared the shit out of me. Pulling my arm like that. You should've said . . ." Her hand reached out, then dropped back. "I could've really hurt you, you know. Started you bleeding."

"I don't care," I blurted; couldn't stop it from coming out my mouth.

She stayed quiet, then offered her hand for real, took mine in both of hers. "You are young, aren't you? Linda said you were seventeen, but I didn't believe her; told her you had to be eighteen by now. She's right though, isn't she?"

"No," I said, which was true. I wasn't seventeen.

"Look," she said. "It doesn't change much of anything. That's not why I'm asking. I didn't exactly think you were my age, you know. Not like I could go back to waiting even if I wanted to."

I didn't know what she was saying. I only knew I hated this conversation. She was holding my wrist now. I couldn't make an even bigger scene by running from her, especially since what I really wanted was to hide in her arms for about a year. She put her arm around my shoulders. This put me in real danger of bawling. All my attention shifted to fending that off. I tipped my head back against her arm to keep my throat open. She kissed me, first my cheek, my neck, then my lips. She kept her tongue out of it, like she wanted things clear. I sat still and let her, though it was so hard to breathe.

I wanted us to move on now. The longer she paid me this attention, the harder it'd be to stay glued.

"What time is it getting to be?" I asked her.

She took her arm from around my shoulders. Made a point of looking at her watch closely. "About twenty to seven," she said and then coughed a little because the words had sort of stuck.

"Gus is going to be wondering where I am," I said but I didn't make any move. I couldn't just push past her, and to get out the other side would mean a whole lot more than I intended.

She sat for a little longer, hands back to fidgeting. She was looking down at them now, too. "Okay, then." She patted my leg, was almost rueful about it. Then she opened the door and we got out.

I started to walk, but she stopped me.

"Hey, look," she said. "I'll find somewhere private for us tonight, okay?"

"Yeah, okay," I said, then told her I'd really like it because I could see she was trying hard and I wasn't helping.

We walked across the field then, not quite together. A lot of people had arrived but we'd been far enough away, I figured we were safe. Maybe I played ostrich, I don't know, but I couldn't take the idea anyone had seen us. I gave Tory the power to protect us from that. I sure could see Linda watching us walk back, though, and so I angled my path that much further from Tory's, forced myself not to look again. As I veered off, I could hear their morning talk—not actual words, just murmurs. The distance left me free to invent the worst. I tried instead to believe Tory could protect me from Linda, too, and felt ashamed when I couldn't be sure about this.

"You sleep in?" Gus asked when I finally showed up.

"Guess yesterday tired me out. It's been a while."

"That'll do it. You sore?"

"Sure am," I answered.

"Well, go on and get yourself some coffee. It's going to be another long one."

"Oh, I already ate. I was thinking maybe I could get on one of the horses early, sort of stretch my legs."

"Sure, if you want. Be one less to lunge."

The conformation horses were up first today, so he pointed me toward one of them, asked if I'd mind getting him ready since he'd gotten a late start too. I agreed overpolitely, virtually leaked guilt. He began patiently describing where I'd find things. Didn't seem to notice all the holes in me. I didn't want to give him time to, so I cut him short, said I was sure I'd have no trouble, and then kept myself from walking away too fast.

Searching through the tackroom soothed me a little. The smells mostly, liniment and flannel, yesterday's sweat, that and listening to the horses, their shifting and chewing—these things put something large and comfortable where all the hollowness had been. I stayed longer than I needed. Only got moving when Gus called over to make sure everything was where he'd said it'd be.

"Yep," I answered and grabbed my saddle. Lifting it took a lot more effort than usual. This scared me. I hoisted it onto my arm and looked for the bridle he'd described. It hung alone on a cleaning hook, its big gentle bit gleaming. Gus would put a smooth snaffle on any horse he could. He hated to tear their mouths up, would always give them at least one chance. I took the bridle hoping this horse had already had his chance and earned the kindness. I wasn't up for a struggle, not feeling this weak.

When I saw the horse, I figured we'd be okay. He was large and round, a dapple gray with soft blue eyes. He barely stirred when I put the tack on him. Gus had already groomed him, braided him. He looked the part, that was sure. If Gus wanted me on him first I guessed he was the place horse, making me wonder what the win horse looked like.

I finished getting him ready and led him outside. Ordinarily I'd've asked Gus for a leg up, but I sure didn't want him swinging me into the saddle this morning. He gave you so much loft you tended to come down hard. At the thought alone, I winced. Struggling myself on up there would hurt about as much, so I found a hay bale to stand on, eased into the saddle. Didn't matter. The pain still came, that and a naked feeling from having no underwear on. I tried to see if you could tell, but couldn't really be sure one way or the other.

At first I stayed up on my knees, but my legs were so wobbly I had to drop down. With each jarring, I'd look for blood there. Told myself that wasn't what the stickiness was from, but still I checked. Kept remembering what she'd said about hurting me, that and how stupid I'd acted. I wanted to stay away from her for a while, her and everyone else. The morning activity had picked

up now and the sounds of cars, good mornings, hoofbeats—
everything bruised me. On automatic, I headed for a spot beyond the show rings, further than anyone had bothered to go. I
wanted to be alone with this horse, lock up with him.

Riding over, I pictured my jitters running out my knees and
into the worn saddle leather. From there it seemed this big
pretty horse would absorb them. He had a confident way of
moving; acted older than most green horses. Didn't behave like
some three-year-old right off the track. I invented his history.
Decided he must be a Virginia hunting horse the Cheslers had
persuaded some friend of theirs to sell. He might be new to
showing, but he sure wasn't new to being ridden.

I liked being off by myself with him. This corner of the
field bordered one of those funny Florida pine forests. I kept my
eyes on that forest and pretended we were out for a pleasure
ride. Had to keep myself from heading down a path cutting
through it.

I played games like this—wasn't far from cowboys and Indi-
ans, but still not far enough away. With my soreness, riding was
just about a constant reminder of her hand in me. This hurt
linked up with replays in my head. Memories of fuckings, which
I wouldn't see at first as longings.

She'd been watching me. This morning, again on that crazy
chestnut thing, she worked the outskirts too. She kept looking
over, but stayed away. She'd not given a hint of anger herself,
just sadness. I wanted terribly to make things right again. I
started across to her. Knew it'd look bad probably, but wasn't
quite sure to who.

I pulled alongside her. Her horse's twitching didn't bother
mine. We'd sort of crash together, then hers would dance away.
Made talking hard, but then we weren't really saying anything,
more just gazing. The next time we broadsided, I caught her leg.
Held tight long as I could before her horse pulled away again.

We kept it up as long as we could, but the chestnut was way worse off today and she was having trouble managing.

"Better get old Jammer here back to Linda," she said breaking off.

A weird little barb caught me when she mentioned Linda. I had to stop myself from checking for blood again, though by now I felt pretty anesthetized there. "Sure, okay," I said.

We went through the day back and forth like this. We did our jobs. I didn't do mine so well, I thought, but the results were okay. Passable. Gus told me Mrs. Chesler'd be happy her gray horse won. That was what mattered. She'd be stopping by the next afternoon, he said. Be here for the rest of the week. I disguised my worry about this pretty well. Promised myself I'd pull it together. Nothing seemed to be showing outside yet, at least if I used Gus to gauge it.

Silas could tell, but then he knew me about better than anyone. Seemed a good reason to stay away from him, but he didn't make that easy. At the end of the day he sort of assumed he'd take me back to the motel, which left me making up excuses. Halfway through a lame one I stopped. Said, "Silas, I think I'm going with Tory."

I knew he didn't want to be mad, but I could see his disappointment. It was clear he thought he'd gotten through better.

"Okay," he said, but he was chewing his lip. "I'll be by in the morning same as usual, right?"

"Yeah, of course," I said it real quick and started kind of backing away. He grabbed my arm and I got the same jolt off him as this morning. He'd never felt like this to me, but I figured it wasn't him, it was Tory—that she'd got me hooked up to all that and so I felt it coming off of everyone.

Walking away, though, I wasn't thinking about Tory, but about my little run-in with Ted and then that made me think about Linda and I wondered how low a profile I needed to keep around Carl's stables.

When I got over there, I saw Tim first. He lounged on that same trunk, smoking his cigarette in a lazy, careful way.

"You want Tory?" he asked.

"She around?"

He nodded, then called, "Lee's here."

It sounded so loud and bold I thought I'd crumple right there. I noticed this little quiver darting around my body, taking over my faculties. It only got stronger when Tory came out from the tent.

"You want to go?" she asked.

"Okay," I said, the quiver in my voice now.

"Keep her at bay for a while," she said to Tim and I knew she meant Linda. He looked unfazed, like this was an old routine.

Walking to her car I asked, "He do that a lot for you?" As soon as I said it, I realized how it sounded. I got to admit the really stupid stuff just popped right out when I was around her.

"Done it enough times, I guess, but not why you think."

I wanted to explain myself, tell her jealous wasn't what I meant, but then she said, "Been a hard day for you, huh, Cowboy?"

"I'm all right," I said.

8

Back at the motel, we stopped at her room first. I sat in a chair by the door and waited while she showered. I didn't know if the strangeness I felt was about being near her things or Linda's. Then I realized I couldn't tell whose stuff was whose anyway, so I started checking out the room—seeing which ways it was like mine and K.C.'s and which ways it differed.

After a bit of that I got edgy, worried that any time now Linda'd walk in the door. I noticed a bottle of bourbon on the bureau and wondered if it'd be okay to pour some. I'd make up my mind one way, then change it.

Tory rescued me from this—walked across the room with just a towel around her waist. I stared right at her breasts because, well, they were about eye level. Then, from habit, I dropped my eyes. Had to remind myself I was allowed to look, was even supposed to.

She tossed some clothes on the bed nearest me, then put one foot up and began drying her leg. I hadn't really seen her the night before so it was odd to now. Odder to see that scar of hers in such ordinary circumstances, though it still hushed me. I couldn't take my eyes from it, couldn't admire her in the way I thought she'd probably expect.

She didn't notice my gawking, either that or she was used to this kind of looking. Though it'd clearly happened a long time ago, the thing still looked so sore and ragged. The cut had been a tearing one and deep. I figured someone had really worked to put it there. Had even cut one way and then decided to make it worse. You could just tell it'd been on purpose and so I knew why it'd been impossible to ask about it.

She finished drying herself, pulled on underwear and her jeans. Now the scar was covered, I sat up, embarrassed I'd actually been leaning forward.

We left as soon as she'd dressed. Being out of their room helped. She drove us around to K.C.'s room and we went in. She sat down in a chair that matched the one I'd just gotten up from. I started straightening things on the bureau nearby, even re-arranged K.C.'s cosmetics.

It took a while, but I realized I was stalling; put down the perfume bottle I was holding and began unbuttoning my shirt. I felt her eyes everywhere then. Understood the charge I got and the shyness, too, but I could not account for the fear. Fear so strong I thought she'd feel it, too, and so I left the door ajar to hide it and kept my shower short.

When I came back into the room, my awkwardness was everywhere to trip on. I took my cleaner jeans from the drawer, another shirt, all that stuff. I set it on the bureau, didn't want to pile it on the bed because that's what she'd done.

Of course she watched me dress and so I was very workman-like about it. I sensed that this confused her and readied myself for questions. None came, though. She simply waited until I'd got my clothes on, then stood before me, right in front of me, and held my chin in her hand.

I closed my eyes—not to keep her out this time, but to let her in. She brushed her hand along my cheek. I knew she wouldn't kiss me, would leave that up to me and I would've, except I'd tuned too far in to how her hand felt on my cheek. How definite and unabashedly tender it was. And though I ached just where you'd expect me to, I hurt worse somewhere else and pressed against her to keep that hurt at bay by fixing the other.

She let me do this. Stayed very still and quiet. I dropped my face to her shoulder, felt her hair damp on my cheek, her hands flat against my chest and waiting. My hands, it turned out, were on her ass and when I pulled her closer, she slipped hers down to my belly, tucked one just inside my pants. That's about when K.C. walked in.

"Oh, jeez, sorry you guys." She cringed behind her handbag in a heightened K.C. kind of way. "Tory, honey, I know you said later than this."

"We were on our way out. Isn't that so, Cowboy?"

I looked back and forth between them. Tried to put together what had gone on there. "Yep. That's right," I said.

"Well, look, I won't be but a couple of minutes. If you two want to . . ."

"Honest, K.C. We were leaving." I hustled Tory to the door. We made a clumsy exit and I began questioning her as soon as we hit the parking lot. I started with a tactful "What was that about?"

She shrugged, giving me a "what was what" look, not peevish exactly, but staunch. This left me no thinking time, so I hit the point a lot faster than I'd planned. "It's her room, Tory. I haven't paid a dime for it."

"So? Darling, believe me, she doesn't care."

Her plainness stopped me. Obliged me to either find my

true objection or drop this altogether and by now I was tired of turning her kindnesses against her.

We decided to go over to the motel bar. Seemed the easiest place to wait out K.C.'s departure and, besides, we figured no one would be there. No one we knew, anyway.

She bought us a couple of drinks apiece and we beelined to a corner booth, slid behind a small round table onto crunchy plastic upholstery. The place itself was a bit more upscale than the Landlocked but featured the same schizoid medieval/colonial decor. In case light might come through nonexistent windows, plastic stained glass—mostly amber—covered the upper third of the walls. Dwarfed candle bulbs burned in wrought iron chandeliers. Our table had a genuine candle, but with no wick, at least not that we could find. We kept trying, though, kept searching both for that and for something to say. When we'd pretty well mutilated the candle, we gave up and started drinking. Struck a brisk pace. When we'd downed the second round she said, "Hungry?"

I guessed we really should eat before going further with the drinking or anything else. She took the initiative. Went up to the bar and returned with "pub menus." We looked these over, really took our time with them, and then decided on burgers. She put in the order and came back with a couple of beers to go with dinner. Course we wound up finishing them early and had to get seconds. Good thing the cook was fast or we might've spent the night right there under that tiny little table. She kept her composure; mine, other hand, was slipping badly.

Eating helped, gave me a focus other than her. I avoided anything really grotesque. Kept the food on my plate and in my mouth. Kept my hands off her. Well, I kept them on the outside of her clothes at least. Didn't matter much. We couldn't help but attract the attention of the five or six other patrons. The ones at the bar were content to watch from a distance, but two guys at a nearby table wanted to join us.

They were polite about it, actually. Instead of just bringing their chairs over, they used elaborate hand signals to ask permission. Tory judged them harmless and enthusiastically waved them on. I wasn't much bothered. They looked like mislaid conventioneers—not the big round type, but the tall skinny kind. Any case, they seemed conventional, right down to their fascination with us and our indiscretion.

We hammed it up for them and they kept the drinks coming. Tory gave the usual answers to the usual questions, at least until they asked what we did. When they asked that, she gave a big wink and said we were professional athletes. The taller of the two was caught mid-swallow. He sputtered as genteelly as possible. The other one coughed hard enough to blow a damp cocktail napkin halfway across the table. The two recovered quickly and if anything fawned more ardently. Guess they felt their time wouldn't go to waste if ours could be bought.

Tory moved closer to me and hooked her arm around my shoulders. For a minute I thought she was headed for my breast, but she stopped herself just short. Her arm had tensed so much it choked me a little. I didn't want to shift, though, not then. Was afraid it'd look disloyal.

She started to put them on the spot. Asked them what they liked and how they liked it. Her bluntness embarrassed them and surprised me. She'd taken some turn to where it wasn't fun and games and I wanted her to stop. The guys had really been okay, hadn't so much as put a hand out toward us. I sent them back to the bar, though we still had half-full drinks.

"Thirsty?" she asked.

I ignored this, said, "K.C.'s long gone by now."

She wouldn't let go, though. Wanted to see whatever this was through to wherever she needed it to go, which for now meant she wanted to follow them back to their room and then drop them. I knew if it went that far it'd go farther, so I kept at her, really had to coax before she came around.

We got ourselves out of the booth before the fellows made it back. I kind of felt bad for them. They looked so desperate, hurrying across the room, their hands tied by the drinks. By the time they reached us even the swizzle sticks looked wilted.

Fortunately, Tory was less softhearted than me. "Nice meeting you both," she said.

All their protests rolled together into one big gasping "no." The taller of the two gave the other a "you've got to do something" look that would've melted most.

Tory'd already started out and I followed. We made it to the doorway before the shorter guy caught up with us. "Hey, my friend over there, he . . . Look, why don't you girls just come on back and finish your drinks? We have money, we're not . . ." He clutched at my arm and soon as he did, Tory sprang. She grabbed his wrist and twisted. For a moment I thought she'd put him up against the wall, but instead she turned real calm and said, "My friend and me, we're leaving now. You got that?" She twisted just a little harder before dropping his arm.

"Bitches," he said soft enough you could ignore it.

I walked Tory away fast before she could hear whatever came after. Looked back once to see him still standing there, muttering and clenching like he was trying to decide whether to yell something.

Even when I got Tory outside she didn't talk. She stayed off on her own, so I just followed her. We stopped at her car and she pulled her pint and her pills from the glove box. She shoved the pill bottle in her pocket and started to unscrew the bourbon, then stopped, said, "You want . . . Let's go inside."

I unlocked the door and we went into the room. Soon as I

could, I sunk into that same chair by the door. Figured I'd wait there to see which way her mood went. She headed straight for the bathroom and came back with two glasses. Held them both in one hand, pouring from the pint as she walked.

She offered me a glass, tossed hers back soon as her hand was free to. Then she plunked down on the bed opposite me. Rested her empty glass on the thinning bedspread and took the pill bottle from her pocket. She downed two with the last of the bourbon and I saw her body slack way before the pills could've had anything to do with it. She handed them to me.

I'd finished my drink so I went to get water. I never could get the hang of taking pills dry, always choked on them. So, anyway, standing over the sink I noticed the script on the bottle. Methaqualone 300 mg. Well, that part I'd figured out the night before, by the size of them. And generic made sense. What startled me was the name on the script. It's not like I expected Tory's name to be there or anything, I mean I was surprised finding a label at all, but what got me was Linda's name on it. Fussed with me like she'd walked in or something, like she was watching.

I popped the cap and took a pill, one seemed about what I could handle. By the time I came back, Tory'd stretched out on the bed. I set the bottle on the table nearby and lay down with her. I wanted the pill to kick in and take me down a notch.

Tory seemed okay, the altercation already a joke to her.

"You see the look on his face?" she asked. "And that other one. We really should've seen it through." She turned and looked at me. "You all right?"

This question needed an answer so I nodded. She looked closer. Propped herself on her elbow. I stayed on my back, concentrated on the weight pulling my limbs, tried to make it heavier. I didn't know why I cared how the night had started or why I cared that she didn't. She was stroking my hair now, and my neck. What with the drug and all, I was paying close attention to this.

I let her handle things. Lay very still when she undressed me and didn't even try to undress her. She turned off the lights, but kept her clothes on. I felt her weight on the bed, her tongue on my arm first, then on my breast. Her teeth there. She stayed beside me, didn't touch me except with her mouth, so when her hand slipped across my stomach I flinched too much to hide it.

I felt her smile and then she slipped her hand down further. Tugged the hair between my legs so I flinched again; closed my legs on her hand and she pulled harder, pulled me on top of her. She put her finger just inside, then took her hand away completely. Her jeans felt soft at first and I rubbed up and down the fly, pressed into the buttons. She let me do this awhile. Shifted underneath me and put her hands on my hips, my ass, then turned the whole thing around so she was on top and pressing down so hard it hurt. I grabbed her hips, tried to keep her just a little further away. I don't know if that's why she stopped. I don't think so. Any case, she got up. After a pace across the room and back, she asked if we kept a bottle.

I told her no. Asked whether she wanted to go get one. She didn't answer, I just heard rummaging from the bathroom. A little while later she came back, said, "Think if we called room service, we'd get anywhere?"

"Worth a try," I offered.

She sat on the edge of the bed and turned the light on to see the phone. I felt funny, being the naked one and all, so I got under the covers. She helped pull the bedspread up, ran her hand along my hip and gave me a pat on the ass, all while putting a shine on some reluctant motel employee.

"How much cash you got?" she asked me.

"How much you need?"

"Thirty dollars?" she said to the receiver, then cocked her head my way.

I nodded.

"Done," she said and hung up. "Take him a while probably, but he'll be by. Guess it's later than I thought." She sat there not quite looking at me.

"You all right?" I asked.

"Oh yeah, sure. Just should've remembered a bottle, is all. Thought there was more left to that pint."

She got up again. Sort of wandered around. She had this easy way of moving; "agile," the magazines always called her. Even in a funk, walking around this stupid, too small room she looked smooth. Eventually she stationed herself at the bureau, picked up every single bottle K.C. had there. Some she commented on, but most she just set back down. The knock on the door interrupted her.

She took a ten from my jeans and a twenty from hers and traded the money for the bottle. You could see she'd felt better as soon as she knew the booze was on its way. Now it was here, she was truly fine. We had a drink or two but the drinks themselves weren't as important as knowing they were there.

After the second one, Tory turned the light out. This time, she took off her clothes and got into bed beside me. I'd never been in a bed with anyone before. I'd had sex and stuff, but not in beds—on them sometimes, but not in them, not with my clothes off, with someone else who had her clothes off, and while I still wasn't anywhere near sure what I wanted from Tory, having her next to me like this, well, it seemed close.

She started kissing me the same as she had earlier, except it felt different. This time I knew whatever I did would be okay, not like before when I could tell she wanted me quiet, wanted me still. It's not that I moved, because I didn't at first. I just lay there, and gave in to her hands, and her mouth; she seemed to like what she was doing, liked doing it to me. Before, I wasn't sure who I was for her. This time I was pretty sure I was me and I liked that and liked that she liked it. Mostly, though, I liked that she had no clothes on, how I could feel the whole length of her beside me and then on top of me. I couldn't get enough of that. Could've stayed homed in on that part for the rest of my life.

I was holding on to her, but I didn't want to act childish, so after a while I started getting more earnest, began sucking her breast, started fingering her. She was still on top of me, so I'd slid down a little, grabbed her ass instead of her shoulders, put some fingers inside. She moved a little when I did, made it easier, shoved her thigh between my legs, then put her hand there, too, used her thigh behind it.

The more she played around with my cunt, the harder I sucked her. Finally I gave up trying to fuck her ass. Fell back and felt sort of girlish—clutching at her shoulders, waiting for her to fuck me, moving around so she'd do it without me asking. She clearly liked this part, started teasing to make me move more and along with the girlishness I felt sort of rugged.

When she finally put her hand in, it was pretty rugged all right. I still sucked her breast and took more into my mouth then. Somehow having almost enough to smother me balanced off how much of her hand she'd got inside. I guess she understood this because when she moved her breast away she put her other hand in its place, let me suck on that.

I let go of her entirely. Clung instead to the blankets, which were underneath us, now, caught up in bunches. She pressed harder into me, but I fought her. Didn't mean to, just couldn't not. She fought back. Gave a lunge that nearly split me and put her other hand down my throat until it tasted like my mouth. I choked on all that sameness and she laid off it then, clear she'd gotten as far and as much in as she could.

She took her hand from my mouth and tucked it underneath me, stroked me until I'd calmed some, kissed my thighs. I didn't like that she wasn't right up near me. It felt lonely. But at the same time I didn't want her seeing me and while I knew she would watch, I could pretend better with her further away.

She tried getting her hand a little further in, but I closed against her, so she stroked me again, coaxed me. She put a finger in my ass, but that didn't work at all. That's when she started kissing me, kissing my thighs. She did this a long time. Never moved her hand, just kept it inside me, began to kiss around where it was. Began licking me there. This worked better. I dropped my head into the pillow while she eased my legs apart.

She began pushing her hand slowly, but very steadily so I knew she wasn't going to stop this time. I opened my eyes long enough to see her watching, then closed them. Had seen what I needed. Her savor gave me a kind of license, but it was her certainty that let me drop into the bed, let me open my legs. Once I did I felt only her sure, constant pressure. I moved toward her now instead of away; arched a little and felt her hand ease in and fold up. Then she stayed absolutely still and I felt myself close around her wrist.

Now she was in, she came up closer to me; was sort of over me. "You want me to stay quiet like this?" she said.

I nodded. Didn't want to talk because I was afraid I couldn't, not without starting that tightness in my chest, that thing where I couldn't breathe.

After a while, she began moving her hand a little. I knew she would, not like I didn't want her to or anything, it's just I knew she wasn't going to stay still. At first all she did was sort of turn her arm, real gentle and slow. Then it got harder. I flinched a little at first and as soon as I did, she grabbed my thigh, just held it. I must've shifted more or made her worry somehow, because soon after she leaned into her hand and pinned my leg for real.

That's when she started. I stayed with her for what seemed a long time. The pain was there from the start—big and solid. I swallowed tides of it. Opened to more of it, to its weird safety. But then she got way up inside me and the pain became big enough it took time to manage. I kept pushing it back, but couldn't get to anything else and finally she gave me a hit I couldn't stop.

I hunkered down, but I couldn't stop the blows that followed. Not any of them, and it hurt to try so I gave off trying. Let her pound me until I felt swaddled by it, until she'd put her fist so far up into the center of me she brought me close to crying and I guess I did cry out because she stopped and asked was I okay and did I want more. I said yes, though if she'd asked if I wanted to stop I would've said yes too. What I couldn't seem to say was no.

We went on like that until she saw I couldn't take it. When she stopped, I felt her hand drop down as far as I'd let it. Her other hand was on my thigh first, then touching me. What she was doing worked. The more her fingers played with me, the easier it was to let her hand go. Even once she'd got it out, or could've, she kept some fingers inside me, kept working me with her hand until I came in this necessary, basic sort of way.

I fastened myself to her then, sinking into every bit of her skin. She indulged a lot of this. Whispered to me and kissed and petted me. She showed me such tenderness that when I opened my eyes and saw the greed still left in her I got scared, even let out a little sound that brought her fingers to my lips. Then she pressed her full weight into me. Rubbed hard where I was already sore.

I was having trouble and she could tell. I knew by the way

she kept roping herself in, by the way she grabbed my hair and let go at once. She seemed embarrassed to be caught needing, and so bluntly. When she came she held on tight and afterwards kept holding on and I did too and we just lay there like that.

It took a long time, but finally even I'd had enough of this to start talking. Or maybe more rightly I had enough to where I needed to start talking. I don't think I planned what I asked. I just said, "So, what's dope like?" and my own question surprised me not because it was something everyone seemed scared to ask her about, but because I hadn't thought I wanted to know. It surprised her too because she gave me a funny look like weighing whether to tell me or whether I was misusing her, voyeuring.

The look went away, though. She thumped my chest like she had the last time she was telling me something she thought I already knew.

"It's like this," she said and she flattened her palm on my chest. "Like this afterwards part mostly, but like coming, too. A little bit at first anyway."

I thought she was going to stop there and she did for a while, but then she said, "It hurts when you can't have it. It hurts a whole lot when it's not there anymore." She reached over for what was left of her drink, took a swallow, and then rested the glass in the hollow beside her hip bone. "But then so does this," she said. And because she still had the drink in her hand, I didn't know if she meant booze or sex. Couldn't be sure anyway.

She filled her glass and handed it to me. I purposely took a huge swallow. Wanted the bite to reach my belly and remind me of her. The liquor traveled like a backwards echo of her hand. It spread out, bathing and opening tissue. But it didn't reach down far enough and draining the glass didn't push it any further.

She took the glass from me and put it away. We were both a little gauzy and she spoke with her voice still lost there. "Don't let anyone tell you it's not worth it. Anyone tells you that's a liar."

9

Silas's horn woke me sore and sleepy and way before I wanted. I started from the bed, but Tory pulled me back.

"Where you off to?" she asked. "And who the hell is honking?"

"It's Silas. I overslept."

"Hell, it's not light yet, girl. What're you talking about."

"I got to go," I said, more scared by the minute he'd be at the door and knocking.

She didn't let go, though. "This is stupid, Lee. You tell him I'll take you."

I couldn't answer her and once he knocked it was clear I wasn't moving.

"Look, I'll take care of it," she said.

I watched her pull on the nearest clothes, some of which were mine. She opened the door and I could hear their voices. She was making it sound like the most ordinary thing in the world. We'd had a late night, she'd bring me over later, sorry for the inconvenience.

Maybe it was ordinary. Maybe Silas had been worrying too much. Still, I felt bad hearing his voice. Could hear this sadness in it, though not the actual words.

She closed the door soon and I heard him drive away. I'd put them both in an awkward spot but she came back to bed like she hadn't noticed, had those clothes off and was beside me as if she'd never left. "Why you been going over so early?" she asked, hauling me on top of her.

"I don't know. Makes a good impression, I guess, with the Cheslers. You know how they are." I queased a little, remembering Mrs. Chesler was due that afternoon.

"The lady got you on a short leash, Cowboy?"

I dropped my eyes, didn't feel right joking.

"What? You think you owe her? Think you're some charity case?" She turned my face to hers. "Darling, you're a commodity. No different from the rest of us. And Mrs. Chesler, she's a businesswoman. With a longer arm than most, I'll give you that, but what you think she's going to do? She knows a good thing when she sees it. You just remember you're that thing. And her interest's not in you, but what you do for her. You're a hell of a property, darling. Sooner you get that, safer off you'll be."

I didn't agree with her on this. Least I didn't think I did. Okay, a lot of it was probably true, but I still didn't think Mrs. Chesler saw me that way, least not only that way. I could tell Tory thought people saw her that way, but I didn't want her to put this on me and when she pressed her leg up between my legs and acted playful, I didn't play back. She wanted me to, I guess, because she pressed harder, pressed until it hurt. I shut my eyes to push back the pain and she dropped her knee instantly, caught me in her arms.

"You hold on, now," she said. "I promise this part goes away."

I let her fuss over me. But while she did I started thinking things I didn't want to. I was so bruised I couldn't see how I was going to get through the day. Yesterday had been tough enough and now I had to make it look good for Mrs. Chesler, make myself look good.

That wasn't all of it, though. There was this other thing, too, and I'd thought it last night; had wondered how Tory came to know so much. Who'd torn her up like this. And, in that way you do sometimes, I felt jealous—both wishing it'd been me and wishing I could've stopped it.

I'd rolled off her and lay on my side buried into her. She hooked her leg around me and I held onto it. Hid my face in her chest, which made it easier to leave my hand on her scar once I found it. The way she tightened up would go right by you if you weren't waiting for it. The slightest tremble rolled once beneath my fingertips, then disappeared. I kept still, with my finger resting along the smooth ridge.

Slow at first, I slid my hand back. Followed the ridge, not down her thigh, but between her legs. She stayed real tightly wound, so I took it easy, but definite. Used an assurance I'd copped off her. I wanted to look at her face, see how well I was managing, but knew I'd lose it.

Instead I slipped over a little, let her turn onto her stomach. She pulled the pillow around her face and left her legs apart. Along the inside of her thigh the thing got saw-toothed, fits and starts of barbs, and her breath got that way, too; jerked away from my touching. I reached my hand underneath her, followed to where the scar came around the front and turned in. It cut higher than I'd realized, then turned down and went further in, came much closer to having fucked her up for good.

Now I was breathing bad. Could no way turn this around. I pulled my hand away and lay full length on top of her—just lay there. I wished I could act tender, cover the whole thing in that sort of light, but I couldn't. I'd wanted to see how far I could push. What she could take. A whole lot more than me, apparently, because now I wanted her deciding what came next.

I kissed her once before getting off her. She stayed how she was for a while after. I almost believed she'd fallen asleep. Now I was the one reaching my hand out and pulling it back, not sure when I'd feel allowed to touch her. She grabbed my hand and made me. Yanked me back where I'd been. She'd turned on her side now, held my hand to her lap and watched me.

I met her eyes; knew I had to. They weren't hard. Actually she looked disarmed. At first I thought I'd somehow done this to her, but understood quickly this was something she was letting me see. Her hand held mine in a clumsy way. She forced my fingers over the silky flesh, over and over.

After a while she closed her eyes and lay back. Let go of my hand. I curled against her, kept my hand where she'd put it, and watched her sleep or pretend to. This left me in not such a great place. Touching the scar had got me thinking. Opened me to stuff I usually kept cordoned off. Not the stuff when I was little, but how things changed when I turned ten and had that growth spurt. That stuff before didn't matter. Not so's I had to spend time not thinking it.

It was true what Jeannie saw when she looked at me; what my mother saw. I knew how to do things and knowing how got me through. At first it did. Like I knew how to suck him off. It was like I'd always known. And if I stayed down low on his body and kept my eyes closed I could forget who he was and play with his balls and taste him about ready to come off—almost.

But, thing was, he'd never let me jerk him the whole way. Instead, nearly there, he'd go from running his hands through my hair to holding my neck; shove me off him and onto my stomach. Get around behind me and take the dick I'd just made hard and put it up against me. Play me like he'd put it in. Slide against me until I was sliding back and both of us slippery.

He always put it up my ass now. I think this was for my mother. See, I'd got my period—got it young—and my mom, she made sure she knew when. Then she made sure I knew to get an abortion if I got pregnant. So my father, I think that's why he started fucking me in the ass, tried to keep it to that.

My mother's concession to him was the full-size bed we now fucked in. She pretended it was for me. That it was something I'd asked for and wanted—that and the new paint on the walls. I didn't remember asking for any of this. Only knew that since my twin beds were gone, I'd stopped staying up nights rearranging my furniture. It wasn't just because she'd told me not to, told me I'd mark up the walls, I'd already decided to quit. Was grown up enough now to see it didn't change anything. Grown up enough to see how things worked and to work them. Work him, though I had a harder time of it with his dick in my ass.

Still, it was fast becoming something I needed and so it wasn't what drove me away. That thing, the thing that did, I don't think it started right off. I get it confused with his crying, with his saying how sorry he was, though it doesn't bear much resemblance to that. Besides, that part had been going on all along.

This other thing he built up to. Started with saying how good I was at sucking, what a good girl—you know, stuff you can tune out. But that turned pretty quick to who else was I fucking, which he'd say a lot louder, which made it hard for me to do this my way, which was staying down on him and not listening.

He kept busting into my head, wouldn't let me alone. See before, in the twin beds it'd been about me and him and we'd been close and it was gentle—well, most of it—and so I'd come to depend on it. Now what it was, was about him and me staying separate and even that was okay because I could go into this thing it seemed I'd always known how to do. Could be who I thought he wanted. But what happened instead, he couldn't let it. Started yelling this stuff about who was I fucking and how he'd show me.

Then he'd forget and smack me over so I'd be looking at him and he'd start smacking me some more, back and forth across my face. And now, since I was on my back, he'd be on my stomach with his dick up the wrong hole, showing me what a bitch and a cunt I was. The words got caught up with how his dick was hitting me, way up inside and hard that way that's like coming, but not—that way that's better. Finally he'd stop yelling because he couldn't with his tongue in my mouth and I'd arch my neck so he'd put it in further and harder because I needed something to suck on.

Afterwards came the crying and all. His, not mine. Me, I'd get gone. I mean I'd have to sit there and listen, well, pretend to, but I didn't comfort him the way I used to because none of this was about me anymore and that single thing sent me running to Silas. Maybe Jeannie was right to worry. Maybe what I wanted from Silas was that old thing. Where it's—it's about you and they hold you and they put it inside because you want it there or you want the rest badly enough you get to want this part, too, and anyway it doesn't hurt. Like I said, I don't believe Silas would do this. Maybe that was the problem, that and knowing even if he did it wouldn't anymore be enough. Tory, I figured she could give me all of it.

I curled closer to her and shifted my hand. Put some fingers inside her and she started soon as I did—a jerk before she slipped back limp just as fast. I put my hand further in. I just held it there, held it still, and she kept her eyes closed but her breathing changed.

She slid her arms up over her head. Looked lazy about it but she had a real grip on the headboard and I couldn't keep my hand still any longer. Not with the way she pushed against me and how soft she got inside. So I gave her as much as I could until, like the other night, I just couldn't. Took my hand out and then she got up real abruptly and I worried about this way I kept letting her down. Worried mostly because I'd some idea where it left her.

She spent some time in the bathroom. I heard water running, the toilet flush. She came out a little damp. I contemplated the bourbon still on the table beside me. She simply walked over and poured a short one.

"Got to get moving," she said, offering me the glass.

I took it from her and drank what was left. Was what I liked best about her—she'd never ask because she knew it all already and she could fuck me to some place where it didn't exist. I just needed to get to where I could do the same thing for her.

I put down the glass and got myself up. She said she'd head to her room, then meet me back here. I didn't want to be without her for even that long, but wanted less to be in her room again; in Linda's room. She gathered her clothes, her pills, left the bourbon.

10

I got myself together a whole lot faster than she did and so passed some time sitting on the hood of her car. I hoped I wouldn't see anyone, but couldn't make that sure by staying in the room. Outside I could breathe better. The weather'd stayed cold and damp and I was glad for it, glad for the chill on my neck.

I hadn't seen anyone and had just about decided I wouldn't when Ted Bergan stepped out of a room three doors down. He tossed the toothpick he'd been sucking, traded it for a cigarette, then rolled the pack into his shirt sleeve. He looked like he had the day off. Or at least the morning. I wished I did. That I could spend the day in my Levi's watching other people work. I wished it hard, but nothing happened.

Ted stood there, arms folded across his chest, straw cowboy hat low on his brow. When his cigarette burned down a ways, he raised his hand to flick the ash. He had on sunglasses, though there was no need for them. Well, no regular need, still overcast as ever, especially so in this parking lot. With the glasses, I couldn't tell what he was looking at and I sure didn't think it was me until he turned his boot heels slightly, sort of listed my way.

He appeared to be deciding something. Least he would

waver a little, then fold his arms again, puff hard. Finally he cocked his hat back, started walking over. He didn't get far before Tory came around the corner. She didn't see him, least she acted like she didn't. He turned back, went inside. The door shutting caught her attention, but just for a moment.

We were about halfway to the showgrounds when she said, "What'd Ted want?"

"Never got the chance to find out."

"Yeah, well, be best to keep it that way."

I must've looked funny, showed my hurt, or whatever, because she softened her voice.

"He's not the kind you want near you, all right?"

I nodded, not sure what I'd done wrong. I disliked Ted about as much as you could dislike anyone you'd not yet spoken to. Course, sometimes that's the easiest way to hate. Any case, it bothered me she couldn't see I didn't need convincing.

Since we were late, she parked right up by the tents, next to Linda's car. I took off for the Cheslers' stalls, worried what Gus would think. Found him sitting on a hay bale talking with Reb. Reb nodded hello and so did I. He wasn't as tall or thin as his father. Made him a good size for most horses. Since I'd walked up, he'd taken a rag from his pocket and started buffing his boots. Most everybody wore black boots these days, but the Cheslers had put Reb in brown a long time back and they'd kept it that way. He'd wear green coats in the summer and tweed when it got colder. Was about the only one still wearing tweed. Part of the Chesler signature. I'd actually wondered if they'd put me on the gray horse because my black boots would look better on him than Reb's brown ones.

Any case, Reb kept busy with his boots and I was just as glad. Always felt nervous around him. While Gus's southern gentleman stuff was the real thing, Reb's came off forced. Don't mistake me, he could put a shine on you better than most. Came second nature to him. But that was the thing—it wasn't his nature exactly.

I would've felt jittery with Reb there or not and so spoke up bold to hide it. Gave Gus a big loud good morning. He teased me for still looking achy and laughed off my lateness. Even said to Reb how he'd been wondering when I'd quit "rising with the rabbits" and act like the rest of the riders—Reb included.

It was true most riders never turned up much before seven, so maybe I was okay. Had worried over nothing. Of course, this thinking worked only if you truly had nothing to worry about.

Gus was still teasing me. "Nothing for you to do here," he said. "Why not go get yourself some coffee. Looks like you could use it."

I laughed along with him, then started off.

"And Lee," he called after me. "Eat something, will you?"

I took the short way round to the concession stand and felt bad for hoping Tory wouldn't be there getting food. Tim would probably have taken care of it, though. I hoped I wouldn't run into him either, or Silas for that matter. At least I knew Mrs. Chesler wouldn't be arriving until afternoon.

After all this fearing and calculating, I came around the corner of the tents and literally smacked into Ted Bergan. He backed me against a wall so his arms stanchioned my neck and his hipbones pressed into me. "Was looking for you," he said, bringing his face closer with every word until his lips touched my ear. He whispered, now. "What I want to know," he said, "is you sucking her pussy, or is she sucking yours?"

I couldn't move, not that he was really blocking me, I just couldn't move. In this hazy way I wondered should I be answering him, but the question made me sleepy. I closed my eyes and he said, "My guess is you're sucking her. My guess is you're good at it." I felt his tongue in my ear and him getting hard from rubbing on me and me opening my legs just a little and then someone else's hand was on my arm.

"Girl doesn't want to talk to you, Ted."

It was Carl's voice and so I figured it was his hand on my arm, jerking me away and then on the small of my back guiding me along. We walked awhile before I opened my eyes. When I did, Carl said, "He didn't hurt you, darling."

I shook my head, though it wasn't a question. He clamped his arm around my shoulders and kept us moving. I wanted to feel safe walking with him, but something about the force of his arm had me completely cowed.

"Stay clear of that one," he was saying. "He's been looking for a way to settle up and we don't want him deciding you're it."

"Yes sir," I said, thinking how I never talk that way. Even at school where you were supposed to call the teachers sir, I never did, couldn't stomach it.

Soon enough he'd bought me breakfast and we were sitting at a table overlooking the grand prix ring.

"You happy, Lee?"

The question threw me off. It seemed he genuinely wanted to know, but at the same time knew already. Like his point was to find out whether I knew. I didn't answer right off, sat there weighing one thing against the other. Wanted my answer to be the right one, same as his.

Just when I was going to try and say something he said, "Don't worry yourself about that now." Then he got up. "You think instead about coming to work for me. Be the best thing for everybody."

I kept my eyes even with his while the rest of me squirmed. I blamed the morning damp on the chair. Wanted to get up too, but if we both were standing, it'd maybe drag this out. I settled for shifting a little.

"You let me know," he said. "I'll take good care of you." And when he walked away, his footsteps rattled the aluminum riser, my flimsy chair, even set the table shaking. I sat staring at another uneaten breakfast and sipped coffee to stop my own shivering. Soon as he'd said it—the part about taking care of me —my shaking started. Now I couldn't get it to quit.

I decided moving might help. Walking across the riser, I jostled it the same way he had. It helped to know the floor was actually moving, but by the time I reached the stairs, I had to hold the railing to make it down. Even so, hitting the ground caught me up short, upturned my stomach. I kept walking despite a powerful urge to sit down in the dirt.

Some ways away I realized I'd left the remnants of my breakfast sitting on the table. I hoped that on top of everything else people weren't going to think I was someone who littered.

11

I hadn't known where I was headed, but soon found myself by Tory's car. From there it came easy. Opening the door, the glove box, finding the pills there. I took one from the vial and halved it. Put one half in my breast pocket, the other in my mouth. I couldn't swallow, so it began to dissolve.

I found a hose by the front of the stalls. Someone'd left it running. I took it round the corner. Choked on the water. The bitter paste clogged my throat instead of washing down. I kept forcing myself to swallow and by the time I got the pill down, I'd burned my throat pretty good.

I wanted the trembling to stop right then—magic. When it didn't I looked up. Found Tim standing there watching. He maybe had been all along. I couldn't know. He turned the faucet off. Offered me a towel. I buried my face in it. Peeked down at the mud puddle I'd made, the splatters up and down my boots. I leaned over to clean them. Tim steadied me. His hand on my arm wanted nothing from me.

"You all right, now?" he asked.

"Thanks," I said, not willing to admit I'd been in trouble. We walked around front. Sat on the trunk there. I needed this—just sitting, but not alone. I remembered wishing for the day off. A funny, soothing kind of thought till I remembered that seeing Ted had started it.

I was up and partway around the corner before I knew why. Then I threw up.

Tim let me alone, though he turned on the hose again. I rinsed my hands and mouth, my whole face. I'd have to take the rest of the pill now. It seemed a waste, but there it was, done, and the most concrete thing to focus on. Course I'd spilled water down my shirt, so I was lucky the crumbling little thing hadn't melted. I swallowed it fast. Didn't want the time to lose it.

Afterwards, Tim took me back to the tackroom. Helped me onto the cot. Hell, he practically tucked me in. I stayed how he put me. Lay flat on my back, afraid moving would turn my stomach. I couldn't quite rest, though. I fidgeted from the neck up, turned my head this way and that.

Tim stayed at the doorway, facing out like he was guarding me. At least I imagined it that way. Felt hugely cared for by him. Whatever the truth of it was, my version settled me, left me still so I began to notice things around me. The cot smelled musty, but better than anything outside. The pillowcase had a familiar commercial laundry smell. Was stiff on my cheek, reminded me of the guy on the plane—his shirt collar. That made me restless again so I focused on things further away.

The little room seemed sparser than the other night. Then, shadows filled the gaps and Tory loomed larger than life. Now the room seemed larger, but the more I concentrated on the spaces, the smaller they became. Some place inside me wanted air—great gulps of it. The pillow's laundry smell held me down, the sick-sweet starch smothering me until I bounded off the bed and out past Tim.

I slowed myself once outside, walked a few yards then rested against a tent rope. I rubbed my back along it. Ducked so the rough fibers crossed my neck, burned the skin a little in a good way. I started walking again. Figured by the time I walked the whole way around the tent Gus would need me on a horse. The morning'd go on normal after that.

By afternoon, I'd brought myself under control. When I have to, I can. My body works that way. Of course, another Quaalude stolen from Tory's glove box didn't exactly hurt. I'd managed to hit a place with the right amount of ease and sharpness, which was good because now there'd be Mrs. Chesler to deal with.

Gus and I were walking the three conformation hunters to the ring. I led Mrs. Chesler's special gray one. We didn't talk about her—Mrs. Chesler, I mean—but it was clear she'd arrived. Gus carried his long frame a little straighter and he spoke carefully and humbly, like he was practicing on me.

He'd slung coolers over the horses. First time he'd bothered with that all week. The weather'd stayed cold enough for flannel ones. Good thing, too, since the Missus preferred flannel to fishnet. Said it gave her a chance to really see her colors—navy and white. The gray horse looked especially good in his.

I wished the conformation class wasn't first. It would've been nice to have a warm-up before the showdown, before I had to give the performance Mrs. Chesler'd come expecting. At least I didn't have to get on the gray horse right away. Their little chestnut mare was up first. She was docile enough to help me get settled. By the time I got to the gray, I'd be all right. I tried to remember his name so I could work it in when I spoke with Mrs. Chesler. She liked you to know her favorites. Be a while before I had to do that part, though. She always stayed in the stands. Afterwards you'd go calling—haul the trophy and the ribbons, the prize money, which she'd give you back, tucking it in your pocket like you were her hairdresser. It had always been done this way, went easier on everyone.

So we were both nervous, Gus and me, and on our own for the moment. He tutored me on the course a lot longer than he had to. It was another easy one, just the flip side of yesterday's. Simple, I told myself—tour the ring and get out.

Soon as the groom arrived to hold the horses, Gus put me on the chestnut. I felt big on her. Most of the horses I piloted were big ones, while this one couldn't have been more than fifteen hands and fragile, too. Felt like if I squeezed my legs too tight I'd break her in half.

Anyway, I worked her around and then Gus got us started with some fences. He'd stationed himself by the vertical and now dropped the top rail on one side, making a little fence for us to jog to. We did this easily, the little mare acting like she just woke up. Might have been my Quaalude, though. I turned and took us back over it, careful to get more steam going this time.

Gus put us through the rest of the motions, but none of it prepared me for how I felt catching my first sight of Mrs. Chesler. From the in-gate I saw her legs—well, those white stockings of hers. She always wore white stockings, sheer ones, and somehow, even with all the dust and dirt and muck, they stayed spotless. K.C. said she had a Dustbuster plugged into her car's cigarette lighter and vacuumed herself several times daily. Reb said a lady-in-waiting hid in the trunk—even claimed he'd seen her. Just about everyone had noticed and had a theory. Mine was touch-up paint.

I watched those legs for a while, then moved my eyes to the patent leather shoes, the navy blue knit suit with white piping— the Missus liked to wear her colors, too. I didn't quite look at her face—was afraid to meet her eyes before the class. Thought it'd jinx me somehow.

When I got into the ring I put the mare right into her circle.

Figured getting busy fast would keep me from noticing any more of Mrs. Chesler. Didn't work, though. The ribbons flapping from her straw boater caught me. The little horse saw them, too, so I jerked the reins to bring her back to me.

Coming out of the circle to the first fence, I decided I'd figured the jinx wrong; had better face Mrs. Chesler. When I did, she nodded, not that she moved her head or anything. It was all from the eyes. I tipped my hat in return, barely touched my fingers to it but she noticed, her smile told me so.

My gesture surprised me. It was something the real pros did. I'd never had the gall before, but today it sort of slipped out. Was clear the Missus felt it belonged on me, which made it a keeper. I'd be tipping my hat till the end of my days, which'd come pretty soon if I didn't pay attention to where I was going.

We were almost down on the first fence without a spot. Least I didn't have one. The mare worked it out herself, taking us safely into the course. I had this sense of picking her off the ground at each fence, carrying her over. Wasn't fair to see it this way, especially since it was the other way around. I couldn't help it, though.

We took all the safe distances. No decisions to make, just get around without goofing up. We did fine, nothing spectacular, but then spectacular wasn't in the offing. I tipped my hat on the way out, too. You can't do one and not the other.

Gus held the chestnut while I hopped off. We didn't even talk about how she'd gone, I just tied her number around her neck and headed for the gray. He stood there calmly, big and soft as a baby-sitter. The groom pulled my saddle from the chestnut, and soon as he had it transferred to the gray, Gus helped me aboard.

When I hit the saddle, I remembered his name—Toreador. No wonder I'd had trouble. It sure wasn't something the Cheslers came up with, so that meant a bloodline name. No question there were special plans for this one—a bloodline horse who'd never raced. I got a sudden fear they planned on me taking this horse into the future for them. I brushed some gray hairs from my navy jacket, straightened the collar of my white shirt, all the while wondering how much of me Mrs. Chesler figured she owned.

Gus jostled my knee, reminded me of things a little closer at hand. "You're all right now, Lee?" he asked.

I swallowed and nodded; knew he'd hear the shake in my voice if I spoke. I ran my hand along Toreador's neck. Touching him helped; still I feared he'd feel my nerves instead of calm them. He showed no signs of fretting, though. Hadn't since I'd met him, and I'd exposed him to worse than this. I relaxed a little and wished for another half lude to keep me there. I stopped short of searching my shirt pocket for powder, but only because of how it'd look.

We trotted a couple of times around the schooling ring, then moved into a canter and he turned into this giant rocking chair. With him soothing me, I began to feel even more okay. Like maybe I wouldn't have to pay for the things that had happened. It could start here with this horse, with Mrs. Chesler in the stands. She'd seen nothing that'd come before and if we nailed this class, then who could sway her against me?

Gus put us over some fences. Not a single hitch, just easy all the way. Before I knew it we were waiting at the in-gate. I couldn't help searching for Tory in the stands. I knew she'd be over on the other side where a jumper class was starting, but I still looked. I didn't find her, but on my way into the ring I saw Linda. No mistaking her.

I lengthened that first circle as much as I could. Gus had told me to show off the horse this way, but I did it more for time. Needed to get used to the idea Linda would be watching me now, every chance she got. I wasn't sure if Carl'd put her up to this, or if it was her own thing. Either way, I knew it'd be this way from here on in. I could just tell.

I took Toreador for as long a tour as I could without being accused of trying to show him the course. You had to watch that sort of thing, they'll bounce you right out if they think they've truly caught you at it. The line's pretty thin and I knew I'd coasted near it, so I turned the corner with him moving at that nice rocking canter.

At the pivot, I tightened him a little; made sure we were seeing things the same. Once I had him gathered this way, I tipped my hat. I could hear Linda's account of that. No doubt she'd wait awhile before she gave it. Launch in just when I believed she'd let it pass. I didn't know who I thought I was and I sure hoped she didn't ask me to explain it to her.

I couldn't be the unwitting passenger for another first fence, so I buckled down; made sure I knew what Toreador needed. He seemed only to want my assent. I guess this bighearted fellow had good manners about taking over. I gave him a little extra leg as a go-ahead and he took the cue. The rest was picture book. Easy and dreamlike—the kind of ride that humbles you about your partner.

Making my exit, I looked for Linda. Even considered touching my hat to her, it'd been that good. She'd gone, though, and her empty place at the rail turned the magic I'd felt back to business. I finished out the class that way. The last horse was a big showy chestnut I had no feeling for anyway. Another mare, but the turned coin of the first one. Solid and tall with a big blaze splashed across her face and four white stockings to match. This one had her future secured already, just not the best manners yet. The Cheslers had probably yanked her from the track with the hook end of a crowbar and they'd never be sorry for it.

We turned in a nice steady trip with me keeping her from

playing on the turns. Anything more than that and she'd have a chance of edging out Toreador. Was delicate sometimes when the Missus had such a clear favorite. Most often you could keep her top two bouncing back and forth and it'd not matter who won. Then times like this you could lose for winning if you didn't shave a little here and add it there.

Coming out the ring, I knew I'd played this class just right. Gus knew it, too. He held the chestnut while I jumped off and then I just started walking. He let me, probably figured I needed to cool off some and I did, but there was something else, too. I wandered away from the ring, the schooling area, caught myself veering toward the other schooling ring where Tory'd be.

I stopped myself; had to stay out of trouble until the end of this class. Wouldn't be long before they'd call the numbers. Then I'd have to jog Toreador and stand him for the conformation part. It counted twenty percent, so I couldn't just blow it. I turned myself around and headed back to Gus. He clamped his great big palm on my shoulder, said, "You did just right, Lee."

He said a lot of other things, too. Called me by name a lot, was building me up and taking my nerves down all at once. He'd handed the big chestnut over to the groom, who was busy rubbing her down. The little one stood patiently under her cooler, waiting it out. Toreador waited too—calm and handsome as ever. Gus held him with one hand and me with the other.

Soon enough, the last horse went into the ring and that was our signal to get ready. I still wore the mare's number, so Gus quickly traded it for Toreador's. I felt six years old with him tying strings around my waist. He gave me the reins and pulled off Toreador's cooler, gave him a last rub with a towel, while the groom painted those great big hooves.

They called the numbers just as if we'd told them how. Toreador first, followed by the big chestnut and then the little mare a respectable, maybe even lucky fourth. I jogged Toreador into the ring and set him up fast. I knew if I got him set straight away, he wouldn't move. Sure enough, he posed like a pro, leaving me just to hold the reins and wait.

Gus had less luck standing the mare. She kept twitching and breaking out of her stance, till finally the judges switched her and the number three horse. The little mare kept her fourth place and of course Toreador kept his win. That made wins in all three of his classes so far. This was good, of course, but also bad. Now Mrs. Chesler'd want him to win the last class tomorrow. That'd not only sew up the division championship, but the overall championship for the green divisions.

The championships wouldn't mean so much to her, though. It'd be having the win in all four classes that'd matter. Not many horses pulled that off anymore, especially not green ones. Used to happen, but these days things came in tighter. The first two or three point horses most always slugged it out and while these rivalries were good, Mrs. Chesler loved having a superstar. If Toreador debuted with an old-fashioned sweep, he'd get everyone talking. And Mrs. Chesler'd get to remind everyone how things used to be when her horses were the main attraction and jumpers just a tacky sideshow. So winning tomorrow'd keep the Missus happy. Problem was, after that there'd be no place left to go but down.

The ringmaster pinned the blue ribbon on Toreador's bridle and handed me the trophy and the check. I knew my manners, so I didn't look at the check. Anyway, I didn't need to—yesterday's was for fifty dollars, so this one would be, too. Tomorrow's stake class would pay a hundred for the win, so I guess I had my own reasons for winning it.

Once we were out of the ring, Gus sent the horses back with the groom and handed me the ribbons along with the rest of the loot. I put it all into the trophy, which was, no joke, a silver wire

bread basket. Gus mumbled something about paying our re-
spects and so we headed over to the stands, to Mrs. Chesler's
table.

As we walked, I couldn't help but notice Tory schooling that
nutcase of hers. Carl stood beside a huge vertical as she barreled
down to it. She pulled up just in front and backed the horse. I'd
caught my breath for her and now was having trouble letting it
go so I looked away, over to the jumper ring. I couldn't miss
Linda. She worked the in-gate hard, cajoling a hapless official
into rearranging the order. Tim stood not far from her holding
Huey and the three other horses that made up Tory's string.

That sight'd be enough to bring most gatekeepers to their
knees. Huey probably could've swayed the guy all by himself,
but his three heirs flanked him: Flexible Flyer was a sleek
black daredevil Tory'd nicknamed Frisbee; Mr. Clean, a muscu-
lar white horse who'd started off well and then plateaued; and
Lazy Boy, announcers called him the easy chair with wings.

Gus sure wasn't the only one who knew how to stack a deck.
Hell, Linda could probably teach him a few tricks—you needed
a lot up your sleeve to mess with a jumper class. See, no one
could prove the order mattered much in hunters, so it was more
about manners. But in the jumpers, everyone knew going late
gave you an edge; meant you knew what to beat. This edge paid
off big in jump-offs. You'd know if and when to shave time,
whether to go for broke or play it safe and clean. A tenth of a
second could make your win, and going last handed it to you. If
you could deliver, that is.

And when you won a grand prix class, it wasn't just about
ribbons and silver baskets. The stakes were a hundred times
what they were in hunter classes. Then you add the boost to
your animal's price tag, a price tag that already had an extra
zero, and you can see how it'd get under the skin if someone
were too obvious about fixing the order.

But Linda knew how to fix and keep everyone smiling. It was fear really, though no one let on, so she kept fixing and Carl's horses kept winning. At least what they called the big-ticket classes. They'd throw a few of the smaller ones, or not even enter. Sort of keep things square. To Linda and Carl, and Tory too, I guess, this was all just part of the game. Same as a good ground man or a well-timed needle. Getting caught was the only thing against the rules.

Gus tugged my sleeve as we climbed the stairs. He knew where I was looking and didn't like it, so I stopped. It was then I noticed people watching us. Some offered approving nods, a few nice words. We glad-handed our way across the riser, each tossing the praise back to the other. Neither of us had ever learned too well how to handle this. For myself I was glad the riser didn't shake the way it had this morning. There were enough people now to hold it steady.

When we reached Mrs. Chesler, both of us breathed different, though not necessarily easier. She sat at a big round table surrounded by an entourage. Today's group included two pipe-smoking men accompanied by white-gloved women shod in spectator pumps. All four approached Mrs. Chesler's age but weren't there yet, which partially accounted for the heavy smell of deference coming off them.

Another couple rounded out the group, younger and less conciliatory. The man was Mrs. Chesler's "nephew." She'd taken him in when he was twelve and had remained blind to almost everything about him. Right now she kept her eyes from the impatient woman who groped him under the table. Seems to me there's something about people with acute vision that makes them lump all their bad judgment in one place. It's like they need somewhere to rest all that sharpness and it feels best to put it someplace unusually dull. That place for Mrs. Chesler was Jerry.

His role as nephew differed from mine and Reb's as employees, but the ways were subtle, having to do mostly with the number of chances doled out, the possibilities for forgiveness. We served different purposes. Reb and I were supposed to generate income, while Jerry was to siphon it off. True to form people whispered about him and patted us on the back. All it really amounted to was each of us doing our job.

Mrs. Chesler had chairs brought for me and Gus. I sat between the two of them and handed over the basket first thing. I tried not to, but when I heard the announcer launch into the familiar list of Tory's accomplishments I looked past Mrs. Chesler to the jumper ring. Tory was on Mr. Clean, so I knew I didn't have to worry. While I still didn't believe they'd put the chestnut into a jumper class, I didn't know. They sure were giving him a lot of play. I saw Tory take the first three fences, then Mrs. Chesler crashed in.

"Well, dearie," she began. "You and my Tory make quite a formidable pair. I suppose you've guessed he's my special onc."

My breath left both lungs and a prickle replaced it traveling fast through my belly and down between my legs. "Caught," I thought for an instant, even though I knew what she meant, knew Tory was the nickname for the gray horse, Toreador—I mean, what else could they call him?

"Yes, ma'am," I said, recovering. "I like him real well myself."

While Gus went into an overly cautious way of speaking around Mrs. Chesler, I went into a folksy, "aw shucks" mode. It startled me every time and then embarrassed me. Still I did it. No matter how cheap and foolish I felt about it, it worked. "You two have much ahead of you," Mrs. Chesler continued. "I expect we'll see you take home the Governor's Trophy at the National this year."

From here on in it'd be autopilot, though I hated when she got to planning so far ahead. The National wasn't till November, but this kind of long-range goal helped her keep you on a string. She usually didn't set in to this talk quite so soon and it got me wondering how much attention she'd paid to my wandering eye; how much she'd heard.

Gus and I had cocktails with her; well, Gus did. Not surprisingly, the Missus didn't acknowledge I drank and so always ordered me ginger ale. After we'd all been sipping awhile, she fished the checks from the basket and tucked them in my pocket, along with a white envelope. "Now, I know you've had a little setback, dearie, so you'll find a little extra inside. Anything else you need, you know just to ask."

It was all expected, but like before when she called the horse Tory, I had feelings I thought I'd planned for and so prevented. I wanted her help, needed it, but at the same time wanted never to take anything from her again. Maybe it was because I felt a tug that said extra help now meant a payback lasting through November. I began thinking about the things Tory'd said this morning. Believing them made it a whole lot easier to think about Carl's offer. Made everything easier.

Mrs. Chesler put her bony hand onto mine and squeezed. It was my signal to lean closer while she kissed my cheek. This ritual had always meant too much to me and today, when I was supposed to kiss her I only brushed my cheek against hers and then got to my feet, fighting the urge to dump a drink down Jerry's girlfriend's dress. And while the urge didn't trouble me, the target did. I'd sighted the weakest one available.

By now, the jumper class had finished. Tory'd won it with Frisbee. Huey'd clipped a rail on the second fence, so after that she'd taken him around letting him rub everything. Mr. Clean made it to the jump-off and came in fourth, Lazy Boy sixth. All this I'd managed to figure out while holding my own with Mrs. Chesler.

Once freed I headed for Carl's stalls and would've continued dumbly on that way if I hadn't seen Ted and Linda standing at the water spigot near the tent. I veered close enough to hear Ted saying, "How you know what she wants, she practically . . ."

Linda cut him off there. "I don't care if she pulled you by the dick, you touch her again and I'll fix it so you can't even buy aspirin."

"What's this to you, you next in line?" His voice had gotten louder, while hers was getting quieter.

"We've got an interest here, Ted. You want to line up against us, it's okay by me."

I'd heard enough. Began heading for the parking field. I saw Silas's truck still there and gravitated toward it, but before I got there, I saw Tory's car.

I stashed myself in her passenger seat and waited with no idea how long she'd be or how I'd find her when she found me. Reflexively I went for another lude and had swallowed part of it before I realized I didn't need it, that all the twenty-hour days back to back had done enough, especially now the pressure was off until tomorrow. I got out of my jacket and put on a gray sweater I found on the backseat. Then I curled up to wait.

12

I'd dropped asleep waiting for Tory, so when she finally came she shook me awake.

"Christ, Cowboy, what you doing here? I been looking all the damn place over."

She didn't seem to expect me to answer, so I didn't. Instead, I tried to adjust my eyes to the dusky light while she got the car started. We went back to the motel and through the same routine as last night—stopped at her room first, then mine.

We passed up the bar altogether and wound up in the dining room, which was okay since they had plenty of drinks in there too. I drank my first one trying to decide what I most needed to find out about—what Carl'd said or what she knew about the thing with Ted. We hadn't started talking yet, so I still had a chance to steer things.

By the second drink I'd decided the thing with Ted was keeping her quiet and while at first it seemed that meant I should talk about it, soon enough I'd started in the other direction.

I began by saying, "Silas is leaving Saturday."

She'd been stabbing her swizzle stick this whole time, now she prodded ice cubes with it. "He getting an early start for Tampa?" she asked.

"No. He's going home. Didn't have the money for the whole shebang."

I kicked myself for saying this. Knew Silas wouldn't want it getting around. One thing if everyone knew, but another to confirm it for them. I looked at Tory. She looked sad instead of eager to hear more and it reminded me she didn't traffic rumors. Enough going round about her, I guess.

"Silas always been one of the good ones," she said. "Shame seeing him go out this way."

She only said what was true. Silas was on his way out. Still, I wanted to spar with her about it and nearly chewed my cheek to keep from starting something with her.

She chewed her stick now, then sucked it. Said, "Carl talk to you yet?"

"Uh huh," I said. "Sort of."

"He's had his eye on you a long time, you know . . ."

She said it like I owed for it, but I didn't say anything and she kept talking.

". . . so if Silas, if he's lost his claim and all, well, kind of gives us a clear path, don't it? Carl, I mean."

She pulled her swizzle stick slowly through her teeth, then tossed it on the table, said, "Shoot, Cowboy. You're not going to spend your life becoming the next Reb Taylor, are you? Somebody's got to take you into the jumpers, and . . . it just ought to be Carl."

She discovered she'd been leaning forward and so sat back, said, "I got too many horses now, anyway. Can't be riding ones like Jammer."

She kept talking some more about how she had too much to do and how Linda and Carl planned to go on a spending spree after the Tampa shows.

"God knows how many they'll bring back," she was saying. "I don't have time to weed them out. Not and do justice by the string I've got. So you can see what we need."

"Just like that?" I said.

"Nearly. In fairness, we got to put you up and see what you do against some height. Let you take one for a test drive."

"You mean test me."

"Yeah, well, that's about how it'd be."

I backpedaled, now. I knew what she was offering. That I could take their test tomorrow. At least, I had presence enough to remember what it'd cost me if I blew it.

"I'd have to wait," I said, "until the Tampa shows have finished. Mrs. Chesler's got me least until then."

"You want her to have you forever?" She'd chewed her swizzle stick flat and now tapped her glass with it. Her sulking surprised me and maybe her too, because she quickly said, "Look, I didn't mean that. It's just I can see where you're going and you can't and it tires me. Believe me, darling, you'll wonder why you ever gave that woman the time of day."

There was something between her and Mrs. Chesler and I didn't want to know about it. Not now. We had enough at hand.

"Listen," I said. "For now she pays me. Without her I'd be going north with Silas this Saturday and then where would we be?"

This last thing sort of slipped by. I'd no intention of putting our fortunes together and now that I had I wanted to get up and walk around. I didn't know what I expected from her and at the same time I knew this whole thing was about our staying together. Knew it so much I wondered whether she was twisting Carl's arm to get me signed on.

She just said, "You're right."

I didn't hear what came after and so had to ask.

"I'll talk to Carl," she repeated. "We'll set something up. Lookit, don't worry. It's not going to surprise the lady any, but we'll be careful and keep it quiet. After Tampa's better anyway. I mean, there's no sense tipping our hand and there'd be nothing for you to do until we got home."

Ocala finished out pretty much like it was supposed to. Toreador made his sweep; wound up green hunter champion —both conformation and overall. After that Mrs. Chesler insisted I continue on to Tampa. Silas couldn't argue much, not with her standing there beaming and telling him she'd look out for me. It left him nothing to do but head home. And it left me right where I wanted to be—in Tampa with Tory.

13

I was done with my last class for the week. Done period. Just a presentation to get through tomorrow. One of those things where I'd stand around with Mrs. Chesler and Toreador while people took pictures and we took the haul. Other than that I had nothing to do and this nothing made me both easy and edgy. Feeling this way made me need to get moving so I left Gus standing by the hunter ring and just started walking around.

These Tampa shows had gone okay for me. Toreador won almost everything he could. Not flawless like Ocala, but no one could expect we'd keep that streak going. So there were a couple of red ribbons mixed in with the blues. Both weeks they came in the first class, making me sweat the rest of the division. It was okay, though—kept my mind on my work and that made things easier.

Having Silas gone made everything easier, too. No one pointed me to my concerns and so I had fewer of them. K.C., she eyeballed me funny sometimes, but she'd stayed pretty scarce lately, at least it seemed so. But then maybe I was the one laying low. Maybe it was just that since Tory'd got us our own room, we didn't bump into K.C. all the time. I guess I sort of missed her.

I walked until I decided it was late enough I could go over and hang out at Carl's stalls. Late enough no one'd see me there. I didn't know who I was worried about. Mrs. Chesler never hung around this late and who else did I have to care about? I went and sat on some feed sacks outside Carl's stalls and waited for Tory.

I'd just closed my eyes for a minute or two when she showed up. I felt her lean against the bags, then she gave me a little shove. "Come on and wake up," she said, her voice husky and sure like always.

"What?" I said, keeping my eyes closed. I liked this so far, her touching me, the sound of her voice.

She gave me another shove and I opened my eyes. She'd taken down her hair and the dark curls fell across her shoulders. I reached out to touch her, but she pulled away, grinning. "You got no time for that, Cowboy. Carl's got something he wants you to do."

It took me a minute, but then I understood everything except why she was grinning. I think I'd convinced myself this test would never come, that these last two weeks would just go on and on forever, but now here we were already at the end of them.

I still hadn't moved, so she yanked me up; said, "Get it in gear, baby. They're waiting on you."

I followed her into the tent. She got Huey out of his stall and put him on the crossties. "Come on, give me a hand," she said.

I took the brush she handed me and started working. She went to get his bridle and when she came back I said, "You mean I'm riding Huey?"

"Yep."

"How come?"

"What, you complaining?"

"No, just why?"

"He's the best, so we give you your best shot. Get it?"

I nodded.

"Okay," she said. "Go and get my saddle."

Sooner than I wanted, we had him put together and she took him outside. I lagged behind a little, but not long enough she'd have to call me or anything. I'd taken my jacket off earlier and left it with Gus and now I felt funny without it. I wanted it more for protection than appearance, but still I asked her, "Do I look all right?"

"Yeah, fine, but come here."

When I did, she looped Huey's reins over her arm so she could fuss with my shirt. She took the choker off and shoved it in her pocket. Then she unbuttoned my collar, letting her fingers slide along my neck until I was trembling.

"That better?" she asked.

"Uh huh," I said.

"Come on, let's put you up."

She gave me a leg up and I hit the saddle still shaking. He was physically larger than any horse I'd ever been on. I felt like my legs must be sticking straight out to the sides, though the truth was she had to lengthen her stirrups a hole and I knew she didn't look so small on him. I guess I just felt small, and so I was glad when she put her hand on the reins and led us to the schooling ring.

As we got nearer, I could see Carl and Linda talking with two men and a woman. The sight started something new roaming around my stomach. "Uh, Tory," I said. "Who are they?"

"Buyers."

"Quit," I said. "Since when is Huey for sale?"

"Darling, everything's always for sale."

I swallowed this at first, but it didn't stay down long. We were getting close enough to them that if I was going to press her I had to do it now and quick. "Come on, give," I said.

She stalled a bit more, smiling all the while, but finally she let on that Carl wanted to work these people. They'd come down representing some business executive who wanted to tell his clients and weekend guests all about the horses he owned. Thing was he didn't own any yet. He'd read about Huey in some magazine and decided to buy him. When he'd called, Carl'd decided to play him a bit. See what he could get. This was the first stage of the game, was all. Nothing to worry about, she said.

Right.

I stared at the group again. The two men wore blue suits. One looked bony and fearful. He kept peering down at wingtips coated with dust. The other man, taller and broader, talked easily with Carl. Somehow, on him, a three-piece suit seemed the sensible thing to wear in the middle of a schooling ring.

The woman had bigger hair than I'd seen in a long time and her heels kept punching through the dirt, throwing her off balance. Linda was pretty off balance herself; nevertheless she attempted some kind of girl talk. I'd've had trouble imagining two people with less to say to each other, but they pressed on gamely. Linda kept her thumbs tucked into her belt loops and we'd come close enough by now I could see the muscles of her forearms. They'd popped up clear as if she'd been boosting a bale of hay; gave away her discomfort. That and the way she kept watching the ground while she used her boot toe to shift dirt back and forth between two little piles.

Carl, he looked comfortable. He rocked back on his heels now and then, arms folded across his chest, his low voice breaking into easy laughter. I knew both him and Linda hated outsiders, but Carl enjoyed hating them.

I watched as he brought the woman into the conversation, his eyes probing and discarding her. Linda had the same eyes, fierce and green, near dark as sea glass. She'd given me this same once-over a couple of times. I recognized the insult behind it, but this young woman would always think Carl'd been admiring her.

Linda made a break first chance she got, escaping over to me and Tory. She pretended to adjust Huey's bridle, but really just fiddled. "Assholes," she said, spitting into the dirt.

It disappointed me she'd got herself back so fast. Watching her off base was the only fun I'd found in this so far and losing it made it harder to see Tory joking with her. Still, like always, I hung back. I never mixed into what went on between them. Tried not to, anyway, though sometimes my being there at all was enough to get Linda going. Then I'd have to think about Tory's tie to her and how far it went. I didn't like doing that so mostly I'd keep my head down and my guard up, which right this minute meant listening more to Carl than to them.

"Linda," he was saying, "she's my right hand. Runs the barn. Bit of a veterinarian, too. Well, and, let's see, you know Tory. She's a little tired today, so Lee, there, she'll be doing the riding for you."

"Listen to that," Linda said, with enough bite you couldn't miss it. "Every day he sounds more like he's dealing cars."

"Come over here a minute, Lee. Say hello to these folks."

"Jump off," Tory said, squeezing my knee.

I did, hitting the ground stiff-legged. Tory sort of pushed me toward Carl and, from there, I used his red polo shirt as a beacon. My stomach flopped the second he clamped his arm over my shoulder. Last time he'd done that was when he'd taken me away from Ted. Now he had me shaking everybody's hand, while their names rolled past.

I wanted to go back to Tory and Huey, even Linda, but knew when I did I'd have to start riding. Then I'd either make it or blow it. What I'd done so far had already finished me with the Cheslers. Just getting on Huey's back had settled that—I'd never ride for them again. No way to take it back or hide it, so in a way I had nothing to lose. Or I'd already lost it and now had this one way of getting it back. "It" seemed to be Tory, not riding horses.

I realized I'd been staring at Carl's boots, so I looked up and they were all staring at me. Carl said, "Go on now, girl. These nice folks waited long enough."

I jogged back to where Tory and Linda stood with Huey. Soon as I got there, Carl called Tory and she went off to do her glad-handing.

That left me with Linda. She tossed me into the saddle and I gathered up the reins. As the leather rubbed Huey's neck, some lather foamed. The salt-sweat smelled steamy and bitter; stung the cuts on my hands. My own sweat rolled down my stomach, smelled worse to me than his.

I felt Linda's hand on my thigh and tightened my muscle against it. Caught myself pressing into the saddle, rubbing myself on the pommel, and I think she caught me too because she smiled and left her hand there longer than she needed.

After she'd checked the girth, she guided my leg back into place. Got her fingers between my thigh and the saddle.

"You tight?" she said.

And when I didn't say anything, she laughed, said, "I'll bet you are," and she left her fingers there right up until I rubbed against them and then Carl came over and she went to help Tory fix fences.

By now, Huey was grinding his teeth so hard you could hear the bit rattling in his mouth. Carl smacked him once hard, hit his mouth. We both jumped from it, me from the sound, Huey from the blow itself. I felt a tiny tremor run through him and then he stood quietly. Carl said, "Mind your manners now, son. We got company."

My own trembling started on the tail end of Huey's. Carl came over beside us. Put his hand in the small of my back. It felt heavy, pressed my damp shirt against my skin. I leaned down closer to him. His breath smelled of cigarettes and the peppermints he chewed. He moved his hand, tucked his thumb into the waist of my breeches, and rested his palm on my butt.

He said, "You do exactly what I tell you and this'll go smooth as silk." Then he yanked hard on my breeches. "You hear me, darling?"

I nodded.

"Good," he said loudly and slapped Huey on the rump. "Work him around a bit."

I watched him walk back to where the buyers were standing. They'd claimed the narrow strip of grass that ran between the schooling ring's dirt edge and the jumper ring's fence. Then I looked over to Tory and Linda standing by the one vertical on the other side of the ring.

Once I'd located everyone, I pressed my calves into Huey's side. He took a few steps at a walk and then moved into a jog. We trotted around the edge of the ring. I wasn't used to his gait. It felt rough and choppy at first, not like Toreador's. I hadn't realized how much I'd gotten used to Chesler horses.

As we warmed up, the few people who'd been schooling this late moved out of the ring and onto the grassy area across from Carl and the buyers. Soon more people began to gather there. I guess word had gotten round. It always did when Carl was doing business. Trainers, riders, owners—anyone who knew anything studied Carl.

The crowd grew big, especially for this late in the day. I swallowed back a sickness that climbed my throat, burned it. I looked for Tory; wanted her help, but she'd turned all business. That left me nothing but to stick to business myself.

I eased Huey into a canter. Tuned out everything but the sound of his hooves. He cantered smooth and the steady loping soothed me, drowned out the hornet noise coming off the crowd. Their numbers still grew. People now circled both ends of the ring, but not one of them dared share the strip of grass Carl and the buyers occupied. This sort of deference disgusted Carl, and at the same time he demanded it.

My eyes darted from the crowd, to the buyers, to Tory, and finally to the fences. A single vertical stood on the side near the crowd; a combination of two spreads on Carl's side. I'd taken the Cheslers' horses over these fences hundreds of times in the last two weeks. Didn't matter, though, everything'd changed.

Even my sweat stiffened when Carl's voice boomed at me. "Next time around come up over the vertical," he shouted. "You take it nice and easy, now."

I shortened the reins and shifted my weight forward a touch. Huey's ears pricked and he picked up the pace. I sneaked a look at Carl and the buyers as we came off the turn and down their side. Carl still had his arms folded across his chest, his feet planted squarely. The larger suit stood near him but looked less at ease than before. The other one and the woman had backed as far away as they could.

I caught this much, but then Huey and I had passed them and were rounding the bottom of the ring. I needed to start finding a line to the fence.

At first Huey felt unwieldy—too big for the space we had. I

didn't know how many strides he'd need or how to gauge the distance. Suddenly I'd no idea why I was doing this or how to do it, so, actually, I more or less panicked. Huey took over then, saw his spot and moved easily toward it. And almost before I knew what he'd done, we were airborne.

He way overjumped it—left plenty of room to spare and we seemed to hang for minutes before landing. Once we were down and off the turn, I heard Carl's big, roaring laugh. "I guess he's bored with that," he said. "Go on and put that fence up where he can enjoy himself."

Linda and Tory raised the fence. It hadn't been more than four feet before. Now the top rail was at Tory's eye level, at least five three. I'd never jumped anything that high and the prospect set two separate currents running through me. One, jittery and tight, wrapped bands around my chest; the other busted them.

"Come up over it again," Carl yelled.

This time I kept my eyes ahead of me, ready for the turn. I picked my line early and Huey flowed forward, seeing it too. We closed on the fence, hit the spot and Huey rocked back, then surged up. My stomach leapt with him, filled my chest. I heard the saddle leathers creak, then perfect silence surrounded us.

We hovered in earnest. Shivers started in my chest. Bunched there before trickling through my limbs, darting just below my skin, down my thighs, my forearms. Felt too big in my hands, so I pressed my fingertips into Huey's neck to try to let them go. I knew instantly I wanted to feel this over and over. Nothing else mattered. Not the buyers, not the crowd, maybe not even Tory. Just this feeling pumping me like a rush.

As soon as we landed, Carl had them raise the fence again. My heartbeats melted into Huey's hoofbeats. The two sounds lodged deep in my eardrum, protective, blocking everything else.

"Again," Carl called. But his instruction came like sound underwater. I more read his lips. Followed the motion of his arm as we cruised past him, past the buyers, past the blurred crowd.

I didn't cut the turn right this time and the fence came too fast. Huey'd trusted me, so he couldn't recover. We got under it a little and he lurched some taking off. But then we were up again and the rush came on, nearly good as last time. Before we'd even landed I wanted to move on to the combination. If a single vertical could give this kind of head, I wanted to know what two spread fences could do.

Carl read my mind. He was already helping Linda and Tory adjust the combination. I'd always liked combinations best. You hit them right, they just happen. And I had a knack for hitting them right.

Huey and I circled while they worked. Linda had pulled the spreads out to about five feet, while Carl and Tory raised the first fence. Squared it off at about five three. Linda had the second fence stepped, so the highest rail cleared her head. I was with her on this, but I saw Tory glare. Linda just shrugged, but she dropped the fence down some.

As we came alongside the combination, I took a good look. Made Huey look, too. More for me than him, though. My buzz had gone jittery. This was a big fucking fence.

Carl seemed to read my mind again. Said, "Nothing to it, Lee. You just take it by itself the first time, darling."

I came up the side and started off the turn, but Tory waved me off. She walked the stride between the two parts, complained it was too tight for Huey. I could see she wouldn't want him pretzeling himself the last minute. Still, I didn't like her stalling me.

She walked it again shaking her head, so Carl helped her move the second fence further back. I slowed Huey back to an easy canter, imagined he chafed as much as I did. After they'd fixed the fence, Tory must've walked the distance a dozen times. Carl waited till she was satisfied, though. Finally she nodded to him and he said to me, "Plenty of room in there now. You go on give it a try."

I nudged Huey and he picked up speed. As we flew past the crowd, we both eyed the combination. I gave little tugs on the reins to steady him. This end of the ring gave us more room to maneuver. I picked up a line and a spot early. Huey snorted in assent and we moved down to the first spread fence slowly, almost too slowly given the height. I trusted his rhythm, though, tried not to interfere.

He met the fence, rolled back on his haunches and sprung into the air. I lagged behind, had to grab his mane to get up off his back. I ducked my head to his neck, could hear his breathing. We touched down then soared up again. My heart pumped my chest looking for more room. Blood pushed against my veins, floods of it traveling wildly. I wanted down on the ground just to go up again, keep it going.

When we did land, I felt powerful. More powerful even than Carl. "Add the vertical to it," he yelled, as Linda and Tory widened the spreads, raised each part. They couldn't set it fast enough or high enough to meet my pulse. The rhythm kept building in my body. Huey accelerated to match it. Lather coated his neck; slippery on my hands, on the reins.

We turned to the vertical too suddenly. Hit it way short and Huey struggled over it.

"Relax, now," Carl shouted. "No one's in a hurry here."

His voice sounded edgy, busted my fix on the combination. I tried to calm down.

We rounded the turn to the double and I saw a spot that looked perfect. I pushed Huey toward it. We bore down to it at a fast clip. Meeting it, I urged him off the ground. He hurled us into the air. That slow motion feeling came over me, but held on too long this time. I started to register there'd been a hitch. Huey grunted as we pitched forward. My heart plummeted into my stomach. We were going down head first.

Huey hit before me. I heard him squeal, then heard the rails splitting as his tremendous weight crashed into them. I landed an instant later. My elbow took the brunt of it and I rolled away from the pain. Looked just in time to see Huey come up and run. I saw blood on him and my stomach heaved. I couldn't tell how much blood or where, but I figured I'd just crippled Tory's best horse.

I rolled back, lay flat just to keep from throwing up, and when I swallowed I tasted my own blood. Enough so I had to try to spit it out. Tory knelt beside me now. She kept saying, "Don't move. All right? Just don't move." And when I didn't listen I felt her hand on my chest holding me down. "Lee, baby, would you please just lie still a minute."

I gave in then. Something about her voice let me sink back against her. Her arms tightened around me, rocked me. Her hand felt soft on my lip, though at the same time I couldn't feel it, could just feel the swelling there, and then could see the blood on her thumb.

"Jesus," she said. "Can you see?"

"What?"

"Lee, did you go out?"

I couldn't follow her, though I knew what she was asking. I tried to look at her, look at anything. My neck felt too stiff to bother and when I blinked, some blood dripped into my eye. I figured I probably looked bad, though I didn't feel bad exactly. A haze bathed everything. Kept everything away except Tory.

Her voice quavered, now. "Lee, can you see?"

She was asking me again and I knew my not answering had

scared her. I didn't mean to, it was just this stupor kept pulling me under and I thought she could see inside it. "I'm okay," I said finally.

"What did you land on?"

"My arm, but it's fine. I'm okay." I knew I had to act it if she was going to believe it, so I sat up a little. Now I could see the crowd, swollen from word of trouble. People had been pushed off the grass and into the ring. Seeing them watching, looming over us—now even Tory'd come too close. I tried to push her away, said, "Please, will you just . . ."

"Look," she started, then tried to steady her voice. "It's okay, Lee. Everything's going to be okay."

That's when I knew how bad it was. Understood all of what I'd done and that it'd really happened. "No it's not," I nearly screamed. "You know it isn't."

I wanted for her to disagree, but she didn't and so I had to get away. When I tried to get up, she didn't stop me, but I couldn't stand. "You got to help me, Tory. I can't stay here."

I felt her waver, but then her arm was firm on my back, lifting. Once she had me on my feet, she said, "I'll walk you."

"No. All right? Just leave me alone."

She jerked back, same as if I'd hit her. I felt like I had. Didn't know how to help it. I broke then, pushed my way through the crowd and was running. The ground kept pushing toward me, bumping up at me. It wobbled me a few times, but I kept my footing. Made it back to the tents, Carl's stalls.

I ducked into the tackroom. Threw myself onto the cot and burrowed into the pillow. I tried to curl up, hide against the wall, but my left arm felt leaden. It didn't hurt, but it wouldn't move. I pulled the pillow closer with my right hand, tucked my face and sobbed.

The crying seared my throat. What couldn't get out pummeled my head from inside. I punched the pillow trying to quiet it, but it only got louder. I couldn't stop, though. I tumbled off the cot. Fell on my knees beside it. I hit hard as I could, my left arm dangling, useless. I pulled myself up and flailed against the wall. The horse on the other side cried out and staggered to his feet. Began weaving. I fixed on his noises. Heard other horses join him. They kicked the walls, snorted low and rumbly. My hammering blended with theirs. Their cries muffled mine, let me wail.

I clouded over. The burning of my throat and the burning of my knuckles were the same. The pulse splitting my head drove my fist, split it open against the wood. Then I heard no sound at all. My blows began to founder. My legs doddered suddenly and I felt Tory's arms come round me from behind. She all but held me up. Made little cooing sounds as she drew me closer.

She held me a long time. Finally her hands coaxed me to face her. I hid myself in her shoulder.

She rubbed my back while I cried more. Finally she said, "It played out different than you think."

I didn't move, didn't want to get caught short hoping.

"Carl blames himself. Said he should've known better than to put them up so high. Shoot, anyone could've seen it coming. Your first time out. Jesus. We all know something else takes over. Can be fear or boldness. What you tried came from being bold. You won him over."

I stood back from her. Needed a look at her face to believe her, but even then didn't. "How?" I said.

"He said he could use someone with guts. Then he looks at me, right? Says, 'And who has the brains to do what I tell her.' You're signed up, Cowboy."

"What about Huey?"

"Skinned knee. Nothing Linda can't fix. We're set, baby."

She grabbed my arms, began to pull me toward her. I yanked back. Had no time to hide it. She dropped my arms and stood not knowing how to touch me.

"I knew that fall was bad," she said. "I didn't like the way you went down. But, damn it, you never said anything. Why didn't you tell me?"

Her face wore such a look of betrayal I wanted to find an answer that'd satisfy her. While I tried she kept talking.

"You act like you're okay and a thing like this gets worse. You get racked up for good that way. Then where are we?"

She circled around these points a few more times, stopped herself just short of talking nonsense; put her hand on my cheek. "Come on," she said, "we better get you taken care of."

14

Do this long enough and you get to know your way around hospitals. Like airports and motels, they're all pretty much the same wherever you go. Tonight, our familiarity gave us an edge and so we went through the motions quickly. Good thing, too. My arm ached pretty nonstop now and my stomach had started queasing from it.

They took me into one of those curtained cubicles. Tory knew better than to follow. I felt a guilty gladness at being alone. I sat on the paper-covered table, ran the fingers of my good hand along it. Crusted blood covered my knuckles. I tried to make a fist, but the top of my hand stuck together. Still it moved some, so it couldn't be too bad.

The doctor noticed the hand first. He picked it up, then turned it over and back with a well-worn motion.

He looked at me, then his clipboard. "Says here riding accident. You did this in a riding accident?"

"Yes, sir. Scraped it on the dirt." I always put on my best behavior for cops and doctors.

"Doesn't say anything here about the hand."

"Guess I forgot about it. My other arm's the real trouble." I wanted to prod him along. Couldn't see why he had to act so suspicious so soon. Wasn't like I'd asked for anything, though believe me I could've used it.

He kept dawdling, though. Writing notes, asking useless questions. Finally he popped his head out the curtain and a nurse came in.

He told her to cut the sleeve off my shirt. She tried cutting around the top and then yanking it off, but my arm had swollen too much, completely filled it. It meant she had to cut the whole length of it. I could feel some pressure, but as if it came from inside my arm. I had no sensation of the scissors touching my skin. Once she got the cloth off, I had to admit it didn't look so great. They didn't waste any time sending me down for x-rays.

By the time I got back to have my arm set, I'd chewed my cheek raw. See, I'd still had nothing to help the pain and was coming close to acting ugly. I held off, though. Knew it'd be better not to ask. They finally stuck me three times, twice in the bad arm, once in the good. Whatever it was came on fast. Good thing too because they didn't waste any time before doing a quick snap and jerk. The doctor gave me an envelope of Percodans and a script that'd last a month. He left me with the nurse. She cleaned my hand and bandaged my knuckles. Then she sent me for plastering.

Because the break lay just below the elbow, the cast was cumbersome. The doctor'd kept saying how lucky I was. That he didn't see how the joint had stayed intact. I knew I'd been drunk with bliss when Huey started to fall. That it'd saved me being worse off now. But even whacked out on all the shots, I knew not to try and tell a doctor about it. One little listen to that sort of talk and they keep their script pads in their pockets.

Tory stayed quiet the whole way back to the Ramada but then I talked almost constantly. When she turned into the parking lot, she grumbled at how full it'd gotten. We had to park pretty far from our room and the whole way across the lot she held on to me as if I'd fall otherwise. The night air quieted me, felt soft and warm on my face.

She helped me into the room. I'd gotten heavier, was leaning on her pretty good now. She got me onto the bed. Lying down that minute seemed the greatest pleasure I'd ever known. I welled happiness, made part by this, part by the shots, and part by knowing I wouldn't have to do anything for a while. My arm put me on layaway. Nobody could want anything from me, at least not for now.

Tory stood over me. She was grinning at something I'd said but couldn't remember. "Come on, baby," she said, patting my thigh. "Help me get your clothes off."

I smiled while she pulled my boots off and then my socks. I was starting to enjoy her taking care of me.

She unbuttoned my breeches. "Help me out here," she said trying to pull them off. I lifted my hips a little and she slid them down and off. I closed my eyes, felt her hand slide into my underpants. She tugged at them, teasing me. "If you're so hot and bothered, you want these on or not?"

I wanted to go along, had been right with her, but just now something shifted. "What?" I said, buying a minute more to try and sort myself out.

"You want these on or off, darling?" She gave another tug.

"Leave them for now. I promise I'll let you take them off later." I tried to sound playful but, truth was, her taking them off scared me.

She didn't notice my switch. "Believe me, darling," she said, "you're not going to want any later."

I moved my legs and tried to pull the covers down with my good hand. I wanted to get underneath them quick.

"Hey, hey. Hold on a minute. I'll do that." She sort of tucked me in and then started walking over to the bathroom.

"Where you going?" I said. The way the words leapt out confused me.

"I'm getting some scissors, darling, I'll be right there."

"Why?"

"How else we going to get that shirt off you?"

"You want to cut my hundred-twenty-nine-dollar shirt?"

"You didn't mind them cutting it at the hospital."

"That was just the sleeve. Who's going to see the sleeve's missing underneath a jacket?"

"Look," she said, speaking slowly, patiently. "I'll cut along the seam. Besides, Carl'll see you get some more made. He'll take care of all that stuff now."

This last bit I still didn't believe. "You be careful," I called, trying to figure where all my well-being had gone.

She came back from the bathroom with the scissors.

"I'll take it real easy," she said, sitting down beside me.

She cut gently, held her hand underneath the path of the scissors. When she pulled the fabric away and eased the shirt off, my tears started. She held me as close as she could without hurting. I burrowed my face into her shoulder and her hair fell against my cheek, cool and soft, with little matted places from my tears.

"It's over," she said, stroking my neck as she spoke.

I let myself sink into the sweet-salty folds of her shirt; licked the first skin I found.

"Let yourself rest, baby," she murmured. "The hard part's over."

two

15

Seemed ever since that fall in Tampa, Tory'd been carrying me from one bed to another, with each one getting softer. That I'd found this last one, which was Tory's own, in Linda's house—well, at first, it kind of threw me. Then I got used to it. I can get used to almost anything.

Anyway, I got used to living here, which so far meant lying in bed and watching TV and taking Percodan. And I got used to Tory taking care of me. Got so used to it I could almost believe it'd never change. Made believe Linda and Carl would never come back from their buying trip and my arm'd always stay broken and so Tory'd have to take care of me like this forever.

There was one thing queered this, reminded me how short-lived it'd all be. From day one, practically, Silas had been calling. First filled with worry, wanting to know was I all right and what had happened and what was I doing down here when I was supposed to be up there with him and why hadn't I called—why'd he have to hear it from Gus. The Percodan helped me keep my distance, helped me act like nothing I was doing should upset him, but it didn't stop his calling.

His were the only calls we got except Tory got one from Linda a couple of days before she and Carl were supposed to come home. That same day I got another one from Silas. He told me he caved in and gave my father Carl's number. Said he just couldn't hold him off any longer and I thought, well, that's true to form—thought it because I needed to be mad at him, but behind his back, what I said to his face was I understood, knew he always did his best, that I'd gone and put him in another impossible situation. He didn't call again after that.

That other call, the one from my parents, came late the next evening and since I was expecting it, I'd had enough bourbon on top of Percodan I figured I'd handle it smooth. I went into the kitchen when Tory called me because that's where the phone was—right there on the wall next to the refrigerator. I took the receiver from her and she hesitated a minute before she left, but she left. That's when I started wrapping myself up in the cord, which was a nice extra-long one, and just before I said hello I leaned back into the refrigerator because I wanted to make sure I kept my balance.

"Lee, is that you?"

This was my mother's voice, which startled me, so it was another little bit before I said yes.

"I've been calling all over trying to find you."

This didn't make sense until I remembered she liked doing my father's legwork. It let her keep a hand in and play it first if she needed to. Anyway, she kept talking.

"I called Silas and he wasn't sure where you were, but finally your father called and got Carl Rusker's number. I talked to his wife, who's very nice incidentally, and she gave me this number. You're in Virginia?"

"Yeah."

"Well, is everything all right? I got a bill from a hospital in Florida. It was stamped paid. Is that right?"

"Yeah."

"Because when I got it, I didn't know what it could be. Says x-rays and, well, other things. Carl paid it?"

"Yeah."

"Well, do I need to send him anything toward it? I was going to file the insurance. I guess that's why they sent it to me, you must have shown them your insurance card or given our address. Now, you're sure I don't need to send Carl any money for this?"

"No, Mom."

"Well, if you're sure you don't need the money, I thought I'd use the insurance check then, if he doesn't expect it. You are all right and all? Nothing too bad?"

"Yeah, yeah. You keep it, Mom. I don't need it."

"Well, if you're sure. We'll straighten it all out when you're up here. Oh, wait a minute, your father's right here. He wants to talk to you."

I'd wrapped the phone cord around myself three times by now; was facing the refrigerator. Soon as I heard his voice I stopped winding the cord and coiled myself instead.

"Darling, we've been so worried about you, and when your mother got that bill we didn't know what to think."

"Everything's fine," I said.

"You're sure you're okay? Really now?"

"Yes."

"Well, I . . . We miss you, darling. How soon you getting up this way?"

I didn't answer him. Instead, I opened the refrigerator, then the freezer door too. I actually stuck my head in the freezer, like the cold could burn his mouth off my ear or something. I felt him same as if he was standing there and holding my arm too tightly and his mouth too close, his breath hot and sticky like his tongue.

"I'm not sure, Dad. I'll let you know."

He backpedaled, wasn't going to let me off so easy. I could feel him gathering himself, could feel him shift. "What's this Carl Rusker like?" he asked now.

"I don't know."

"Your mother said he got some girl pregnant, ruined her career. So what is it you want with him, or should I know?"

I almost bit. Was primed to get in it with him—a tinderbox and him tossing the matches.

I'd let my arm rest on the freezer shelf until it'd sat there long enough to stick. I pulled it off now, hoped the feel of this would stop me from what I knew I was about to say. I said it anyway.

"He's teaching me to ride." I said "ride" so he couldn't miss what I meant by it and then felt bad dragging Carl into this.

"I thought you knew all about that," my father said.

He said "all" so I couldn't miss it. It was always this way with us, the double meanings, nothing straight shot, and I kept up my end, said, "Yeah, well, this is the real thing. Big stuff. See, Carl, he's big."

I picked this last thing because my father's not big, one of the ways I explained him to myself when I was still trying to. I thought he was big when I was young because him getting in hurt so much, but later I knew it was just I was small.

"He's good too, Dad."

And here I thought I had him, that I'd won the round. Instead he said, "Well, I'll see for myself in Connecticut."

"Huh?"

"That show there in Darien, your mother and I thought we'd come see you. Maybe you'll be ready to come home by then."

I couldn't pretend we wouldn't be there, couldn't think of anything else, so now I backpedaled, saying, "I don't think Carl'd want me going home, he needs me."

"I don't think this Carl knows how old you are."

Now I had nowhere to go, so I went further into the freezer but even with all that cold I could still feel him. I heard him waiting, heard his breathing, and then he was saying, "Lee, you hear me? I know that you do." And I heard him chuckling. That's when I put the receiver down. Rested it on the frozen beans and rested my head on my arms.

Next thing I knew, Tory'd come up behind me, which was good because I could have her be the one who'd made me hot inside all this cold. She untangled me from the cord, then she hung up the phone; took me into the living room and put me down on the couch. She sat on the coffee table, opposite me so our knees touched. At first she just watched me while I tried not to look at her, but this was hard because of how close she was and where she was sitting, but she didn't touch me, not right off.

I don't know how long before that part started, before she got down on her knees, started unbuttoning my shirt, but from the bottom up; was kissing my stomach. I liked it, except at the same time I didn't want her doing it now and so I fidgeted. I knew she was comforting me, trying to, so I wanted to let her. For that to happen I figured I needed at least to be in her bed and needed another pill on my way there.

Instead, I rested my bad arm along the back of the couch; made it easier for her to get where she wanted. I used my other arm to pull her closer, encourage her. Pretty soon, she'd unbuttoned my pants and by then I didn't care so much where we were, though I still wanted the pill.

She was still mostly kissing when she pushed down my pants. This wasn't something we did a lot, this particular thing. I guess that was more me than her. Usually I'd stop her because I couldn't bear how gentle she'd get; how it'd slow everything down so, and then I'd be feeling more than just my body and it'd make me want something rougher, something I could get a better hold on because I knew what to do with that, how to manage it.

With her on the floor like she was she seemed so close to me and that made it better for a while, maybe even better than the roughness I thought I wanted. I couldn't be sure, though, because I hadn't given up on asking for that, only hadn't asked yet. Still, I moved my hand along her back, kind of rubbing, and soon I'd grasped her neck instead; pressed her head into my lap and pressed myself against the force of my own hand pushing her.

She shoved the coffee table away and I leaned back, while at the same time sliding toward her. She eased me a little further off the edge of the couch and while I knew I heard the door—the front door—and even tried to get up, she held my legs.

I told myself she must not have heard. I thought I would tell her, but it didn't matter so much to me now, so we just kept on. Even when I knew Linda was in the room with us, felt her standing in the doorway, we kept on and, if I'm truthful, her standing there, the smoke from her cigarette, and my looking at her and her looking back—that's what made me come. And while I can do this real quiet, I didn't.

Right after, I felt just as low as Linda probably intended and mostly because of what I knew I wanted from her. I don't know what Tory wanted. I can still convince myself she hadn't realized or that I got the whole thing confused. That it didn't really happen. They both helped me with that. Even while I was pulling up my pants, I began doubting it. Couldn't see how Tory got from between my legs to sitting beside me on the couch. How Linda came to be sitting on the armrest. Neither of them acknowledged anything awkward and so I couldn't see anything to do but go with them.

Tory started right in asking about the trip and that kind of thing. I didn't hear any of it, except that Carl wasn't back yet, wouldn't be till the day after tomorrow. Tory didn't ask how come, seemed like she already knew, and then I remembered she'd talked to Linda and not so long ago. I'd've been stupid not to realize Tory'd been expecting her but I didn't like where that left me so I went for the pills.

I'd been heading there anyway. They were in the bathroom —right out on the sink last I'd seen. I could still hear Tory and Linda talking so I closed the door and for the first time tried to lock it. Discovered there was no lock. No pills either. I opened the medicine chest and started taking stuff out. Spread things all over the sink. I got so caught up I didn't hear the door, though it was inches from me.

"Looking for these?"

Linda's voice made me knock the mouthwash into the sink; broke the bottle. The smell burned my nose, made me almost retch. I started picking pieces of glass from the basin.

"Wait a minute, there. You'll cut ribbons."

She sounded kind, which confused me. I wondered where Tory'd gotten to and couldn't stop myself from asking.

"She went to the store," Linda said. She put the bottle of pills in my hand. Then she put her hands on my shoulders and steered me. She sat me down on the edge of the tub and, when I didn't do it, she pulled two pills from the bottle and handed them to me. While I took them, she began picking glass from the sink.

By the time she'd finished with that, I'd gone pretty woozy. The pills seemed to come on faster and stronger and I was sort of weaving back and forth on my perch. She'd lit a cigarette and the smoke filled the little room fast, made everything fuzzier. She caught hold of me the next time I tipped back, grabbed me around the waist and hoisted. Her cigarette hung so close to my ear I could feel it burning, heard some hair crinkling first and then smelled it.

She leaned back a little but I just slumped into her. She grabbed my pants, grabbed the waist of them, and pulled me up, and when I held on to her and pressed into her she just laughed at me. I'd rested my chin on her shoulder to hide, but then Tory opened the door. She just stood there watching and Linda just kept laughing and so I opened my mouth like I had something to say except I didn't.

Linda wheeled around, pushing me out in front of her, pushing me into Tory. "Here," she said, letting go of me. "Someone's got to take her to bed."

16

Linda cut my cast off the next day and Carl got home the day after. The day after that we went back to work. Linda drove me and Tory over to the stables and I felt young and stupid in the backseat, popping my head between them to ask questions. Seemed odd now that Tory and I hadn't bothered going over before. I'd never even wondered what the place looked like, but when we drove down the long gravel driveway and I saw these huge spans of crisp green lawn cordoned off with simple white racing fences, I realized this was exactly what I'd pictured.

When you got far enough down the drive you had two choices: either go right and wind up in front of a big Georgian house, or bear left, which is what we did. The gravel turned to blacktop as it curved round back of the house to a parking lot. Two horse vans sat next to each other, one I recognized, the other spanking new. I remembered Linda and Carl's argument about buying a new truck. Seemed she'd won that one.

We parked right up next to the barn. Linda got out first; said she was going to the house to see Carl. It was clear we weren't supposed to follow. Myself, I guess I would've spent the day gawking from the car except for Tory waiting on me.

I walked a few feet behind her as she headed around back.

She stayed on the blacktop, stayed close to the barn, but I found myself drifting—first walking in the wide concrete gutter, then veering further off.

I stared up. Kept trying to see the highest point. I walked further away before I finally saw the weather vane. A winged arrow held steady above the name Rusker. Big, blocky wrought iron letters. I guess I wanted a horse up there or, hell, even a rooster. The sheer size and weight of the letters made them hard to look at.

I caught myself from dizziness. Refocused on the barn, its span instead of height. Seemed to go on forever, though walking further along the side I could see the whole length of it. The two sliding doors were open and I started counting stalls, got to fifteen before my view was blocked.

I backed further for a different angle and felt myself climbing a gentle grade. It was then I looked over my shoulder at what lay behind me. The slope I'd started up grew steeper, led to a fenced-in schooling area bordered by a paddock.

Everything back here was as torn up and shabby as the front side was manicured and grand. I could imagine the view from the house, protected as it'd be—the barn pristine, too big to see around. You knew instantly that the buyers, if and when they got here, stayed on that side. I pictured a lawn between the house and barn. A circle within it made from more bright, white fencing. A private backyard auction block.

I walked further up the hill still thinking I'd missed something. That no way could everything happen in this one battered ring, sloped and rutted from what I could see and with just two broken-down fences. I looked over to the sparse pasture beside, watched the five horses roaming there, and soon realized one of them was Huey. When I recognized him, a little charge ran through me, reminded me what I was doing here and tweaked me a little, too. What did it matter how things looked?

"Want to go up there?" Tory asked.

She'd come up behind me and I jumped a little from her voice. She put a hand on my shoulder, smoothed me first, then started walking me. As we started up the hill, Huey jogged over to her. Could've been a scene in a bad movie. She fussed over him a little and then he followed her like a dog would've. I didn't say anything, but I'd never seen a horse actually do this before. Come when you called maybe or wander somewhere near you, but this horse heeled. Kept it up, too, until she finally grabbed him by the nose and pushed him away.

"A real brute, ain't he?" she said.

I smiled at her, but she laughed at me when I did.

"Too much to get used to, Cowboy?"

"A lot, anyway," I said.

"You get on those horses, you won't think of nothing else. Won't have time to, probably."

She said this as we came up beside the ring. I saw that besides the two fences you could see from below there were four more, but they ran down the other side of the slope. A tarped-over pit sat pretty much in the middle of things—had to be a water jump. My eyes went to the downside of the hill and then my stomach went downhill too and then came fast back up.

She was still talking, said, "You know they brought about a dozen back. I expect you'll get half. Maybe I'll take one or two. I don't know. How many you want, anyway?"

"What?" I said. I'd heard her, but was looking at those fences —the ones planted on the gradient. The charge I was feeling became a buzz. Going downhill over a five- or six-foot fence? I sort of couldn't wait.

We both heard the gate then. Tim was leading a willowy black mare. She looked like Frisbee, but smaller and with a fleck of white on her chest—a nothing kind of mark just splotched there.

Tim had my chaps hung over his shoulder and I saw my saddle on the mare's back. I wondered who'd gotten my stuff from Gus; realized there was a lot I hadn't been thinking about. Like what the Cheslers knew about the accident, for one.

I hadn't asked Silas—couldn't act both worried and not at the same time. He'd pretty much told me, anyway. Told me Gus had seen it along with all those others and that he'd been bewildered by it. Bewildered because he couldn't understand how I'd do a thing like that without a word to them. "Not a word after all those years" was how Silas said Gus put it and I knew Silas was talking partly about himself here. He'd said nothing about Mrs. Chesler but if Gus felt bewildered, I knew she'd feel betrayed. Once that woman got there, repairing things was impossible. Not that I wanted to or needed to, but it made me queasy to know that even if I did, I couldn't.

Anyway, my stuff looked like it'd been packed in a hurry and then left to sit. Both the chaps and the saddle were still stiff with sweat and dirt. Tim tossed me up and that stiffness along with my own made me that much worse for all the downtime. He tightened the girth, checked the leathers. His hand on my leg comforted me. I looked down and he grinned up at me.

"You're fine," he said, but he had the boss-is-back jitters running his voice; kept hold of the reins until Tory called him. I watched him walk across the ring, swimming in baggy overalls and nothing else. His arms and shoulders had gone pink and freckled, that white-blond hair down past his shoulders now and looking thicker and shinier, even whiter.

Tory sent him to check fences and then came alongside me. Her hair had grown too this past month, but I hadn't noticed until now. She'd tied it back but, like always, bits escaped and she kept pushing them from her face and away from her eyes, which seemed darker to me, but gentle in a worried way.

Her fingers felt trembly on my leg, too, so much so it was

catching. I shifted my weight in the stirrups trying to get the shakes out. Didn't want to start from here, especially since the mare acted twitchy enough without my help. She was looking at everything. Seemed to fear the ground itself and when we heard the gate again, she nickered and swung her head. I looked, too. Saw Carl and Linda.

We didn't waste any time with hellos and how are yous. The only thing close to it was Carl asking about my arm, but he asked Linda, not me, and it was clear it was just about how much and hard he could work me. Once he'd settled that, he said to get the mare warmed up and so I did, glad for something to do.

I took her down the hill and worked her around down there for maybe ten minutes before Carl yelled, "Enough of that. Bring her up here."

He and Linda stood by that single fence at the top of the hill. Tory and Tim roosted on the post-and-rail. Tim lit a cigarette and I wanted to smoke it for him. I noticed one in Carl's hand too, but it wasn't lit. He held it like it was, though; kept rolling it back and forth in his fingers, tucked it into his palm like to shield it, slow its burn.

I headed the mare for the fence—a small little cross-rail. She trotted jerky, fits and starts all the way. But as she jumped it, she arced up, did this in the air it felt like. A second burst. We took the fence again and she gave the same loft. Coiled, then grew big and round underneath me.

She landed quiet, but then tried to run down the hill. I turned her fast, tucked her into such a tight circle she could've licked my knee if she'd wanted. I kept her turning like that until she almost stepped onto the tarp that covered the water jump, so I had to jerk her quick around the other way.

Carl kept us at the one fence a little longer, then moved us on. He had us jump the line on the far side of the ring—just two verticals. First up the hill then down it. The fences weren't high enough to get me going anywhere and since the mare still wanted to charge downhill that was probably good.

While Carl kept me working this line, he had Tim and Linda make a combination on the other side of the ring. I stretched out the time after each try at the verticals. Watched them building the spreads. Tory stood with Carl now, went back and forth from watching me to watching Tim and Linda.

Carl had me do the line once more before he and Tory raised the fences. By now, the mare'd given up bolting. I had tried different things, but Tory solved it for me. She told me to snatch her back in the air—jerk her mouth with all my weight before she even hit the ground. The first time I did it, I nearly pulled her feet out from under her, but two more times and it worked. It felt cruel but it worked.

Tory and Carl'd set the fences pretty high and since we were coming uphill they looked even bigger. I steadied the mare because like me she seemed to want to run at them. I almost broke off and circled, but I knew they'd see no reason for it. Carl'd see.

Instead I drove the mare right up into the grasp I had on her. Let her build steam, but choked it so when we hit that first fence, she curled every piece of herself. I kept feeding her the reins so she'd let her neck go. I gathered some of the slack before we landed, and then took back more between the fences; still, she'd taken enough to run with.

"Shorten her," Tory yelled.

We hit the other fence tight, but okay—lurchy, nothing too bad. I'd been too busy to pump up much. The first fence might've sent me, but not this second one. I wanted to come down to the both of them, figured that'd get me going, get me that feel I wanted. Tim and Linda'd finished with the combination by now. They stood beside it watching the rest of us. Carl had his arms folded across his chest, while Tory spoke to him.

I couldn't hear anything, but I saw Carl shaking his head. Then he called to me to take the line downhill this time. I'd kept the mare cantering so now I circled her once more before heading for the line. She took it easy off the turn, still I held her pretty tightly. She'd lathered by now; was breathing heavy. I didn't trust her not to start dashing again.

We met the first fence from a ways out, so I gave her some slack, but not much—grabbed her mane off the ground, then let go in the air; dropped my arms low and hugged her neck to give her room without feeding her rein. My wrists slithered around in her lather and so I hugged tighter until I felt a pulse I swore was hers even knowing it was my own.

I leaned back, landing. Was all the adjustment I needed to make. We came evenly to the next fence, but she scuffled at the last moment, gave an extra burst off the ground. I clutched her mane to catch up. Ducked my head over her shoulder while my hands slid to her neck. I kept slipping her the reins like I believed we would stay here in this stillness, caught in the air.

It stopped me completely. When she came down, I stayed forward. Nearly tipped her balance perched on her neck that way. I straightened up sharply, finally heard Tory's yells through my daze. I wanted to blame pills, but hadn't had them today. Maybe I could blame not having them. Good thing the mare didn't run. Maybe she only wanted to if she thought I'd put up a fight.

I brought her back to a walk. Let her catch her breath. She smelled as steamy and dank as the swamp. I did, too. Sweat had gathered at my waist, was trickling down my back. I examined the blisters on my palms. There was one at the base of each finger. The largest had filled with blood, the others were mostly open but not bleeding.

Carl worked another cigarette in his hand. He let me keep walking the mare, let Tory keep talking to him. I still couldn't hear her, wasn't really trying, but I saw Carl was still shaking his head. Finally he held his hand up and she stopped; wrapped her arms tight across her chest. Soon after, Carl told me to try the combination.

I was almost to the first spread fence before I realized what was bugging Tory; understood she feared a replay of Tampa. I could've gone under to this myself, but didn't have time to. Already, the mare leapt at the first fence. Then she caught herself and rounded out only to twist again in the air. We landed on an angle, were headed for the standard, not the fence. Before I could stop her, she ducked hard right to finish it. Cruised past the fence instead of over it and almost wrong-wayed me out of the saddle.

I held tight and stayed with her. Yanked best I could to correct her, but that was my bum arm, so I didn't get too far. Everyone'd gotten quiet. We watched Carl. Even Linda did. He tossed his cigarette down. Crisp still, and round, it rolled in the dust. I watched it till his voice snapped my head.

He didn't speak loud or even mad exactly, just said, "We'll fix her of that right now."

I was suddenly thirsty.

"Lee, you take her down the hill again. Linda, go on, get one of those rails. You too," he said to Tory.

Linda was already moving toward the rails, piled on the far side of combination. She grabbed the closest one and stayed over there, blocking that side.

Tory didn't move from Carl's side. She talked fast now and loud enough I could hear it.

"Think a minute, would you? She's not ever . . ."

"Get the goddamn rail, Tory."

"No. She's . . ."

"She's fine. You're the trouble. You and your coddling busting me every step."

"Yeah sure, Carl. You keep your hands over your balls, keep them nice and safe while we all watch you bust her. What good it'll do anyone I don't know, but . . ."

"Go on, do it," he yelled.

His sheer volume caused the shift. She started toward the rails, every bit of her tight and tied.

Linda'd upended her rail, had been leaning on it. Now she tossed it across to Tory. The rail landed at Tory's feet. She rolled it underneath her boot until it caught against the heel, then she rolled it forward.

"Pick it up," Carl said, his voice quiet now.

She did what he said and I knew I'd better stop gawking before he turned on me.

I took the mare down below and began circling her. When Carl waved me on, I started up the hill. I looked everywhere. At Carl, Tory, Linda, everywhere but ahead and for my takeoff. I serioused up just in time. Got us an okay place to go from, but the same thing happened. In the air, she pitched right. I tried to pull left, but she pulled back and harder. My arm was too scrawny to stop her. Hitting the ground, she went for Tory. Tory held the rail up but then she backed off and let the mare dodge out again.

I yanked her back the other way, had to hand-over-fist it, use my right arm instead of my left. I tucked her into another tight circle so she was kissing my toe. All this time I kept my eyes on Carl and Tory. He'd come up close to her, was talking low and mean to the side of her head because she wouldn't face him. I couldn't hear a word, but was straining to. I could only see. Saw his spit on her cheek and her rubbing it off, her rubbing her arm when he let it go. Time for me to get back down the hill again.

Carl didn't let me circle so I came straight back up—looked ahead and found my mark. I drove her for it. Thought maybe if I got tougher, she'd behave, but when we went off the ground, she pulled again that same damn way. Before we'd even landed, I heard her squeal; saw Tory moving toward us, then throwing the rail. It thumped the mare's shoulder, then pivoted; came back against my leg and her side. She headed the other way. Put us into Linda's rail.

Linda didn't let hers go, she smashed it into us and kept coming. Got us backed against that first fence so it tumbled down. The mare squealed again. Couldn't go backwards or forwards, so went up, rearing.

Linda dropped her rail then. Yanked the reins from me and jerked her down, but she went up again, pulled against Linda's hold.

"Lean back," Linda was yelling at me.

I did what she said from reflex, hadn't thought where it'd put us.

Soon as I moved, the mare lost her footing, balanced against Linda instead of fighting her. That's when Linda let go.

We started falling backwards. Rails clattered under her hooves while she teetered back and forth. I closed my eyes and all I could see was landing on my back with her on top of me.

But she quieted suddenly; got her balance back. I opened my eyes and saw Linda'd caught the reins. That she was the one who steadied us. The mare dropped quickly down on all fours and Linda started walking us. After a bit, Tim brought another horse. As I jumped off, Linda caught hold of my hand. Looked at a bruise already coming up on my arm where the rail'd hit it.

"Jeez, you're a fragile one," she said and I just stood there, as confused and docile as the mare.

17

I stayed pretty altered the rest of the day. I kept riding horse after horse, but stayed tuned to the stuff bumping around in my head like why was I mad at Tory instead of Linda and shouldn't I really be mad at Carl or maybe I shouldn't be mad at anyone. I stayed mad, though. The anger sharpened my focus. Zeroed me onto my riding and so it kept other things down. Let me think I wasn't watching Linda all the time and since I wasn't doing it I didn't have to feel anything about it.

All this kept working until we'd finished for the day and her and me and Tory were driving home. That's when other stuff began bleeding through. We stopped at the store and picked up groceries. The two of them had gotten back to a routine I didn't know, so when we got home, I sat at the kitchen table and pretended to read the paper Linda'd left there. It was a *Racing Form*, so I didn't get very far—never had learned much about the track. Still, I could look like I was reading, have an excuse to keep quiet.

Tory started cooking, something I'd never seen before. She looked odd fussing in the kitchen. Linda went back out to her car. She came back in with those drug boxes of hers. Over the top of the paper I watched her turn the corner toward her room, then heard the door close so I put the paper down. Watched while Tory butchered a chicken and dipped its parts in batter while oil heated in a big cast-iron skillet.

The hissing and popping made me hotter. Tory got a couple of beers from the fridge, opened them, and handed me one. I ran the bottle across my forehead. I looked for a window to open, but all of them already were. I leaned my chair back and cracked the back door. For a second there was almost a breeze. It was late enough to be turning dark. You could hear every bug and frog in the county and close enough you'd've thought they were screaming because we were frying them in that great big black-iron pan.

Tory put in the first few pieces and I could feel the whoosh. She'd plopped them in with her hands but now as the oil started to splatter, she fished through the drawer and pulled out tongs. An oven mitt hung by the stove but it looked like it'd never been used. As if maybe some relative had given it to them, or even the real estate agent, because I sure couldn't picture either of them buying it, let alone wearing it. Something about the design, which was pictures of herbs with their names scrolled underneath.

I could hear Linda banging around in her room. I started thinking about what stuff was probably hers and what stuff Tory's. The same game I'd played back in that Ocala motel room, only this time with furniture. I didn't get very far; felt like none of this stuff belonged to either of them. Like they used it because it was there. None of it actually looked very used at all, though I hadn't noticed this before. Before, maybe, it'd all seemed like Tory's.

I began to take big gulps of the beer and then pressed the bottle to my face again, used the cold as fuel to get up. I pushed the screen door open. Settled into an old wicker rocker on the back porch. The furniture out here seemed used, maybe even by them.

Soon I heard their voices in the kitchen. What little I could make out seemed to be about the horses I'd ridden that day. As they talked about them, I had trouble sorting which was which and me the one who'd been on them all. They worked back to the mare.

"Best of the bunch," Tory said.

"And the worst behaved."

"Gives you something to do." Tory laughed after she said it, but more mean than anything else. I could almost feel her giving Linda a little jab and then, too, I didn't know quite what she meant. It put me back thinking on what they'd done to the mare and how it left me feeling—mad at Tory and some kind of grateful to Linda.

She was the one came out on the porch, Linda was. She didn't sit down, though. Instead she leaned against the rail and so where I'd been looking out over it, now I was looking at her and her looking right at me, too, drilling me the whole time without a single word passing between us. We stayed just like that until Tory called us in.

We ate at the dining room table. This was new, too. Tory and I had stuck to the bed and the couch. The two of them kept up their sparring and I wondered if it'd be like this for the next month—the three of us sitting around while the two of them poked at each other.

After dinner, Linda started cleaning up and I followed Tory out onto the porch. She sat in the rocker I'd been in before, so I took the big old wooden one next to it. It had wide, flat armrests and I spread my hands out on top of them, kept trying to get my fingers all the way around until Tory pressed her beer bottle into the back of my hand. It felt cool and good before it started to hurt.

"You're quiet tonight," she said.

"Just tired."

"Right, I guess you would be," she said, but with the same tone she'd been giving Linda all night.

She still held the bottle to my hand, pressed harder before she slacked off some.

"What's wrong with you?" I asked.

She mashed the bottle into my hand again. Said, "You seem to know everything already so why don't you tell me?"

"Tell you what?"

"Or maybe we should get Linda out here."

Just hearing her name put me squirming. I tried to pull my hand out from under the bottle but Tory pushed down harder, then leaned closer, held my wrist with her other hand. She said, "Listen to me for a goddamn minute, okay? Her and Carl got one way of doing everything. Neither one's ever been on the back of a horse, not once in life."

Now I wasn't sure where she was headed. I'd thought she was going to get after me about Linda. I'd been waiting for that since the other day when she found us in the bathroom. But instead she was starting here and so I didn't know which thing she was really talking about—the thing with the mare and how I'd acted mad at her or the thing with Linda. Or was she going to talk about one as a way of talking about the other?

This last possibility was the one made me ornery. "So?" I said and I knew just how it sounded.

"So, maybe I know some things they don't. Maybe I know things you don't. I can sure see you haven't got a clue what you're doing yet."

I smarted at that and she let go a little. When she began

talking again her voice was gentle, which only made it worse to listen to.

"Lookit," she said, "you can't only care about getting juiced. But Carl, he likes that about you. Wants to find you a horse just as hot-blooded. He never sees why that won't work. Seems you can't either. Don't you see, Cowboy? We're the ones supposed to cool them down. Otherwise you and the horse keep pumping each other up and nobody puts the brakes on. Best way that turns out already happened in Tampa. Is it so terrible I don't want you getting hurt?"

I started to look at her but then couldn't. She was stroking my hand now and I concentrated on that, how the sore left from the beer bottle made her fingers feel softer. She took my hand and we went into the house, headed for her room. When we hit the hallway I saw the door to Linda's room was open. She had the light on.

I tried not to, but I hesitated. Stalled long enough Tory caught me looking. She didn't say anything, though, not even when we'd gone into her room. I genuinely believed she'd let it pass. Took off my clothes believing it, and got in bed. At first I thought the comfort would swallow me, that I'd sleep before I could stop myself from falling into it, but nearly as soon Tory got into bed beside me.

She pressed close to me; stayed soft until I turned my back to her, then she switched. After that, every place she touched, her fierceness wrangled me. She hadn't come at me this way since I'd hurt my arm and then the arm itself put things off kilter. There was no way for me to take over from her and she knew it, and so I had to just let her.

She moved in quick jerks, snatching and pushing. Then she tried to turn me on my stomach, but my arm wouldn't bear it. So she lay down on me and I felt glad for her weight, how sure and solid she felt. And how it felt when she tucked her arm underneath her body; got her hand inside me and used her weight behind it.

She was breathing hard, her mouth close to my ear, her face ducked into the crook of my shoulder. She behaved so single-minded, it put me aside. I wondered what I could ask for without vexing her more. Settled on saying nothing, not making a sound. But then with the way she clobbered me I couldn't help it and like I said, I'm used to deciding whether I make noise or not.

I wondered what Linda could hear. Knew her hearing was part of the point and this made me try still to keep quiet. But soon Tory'd gone far enough I couldn't consider anything except what she was doing. Not like usual, though, not so it helped. This wasn't working for me.

Her hand moved blunt and heedless. I tried different things to slow her. Held her tight as I could, thinking that would make it hard for her, but it didn't so I tried the opposite; pushed her away. This got her off me, but that just gave her more leverage.

I couldn't speak, just cried out. I still tried to keep from too much of this but, the thing was, it helped. Letting the sound come left me looser, helped me not to fight her so much. For little bits at a time anyway. Long enough to keep from crying. I wouldn't do that.

When she'd finished, I turned on my side away from her. She curled against my back, touched my shoulder, then kissed where she had touched. Her gentleness, coming now, just wound me tighter. I turned my face further into the pillows, further from her. She moved her hand along my side, my hip, then pushed me a little so she could get at my ass.

I liked how she felt despite myself. Tucked my thigh up like she wanted and only flinched when she put her hand in from behind. She'd smashed me up pretty good and there was no way I'd handle more, even if she was kind about it. She didn't push me. Slipped out; let just one finger stay. This one she moved so soft and slowly I could almost believe she'd done everything before to let me feel this so distinctly.

At first, I made no sound or movement, wanted nothing to take away from feeling her. She held very still and quiet too. Nudged slightly when she wanted me to turn over more and I ducked even further into the pillows at my head.

Her laying me out like this worried me, but all she did was what she'd been doing and then that worried me, too. She sat up a little. Was holding me with her other arm, while that single finger kept stroking until I'd drifted so close to its motion I wouldn't be getting myself out. She kissed my back, licked down my spine, licked my asshole. All I felt was her tongue and her finger. And then she had more than one finger inside me but still so soft I wanted her whole hand, or thought I did and opened my legs.

She kept things where they were. This same slow fucking until I was sure I wanted it harder. Wanted it rougher because this tenderness seemed so much harder to bear and maybe it showed because right then she pulled out altogether. Began touching me as soft as she'd fucked me and that was easier— easier enough, I didn't care except about her tongue, and the way her other hand kept coming closer to it until I couldn't place anything else.

I rubbed against her, pressed my face to the pillows and her licking me, all of this put me back anxious and so I started thinking about Linda until I wanted her watching, was imagining she was and then that got me off. Or maybe what did it was this morning, her coming at me with that rail and then calling me fragile like that interested her. I couldn't be sure because it'd sort of all run together.

Tory waited a bit and then crept up beside me. I stayed on my stomach, kept my face in the pillows. Her closer arm dangled across my back and she kneaded my ass, was real lazy

about it. I stayed put. I wanted to be sure when I turned I'd see her and not Linda and this took me some time. When I finally rolled over, she petted me and I nestled into her.

"You feeling good?" she asked me and I nodded, though something big and gummy had hit my throat and that made it hard to move my neck.

18

The days and nights kept on rough like that and then they got smoother, turned into weeks. By now we'd weeded the horses and found the ones we'd take on the road. The mare stayed the best of my six. Tory only took two of the new horses, but she started fussing with Jammer again. Claimed she wanted to bring him along with us, though I think what she really wanted was another reason to fight with Linda.

Things kept building between them and I knew it had to do with me, but not really. Like I was just the next level down after Jammer. Something to say was the matter, but not the real thing, not exactly. At least that's how I looked at it because I couldn't carry the whole weight of their anger, I just couldn't, and so even though I knew that what happened with them determined how Tory fucked me, I didn't know. Didn't let myself.

I knew this much, though—if they had a whole day not saying things, I'd spend the night on my stomach and her in up to her elbow. If they actually fought, well then I'd be on my back and it'd go easier. Hardest of all was when they got along and then Tory'd treat me so gently. Looked like today might end up this last way because so far they'd been talking but not yelling. And I'm embarrassed to say it, but that got me thinking about fussing with Linda because I knew it'd get Tory started.

We'd gotten her horses done already and so were on to mine. I was on the black mare, rode her first just about every day. I was working her around getting her warmed up. Carl'd pulled the tarp off the water jump that morning. He'd had a hose running into it ever since and it was about full. Would've been sooner probably except Tory kept splashing us all every chance she got. Tim was the only one besides her still laughing about this.

I wasn't really so cross at her, just a little nervous. I'd never jumped water, didn't know how to, but everyone seemed to have forgotten this and I didn't want to say anything. Would've been okay if the horse knew anything about it, but she didn't. And while her nerves had settled some over the weeks, all the splashing and yelling had got her going.

Carl put us over some other fences first, but not too many. Pretty soon he told us to give it a try. I galloped her to it because that's what I'd seen people do. Anyway, she didn't try to run out, she'd never tried that again. Now if something scared her, she just went right through it. With fences, she'd do that once. It'd hurt. And the next time she'd go over them. But when she ran through the water, well, it maybe startled her, but it didn't hurt.

Carl let her wade through it a couple more times, but then he lost patience. Tim'd left the tarp piled on one side and now Carl kicked it further away; finally he stooped over and lifted it. Underneath was a car battery. I started to feel current soon as I saw it. Must've passed that on to the mare because she was stomping a foot and every so often she'd nicker.

I looked over at Tory. All the joking'd gone out of her face. She stared at Carl who was fussing with cables, running them between the battery and what looked like a transformer. I started staring, too, until Linda came over to help him, then I let my eyes follow the cable to where it disappeared at the edge of the pit. Well, it didn't really disappear, just the black coating was stripped off leaving copper wire that'd long since turned green.

Tim stood near Tory now. He'd lit a cigarette and every so often he'd hand it to her and she'd draw on it and hand it back and I wanted to pull on it too, but then Carl and Linda had finished. That's when Tory started walking. Right straight at Carl until she was practically standing on his boots.

I took the mare a little ways down the hill because I didn't want to hear what Tory was saying, though this time I wanted Carl to listen to her. She kept leaning into him until he actually started backing away from her. Finally he held up both hands. "Fine," he said, "you go ahead have it your way."

I heard this because of how loud he yelled it. She just stood there.

"Go on," he screamed at her and then she was walking towards me and the mare.

"Get off," she said.

I almost crossed her, thought for half a second about opening my mouth. She was next to us by then, had her hand on my thigh. Said, "Come on, let's go."

I swear I could feel the heat of her hand through my chaps and jeans. Jumped off before she said another word.

Soon as I was down, she said, "Give me your chaps."

I yanked at the zippers. Handed them to her fast as I could; held the mare while Tory put them on. I shivered now, tugged at my jeans where sweat had them plastered to my legs. Drafts seemed everywhere, running through my damp clothes.

Tory gathered the reins and I grabbed her leg, boosted her into the saddle. The mare sidestepped away, feeling her new pilot. Tory jabbed her a couple of times, quick jerks on the reins.

When she saw me still standing there, she said, "Go on back up there to Carl and them."

I hustled up the hill, stung and shaky from her voice, but too fearful to be mad about it.

She didn't waste any time. Yelled to Carl she wanted to try it once without the juice just to see what she was dealing with. He said it being her show, she should do whatever she wanted. She flipped him off then ran the mare up the hill to the pit. The little horse didn't even pretend to jump—she just galloped right through it.

"Satisfied?" Carl asked.

I'd drifted over to Tim. He'd lit another cigarette and so I was getting my pulls, taking long ones.

Tory ran the mare back through it the other way, I think just to piss Carl off more.

"Enough," he said and turned on the transformer.

Linda was standing with me and Tim now. She had her own cigarette and I found myself reaching for it when Tim took his back. She didn't let it go, but let me draw on it while she held it and I could feel her fingers against my lips.

Tory circled the mare down below. Jerked her mouth as if to let her know what she was in for.

"You got that thing ready yet?" she yelled.

"Waiting on you," he yelled back.

They came up the hill even faster this time. The mare's hooves hit the ground, digging dirt and raising dust. She'd barely touched the water. I didn't know she had and then the next thing came too fast to see, except in sparks and pieces.

The mare pitched forward then sideways. Ankle deep in water, then not anywhere near it, but in the air, then on her side, skidding across the ground with Tory jammed up underneath her and not able to get clear.

Slamming a fence stopped them. Tory's back hit first and the whole thing shook but didn't come down. The mare just lay there. She didn't try to get up. Tory didn't either at first, but soon she wedged her top foot against the saddle and pushed herself out from under the mare.

No one else moved. Tory staggered a few steps then fell back into the fence—sent the whole damn thing crashing. The mare bolted up, squealing like she'd just now realized what it'd felt like. Then she ran—ran from one side of the ring to the other, stirrups flailing, the reins still over her neck but drooping low enough she could trip herself.

Tim moved first, went after her, but Linda called him off. Said, "Stay away from her. Let her stop herself."

You could see a kind of trench in the ground marking their slide. I looked from that trench to the mare, still weaving, trying to run, but tottering. Then I looked at Tory. She was watching the mare, lost her balance watching her and fell again, this time forward. Landed on her hands and knees.

I started for her, but Carl caught my arm, held me off. It was Linda who picked her up. She held her tight around the waist and walked her. Talked soft to her, saying, "You're just shook, now. Listen to me, you're not really hurt."

She kept her walking and I kept listening to her, feeling jittery and funny, like I was going to fall. It stayed this way for what seemed a long time and then other things began to creep in. I could hear Carl. Could feel him still holding me, noticed I was leaning into him pretty good.

I still hadn't said anything, but wanted to. I couldn't find what it was, though, and then I realized he was trembling and this troubled me more than the rest had.

Linda was walking Tory down to the barn. Carl and I followed them. Left Tim to collect the mare. Walking behind like we were I could see Tory limping, sort of favoring one leg, but covering it pretty good at the same time.

Once down there Linda took her into the tackroom. Carl kept me in the aisle and because I wasn't sure, I said, "That's not supposed to happen?"

Instead of answering me he lit me a cigarette. The smoke felt good, but mostly I liked having something to suck on.

Pretty soon Tim brought the mare in and soon as he hooked her to the crossties he started taking the tack off her. Carl called for Linda, but not mean or anything. She came out of the tackroom with something tucked up under her palm. I hardly saw the needle before she stuck the mare. She did it so fast and smooth the mare herself barely noticed. Tim put two flannel coolers over her. I was cold too; realized it when Linda put her arm around my waist and I started shivering. Everyone else seemed to be sweating.

We all stood there like that until Tory came out. Soon as she did Linda dropped her arm from me. Still, Tory acted funny like she didn't know whether to come near me. It was up to me to go to her, I guessed, so I did. Tim was leading the mare to her stall and Tory watched them go. Linda went back to the tackroom. Carl just shrugged and said, "Guess that'll be it for today."

I felt Tory bristle, but she wasn't going to start anything. We walked out to her car. I got in on my side, but she came around and said, "You drive us home. Okay, Cowboy?"

"Can't," I said.

"Come on, darling. My leg hurts and . . ."

"No, I can't drive."

"What?"

"Can't . . . Well, I can . . . I don't have a license."

"You and half the state of Virginia," she said and handed me the keys.

I moved over behind the wheel. When she got in, she had to sort of pick up her leg and put it in the car. It looked bad, but I wanted to believe she was okay, that she knew what she was doing, so I just got the engine running.

"How come you never got a license?" she asked, once we were out on the road.

"Just never had time," I lied. I knew she was closing on me. Would be there soon as she wanted.

When she spoke it was careful. "Best we get you one while we're down here. It'll be easier."

She let that hang too long then said, "I mean proving residency and all."

We both knew she meant age and that we'd skirt around it. The trouble was, right this minute I felt my age or maybe even younger.

19

When we got home we both headed for the refrigerator. I got a beer and went and sat on the couch. Tory followed with her own beer and a sack of ice. She pulled off her pants and I saw the bruising that'd started around and below her knee. There were cuts, too, and some scrapes. I stared at them so long I almost didn't see the puncture, but once I did I couldn't look at anything else, not until she covered it with the ice. Even then, I didn't stop staring and so when she sent me to get some peroxide I was slow off the mark.

I brought the bottle in and she dumped some on her leg. She jerked like it hurt more than she expected. The hole lay just above her calf on the inside. I watched the stuff fizz inside it— saw little shards bubbling out. It smelled bad, thick and warm, and I began to feel sick.

She kept tipping more into the puncture. Let the excess drip onto the carpet and the couch. She'd dumped more than half the bottle before I took it from her.

"You're making a goddamn mess," I said. "Maybe you should be lying down or something."

She just picked up the peroxide again and poured the rest of it into her leg. Then started pouring beer.

I grabbed her wrist, but she jerked away. Had thrown the bottle before I knew it. It didn't break, just bounced off the wall and then rolled to a stop, foamed all over the carpet. Some wet spots marked the wall.

She didn't say anything. Not then and not when I got up and went to the bar. I tried to pour her some bourbon. Was shaking so bad I slopped it everywhere but the glass. I thought of the Percodans, for me or her I'm not sure. I put the bottle down in the puddle of bourbon. Stared at it awhile, at the mess I'd made, then started again. Poured us both drinks this time and carried them over to the couch.

We sat there nursing ourselves until we heard Linda's car and then another one right behind it. Carl walked in first. You could tell right away he'd lost the shakiness he'd had earlier.

"Christ damn," he said. "This the fucking gimp ward? You should see yourselves."

I could see what he was really looking at and so could Tory. She pulled her jeans closer to her first, then put a cushion across her lap, tugged at her underwear like if she pulled at them they'd cover more.

"Jesus, Markham. Let me get you another drink."

She held her glass out to him. He pushed his hat back, then took it off altogether; dropped it on the coffee table before he took her glass.

He said nothing about the mess I'd left on the bar, just made Tory another drink and then one for himself.

He handed Tory her glass then pulled a chair up. Put it right across from her. As he settled into it, he took all the air from the room and when Linda came in a few minutes later I thought the fucking house would explode from the force of the two of them in that one close space.

"Better get your Kildare bag," Carl said.

He handed Linda his glass. She took the drink but didn't

quite seem to know she had. Soon as she noticed it, she put it down. Then shoved the coffee table back so it hit Carl's shins. While he cursed her she sat down on the table, blocking his view. She ran her fingers along Tory's knee, then lifted her calf. Even I could feel the stiffness when Linda tried to move it.

"Good god," she said and then was up again and out the door.

Carl took Linda's seat as soon as she left. He ran his finger along Tory's thigh to her knee. His voice came in this quiet way. "Got to hurt like a son of a bitch but then, if I remember right, you like that."

Tory didn't say anything, so he turned to me.

"Isn't that right, Lee?" he said. "Am I right? Help me out here, girl."

I couldn't say or do anything. Not now. Already it'd gone too far. Even if I could've tried, there wasn't anything that'd ease this. I just hoped I could stay out from between them, hoped he wouldn't keep dangling stuff my way.

I looked at Tory, to keep from looking at him. Her face had been growing a darker and deeper red this whole time. First with embarrassment, I'd thought, and now I wondered if it'd been something else all along.

"Neither of you talking?" he said and she slumped back, let the pillow slide off her lap. Then she stretched her bad leg a little, and the other one, too.

His feet had been outside hers, now he had room to put them in between and he took it. Then he leaned back a little, too. Stretched his legs, so they were pushing hers and when she didn't flinch from the pressure, he eased off on her bad knee and held his glass up like to toast her; took a long, slow sip from it.

I couldn't look away from them, couldn't get up. It was like I'd short-circuited. I could think what I wanted to do, but when I tried to do it, nothing happened.

Carl kept leaning his one leg into hers. She rested her drink between her legs. Started stroking herself with the glass. She tucked her fingers inside her underwear, pulled it aside for a moment, then let go, said, "Never tire of what you can't have. Do you, Boss?"

Linda walked in before he answered. I don't know if I'd ever been so glad to see her and mostly because she dulled the ache between my own legs, or at least changed it. She crashed those boxes of hers down on the table—the big red plastic one and the little black metal one, then she pushed Carl so she could sit beside him.

He slid across the table, collected his hat on his way, then was sitting opposite me.

I looked to where my feet were in relation to his because it seemed important, but before it could register Tory handed him her empty glass and said, "Be a dear, would you, and get me another?"

She'd meant to mock him, but her voice sounded urgent and shaky. I thought he'd smack the glass right out her hand. Instead he just took it, but he stared at me a long minute before he went back to the bar.

Linda ignored it all, or seemed to. She snapped the latches on the red box and started rummaging. When she found the bottle she wanted, she said, "I'll start you with some cortisone; maybe that'll be enough."

Tory was still looking at Carl, wasn't paying attention to anything else.

I paid attention to Linda. She'd fished a syringe from the black box and had already got the needle through the bottle's rubber cover. I watched her draw the liquid into the barrel. It wasn't even half-full when she pulled it out. She tossed the bottle back into the box and upended the syringe, then flicked it a couple of times, squirted some out the needle. When she was done, there was maybe half again as much as before. Tory got up and turned around. She put her hands on the back of the couch. Linda slapped back of her knee just once, then had the needle in and out fast.

When Tory sat down again, Linda stroked around the puncture. "You dump all of this in here?" she asked, picking up the peroxide.

Tory was still watching Carl. He'd brought back her drink but wasn't giving it to her. He sat in that chair again, rested her drink on the armrest. Kept dipping his finger in and then sucking it.

"Tory?" Linda said. "You dump this in here?" When she said "here" she poked her finger right into the hole.

Tory snapped her head back. I could see her chewing her lip, working hard at looking smooth.

Linda took this as an answer. "Not exactly the best thing," she said, "but I expect you'll live."

She went back into the red box and brought out some gauze and a big jar of paste. She put some of that on the gauze, poured something else powdery right into the puncture, then pressed the gauze on top and tied it there.

I reached for my drink and realized how long it'd been since I'd had anything to file my edges. Thinking this got me up and headed for the bathroom. I figured I'd hunt up the Percodan or maybe Tory's Quaaludes. Once I got there, though, I took off my clothes and got in the shower. Let the water run hot even though it was so muggy.

Sweating under the water felt so good I just stood there awhile not thinking what it was I was doing or why and when I heard the door I didn't think I cared who it was until Carl said, "Fucking steam bath in here."

I could hear him peeing. Could see him pretty well through the shower curtain, something I knew worked both ways except he didn't seem to be looking. He shook his dick before he put it away, put it away before he turned towards me, and then he was looking and he flushed the toilet and so the water got that much hotter and now it was me trying not to flinch from him.

He didn't do anything, though. Just stood there looking awhile before he left. Soon as he did, I jumped out of the tub. I pulled my T-shirt on, felt it stick to my back. Pulled my jeans on over nothing. Everything was damp from the humidity, the steam, the water I'd left on my body. I buttoned my pants and hid my underwear under a towel.

When I got to the living room, I hung in the doorway and Tory said, "Hey, Cowboy. What you been doing?"

Her hand played absently with the buttons on her jeans, which still sat there beside her. It looked like she wasn't going to put them back on, but then I looked at her leg and figured she couldn't even if she wanted to.

Finally she let them go and patted a place beside her. Said, "Come and sit with me, baby."

Linda got up to let me pass. She left her boxes on the table, but she took a chair near the door.

Soon as I sat down I felt Tory's hand on my back.

"You're wet, baby. How'd you get wet?"

Carl's chuckling got me looking down and away. I saw her leg first. She was bleeding through the bandage and the blood where it'd mixed with the salve made an orange blob, but then in the middle was this black-crimson dot I had to look away from. It was then I saw the second syringe on the table.

By this time Tory'd got what Carl was laughing at. She said, "You wet there, too, darling?"

You could hear the drug in her voice and she was grabbing at my jeans, had opened some of the buttons. I shoved her a little, said, "Come on now, quit."

"What'd I do?" she said and then Linda was lighting a cigarette off the one she was finishing and Tory said, "Let me have one."

Linda just said, "You don't smoke, dumbass."

"Come on and give me one anyway."

Linda came over and lit Tory a cigarette. "You want one, too?" she asked me.

"Okay," I said.

She handed me one, then leaned across Tory to light it, rested her hand on my thigh. I looked down when she did. You could see my bush through the open buttons.

"You're not breathing," she said very quietly and then she flicked her lighter.

I took the smoke into my lungs and held it until I'd burned myself. Linda still loomed over me and I started coughing and she dropped her lighter in my lap. I scrunched further down on the couch. Felt my pants press my crotch, felt her take the lighter. I tipped my head back, but righted myself, stopped just short of catching her arm and then she'd pulled away and I'd opened my eyes and Carl was the one looking at me and he kept looking until his cigarette burned far enough to get his attention and that made me look where mine was.

Lifting my hand dropped the ash on my leg and I was rubbing it into my jeans when Tory tried to get up. She fell right back down and Linda started for her, but Carl said, "I'll get it."

He came around the table and picked her up, not all the way, just enough so he could walk her.

"Where is it you're going?" he was asking her and she said she needed to go to bed and he said, "Is that what you need?" and then I couldn't hear them, not what they were saying.

Linda'd taken Tory's place on the couch. She took bottles from the red box and syringes from the black one.

"Come on and help me," she said.

I didn't say anything and she tossed a handful of plastic packets into my lap. I didn't move right away, was still straining to hear anything coming from Tory's room.

"They don't ever really do anything," she said.

I pretended not to know what she meant.

She ignored my pretending, said, "She won't let him and he can't bring himself to just take it. If he'd just gone and got that over with a long time ago it would've been easier on everyone."

I didn't want her to keep talking this way so I said, "What do I do with these," meaning the packets.

"Just open one," she said.

I picked one up. My fingers had gone rubbery and so I had trouble tearing the wrapper. Finally I got that first one open and slipped the syringe out. I looked at it wide-eyed, turned it over in my hand.

"Like the feel of it?" she asked.

"What?" I said, even though I'd heard her clearly.

"Just take the cap off, darling."

I popped the cap and handed her the syringe. She took the nearest bottle and stuck the needle through the rubber covering the top. Then she drew clear fluid into the barrel.

"Give that cap to me now," she said.

I wasn't sure where I'd put it, then realized it was still in my hand. "Here," I said, holding it out to her, and her fingers brushed my palm when she took it.

We did this at least a dozen times. Each time she placed a colored labeling dot on the syringe's barrel. Sometimes a few got the same color.

"What color is Huey?" I asked.

"Blue," she said. "But he doesn't get much these days. A little bute when he's sore. Most of this is for yours, well, and then there's one for Frisbee."

She put a rubber band around the bundle of needles, checked the caps and put them in the bottom of the black box. Put the little tray back on top.

I had one packet left in my lap. I put it on the table next to her cigarettes and we both watched it for a while until she leaned over and pulled a bottle from the box beside it and read the label. Then she set it on the table on the other side of her Winstons.

I reached, I thought, for a cigarette but I came back with the bottle. Stared at the label, which said Hydromorphone.

"What is this stuff?" I asked.

"Horse horse," she said and I guess I must've looked dim because she said, "Horse heroin," then added, "It's a synthetic."

I took that to mean not genuine, so I put it back down. Took a cigarette this time.

She said, "They give it to people, you know, they just put a different name on the bottle."

I put the cigarette between my lips but she made no move to light it. I rolled it back and forth with my fingers, but then my hand was shaking so I had to put it down.

She picked it up, that same one that'd been in my mouth, and she lit it and then held it to me.

"Did you want this?" she asked.

I nodded and then she put it in my mouth; let her fingers brush my lips. This started a hum between my legs that matched the one already going behind my eyes. I thought of closing them, my eyes that is, but then I might miss something.

She smiled, was patting my leg now, asking me, "So you want to go for a ride?" and for a minute I thought she meant a drive and her hand was still on my leg and I was nodding but then I knew what she meant.

I began to fidget. She let this go on awhile before she picked up the packet. Once she'd done that she became quick and efficient. Tore it open and uncapped the needle in what seemed like one motion.

She drew the liquid into the syringe the way she had before, but less of it; squeezed only a couple drops out the top before she extended her hand.

The syringe lay across her open palm. It looked small. I wanted to take it, but couldn't. Only felt this simple fear and she saw it. Capped the syringe and put it down. Said, "It's all right, darling. Not like you have to or anything."

Her voice sounded so soft I wanted to curl up inside it. Couldn't stand listening to her sounding like that, so I said, "Let's just do it."

She reached her hand over to me and I got up. Was standing in front of her. She put her hands on my hips, kept me steady, still I had to work to keep my legs from shaking.

"Stay still," she said and began unbuttoning my jeans.

I didn't understand; grabbed her hands and then felt stupid for it, stood there trembling and embarrassed. Said, "I thought you'd . . ."

She looked up at me and laughed, said, "You bruise easy, darling. We don't exactly want to advertise."

She was holding my hands or I was holding hers, I'm not sure, but either way she pulled free and finished unbuttoning my pants. She had to reach around me for the syringe. I watched her pop the cap off and she put the barrel between her teeth and I felt her hands on my stomach first and then lower.

I locked my knees. Held her shoulders to keep my balance.

She began to pull and press my skin, sort of stretching it and letting it go. Then she pressed hard against my thigh so I had to brace against her. There was an instant's pause. A short prick. My flesh went numb around the needle but then I felt a pulling; saw her draw blood into the barrel. I snapped my eyes shut.

I could feel it going in; felt the liquid fizz in my groin, then my belly, right before the hammer strokes started. They hit my crotch first, then my brain. Swung back and forth until it became hard to stand and then, right then, it changed. It was spreading through my chest; sent pressure bursts down my arms, through my body, shudders, my whole body quivering and, me, I was loving it by now.

I clutched her shoulders. Fell deadweight against her when she got up. It wasn't that I couldn't support myself, I just couldn't imagine bothering. She grabbed me under the arms and held me and soon the trembling quieted. Then it shifted again, seeped outside—an undertow, constant pulling, blissful.

Linda dropped me back on the couch. I lay there and listened to her move around the room. Heard her closing the boxes, fixing another drink. It seemed nothing bad could happen, or that if it did I wouldn't care.

The junk had lodged dead center now—an actual presence taking up space. It felt benevolent, comforting. Like if I tried to get up it would put a hand gently but firmly on my chest and say, "Let me get that for you. You just rest, I'll take care of everything."

And so I lay there like that, completely succored.

After a while, I heard only Linda's breathing and my own— once in a while the ice in her glass. She sat on the edge of the couch. Was right beside me where I could feel her. I still wouldn't open my eyes.

I heard her put the glass down and then felt her hand cool against my cheek, smelled her cigarette, but then sensed she wasn't smoking and when I opened my eyes I saw Carl there, in the doorway. Holding himself, which I figured meant he hadn't done anything to Tory.

"Come on, let's get you to bed."

This was Linda talking and then she hoisted me up and when she did I nearly lost my pants what with them still unbuttoned and all. I clutched them with one hand, her with the other, though like I said I could've done all this myself, just didn't want to. This seemed to have more to do with all the drinking than the dope anyway, least that's what I told myself.

She walked me down the hall, past Tory's room to hers. She laid me there on her bed and stretched out beside me; nudged me over so I lay on my side with my back to her. I rested in the crook of her arm. Could feel her breath against my neck. Her other arm slipped around my waist and I turned shy when her hand was there, pushing into my jeans.

Her mouth rested right behind my ear. "Easy now, darling," she said.

I wanted just to let her, but my body fought. Some part of me kept above the junk, wouldn't give to her yet. She caught me by both wrists. Pulled my arms crisscross against my chest and leaned into me; pushed me on my stomach and I felt her belt buckle dig into my back. She tightened her grip on my one arm and let go of the other. I left it pinned under my body. I think I could've moved it, but I didn't try to.

"That's it," she kept saying. "That's right, darling. You just take it easy."

Her voice lulled me. I felt her taking off my jeans, her weight on my legs, and I could smell Carl; turned my head when he said, "So you want help with this one?"

He still had his hand in the same place, was rubbing himself. Linda acted like she'd forgotten him, just said, "You leaving? Get the door then, would you?"

I watched him close it, still heard his boots when she put her fingers up my ass. I jerked away from her, only because it hurt at first. She grabbed my wrist and twisted. Held me close against her and pressed her hand further into me.

"Easy now," she said. "Baby, just ease up."

I let her weight push me down; let my body sink into the bed. I hid my face in the pillow and kept my eyes closed. Her strokes cut through my middle. I clutched the bedspread first, then the mattress—wasn't sure where we were now or what I wanted and then she left off hammering me.

Her hand stayed deep, but quiet. This was familiar and I was crying and I hated her for it, except I didn't hate her at all. She slid her other hand underneath me. I felt it down my belly, pressed against my crotch.

"Shh," she said and kept stroking me. And when I wasn't quiet anymore, she moved her hands. Pulled me towards her like she knew the last thing I wanted was to look at her. Like she knew the thing I wanted most was comfort.

"Easy," she kept saying. "Take it easy. Nothing so very bad going on here."

She held me on top of her. Her lips were on my mouth. Her tongue inside it and when the junk swept in this time, I went under to it fast, let it swallow me.

I put my arms around her. Curled my body into hers and liked the feel of her clothes against my skin. I took my shirt off to feel it more, hid my face in her shirt, then put my hands underneath it. Touched her breasts before I sucked them.

"That's right," she was saying. "That's a good girl."

I had to press against her hand before she'd touch me. Had almost to put her hand there.

"What you want?" she asked. "That what you want?" she said and she was over me, had put her hand in my cunt but then took it out. Said, "Say what you want."

I wouldn't. I pulled at her belt instead. Started to unfasten it.

"That's not going to happen," she said.

I let go same as if she'd hit me. Then she did. Not hard exactly. A smack across the face.

"Say what it is you want."

I tried holding on to her, but her hand came back the other way and then again the other.

She said it over and over until I said it, though by then I didn't mean it. Didn't want it anymore.

I got it anyway.

Got it until I felt split up inside. And maybe I was because afterwards I was bleeding. From my ass or my cunt I wasn't sure. I think both. A lot of blood on the bedspread. Enough to go through to the sheets, I knew this when I pulled back the covers. Felt the dampness when I got under them. Did this while she was still in the bathroom.

I pretended to sleep. Did this a long time, while she didn't. While she sat beside me and kept drinking.

Finally she looked like she was dozing, or had at least gone off somewhere. I got up to pee. Had needed to forever and so it took me a long time, and I heard her in the hallway, roaming around. I tried to clean myself up. Used a washcloth, then didn't know where to put it.

I went back to her, back to her room, but she wasn't there so I wandered down the hall. Found her in the living room. Carl was still there, too. The empty bottle of bourbon sat beside a newer one. I dropped back behind the doorway, but that just made him smile, so I turned tail.

When I'd gotten into the bed again, she came in. I knew she had something in her hand, still I turned my back to her. She rolled me the rest of the way over. Patted me through the covers before she pulled them back.

I felt a quick stick in my hip. Then drops along the crack of my ass. Her fingertip rubbing the liquid where I was sorest until I didn't feel anything there. Didn't feel much anywhere. I remember her putting the covers back over me. And that she patted me some more then. Patted my back until I didn't know who she was and then I could sleep.

20

When I woke up, she'd gone and so for a little bit I could pretend it hadn't happened. Not for too long, though, since I was in the wrong bed, felt practically nailed to it. These little shaking waves rose in my chest, but then stuck to my throat. It seemed I'd be carrying them for a while. My ass and cunt ached, but in a tired, dead way. My groin hurt more, stung and tender. I pulled the sheet back to look, saw a bruise had formed, already purple. My hip was just sore.

I lay there a minute more, then fell from the bed in a sudden hurry. I found my jeans right there on the floor, my T-shirt beside them. I kept thinking Linda would walk in the door. That if I didn't get out fast, she'd keep me there. That it would start all over.

I picked up my clothes. Was out the door and down the hall, into the bathroom, the shower. When the water hit me, I folded over. Heaved spit, but nothing else, nothing was there. I sat in the tub. Rubbed my hands along my thighs, pulled them to my chest. The tub caged me. I pounded the sides halfheartedly, then harder. Finally some pain registered, starting as dull heat then turning hotter, surfacing in cycles through the numbness, mobilizing.

I turned the water off. Pulled a towel into the tub with me and lay there covered by it; drifted in and out. I was wishing I had something to hold when I heard the door. She stayed in the doorway. Was standing there looking down at me as if she saw nothing surprising. "Come on," she said. "Get going."

Linda waited there while I stood up. I think I felt more naked than I ever had. I got myself out of the tub and in front of the sink, tied the towel around my waist. She was so close I could feel her breath, felt it moving water around on my skin. I tried to brush my teeth but dropped everything I touched and so she left me alone.

When I'd stalled as long as I could, I started across the hall, then looked both ways down it. I didn't know where to go. Couldn't see opening Tory's door or going to Linda's room. Both seemed pointless and impossible. I wound up wandering toward the living room. Linda sat in the same chair as last night; watched me. I sickened hearing Carl's voice. I'd forgotten him— that part; hugged my clothes tighter to my chest, but kept walking. I couldn't tell which of them said, "Come here, let me look at you," but I went to Linda. Pretended easiness when she pulled the towel off me and then her eyes traveled my body. I felt sure they left streaks in their path, Carl's too. I tucked my chin to my chest, closed my eyes.

"Bad bruise," she said while she prodded me, pulled at my flesh the way she had before she stuck me.

"Going to be hard to find room on you," she said when she let go of me. "You don't hold up so good."

I knew she meant my veins. I wanted to say it didn't matter. That I wouldn't let her again. I couldn't stand how I longed for it.

"Go on and get dressed," she said but I did it right there in front of them because I'd made up my mind I wasn't going into anybody's room.

Carl left before us. I waited in the kitchen while Linda checked on Tory and then we headed over to the barn. She drove fast and I rolled my window all the way down. The wind smacked pretty good, but it stayed thick and warm, had no edges, and these big flat sheets of air were hard to swallow, smothering even.

When we got there, Linda went into the house and so I was left on my own. I went around back and found Tim. He had Huey out on the crossties, said, "He's all set for you. You're supposed to get him done first."

"What?"

"Carl said I should get you up to the schooling ring soon as you got here. You know, what with Tory out, you've got that many more to get to."

"Oh yeah, right," I was saying and then Tim was helping me up on Huey. I eased myself into the saddle, tried to find some way I'd be comfortable.

"Hey, you okay?" Tim asked.

"Yep," I said, but really I felt Linda's hand so far up me I choked. I grasped the pommel to keep my balance as all that soreness spread out. I held on like that all the way to the ring. Let go only once we'd got up there and I saw Carl and Linda following behind us.

I started working Huey. Couldn't help thinking how I hadn't ridden him since Tampa, not since I'd crashed him. I kept telling myself I had nothing to lose. But since this was because I'd lost everything it wasn't so comforting.

As Huey and I circled the ring, I tried to hear what Linda and Carl were saying to each other. They were leaning against the fencing near the gate and I'd get snatches each time I came by but had trouble putting them together, trouble focusing. Every time my butt hit the saddle, I felt Linda's hand up me and that took all my energy to manage.

I gleaned this much: I'd be riding everything for the next few days until we went on the road, then I'd keep Tory's horses and they were going to hire someone to ride mine. Hearing this, I realized they'd had a choice—could've hired someone to take Tory's string instead of the other way around.

It was a little later I realized this meant Tory wasn't leaving with us, was maybe a lot worse off than I'd thought. I couldn't ask about her, though, because I couldn't stomach what I knew they'd say. Instead I was busy trying to find another explanation for what I'd overheard. One that meant Tory coming with us after all. I needed to believe for a little longer that last night hadn't happened, that it wouldn't be happening again.

By the time I came round past them again they'd stopped talking and then Linda and Tim fixed some fences. Soon as they had them set, Carl got us started. We didn't face anything too scary right off and Huey was good to me. Apparently he wasn't holding any grudges.

Once we'd got going, I found this funny kind of calm; tapped into it as much as I could. I told myself it was the remnants of the junk. Believed that if it'd been put there from outside I could depend on it.

After those first few fences, Tim and Linda raised them. I guess I'd gotten used to the height by now, but this day I noticed it—maybe needed to notice it. I figured as long as I stayed on cruise control I'd be okay. I let my legs meld with the saddle, my hands barely held the reins. I tuned in to the creak of leather. Could smell the salt-sweat lathering Huey's neck now the sun'd burned off the fog.

Carl's voice blended with the rhythm of Huey's breathing, his hoofbeats. I kept my eyes tunneled. Anything to the sides slid by in a blur while I focused dead ahead; registered the fences and nothing else. Even then, I let Huey make all the big decisions—just measured some of them.

I rode all of them this way. Only Frisbee needed more and by the time we got to him, well, a couple of hitches, but not much else. Then it was over and Carl was telling me I'd done good. I registered no relief because there'd been no strain, except in my body. When I hit the ground off Frisbee, I staggered some. Handed the reins to Tim because I thought I might let go.

He looked at me curious, but he'd been doing that all day. "Something's wrong with you," he said.

I started to help him bathe Frisbee, but he said, "I can do it. You go and sit."

I did what he told me. Sat on a trunk and when he'd finished, he sat down beside me and pulled out a pipe, his old corncob one, and handed it to me. I rubbed the bowl against my palm, liked the roughness, how it'd yellowed brown, the pipe part had too, and I started to suck on it.

Tim took a wad of foil from his pocket and started to unwrap it. Then we both saw Carl coming.

"Shit," Tim said. "No rest for the fucking weary."

He pressed the foil into my palm and disappeared. I bent over to unzip my chaps like that's all I'd been doing all along. I couldn't help but notice the little hole on the inside of one leg, the dark stain around it. I looked away from it; shoved the foil in my pocket and wrapped the pipe up in the chaps.

When Carl got closer, he said, "Come on, girl. Let's take a walk."

He didn't wait for me, so I had to catch up. Once I did, he put his arm round my waist, steered me out the barn and back up the hill. His hand felt large and warm pressing my back—and gentle—and that made me want impossible things like to turn into his shoulder and for him to hold me.

Instead he started talking. I listened while he told me everything'd go fine. Finally he said, "How're you holding up?"

"I'm all right," I said, but I looked away from him.

He tucked his hand into the waist of my jeans. I could feel his fingers on my skin, though he seemed genuinely not to notice what he was doing.

"She'll be okay, you know, just racked up for a bit."

"How long?" I asked.

"I don't know. A few weeks maybe."

I still wasn't looking at him and I kept it that way because I didn't have a very good hold on myself. A few weeks felt like forever but then, too, after last night I feared it might not be near long enough.

21

Linda dropped me off and then went to the store. That left just me and Tory in the house. I knew I should go in and see her, but I stalled awhile first. Thought about having a drink but it didn't seem like what I needed, even Percodan didn't seem right, so finally I just went in without having anything first.

She looked the same. Same as last night anyway. I seesawed in the doorway before going over to her then watched the carpet the whole way there.

"Hey, Cowboy," she said, and when I sat on the edge of the bed she tried to pull me closer.

I hated how this felt, her not being able, so I scooted over next to her. Her body gave way into mine and when I put my arm around her, she lay her hand along my cheek. I turned my head just a little and kissed her hand, but what I wanted was for her to take it away. Soon she did—let it fall away from my face and her jaw sort of twitched, though she made no move to speak.

I felt clumsy then and cruel, worse still when she held on to me and untucked my shirt; began kissing my stomach. She couldn't reach well because of her leg and so I would've had to help her. Instead I held her down. Began kissing her to keep her from kissing me. If she were gentle to me now I knew it'd smash me up. I figured then she'd know about me and Linda. Hell, she'd know that if she got my pants off, what with the bruise still there and how torn up I still was.

All she had on was a T-shirt so I got her undressed pretty fast and then got between her legs. Her bad one was propped up on a pillow and I kept asking her if it hurt and she kept telling me no, still it made me think before everything I did and so mostly what I did was lick her. I did this a long time. Even after she'd started moving in a way I knew meant she wanted me fucking her. I finally did that when she asked, though I stayed real soft about it.

Afterwards, I held on to her while she drifted in and out. She did a lot of that before dropping off completely. The sheet only half-covered her and I found myself staring at her leg. To make myself quit looking I sort of tossed the sheet the rest of the way over her. Nearly as soon as I did I began looking at her jeans. Either Linda or Carl had left them on the chair by the bureau. I couldn't stop myself from sliding out of the bed and then picking them up, searching out the dime-size hole that matched the one in my chaps. This one had a bigger stain around it, though.

I crept back into the bed afraid of getting caught at this. She was dead away, though. So much so I put my arms around her again without her stirring much. I stayed with her this way until Linda came back. I heard her in the kitchen first then in the hall. I jerked from the sound when she opened the door and either my movement or the noise woke Tory.

Linda put her metal box on the bedside table and then she told me to leave. I didn't want to but I couldn't find any way to argue with her. This didn't seem to worry Tory, but I felt scared to leave her there. Wanted at least for her to put her shirt back on, wanted to do this for her. What I did, though, was exactly what Linda told me—waited for her in the living room.

I knew she was giving Tory another stick, that then it'd be my turn.

████████ It kept on just like this with me going back and forth between them. Kept on right up until we went on the road—Linda and Carl and I did, leaving Tory behind and Tim, too. He was supposed to take care of her. Make sure she showed up once her knee healed.

Carl took on extra help just before we left. He'd been planning to hire this guy Jamie since there'd be twice as many horses as they'd taken to Florida—too many for Tim and Linda to manage by themselves—but what with Tim staying home for now, he hired Jamie's wife, too, to take up the slack. She was a ghosty woman named Deb who got me sad every time I saw her, though it'd go away some if we talked. I still didn't know who Carl was getting to ride my horses.

So Jamie and Deb had the truck and Carl took his car while I rode with Linda. She was driving fast even for her because she wanted to beat the horses, and this guy Jamie, he ran sort of hot and so she didn't know how fast he'd get the truck there. We'd left Sunday evening, be driving through the night. Was faster this way and calmer for the horses. Calmer for me, too, except I hadn't gotten my hit and was already missing it, though I guess I can admit it wasn't the hit so much as what came after, not that I could really separate the two. One was the necessary way to the other and not just for her.

We were headed for Connecticut and since that's where my father'd threatened to show up, I had plenty to think on. I knew he'd do it, too, just didn't know when, and my mother'd be with him. I could count on that. She'd be there to make sure I didn't come home.

So, anyway, while we drove I pared things down, wanted to determine what mattered. Linda had a cigarette in her mouth and told me to light it, which was about the only thing she'd said so far. I lit a match but my hand didn't stay steady so she clamped hers to my wrist, held me still. When she let go, I got my own cigarette and then tossed the pack back up on the dash. I was trying to act easy because I'd noticed there was something I wanted to ask her.

I waited until we crossed into Delaware, I guess because I figured we wouldn't be there long and so could leave this there. It was very dark by then and the traffic had thinned.

All I said was, "How'd Tory get cut up?" and soon as I said it, the quiet between us changed and then she pulled over.

We sat on the roadside and she didn't say anything and then two trucks passed one after the other, blasting their airhorns. The draft nearly shook us from the shoulder to a gully. I was shaking from all of it and couldn't stop myself. She put her hand on my neck and it froze me. Stopped me moving, yeah, but also made me feel very cold.

"You think it was me."

This was not a question and it struck me she didn't sound mad. Tired was mostly how she sounded, tired in a way that'd make another person sound broken.

"She's never told you?"

"No," I said.

"You never asked her, though, did you?"

"No."

"But you're asking me."

Now she was angry, though I wasn't sure she was angry at me. Didn't matter much since I was the only one there.

She got out of the car and walked down the shoulder. I stayed put at first, then stepped partway out. Leaned back against the car and rested my arms on the door. About then she started walking back. Walked right up to me.

She pressed the door against me so I was squeezed between it and the car. I wedged my knee to keep the weight off me, slid my hands onto her shoulders before I knew I had. Tried, I guess, to push her back, but instead my foot slipped and this left me sort of squished.

She said, "I'm the one sewed her up afterwards. The one who took care of her. You get that, Cowboy?"

She'd never called me that before and I wished she hadn't now. "Uh huh," I said and thought maybe it'd end here.

She hit me hard enough I could hear it but couldn't feel it. By the time my jaw hurt, she'd pulled the door away and socked me in the stomach. That one, I felt. It doubled me over. Put me down on my knees. I saw her draw her foot back. I flinched before she stopped herself and then she walked around the car and I heard her get in, heard the door close. I stayed on my knees a long time. Listened while she lit a cigarette and could taste the smoke as it drifted from the open door behind me. Was oncoming headlights that got me to my feet. We didn't need anyone stopping. Didn't need any more trouble.

I hustled into the car and slammed the door. Linda didn't start the engine. She pulled a pint from under her seat and unscrewed the cap. She passed it to me first and I swilled the stuff, spilling more than I swallowed because I couldn't feel my mouth too good. Linda got a bandanna from the glove box and took the bottle back. She poured some bourbon on the cloth, then reached over to me and dabbed my lip. I must've bit it when she hit me but I wasn't sure because I didn't feel much besides swelling. Then the booze burned a little in this very specific place—the same place as when I'd been trying to drink and slopping.

She handed me the bandanna and the bottle. I was sort of pouring the booze down my throat, but when she started the car moving again I thought I might choke or be sick or both so I screwed the cap back on and put the bottle between my legs. Held it there, held it very tightly.

22

The next day was almost like we were still back home in Virginia. They put me on one horse after another—just leg-stretching them really. I locked up with each one. Got the most comfort from Huey and this big scrawny one of mine we called Bronto because his neck went on forever. Anyway, he'd taken the mare's place as my favorite, well, except for Huey, and I was trying not to get too attached to him since he wouldn't be mine very long.

No one much had shown up yet, no one I knew. Most of them were from the Northeast so this one was in their backyard. They didn't need to worry about traveling and then having a day like this to recover from it. No sign of Silas yet either, but his barn wasn't more than twenty minutes away so it seemed likely he'd drop by. My parents' house, well, that was another twenty minutes beyond Silas's. These two things kept me looking over my shoulder until Carl yelled at me to look where I was going, not where I'd been and I thought here's an idea I can get behind.

His voice alone bounced me a bit closer to the here and now, though not all the way. I got stuck when I remembered waking up and brushing my teeth—how my mouth looked okay, good enough I could convince myself Linda'd never hit me. Good enough I thought I could live on that level without dropping down to the next one.

I've come close to this kind of thing before, closer than this. My mother lives her whole life this way. For the longest time I thought she didn't have access, but she does. She knows all of it, but she lives above it. Every time I try that, the same damn thing always happens. Today it was brushing my teeth and how much it hurt. Hurt like the swelling was inside where nobody'd ask and so at least I'd be on my own with it. Alone except maybe for Linda because she seemed to live down here, too, all the time. Tory, I think, lived somewhere between, had found a steady place and worked the drugs so they'd keep her there. I knew already I could never manage that and besides I was trying not to think about her.

I dropped down off the last horse and that new woman, Deb, collected him. They'd already set up bleachers around the grand prix ring and I leaned against the metal piping, tired and not sure where to go. Left myself wide open and he came up on me fast. My mother stood pretty close beside him. I stared at her purse—one of those Nantucket wicker things with the wood and the whale and hers had a chip, was missing part of the tail fin and she'd stroked that bit of ivory until it'd become perfectly smooth.

My father'd clamped onto my arm and wasn't relaxing. I didn't know how to play this. Carl and Linda were nowhere in sight, hadn't been for a while, and so I'd no idea what'd already been said or even if my parents had seen them. This left me not knowing how much I could bluff and then bluffing required talking and already I knew that'd be next to impossible. Silent assent, that's how I'd get read.

I couldn't hear what he was saying. Usually I can pick up the top layer and just stay deaf to the other meaning. See, he talks on two levels, that's how he does it, we do it. But I think maybe I said that already.

My mother I could hear. "Frank," she was saying, "Frank, come on now," like she was coaxing some bullheaded dog.

I needed to get eye level, but couldn't. My head stayed away from his, turned sideways and down. Long as I stayed this way he had the advantage.

My mother started walking away. She'd take a few steps then stop. I knew because I was watching her feet.

I'd forgotten how it is to be with them.

He had me pressed against the bleachers' scaffolding and so different pieces of piping supported different pieces of me. What my mother was doing was working. He'd break a little each time she called him and I got my head up, but not my eyes yet.

He had both my wrists. I told myself he was saying goodbye because it actually was what he was doing. Something about this felt very final, like we all knew it'd been a bad idea.

He kissed my cheek, but couldn't leave with that, and then he was kissing me again and my mother's voice became more insistent, but moved him less and by now I was thinking: just go ahead, get it done.

He put his lips against mine and it hurt, not because of him, it was that sore spot I had. But then he put his tongue between them and it felt better and I opened my mouth because I'd got to that place where, for me, it's too late to do anything else and so this felt like a relief. For this reason my mother's voice jarred us both this time and then it sounded closer and not like her, but then I realized that was because it wasn't her, it was Linda.

She pulled my father off me. He wheeled around, but looked dazed. I felt clumsy myself.

Linda was dead clear. She spoke slowly and quietly. Said,

"I'm not the only one saw you with your tongue down your daughter's throat."

My father regrouped some, came out sputtering. "You don't know what you're saying," he said. He must've thought he was talking to my mother or something.

Linda said, "I know exactly what I'm saying," and then she had me by the wrist, said, "Come on, Lee," and I put one foot in front of the other.

23

She took me back to the stalls; left me sitting on a tack trunk while she went into the tent. I could hear her voice and Carl's, and footsteps scurrying around when they barked. I listened for words; needed not to think about the thing that'd just happened. What I caught was about tomorrow morning. Who to get ready first, what bits to use. Seemed every horse I'd be on was getting a little extra insurance between his teeth, which was okay with me.

Then their voices got lower and I had to strain. Linda was saying she didn't care, she wasn't changing anything with Frisbee, and Carl was arguing with her but she was winning. Said she'd keep trying different things with the new horses, but not Frisbee. I put two and two together. I mean, I knew the test for reserpine was around the corner. Everyone knew that. Well, not the test itself—it'd already been developed. The federation could've used it in Florida, but they didn't, so the question was when they'd start.

These things usually got decided slowly so everyone pretty much assumed there'd be one more summer, or even a whole season because there'd be no convenient time and some strong lobbies were working. Who would've thought they'd spring it like this, before anyone'd come up with a decent alternative? Who'd've thought they had any gumption?

So what Linda was saying was she needed to find a drug that worked, but one they knew so little about they couldn't screen for it. This usually meant something dangerous, or at least unpredictable. But then that's how everyone'd looked at reserpine when she'd started using it to replace whatever'd come before. Now it was so commonplace people couldn't afford to remember that that didn't make it any safer.

Linda'd been looking into this awhile already. At home, the new horses had been guinea pigs, the best three constantly getting dosed. The other ones, strung looser, interested all of us less. The black mare had been the tightest wrapped of the original six. She hadn't stopped shivering since that thing with the battery. Still, Linda'd brought her with us. I didn't know why, and I didn't know why she wasn't getting stuck anymore when, of all the horses, she could've used it the most.

I avoided her as much as I could, which was pretty easy at home, and here Linda'd put her pretty far into the tent, back next to Frisbee. Anyway, I didn't have any reason to get near her and so I didn't. I just couldn't stand the way she paced. Actually what she did was circle in her stall. Go around and around, getting herself in a froth.

I wasn't listening so closely now. Had left off when Linda started joking about how she'd keep people on the ropes this whole show. Embarrass them all before offering them something new. She talked like this was about getting a higher price, but I didn't think that's what mattered. I think she wanted to remind everyone how much they needed her. That without her all their prizewinning horses would be dashing across fields or limping out of the ring. And then, too, maybe she wasn't quite sure what to sell.

So I kept listening halfway. Stayed pretty dazed right up

until Carl said, "Ted's got someone bringing by his saddle. Put him on that skinny-necked thing first."

This shouldn't have surprised me. Who else would they throw my horses to? There wasn't anybody else really. I knew I should be glad he was on mine instead of Tory's, but right then I got it. They'd never put him on her horses so I'd nothing to be flattered about, the whole thing'd been by default. This wasn't what bothered me, though. And it wasn't that afterwards I'd be undoing what his roughness did to my string. What troubled me was a whole lot simpler than all that.

Linda came out with her boxes then, put the red one down beside me. "Come on," she said.

I picked up the box, not quite sure I should, and then followed her. She didn't turn on me, so I guessed it'd been what she wanted. I found myself walking slower the nearer we got to her car. Dropped further and further behind until she was waiting for me, leaning against her car waiting.

She didn't open the trunk until I got there. We put the boxes in and before she closed and locked it, I noticed all these other boxes in there—cardboard ones. I homed to the one full of syringes. I looked away before she slammed the trunk. Knew she must not have cared what I saw, but still felt damned for seeing it all.

We got into the car and she pulled a carton of cigarettes from behind her seat, felt for a pack, then dumped the last two out and handed me one. I concentrated on the red Winston wrapper. It nearly matched the upholstery. I didn't open my pack. She opened hers. Took a lighter from the dashboard and rolled the window down.

I wanted us to get moving because the longer we sat here the harder it was not to think about my parents. Linda was taking her time, though. Even once she'd lit her cigarette, she made no move to start the engine. I reached for the glove box without thinking. Tried it, but it was locked. She noticed, but still said nothing. Was a little while before I knew what I'd been looking for—realized the pills and the pint were home with Tory.

She finished that whole cigarette before she turned on the car—and she smoked it slow. I'd been looking anywhere but at her. Had resorted to reading the cigarette pack. Read it again and again. Twenty class A cigarettes I was reading when she finally started the engine and I didn't stop reading it until we were back at the motel.

She carried the boxes, which left me to unlock the door. Once inside, she kept moving. Me on the other hand, I rested as soon as I could. Sat carefully on the edge of one bed and didn't want to muss anything because it seemed magical to me that the beds were made. I was near to believing maid service had erased the whole day.

Linda went out and came back again. This time she carried a paper bag and a bucket of ice. She set both on the bureau, then got the glasses from the bathroom. She put those next to the ice bucket, pulled the bottle from the bag and poured drinks.

By the time she brought mine over, I'd opened my cigarettes and stretched out on the bed. I figured I looked like someone who can take what comes.

I gagged on the drink and she took it away again. Ran water on a washcloth and brought that to me. I put it over my eyes, liked the coolness. I rubbed my mouth too, and then pulled it away, saw blood there from my lip and it reminded me, not about what she'd done, but what he had and after that she couldn't get the syringe loaded fast enough.

Once she had, she came back beside me and opened my pants but I'm the one shucked them off and my underwear, too.

She's the one turned me over; stuck me back of my knee this time. I pressed into the mattress when it started up. Wanted that soggy washcloth back. Wanted anything cold.

Linda still sat there. She rubbed my back, had her hand up my shirt. I stayed on my stomach because the whole thing felt better that way.

She kept rubbing my back and was smoking, and every now and then she'd take her drink from the table and I'd miss her hand, but then I'd like how it felt cool from the glass after she'd put the drink down and was touching me again.

Things kept up this way and her fingers got me remembering my mother and how she'd smoothed that piece of ivory on her pocketbook.

Linda started rubbing my ass that way, just smoothing her palm against me. Did this very slow and soft and didn't do so very much more. She was waiting for me to cross from nodding into sleep.

Soon as I did, she put her hand up my ass. This time it hurt so much more I felt three years old. I curled my legs up, tucked my head down; pressed myself into the wall and when I found I couldn't go through it, I sucked my arm to keep from screaming because if I did that, she'd kill me, she was killing me I thought there for a minute until I remembered it was me, that I had to ease up and then I could hear her telling me to.

She'd caught me around the waist, was kneeling on my calves, and that helped because it made a different place hurt, forced me back onto my stomach, and then she had her one hand still in me and her other between my shoulder blades and I knew who she was and it let me do what she was saying and that meant she could get her hand up where it felt better, where she could fuck me and then when she got done I didn't have to feel anything.

24

I think I longed for the coffee before I smelled it. Before I realized she'd brought me some. It was light and sweet and while I don't usually like it this way, I liked it now. Wanted to make it last, then drank it quick just the same. Linda was sitting beside me as if nothing had happened these last couple of days.

The truth was I couldn't be sure how many had passed; knew there'd been a day that I'd lost. It'd come and gone and I knew it had but had no recall, and because this left me insecure I pulled the sheet up and tucked it under my arms. I don't know if this was what she smiled at, but I think so. I'd gotten down to the end of the coffee and the sugar was thick on the bottom. Good at first, then too much. I put the cup down, thinking how all the time lately I was trying to keep from throwing up.

Showering helped a little; getting dressed, not at all. It'd been forever since I'd put on breeches and boots. My shirt was new and scratchy. Tory'd been right about Carl buying us stuff. He bought just about everything—food, booze, clothes, and not just our riding clothes. He'd bought us new jeans and some shirts and even clothes for if we had to show up at some party or go out with buyers.

It was just we never exactly got paid. I didn't, anyway. I

mean, Carl'd give us cash sometimes or Linda would, but not regular and not that much really. Tory never acted like it bothered her, but I felt funny about it and this morning I even counted what I had left over from selling my things and from the Cheslers. It was a pretty good wad. Enough to feel sure of, I decided before I rolled it back into its pair of socks. That Visa card still went everywhere with me. Today I put it in the breast pocket of my jacket, seemed more anxious to use it now I had nowhere to go.

On the way to the showgrounds, I looked at every house we passed; kept imagining the people inside and wishing myself one of them. Then we were at the stalls and I was sitting on that same trunk outside and drinking more sweet coffee and this longing for Silas snuck up into my chest. I closed my eyes and tried to suck air down through all that stickiness. Otherwise I would've been paying more attention.

The trunk shook when he sat down. For an instant, I thought he was Carl, but at the same time knew. Then I saw his boots. Watched them kicking against the trunk, then kicking at mine. I jerked my foot before I could stop myself.

"Easy now," Ted said. The way he laughed was enough to get me up and walking.

"Now how am I going to find out about those horses if you're running away?"

I kept moving, but like I said I didn't feel I had so many places to go. Then I saw Carl headed for me. At first I thought he'd be mad, thought I was supposed to be talking to Ted, but the way he held on to my arm when he got to me I knew it'd be okay and then he said it would be.

"Ted, you stay away from this girl, you hear me?"

Ted laughed, "Shoot me, Carl. What did I do?"

Carl let go of me and started walking for Ted. Walked right up to him, his voice getting harder, but not louder.

"You do what I tell you while you're working for me or you don't work for me."

Ted slid off the trunk. Carl took a step back to let him stand, but kept talking.

"Now on, you meet me at the ring. No cause for you coming back here."

Ted tried to walk past him, but Carl shoved him. Then he grabbed Ted's belt by the buckle and jerked.

I understood it would've been better not to see this, but I couldn't take my eyes off them. Even watched Ted walk away. Saw when he put his hand to his crotch to adjust himself and then saw he liked that I'd seen him.

I ducked into the tent and then into Linda. She pushed past into the tackroom, so I picked the feed room across the aisle. Jamie'd tied his dog there—a shepherd who started barking soon as he saw me.

"Shut him up," I heard Jamie yell.

And then Deb scurried in. She started when she saw me, but went right away to quieting the dog. I wanted something to do, but just stood there, afraid of whoever I'd collide with next.

Deb hushed the dog, kept cooing to him. I slumped back onto a pile of sacks, glad for her voice, the low sounds she was making. Glad for whatever calm I could siphon.

"Who the fuck's got Huey standing here half-dressed? Let's get moving." Carl's yelling trapped Deb. She looked to me before she went into the aisle and so I went to the dog. He whimpered a little and rubbed against me. I dropped my hand to him and he licked it.

Deb stuck her head in a while later. "Supposed to get you moving," she said.

Soon as I did, the dog started barking and Jamie started yelling and then Deb and I were outside and she had me up on

Huey and was leading us past all the cars to the rings. Once she had us past the hubbub, she left us on our own.

Being on Huey felt better than anything had in a while. Seemed like they'd made him my baby-sitter—Carl and Linda had. Usually Tory'd ride him last, but with me it looked like they'd keep putting him first. I nudged him into a trot and then kept us to the edges of things.

I knew people stared. I could feel looks from everywhere. Felt a shameful pride because of it and at the same time this rage. There were horses who'd been placid for years tearing across fields with their riders—theoretically some of the best in the country—yelling whoa and yanking the reins and I kept thinking why still stare at me? And I felt glad Linda'd jerked everyone a little, let them all see what life'd be like without all the dope she supplied, the dope that supposedly separated us from all of them.

By our second time around the outskirts, I'd stopped looking at people looking at me. Started Huey cantering and looked at the layout instead. They'd set up the rings like they had in Florida—a riser with tables between the jumper and hunter rings and bleachers around the edges. The tables were still pretty much empty, though a few parties had settled in for the day, some with picnic breakfasts. I knew the table dead center on the hunter side would be the Cheslers'.

The jumper ring was on the furthest side and its schooling ring beyond. When Huey and I came round it this time, I saw Carl and Linda talking with the in-gate man. Right on cue, I saw Deb leading my other three horses and Jamie following with Ted's. If they were bringing them down this early I guessed it meant Carl wanted to send them in one after another. Tory said he liked to do that sometimes with the first class, that it showed him how the week looked. It was fine with me. Maybe the day'd be over early. I wasn't sure if we had one or two classes today, but usually the schedule let you ease into things.

I dropped Huey back to a walk, then circled him around, kept my eyes on Linda and Carl. Now the horses were here, Linda started checking them over. Carl poked his head into the trailer where the announcers camped—parked catercorner to the two rings. Soon enough he disappeared inside to finish his schmoozing.

I was getting antsy. I took Huey over to Deb and she started handing me numbers and then Linda led us to the schooling ring. She started us over some little fences. Not too many peo-ple there and the ones that were gave us plenty of room. When Carl came, we started with the big stuff. I felt okay, actually. This was a lot better than waiting for it and even when Ted showed up and came into the ring on Bronto he kept his dis-tance. He left me alone.

I tried not to notice him, but did. The thing that struck me was how he started doing the small fences on his own. I wouldn't have done that, but I knew Tory did. Made me feel amateur or worse, but I knew there'd be no changing it. Just flicked through my mind really, didn't stay long. Mostly I had this calm and it grew bigger instead of smaller when I got to the in-gate. Linda went over the course with me. It wasn't easy necessarily, but it was easy to remember. I repeated it back to her twice and then I was in the ring.

Soon as I got in there everything hushed but I could still hear it. The announcer's voice startled me most. He was saying all those same things about Huey. I'd heard them over and over through the years. I think maybe it wasn't until then I got it. Understood that this was different than riding Huey around, or schooling him.

As I crossed the beam of the electronic timers, the announcer said, "Ladies and gentlemen, the number one horse in show jumping history."

I needed not to fuck up right now.

Once we took the first fence something happened. The calm had never all the way left and now it took over completely, was like Huey switched to autopilot.

All I did was nothing. I stayed out of his way. Let him decide things. And every fence we took I bathed in stillness. There was this gentle rocking in between, then these swells. Complete quiet while we dangled airborne.

Landing after the final fence, I almost didn't know we'd finished. When we crossed through the timers, it broke and I heard the announcer saying we were clean but with a quarter time fault. I should've cared, but didn't.

Carl did. Soon as we came out he started in. Not mean, but hurried, barraging.

"Can't let him pick the pace," he was saying and nearly faster than I could understand. "Got to make up somewhere for what you lose in the air. Get after him around the turns."

I slid off Huey and onto Mr. Clean all without realizing it. I knew I'd done okay, but knew this one'd require more effort. I tried to shake myself awake. Was blaming the hydromorph then decided I should be thanking it—that without it traveling around in me, I would've had Huey crashing into things.

I didn't know how it would be with Mr. Clean. He felt a lot more alert than I did. With him, my job was reeling in and I didn't do so well with this type of horse. He stayed wrapped tight, but unimaginative, and I could never understand that combination.

Linda worked with us over the small stuff and out the corner of my eye I watched Ted in the show ring with Bronto. I saw them catch a rail at the second fence and liked how it sounded coming down. After that Ted had him bang into everything and, while we all did this, you could see he was doing it for spite, not training. At least that's what I thought until Carl told me to do the same thing with Mr. Clean; told me right before my turn and then I couldn't be sure about anything Ted had done.

I'd gotten pretty good at this sort of tune-up, but didn't like it much. Maybe that was what I'd seen in Ted—he enjoyed it. Anyway, after I buried Mr. Clean at the first fence, I egged him on and dropped him to the second. By the time we were done, the jump crew was groaning. I never exactly could tell why or when Carl thought a horse needed sharpening this way. But then there were things he could see from the ground you just couldn't tell from on board.

After I finished with Mr. Clean, Carl put more of Ted's in before me and Frisbee. That gave us a little time to ourselves. I took him around the fringes the same as I'd done with Huey. Ran into K.C., who looked like she'd just arrived.

"My god, what are you doing up there?" she asked before anything else.

"I've got Tory's this week."

"What's she got?"

"Nothing, she's not here. Look, I've got to get back. Find me later?"

"Sure, honey."

As I rode away, I looked back to see her watching us. She was holding her hat to her head even though there was no wind.

    ━━━━ I wound up giving Frisbee the best ride of the day. We went clean in the time allowed. Took some of the sting out of picking up more time faults with Lazy Boy, though by now we knew the course designer had cut things close because way too many people were going over time. Anyway, I felt good about Frisbee. Could see why he'd become Tory's favorite besides Huey.

It meant a jump-off since Ted had gone clean with his third horse—the chestnut I liked second best to Bronto. Thinking this, I almost wondered if Carl'd had him screw up with Bronto to someway make me happy. Like I wouldn't like Ted doing well with my favorite. Soon as I wondered it, I decided Carl wouldn't even know Bronto was my favorite.

As the jump-off got closer, Linda got edgy. She kept talking with Carl. Well, whispering. I kept looking at the course diagram to stay out of their way. Finally, the last horse finished and then the jump crew began pulling out fences. That's how they do it—the fences that stay are in the same place, but others get dropped out all together. Trick is how to get to the ones left because, assuming everything stays up, all that matters is time.

Ted'd go first, I'd go second, and then there'd be two more after me. A lot of times, you'd go reverse order, but this time it'd be original order, which was okay with me. Gave me the edge over Ted and he was the only one I cared about beating.

Carl schooled us together. Our last fence each, he and Linda held the top rail and thwacked it into the horses' shins. Carl liked to send them into a jump-off smarting a little.

Looked like it worked. Ted's chestnut kept his knees up by his eyeballs the whole way around. They'd gone pretty fast, too. My stomach pitched when the time was announced, I'd been hoping just going clean would be enough.

Ted tipped his hat to me when we passed at the gate. I felt sticky around my neck and waist, even where my boots hit behind my knees. Frisbee was sticky, too. Foaming everywhere and tossing his head so some of it hit my face. I wiped most of it. Licked a bit by the corner of my mouth. I hadn't meant to, but then liked having that little taste.

The horn went off, telling me I had thirty seconds to get through the timers. I felt submerged, but pulled myself up. Drove Frisbee into the reins like it'd wake me. I went through the beam; saw K.C. watching as I came off the turn. This helped a lot. Somehow I felt competent.

I knew enough to go for angles, not speed. Especially with Frisbee. If I got him juiced too early, I'd never roll him back. He'd flatten out and start banging things.

We took the first fence already on a diagonal to the second. Airborne over the second, I yanked left. Had to u-turn him, but not too soon. I thought I'd fucked us there. Had cut too close and slowed him down so he'd never take off.

He made it, but landed way slowed down. I yahooed him to the last fence. Chased him till two strides out, then jerked him back. Had to make sure he wouldn't whack it. The angle nearly landed us in the bleachers. I even scraped my leg on the fencing, pulling him around to the timers.

So much of it'd felt slow motion I didn't believe we'd saved time until I heard it. Was only then I dared look at Carl. He grinned ear to ear. Smacked my thigh when he got to me.

"Be hard to beat," he said.

I kept Frisbee walking and Carl kept walking beside us.

"You got any idea what you're doing?" he asked.

I considered faking, then said, "No, sir."

He laughed good and loud then. Stayed right there beside us until the last horse had gone and we'd won the damn class.

He gave my thigh one last squeeze, then Linda took his place. She had me by the leg, too, except it hurt.

"Listen to me," she said. "I don't care what they say to you in there, you don't get off this horse. You act stupid or deaf, I don't care. You understand me?"

I'd nodded at everything she said, but she wouldn't let me go until she heard me say it, so I told her okay, I understood. She said to hightail it back to the tents afterwards. That I wasn't to look like I was hurrying, but I wasn't to stop. She'd handle it from there.

I rode Frisbee into the ring when they called his number. Ted followed two slots back with the chestnut. Nobody asked me to get off and I was glad. Didn't really think I'd say nothing and couldn't think what I would say. Lots of times they wanted you to pose for pictures or had you get off so they could put a cooler over the horse—they gave them as prizes a lot. Was early enough in the week there wasn't much ceremony. They just handed me the trophy and the check, pinned the ribbon on Frisbee's bridle. Then we were out of there.

I shoved the check in my pocket, handed the trophy to Carl and he pulled the ribbon off, then said, "Get."

I did. I went straight past everything and everyone without stopping. Blew off K.C. again and she was only trying to congratulate me. I still didn't know exactly what this was about. I mean, I knew it was about avoiding the drug tests, I just didn't know how Linda worked it. Good thing nobody'd thought to test riders.

When I got up to the stalls, I jumped off Frisbee. Linda waved me into the tent and traded with me; handed me a leadshank and took Frisbee. Said, "Stay right there."

She led Frisbee down the aisle to his stall. Deb trailed behind her. When they got the tack off him, Deb put it in front of an empty stall. It was then I looked who my leadshank was connected to, though I guess I knew without looking, had looked without looking. Knew it was the black mare.

Linda came back to us with a bucket. She tipped some water on the mare, who danced away when Linda started slopping it around with a sponge. Then Deb tossed a cooler over her.

"Won't they notice she's a girl?" I asked.

"Probably never notice one way or the other; they just take the blood and go. She's black, Frisbee's black. It'll be enough."

As she was saying it, I figured she probably liked getting over this way, making morons of the testers. That's when I realized it was the perfect out. Anyone accuse her of pulling this, she'd just say "With what horse?" and if they pointed to this one, she'd say "That's a mare." No one'd admit they'd never noticed such a simple thing.

We didn't know for sure they'd even come round, but probably they would. Linda took the lead back from me, handed it to Deb, told her to act the dumb hillbilly if the testers showed. Then she grabbed my arm and told me to get scarce, that they might try to talk to me and it wasn't a good idea. From how she said it, I figured Tory'd screwed this up somewhere along the line.

I minded what she said. Ducked into the feed room, which was sort of getting to be my hangout. I heard whimpering, but didn't see the dog at first—muzzled, and tied in the corner. The rope was hitched so short he couldn't lie down. I was afraid to loosen it. I didn't go near the dog, not at all; pretended to him and me both I couldn't hear him.

I'd almost decided to go across the aisle and hide out in the tackroom. Problem was, that's where Linda'd gone. And besides you couldn't see anything from there and right about then, through the slats, I saw a man in a suit coming our way. He carried a black medical bag, but he sure wasn't a vet. You'd have to pay a vet way too much to hang around all day poking prizewinners, so they just taught these guys to draw blood.

As he got closer, Deb got shakier. She didn't say a word, even to the guy's hello. Now I realized when Linda'd said dumb she meant mute. I guess this was another distraction and it worked from the look of things. The guy spent more time looking at Deb than the mare. Finally, he just stuck the needle in and out and left like Deb spooked him.

I went out then. Said, "They sure got him up here fast."

Linda was behind me. "Always do with us but still can't never catch up."

Deb'd loosened some, was almost giggly now, but not herself. Linda and I followed her into the tent. Watched while she pulled the cooler off the mare and toweled her, then put her away. Soon after she brought out Frisbee and hooked him to the crossties. The sweat had dried mostly, but he was still heaving a little. Sounded funny, rattly almost.

Deb took a bucket outside and came back with steaming water. Soaked a sponge and rubbed Frisbee hard. This slowed his breathing down, made it smoother. The whole thing absorbed me so, I didn't hear Linda go into the tackroom. When she came out Deb took Frisbee into his stall and Linda went in after.

I never would've seen the needle in her hand if I hadn't been looking so hard for it. She had it tucked up behind her forearm, her palm curled to shield it. I wasn't sure why I knew her sticking him now meant we were done for the day, but I did and I was right.

Soon as she'd finished with Frisbee, we left. We didn't take the boxes, so I guessed we'd be coming back. Or at least she would.

25

Linda dropped me at the motel and then headed back to the showgrounds. Alone in the room, I paced back and forth until I noticed how I smelled. Like sweat and horses and hours of fear. I took off my clothes on the way to the shower. I'd gotten so dirty you could see it roll off with the water and there was something satisfying about this. I unwrapped the little bar of soap, dropped it twice. My hair took a long time. By the time I'd rinsed it I was tired of standing.

I turned off the water and got out. Stood there and dripped, then wrapped a towel around my waist. Didn't even bother trying to dry myself. The mirror started to clear, but I didn't look. Instead I wandered into the room, rubbing my hair with the towel until I felt sort of dizzy and sore. Then I heard Linda banging on the door. Loud. Like she'd been doing it a long time. I couldn't figure why—wasn't exactly like her to forget keys.

"All right already," I was saying when I swung open the door. Took a minute before I saw it wasn't her. Maybe I'd known all along it wasn't. Knew it was Ted before I saw him.

He was in before he'd finished asking; said he wanted to wait for Linda, that she'd told him to come by. Deciding whether to believe him seemed pointless.

"Yeah, well, suit yourself," I said. I tried very hard at this. I was still wearing a towel.

He sat in one of the chairs. I was looking at his boots again, absorbed by the size of his feet, and then, too, his overall length limbwise. He took up so much room. So much, I headed back to the bathroom. Grabbed jeans and a T-shirt on the way and then couldn't get into them fast enough.

I stayed in there even after. Rubbed my hair some more, but then I couldn't stall any longer. That little room was too humid, too close—more so than the one out there.

Soon as I went into the other room, I got chilled clear through, felt my nipples get hard. I was glad my T-shirt was dark, though how much that helped I wasn't sure. It didn't stop him looking. He hadn't stopped that since he'd come in.

"Mind if I have one?" he asked and I swear I didn't know what he meant until I saw he'd picked up the cigarettes.

"Sure, go on." It came out almost bubbly.

"You have one?"

"Okay."

He held the pack to me, shook one loose. I took it and looked around for matches. He had his lighter out already, but he waited for me to ask.

I stood there smoking and he sat there smoking.

"That your bourbon?" he asked.

I figured he knew the answer to that, but I said, "Linda's."

"Oh," he said.

He sat awhile longer, until he'd finished his cigarette. I stamped mine out when he stood up. I actually thought he was leaving, but he said, "Expect she wouldn't grudge me a short one. What you think?"

"Don't guess so," I said.

I'd been leaning against the bureau this whole time, so he

was coming toward me. I squeezed over to the wall and soon as I did, I wished I'd gone the other way. Gone toward the door.

"You're a jumpy thing."

He said this just before he switched direction; before he started heading for me instead of the bourbon.

I couldn't move and had nothing to blame it on. Worse, I couldn't be sure I wanted to. Not once he pressed against me and then pressed me against the wall and when he said, "Got no idea what you want, do you?" I figured he'd gone inside my head and so it took me a little while to realize his was just a different way of saying what they always said.

That while was long enough he'd got his hands down my pants, down the back first. That wasn't so bad to me, was better than what he was saying. He had his mouth up close to my ear the way he had the other time, was saying things that made sense at first, then didn't.

He unbuttoned my pants before he undid his. He didn't try to put his dick in me, he just slid it between my legs. Said he wouldn't put it in unless I asked him, but that I'd ask.

I didn't, but then I didn't say anything else either. I made sounds, though, and I could tell he liked that. He'd got my pants down and I started rubbing myself on his dick. It'd gotten to where that seemed the way out, but then he stopped it. Not the whole thing—this part.

What he did then was push me down. Pushed me onto my knees. He was holding my head, had his dick in his other hand. He was trying to put it in my mouth. The problem for me was I had nothing between my legs and it left me nowhere to go. I kept turning my head until he smacked me and, boy, that felt familiar and from not so long ago. This time, though, was a whole lot clearer. It always is with men, for me anyway.

I guess I would've gave then, except I heard the door. I think she stood there for a while. Let him wrestle me a little longer. I had no way to know what she could see, but she didn't stop him until he'd got his dick in my mouth. All she had to say was "Let her be, Ted," and he did.

He let go of me but I still felt him. Stayed on the floor while she got him gone. I would've stayed there the rest of the week, except she lifted me up. She helped me get my pants back on and then helped me onto the bed; handed me the nearest drink, which was Ted's. I kept swishing the bourbon around in my mouth before I swallowed it.

She'd brought her boxes with her; was setting up a syringe. When she finished, she took my hand and turned it over and back, then stuck me near my smallest knuckle and I felt grateful she hadn't undone my pants.

I didn't feel a bullet this time and would've said she'd missed, except I'd seen her pull the blood. Pretty soon I felt the downside come on. That was the part I liked best anyway. She'd left the syringe on the table and I picked it up. I'd been thinking about filching one—you know, just to have.

Pretty soon it'd got too heavy and I put it down. Now I'd gotten here I'd've let her do anything. She didn't do anything, though. She just sat in the chair and watched me. I tried to go to the junk so it'd stop me wanting her. It wasn't doing enough and so I felt let down by both of them.

Ted kept coming back at me. It was like on the plane—I needed to finish this and I'd thought Linda was going to help me but she wouldn't get out of the chair. It got to where I balled a pillow and curled around it; crossed my legs and pulled them under me. No matter how tight I tucked my body, I kept thinking how in the middle of it, I'd rubbed against him. He'd always have that on me. Even after I'd brought myself off, I couldn't shake this.

26

The rest of that week, Linda stayed close to me, and Ted stayed away. I wound up spending a lot of time with Huey. Linda put me on him first thing every morning, a lot earlier than she needed, and that time with him would get me through the day and then at night she'd stick me and I'd sleep.

The one thing broke through this was Silas but the way I saw it, he'd shown up two or three days too late. Time enough for me to make things his fault and so feel justified behaving like he was no one to me. Afterwards I'd go back to the tents, trying not to hurry. I'd wind up in that feed stall, hugging Jamie's dog. Had to do this more than once because Silas didn't let up. He kept coming every day, right up through Sunday, which would be his last shot because they weren't going on the road. Hadn't even had any horses here.

Sunday, Jeannie came with him. It was the end of the day and so she sat in near-empty bleachers while he talked.

"Come on, Lee," he said. "Plain to anyone you're not doing so well."

I wanted to tell him he didn't know half of it, any of it. Instead I said, "Took second and fourth in the grand prix today, you miss that?"

He didn't even bother to answer me, just said, "You don't belong with them and you know it. I want for you to come with me, now."

It was the closest he'd come all week to insisting, but all I had to do was look over his shoulder to Jeannie.

"I'm not going to," I said, "and you know it."

Then it got even easier because Jeannie'd got up and was coming toward us and then telling Silas they had to get home and, as if I needed convincing, that made it clear about how long I'd last with them. See, I couldn't afford hoping it'd be different this time, that Silas could be more than a way station. Not when my father'd been on me just a few days before. And then Jeannie was saying, "She doesn't want to, Silas. You don't have any claim to her, you know."

He put his hand over his eyes and rubbed his temples. Then he held that same hand out to me. I knew better than to touch him; knew if I did I'd go soft and I couldn't risk that. He wasn't going to walk away so I had to. Wasn't sure I'd pull this off until I saw Linda and remembered the very next thing after this would be getting my hit.

We spent the next week in Lake Placid. I thought it would get easier now I'd finished things with Silas, and keeping away from K.C. seemed to help. At this show, I guess I'd begun avoiding her on purpose, though Linda had me on a pretty short leash. At first Linda's hold on me helped, but soon it began making things harder. Each night with her called things up in me. Stuff the junk never managed to settle. This made me want Tory and at the same time I couldn't see where I'd fit her. Still, somewhere I decided Tory's coming back would make everything better.

That happened our first day in Ohio. I'd just finished working Huey. Had jumped off and was holding him. He saw her first—walked toward her even before I did.

She limped some in a way that looked permanent. I tried to ignore it, but couldn't quite, looked beyond her to Tim. He grinned, but the two of them seemed so weary it was hard to smile back. Then Tory was petting me and petting Huey and before she said anything else she said, "Come on," and handed the reins to Tim and we took off straightaway for her car. Halfway there, she turned around.

"Wait a minute," she called back to me; was halfway to Linda's car already, which made me nervous. She broke into the trunk. I couldn't tell how she did it, but could see she'd done it before. Then she got inside those boxes. I'd tried the combinations a few times myself, had got nowhere. She knew them. Was in and out, and back beside me in seconds.

Whatever she'd snatched she'd tucked into her shirt. I didn't see it until we were safe in her car. She pulled out the syringe packets first—a fistful of them. She dumped them in my lap. Made me feel pretty paltry about the single one I'd finally snagged a week back.

Then she handed me the bottle of hydromorph.

"Won't she miss this?" I asked because it had been my reason for not taking one.

"That's part of it," she said. "Don't you get it yet, Cowboy?"

"I know enough," I said and when she laughed at me, I tried to act huffy but the truth was, it tickled me she'd called me my nickname and I thought maybe I'd been right—that her being here would make everything all better. Because of this, I said, "Okay, so I don't know."

She laughed at me some more than told me how she and Linda played this game about the drugs. That Linda'd let her steal them. Never say a word about it until she decided Tory was taking too much. When that happened, she'd change the locks on the boxes—change the combinations anyway. And then she'd start doling the drugs.

By the time Tory got to telling me this last part she'd stopped laughing. Already things between us got funny. She started the car and drove us back to the motel. Didn't say anything more, not even when we went into the room, which was mine and Linda's.

We were at the edge of the bed, standing. Tory wasn't kissing me but had her head on my shoulder, her chin hooked there and holding very still. She pulled up my T-shirt, but wasn't really touching me either, more just hanging on, pressing. I realized my hands weren't on her at all, not really, though I grabbed at her to keep my balance when she undid my pants. Then I pulled away from her. Began pacing a little. She sat on the bed, pulled a cigarette from a pack Linda'd left on the table.

I knew what my trouble was. I needed to get to the place Linda put me, but I couldn't see an easy way there so I kept walking back and forth until Tory patted a place next to her and what I did was I took off my pants. Lay down with her and let her look at me.

She traced the bruises in order. At least the first few. She got quiet while she did this and I thought maybe she felt like I did—relieved and sad at the same time. Maybe not, though, because she didn't go the direction I wanted. Not right off, anyway.

There wasn't going to be any other way to it but asking. I said it like I already had at least once. Said, "So, we going to have anything from that bottle or what?" and I nodded to the hydromorph she'd left on the bureau with the syringes.

Tory stopped what she'd been trying to do. Cleared up a little. Said, "Why? Is that what you're wanting?"

"Not just," I said and reached over toward her, but she got up. Lit another cigarette before she said anything.

This gave me time to talk, but I didn't. Figured I'd done enough already. I couldn't see why she was starting something from this. Seemed pretty obvious where we were going and that it'd be easier once we got there, so why'd she have to stall? I felt like she was jerking me. I couldn't let myself see anything else behind it.

She smoked and walked around the room same as I had. I'd made up my mind not to say another word. I would've put my pants back on but it'd've meant getting up. I lit a cigarette, though, and that was almost as good as having pants on.

She kept pacing for what seemed like forever but then, without saying anything else at all, she took the bottle and a packet off the bureau.

Soon as she did this, I slacked. Stopped puffing so hard and furious on that cigarette.

She brought the stuff over and put it on the bedside table. Then she sat in a chair, the one further away from me.

I could see what she wanted to know. That whether or not I could stick myself would at least tell her something. At the same time I knew she knew already, but it didn't stop me from picking up the syringe. I figured I'd watched enough times.

This wasn't about bluffing her, it was because she'd made me mad and so I wasn't going to ask for anything.

I did everything I'd seen Linda do. Had gotten to the point of pulling the stuff into the syringe and soon as I did this, I started looking for a place to put it. I was sitting on the edge of the bed by now. Crossed my leg and found a spot on the inside of my thigh, was about to just go ahead on, when Tory said,

"You didn't clear it."

"What?"

"Clear it."

I pressed the plunger and tried to get something to come

through the needle. This was harder than I thought it would be, but I pushed a drop out. Then the only thing left was trying to get the thing in me.

I missed the first couple of times and then when I got it and drew some blood up, I couldn't get the plunger back down. My hand started shaking to where I couldn't stop it, my other hand held my leg still, which was shaking good, too. I looked for Tory. She was already up. I closed my eyes, felt her hands on mine. I let go, let her take over.

"Easy, there," she said. "Careful or you'll lose your shot."

I could feel her pressing. She took forever and then when I thought she'd finished, I felt her pulling more blood and banging it through again and then it hit.

I heard her set the needle down. I held her shoulders because I didn't want her going away. She stayed crouched there for a while before she pushed me over and got into bed with me. We lay there and when she started touching me, I liked it.

She held close to me and the lull came on and she was pulling at my underwear and then pulling it off. Had my knees up and open and she was on hers. She grabbed my shirt. Had a fistful in her hand before she put her other fist inside me. I had fistfuls of the bedspread and wanted mouthfuls of it—anything to stop the sound jamming my throat, traveling a beat behind her hand.

I opened my mouth and when that didn't matter, I opened my knees more, pushed as hard as she did, smacked her back. The longer it went on, the more grateful I was her face was nowhere near mine. I'd gotten to where I couldn't stop anything or do anything and everything she did still hit me a beat behind so I'd feel it when it was already over. Couldn't catch up.

Then she socked this sobbing breath into my chest. Once it got that far, there were all these others and I couldn't stop them either and she didn't stop. Not until I turned on my side, brought my knees together and up, lay there heaving.

It wasn't like how maybe it sounds or how maybe she thought it was. She wasn't hurting me. I don't know if she knew this. I didn't tell her, still I think she knew. She went over to the sink right after. I could hear her running water, splashing it. Felt it cold on her hands when she came back.

She held on to me, which was what I thought I wanted but the way she did it didn't feel right and I couldn't take it, had to push away or start bawling and I wouldn't be doing that again. She had my wrist, though, and was twisting it. The only way to go was back toward her—either that or fight and I wouldn't do that either so what I did was I opened her shirt, but didn't get much further than that. Wanted her breasts but didn't either because it was too much what I'd wanted with Linda. Already I knew I'd be running against this over and over and that nothing could change it. Seemed like there was less and less we could change.

27

I hadn't thought how, with Tory back, I wouldn't have Huey to take care of me anymore. Instead I had to take care of Bronto and the others. Get them to trust me again after Ted jerking them around.

That Tuesday started rough. We tried to go back to the way we used to work—do my horses in the morning and Tory's in the afternoon. That is what we did, it's just it didn't feel easy. Not for me anyway. I had trouble with every one of mine and since Linda wasn't around, Carl and Tory were setting the fences.

Every rail I pulled sent Carl fuming. Not at me, but at Ted. The way he did it, though, and the way Tory began to look back and forth between him and me, I almost wished he'd just blame me. Same time, though, I liked it. Felt protected. That he knew what had happened surprised me, that it mattered to him surprised me more.

I didn't want to explain to Tory and I didn't want her not to ask either. She did ask. Did it after we'd finished with my horses. Everyone else had taken off to get lunch and Tory came into the tackroom. I'd lagged in there. Was fussing with a bridle that didn't need fussing with.

She closed the door behind her and I looked at her. Had to work my way up to her eyes. I started at her throat, which was splotched red. Her face had flushed entirely, her mouth was quavering. Her eyes seemed like they kept getting darker and bigger, especially when she started talking.

"Didn't I tell you stay away from him? Huh?"

This wasn't what I wanted and so I didn't answer.

"You fucking talk to me."

I still didn't. Worse, I looked away.

She came closer to me then; had my arm so I dropped the bridle, so I had to.

"You fucking everyone? Huh? Who else, Lee? Carl, maybe?"

I said, "Why don't you say what you mean," because now she'd gotten here, I understood this was about Linda.

Tory didn't say anything, she just tightened the grip she still had on my arm and I could hear Jamie's dog whining and crying and then I heard someone coming, but I don't think Tory heard. I don't think Tory heard anything. I tried to push past her, but she'd never let go of my arm and didn't even when Linda walked in.

"What are you two yelling about?"

She asked it this real lazy way and Tory let go of me like Linda's voice made her tired.

I knelt down and picked up the bridle and then since Tory wasn't saying anything, I said, "Nothing."

"Didn't sound like nothing," Linda said but she let it pass; said, "Here," and tossed Tory a room key. Then she was asking for mine back. I felt a guilty twinge handing it over and taking the new one from her. Wondered for the first time where she'd spent last night. Wondered even if she'd spent it on the bed next to us and we'd been too dead to know.

That afternoon Tory had trouble with her horses and Carl kept riding her. Linda and I were setting fences and by the

time we got to Huey, I felt too tired to lift the damn rails. Kept making Linda carry the weight and I knew she could tell.

I'd started thinking about my hit when Tory was on Frisbee. That was two horses back now; now I couldn't think about anything else, though funny little things would pop in. Like when Tim brought Huey and collected Lazy Boy, I wondered when he'd bought sneakers because he was wearing new ones. Red ones.

Tory got on Huey and rode him around a long time. Took him for a tour of the whole showgrounds. I watched them circle back. She held the reins loosely in one hand, tugged his mane with the other. She was talking to him and I could tell she used Huey the same way I had and I decided she needed him more than me. This week, anyway. Besides, I had no claim. He was hers.

The two of them did everything right and, though it took him some time, Carl finally stopped hassling her. Linda and I just set the fences and kept setting them higher and wider until I got this current going inside. It was like the three of us on the ground and the two of them in the air—was like we all knew the same thing, felt it at the same time and I remembered the point of all this. For a little while anyway.

When they finished, Carl and Linda stayed at the ring talking, and I went back to the tents with Tory and Huey. I walked real close beside them; took every chance to reach over and touch, first him and then her, and once we got back and she got off I was still standing so close she fell into me.

Soon as she'd given Huey to Tim we went to the motel and soon as we got into the room, she set up a shot. Everything about it was fast until she had the needle in me, then it took forever. She dropped it so slow I thought I'd die waiting and then she finished and the stuff took just as long to hammer.

Longer than usual, which could've been where she hit me—in my hand, at the base of my thumb.

When she pulled the needle out of me, she put it right back in the bottle. Then she stuck herself in the wrist. Slowed down once she hit blood, delivered the stuff that same long way.

Afterwards, she set the syringe down. I was sitting in a chair. She sat opposite me on the bed. I watched her go up and then her comedown came on so marked it took me from mine. Or I don't know, maybe she hadn't dosed me enough because things stayed clear that way, clearer than I wanted. Enough so I was looking around the room and wondering who'd moved our stuff in here—whether Linda'd done it herself or got someone else to.

Not knowing this seemed sort of creepy and so I felt that much more grateful when Tory came over to me, was kneeling in front of me. I leaned back in the chair and closed my eyes. She unbuttoned my shirt and everything she did felt good, but when she put her hands on my chest, it stopped my breathing.

She started kissing me and I closed my eyes tighter. Something happened to my neck so I believed I must be twisting it, or else had something twisted around it, like she'd put a thick scratchy rope there and was twisting it tighter and tighter. Even before I touched my throat, I knew she hadn't, still I kept my hand there until I felt it inside—a thick rope in my throat, twisting from in there.

Soon as she undid my pants, it all got easier. I could handle her hands there, and her kissing my stomach. For a long while I could. Until she tried to pull my pants down. I don't know. I wouldn't let her. Instead, I pushed her toward the bed. Opened my eyes only when we were both on the floor and me on top of her. She didn't try and stop me from anything.

What I did was turn her on her stomach, take her pants down, and fuck her. I held her by her shirt, lay between her legs and fucked her. Fucked her hard so she had to put her hands up to keep her head from hitting the nightstand, though I didn't notice this until later and by then I'd finished anyway.

She'd seemed to like this fine. She seemed really to like it a lot, but I wasn't sure I did. Well, that last thing's not true, I knew I liked it. What I didn't like was how she held on to me afterwards, but at least that got cut short because someone was knocking and we had to get up, or I did.

Tory had her clothes to put on and so I waited until she'd finished before I opened the door. Both Carl and Linda were standing there.

"We're going out for a drink," Carl said.

Tory'd come up beside me. "Suits me," she said and then we all piled into Carl's Thunderbird—all four of us squeezed in the front. Tory was next to Carl this time, and me between her and Linda. I thought I'd die from the heat and Linda rolling down the window was the only sign anyone else felt it.

Tory and Carl badgered each other and Linda smoked. I did nothing until we pulled up to a light. By then, Tory and Carl'd gotten so far into something so old, neither of them noticed when Linda took my hand. She held it up so she could see the bruise in the streetlight. I just didn't think Tory'd given me enough because everything bothered me still. This bothered me. Bothered me most just how you'd think.

I pressed closer to Tory. Pretended what I felt was for her. When the light changed and we got moving again, Linda put my hand down. She didn't let go of it, though. Not right away. She rested it in my lap and held it there. Held it there exactly until I touched myself and then she let go. Left me thinking it was my idea and before my face had even colored, she said, "Things show on you."

She handed me her cigarette and I took such a long pull

that, soon as I let go, the ash broke and fell. She brushed the cinders off my leg. Said, "Fact, you're kind of a mess, Cowboy."

I felt Tory stiffen and when I looked, she was looking already. No way to get out from between them. Not here in the middle of some fucking Ohio strip.

"Shut up, Linda" was how Tory started it.

Then Carl said, "Come on, let's not do this."

"You shut up, too," Tory said, yelling at him now.

I'd never been so glad about anything as when Carl turned into that bar's parking lot. He found a space away from the other cars and soon as he turned the car off, he got out. Then he tossed the keys in and they skidded cross the dash. "Just make sure you lock it," he said before he slammed the door.

I wished like anything I could go with him, but I wasn't going to climb over the top of either of them. Linda lit another cigarette. She still had the window open, but there wasn't any air and then Tory lit one, too. I took the pack from the dash, but just held it. Slid the cellophane on and off; wanted them to get on with it and knew I was probably the reason they weren't.

Linda solved that. She opened the door and got out. Seemed simple enough to slip by her, but I couldn't, not right off. I guess I wanted Tory's okay or something because I looked for it. She just kept smoking, though—eyes straight ahead like I wasn't there. I couldn't stay in that car another second then.

I stumbled past Linda. She tugged my belt loop. Said, "Order me a drink, Cowboy."

I pulled away. Knew they'd be off to it now. I didn't look back, though, and it wasn't until I got into the bar, got halfway to the table, that I worried about more than them fighting.

The place was crowded with all those same faces. Carl sat at a corner table and I took the corner chair. He flagged a waitress and ordered me a drink I didn't want. What I wanted was another hit, a real one, and I thought maybe it showed.

"They fight mean, but it never takes long," he said and clamped his arm around me in a way I mostly liked.

I kept watching the door. The next two in were K.C. and Freddy, a guy she bought coke from. Anyway, soon as K.C. saw us, she plowed our way. Guess she'd tired of letting me keep away because the first thing she said was "Honey, if I didn't know so much better, I'd say you've been avoiding me." She said this while giving me one of those half-hugs and I held on too long. Freddy seemed to notice this, not K.C. He pulled a chair near me and she wedged hers between Carl and the wall.

"How do you get a drink in here?" K.C. asked Carl, holding a cigarette for him to light.

He got the waitress back and ordered their drinks. Ordered another for me and him, too, so I slogged through most of mine to catch up while K.C. segued to earnest flirting. The other times she'd fooled with Carl it'd been play. I didn't think it was this time. Even hoped it wasn't because I suddenly wanted her back closer to me and this seemed a good way. For the moment, though, it left me to Freddy. I saw him looking at my hand the way Linda had and I turned it so he couldn't, then lit a cigarette to go with my second drink. I liked smoking more and more lately.

I kept watching the door and soon Linda and Tory came in and we were all standing and Linda took my chair and Tory brought me another and one for herself. They'd done this so smoothly I didn't realize it until we all sat back down. Then the waitress was helping us push over another table and then bringing more drinks and by this time I was gagging on bourbon.

My head had turned cloudy and for a second I didn't know who's hand was on me, but then knew it was Tory's. Knew because it didn't burn through me. Besides, Linda was fucking with Freddy. Had him stammering and shaking so pretty soon he excused himself. When he came back his face was still wet and so was his hair. He hadn't got his color back, though.

He didn't sit down. Instead he told K.C. he wanted to leave. That he needed to. She handed him her keys.

"Carl, you'll give me a ride back, won't you?"

"Happy to," he said and Freddy got out of there fast.

I'd started letting my drinks pile up and after a while Carl started taking up my slack. We didn't stay that much longer, though. With Freddy gone, Linda'd turned quiet and Tory and me weren't saying anything and that left us all listening to Carl and K.C. too much. The next time the waitress came by, Carl got the bill and then paid it.

On the way to the door, Linda begged off. Said she had something to do and turned back into the crowd. I tried to watch where she went, but I lost her before we even got to the door.

Outside felt better and even though the air was damp and thick, it settled my stomach. Crossing the lot, Tory put her arm round my waist and I noticed Carl's round K.C. She was wearing this short skirt and he had his hand half under it and seeing this gave me a funny upset feeling.

28

The next morning I'd gotten half-dressed in my riding clothes before Tory started laughing at me.

"What?" I said. "What's funny?"

"Was going to wait till you got your boots on. No classes today, Cowboy. We got the day off."

Ordinarily this would've been good news, but though the week would have as many days whether we rode today or not, I was sure it'd seem longer this way. I hoped she didn't want to spend the day in the room. She still hadn't gotten out of bed. I looked for a droop in her eyes. Wondered what she'd done while I was showering, but I didn't see anything. I picked last night's syringe up off the floor.

"What do we do with this?"

"We'll toss it. Don't worry. What you worried about?"

"Nothing."

I dropped it onto the bureau. Undressed and dressed again. Pulled on jeans this time, a T-shirt.

"Where you off to?" she asked.

"Nowhere," I said, walking out the door.

It was true at least that I didn't know. I wanted cigarettes. My own pack and some coffee. The ball of socks I'd pulled this morning had my cash in it and while there wasn't a lot left, there was more than I thought. Not near enough to go anyplace, not that I was really thinking about it. If I was, I still had that credit card.

I went into the motel's dining room. Bought cigarettes at the register. Picked Kools because I was tired of everyone's Winstons. The clock behind the cashier said nine. I took some mints from the bowl, not quite understanding it was morning. I stopped just short of putting them in my mouth and then had nowhere else to put them so they started melting in my hand. I took the closest out-of-the-way booth. Dumped the mints in the ashtray. Ordered coffee. The waitress brought it with a menu.

I opened the cigarettes. Smoked two over that first cup of coffee. Had a third with my second cup. The waitress got less friendly when I asked for another refill. That's why I ordered the food. I still wasn't sure I was hungry and if I was, what for. By the time she brought the eggs and bacon, I'd forgotten what I'd ordered. Was too busy noticing how long it'd been since I'd been alone.

I wasn't alone much longer. I saw Tory in the mirror behind the bar. Saw her see me. She slid in across from me. Looked at me while she took a cigarette and lit it. Got a draw halfway in, then sputtered, "God, Cowboy. Menthol?"

I didn't say anything.

She went to the register and came back with Winstons. I wasn't going to admit I wanted one of them, especially not when she offered. I don't know what'd got me sore, but now that I was I had trouble dropping it.

The waitress brought the coffeepot and Tory turned over her cup; ordered some cinnamon toast. I looked at my eggs; wished I'd thought ahead.

"So what you want to do?" she asked after her toast came.

"What is there?"

"Not much, I guess."

She picked up some toast, the bread drooped from the weight of the butter and sugar. She saw me watering and pushed the plate toward me. I took a piece. Liked how the sugar felt on my tongue. She was dumping another packet of it on the rest of the pieces. Before we were through, we ordered some more and then we walked out to her car. I left the Kools on the table.

We went to the showgrounds because where else would we go? As we walked through the parking field, past all the cars, I saw K.C.'s Porsche, then saw K.C. sitting in it, sort of hunched over the dash. Something didn't look like her and I stopped. Told Tory to go on, I'd catch up.

I opened the passenger door. Stuck my head in, then the rest of me. "What's doing? You that hung over?"

She jerked her head up, scared like. I saw streaks down her face. I don't think I'd ever known her to cry, but she had been and when she saw it was me, the tears started again.

I didn't touch her. I would've, there was just something coming off her that said not to.

She cried awhile longer and I sat there trying hard not to fidget, not to think of other things. I opened and closed the glove box a few times, but other than that I stayed put.

When she quieted, I said, "K.C., what is it?"

I didn't think of Carl until she turned and faced me, looking mad like I should know already.

"Did he hurt you?" I said quickly, trying to make up for my slowness.

"No," she said. "Not exactly. I left."

She had a pack of Winstons on the dash. I lit one for her, then another. Opened my window. I waited until she'd smoked hers halfway down, then asked what happened.

"I don't know," she said. "Nothing. He said things." She puffed the cigarette the rest of the way down. Took a vial from her pocket. Passed it to me when she'd had some. I just held it. Waited for her to say more.

"Lee, are they like that? Is Tory?"

"I don't know what you're asking." I unscrewed the top of the vial, then screwed it closed tight. Tried to unscrew it again but couldn't; thought it'd break in my hands, maybe crumble.

"You're sure you should be with them?"

I saw her looking at my hands, so I put the vial down. She still looked, though. Looked at that bruise near my thumb. She said, "I'm only asking because I was thinking of going home if I had someone to drive with."

That she'd got shook so bad, I didn't know what to do. I still wanted to touch her, but we never had much and so couldn't start now.

I handed her back the vial. She dropped it in her pocket and lit another cigarette.

I stayed with her until I realized she might stay there all day and that I might stay with her, might even leave with her. I had to get out of the car then. I felt bad, but I had to.

I walked to the tents pretty loose-legged. When I got to our stalls, they were all there. Tory and Tim sat on the trunk. Linda leaned against her car. You could see Jamie and Deb lunging horses. He had Huey and she had Frisbee.

Carl, he leaned into a tent rope until it bent round his back. Every now and then he'd haul the rope and then let go and the thing would shake until the whole big top quivered. Least it seemed so to me.

I came up beside him and he slipped his hand onto my back. Tucked it just a little inside my jeans that way he always did. I tried to feel something different about him, but couldn't. He still felt safe to me.

"Where you been, girl? We were about to send a posse. Isn't that right, Tim?"

"Yes, sir, it is."

Carl was waiting for me to answer, but then something caught his eye. He dropped his hand from me and started walking. Then he started yelling as he walked.

"Jamie, what the fuck is it you're doing? That animal's worth more than you'll ever be. You out to cripple him, you lazy fuck? You turn him around the right way or I'll have you running alongside him."

Jamie turned red before he turned palest white. Deb was already so pale that if she was blanching from this you'd never know. I thought she trembled, though. You could see she wasn't sure whether to stop Frisbee or keep him going. And you could see what Jamie was going to do to her later no matter what she did now.

For the rest of us, though, it was over. I'd moved onto the trunk. Had pushed my way in beside Tory and now it was her hand a little way down my jeans.

Linda and Carl didn't stick around much longer and once they'd left Tory said, "Tim's got the day, too. And he's got hash, right, Red-eye? With something extra on top?"

"Yep," Tim said.

"So, Cowboy. What say we take him home with us?"

Jamie and Deb were bringing in the horses. I didn't want to stay around long once they had, so I said, "Yeah, okay."

Tory slid off the trunk and we started for the car. Tim lagged a little behind us. I looked over my shoulder to see him looking over his, but when he turned back and saw me, he got his grin going again. Flashed the foil in his hand.

We spent the day smoking and then took Tim back to the tents. Now Jamie and Deb had signed on they got a room and Tim stayed with the horses, slept on that cot in the tackroom. We all pretended this was about money, but really it was about having someone always there keeping an eye out.

Ever since we'd started this leg of the circuit, what with the new drug rules and all, Carl and Linda had tightened things up considerably. So much so that when we dropped Tim off, we found Deb sitting on a trunk playing lookout. Tory teased her she could knock off now, that the new sentry had come. Deb didn't seem to hear. She just sat there in a way that spooked me but I chalked that up to the hash. The something extra in it was opium and so I'd been seeing funny for a while already.

Tory and I walked through the aisles following Tim around. I stumbled the whole way, practically bumped into things and did bump into Tory a lot. She'd sort of pull me in and then push me away, which only made me lose my balance more. She seemed to like that. At least she laughed about it and kept doing it. Finally she joked she'd better take me home before she had to carry me there.

We didn't talk too much during the drive back. My silence was the kind that's about needing to say something you can't, though I couldn't quite figure out what it was I couldn't say. I blamed the opium for my cloudiness and at the same time wanted more of something to make sure I stayed that way.

When we got into the room, Tory started hunting stuff up. She'd hid that little bottle somewhere, had done it when I wasn't around. She'd hid the syringes, too. Took her a little time to dig everything out but finally she came back to the bed with what we needed.

She was shaking some while she set up the needle and I thought, that's something new. Her hands still shook when she undid my pants but then I liked how they felt on my belly and so I stopped thinking about anything more than that. I leaned back into the pillows and wanted to lay the rest of the way down, closed my eyes so I'd feel her better.

Her hand steadied and I felt her prick me, then the pull. Felt her start it back in and I liked how long the needle stayed. Liked her steady press in and the slowness. It hurt funny, too. My skin had closed on the needle's grabbing me, grabbed it back. When I felt her pull out, I slid my jeans off and got under the covers. She'd taken her pants off too now, and was sitting beside me, her weight held the blankets and sheets tight against me and it felt both good and too close.

I watched each move she made. How much she drew up, how she found where to put it. She'd pressed at her neck for a while and I got scared in a way I knew meant it interested me.

She settled for the back of her knee. I hadn't noticed the knot of scars there before. Never had and felt neglectful. And then, too, there was that new one looking like a bullet hole. Maybe this was why when she came to bed I got so tunneled on her other scar. Why I made her turn onto her stomach and then kept touching her, down her thigh, then between.

It didn't feel like it had before. The skin still felt smooth, but looser than I remembered. Like it was tired. It didn't look so pink either, but this was maybe the light.

"How old were you?" I asked this while I eased her legs apart, while I put my hand up under her.

"Seventeen," she said, said without thinking, and so I thought the rest would come as easy. Believed this, though I felt her get tight soon as she'd said it.

"So how old was Linda?"

She hesitated this time, started to turn over. I leaned into her; held her still. Left off stroking the scar and stroked her. Her body eased up a little, but she didn't, not really. She answered me, though. Said, "Twenty-five or six, I guess. Hey, what does it matter?"

I didn't answer her. I said, "Where was Carl?"

She tried to turn again. Said, "Look, he was different then, okay?" Said it real quick and hot.

I knew if I pushed hard enough I could get it all, but right then she said, "Hey, lookit, get off me."

This stopped me. For a second, I started to do what she said but then her sharpness turned me the other way, made me sharp. I leaned my body into hers, wouldn't let her up.

"Tell me what happened," I said and when I said it I put my fingers into her ass and I kept them there, kept pressing further into her until she stopped struggling with me.

"Fine," she said. "You want to know? You want to know?"

I didn't say anything, just kept my hand in her, used my legs to open hers more, get in more, then I moved my other hand from holding her shoulder to her neck, pressed her into the pillow until she had to turn her head in a way that'd hurt.

I hated how her voice sounded when she began again, not the break in it, but that I'd put it there.

"We were home," she said, and already I began loosening my hold on her.

"It was afternoon and we'd been in bed, me and Linda had, and then she went to the store. I made her go because I didn't want to get up, was too lazy to, and so I just stayed there. I didn't get dressed or anything, I just lay there and then I started touching myself.

"I got a ways into this so when I heard the front door, I didn't care. I knew it was Carl and Ted, knew Linda couldn't be back yet, but by then it didn't matter to me. Even once he'd come in the bedroom I didn't stop. I kept my eyes closed and he sat on the bed. I didn't even pull the sheet up and Ted, he put his hand on my stomach. And I don't know why, but when he put his hand on top of mine, I just put mine over it, put his where I wanted it.

"After a while I let go of him. He'd opened his pants and he pulled my hand over to him. He said he wouldn't put his hand in me unless I took his dick out. And when I'd done that and he'd got his hand in me, I ducked my head down, started sucking him because I didn't want him making me do it, you know? You know what I mean?"

I did know, only I'd never thought of this way around it or how well it might work.

She'd shifted toward me. I could tell she needed to see me so I let her turn onto her back, let my hand slip out of her and then pulled her leg between mine because of what she was saying. I think this someway made it easier for her. At least she kept looking at me when she went on. At first she did.

"Then I heard someone," she said. "I was scared of Linda, but then before I knew it, Carl clocked Ted so hard he knocked him onto the floor. And after that Ted just sat there leaning against the wall and rubbing his jaw, and I thought Carl was protecting me. Then he hit me and when he hit me again, he got me turned over and his boot heels were digging into my calves.

"I figured he'd fuck me. I figured how bad could that be? I kept waiting for him almost and then instead of his dick, I felt this cool against me and when I realized it was his knife, I tried to get loose but he laughed at this. Then he said the only thing he said. He said, 'Maybe I'll make it so you don't fuck anymore.'

"After that his knee was into me like it was up me and I couldn't move anywhere and then he started cutting my leg. It didn't hurt much until he turned the blade, ran it back up the same path and that tore more and I started crying and when he turned the blade again and then turned me over . . . Everything hurt more when he put the blade back.

"I stopped crying, though, and then I didn't feel anything. After a while I didn't even feel his weight on me and so I didn't really notice when he got off, when Linda pulled him off and then got him and Ted out of the house. I didn't know she was there until the needle stick came and then I started crying again. She wrapped me up in one sheet and started tearing up the other one, tying my leg in pieces of it to try and stop me from bleeding."

Tory'd been staring past me and I hadn't been looking at her either. I did now because she'd stopped talking and then her breathing went jerky and when I looked at her, mine went that way too, so I turned away again. Maybe she noticed this because she started talking again.

"I kept holding on to Linda and so she was angry because I didn't want to go on my stomach. Then she'd, she started crying and when I saw that, I let her turn me so I didn't have to see her like that. She pressed more of that sheet against my leg. Everywhere under me was soaked through."

I thought Tory was crying. Then it seemed maybe she'd started but stopped herself. Her breathing got real slow and measured and her voice changed, sounded flat.

She said, "Linda stitched me up and then she moved me out of her room to the one across the hall. She said it'd be easier for me to be in there while I was mending but she never moved me back. She never took me back. Some nights she'd come in—middle of the night usually. I could never tell when it'd be and she was different; it was how I wanted it by then, I guess. I don't know.

"They got rid of Ted. Carl beat him up pretty bad, that same day he did, after Linda kicked them out of the house. Whole thing became Ted's fault somehow. I'm the one who starts it, Carl finishes it. Ted, he just got himself caught in the middle of us, though he blames me for it all."

She looked at me funny when she said this last thing, then she looked mad. Said, "Can I get up now?"

She pushed her way out from under me and went into the

bathroom. I heard the water and wanted something cool. Went looking for ice, but the bucket was all water now and lukewarm even. Still it was wet.

She found me standing there by the bureau. She took my hand and then took me back to bed. This time she turned me on my stomach and I burrowed into the pillows, found this place I was sure no one else could get to. She put her hand on me and I slid down a little. She started to lick me; did this like it was just something to do, which was fine with me; made it easier.

And then it got easier still because her mouth did the same thing over and over, and I could tell she'd lost herself, too. The sheets felt damp underneath me and not just there. I was sweating all over, but in a slow way that bathed me; stayed warm. She tongued me this one way the whole time and then all she did was switch ways. That's all it took to get me shuddering.

I wanted to press against her, but couldn't. Couldn't press or strain anywhere, which let her get into my ass so easy it hurt. Hurt me somewhere and way I didn't ordinarily feel. I don't mean it was painful. I mean she'd gotten so far inside me I wanted to cry.

She slid up behind me, pulled her hand out and put it around me, clutched between my legs with the other one. Held me there and held me close to her and this was worse than anything so far and I started sort of flailing around until she let go; until I got her to get off me.

three

29

After Ohio, we went to Michigan and then all the way the hell back to New Jersey. The last two shows we hit before fall were in Long Island, the first Syosset, the other Southampton.

We kept on winning. Tory even racked enough points with Huey that he was leading the pack. See, all year they tallied points in the grand prix classes. Then in November, at Madison Square Garden, they name a Horse of the Year and a rider. There's money in it, and this year a car. A Mercedes convertible. A red one.

The Mercedes people had been hauling it around to every show. Rumor was they wanted to make it a fence—put greenery around it, standards on either side. I think the idea was a triple bar, but they worried about dents. The Johnny Walker people, they'd already made standards from seven-foot scotch bottles and had a huge panel with their logo. Hadn't made any of us start drinking the stuff, but then I don't think we were quite the ones they were after.

Anyway, Huey was almost expected to win the Horse of the Year thing. Did most years. Usually he had it locked up before he even got to the Garden and it looked like he would again this year. Tory was doing okay in the rider standings, too. That one's always tougher to nail down, what with everyone winning points on so many different horses. Hard to keep track of even.

She claimed she didn't care, didn't even want the Mercedes since it was an automatic. That she couldn't understand a company that made you special-order standard transmission and when Carl said so what, she could sell it, she said, "Yeah, and turn the money over to you, I suppose." That'd been the end of it for that night, but you could tell, whether she wanted the car or not, she wanted to win and wanted to badly.

By this time, I had two horses in the grand prix classes, Bronto and the chestnut we called Joe Cool—I don't know, was just something about this way he had of standing. He looked all the time like he was leaning on something.

Anyway, I had those two going good, good enough to take indoors in the fall. The rest, they were the ones we'd send home with Jamie and Deb. Tory's green ones, too. She'd really gotten nowhere with them. It was like since that thing with the mare, she didn't want to learn anyone new. She barely even bothered with Lazy Boy and Mr. Clean and so once in a while to shake her up, Carl'd talk about giving them to me.

Was just his way of needling, but it got in between us. She'd yell at me, "Go ahead, take them." Then later tell me she didn't mean it.

I understood what she was doing. With the horses, I mean. Partly, I thought I did. This late in the summer you only had so much left. It didn't seem smart to waste it.

In Long Island, Carl scratched all but her top four and with me he'd drop my bottom three from a class here and there. He was resting us. Knew there wasn't much of a break before we had to gear it up for the fall. But he didn't want us to know he was resting us.

All summer, Tory'd kept snagging bottles and, when we ran out, syringes. And every once in a while we'd buy a packet off that guy Freddy and bang that, but it'd usually be pretty brown and wouldn't do much.

I still had the syringe from months back and in Michigan I'd bought my own packet. These things had a place now, like that credit card did. Like I had to have them but couldn't quite use them. Not yet.

We rode through the week okay. At Southampton, I mean. That Saturday night they had this big party. An annual thing K.C.'s family threw. They had a big house out there on the beach and they'd put up tents and hang lanterns. Had all this food and booze laid out on table after table. This was to keep you out of the house. Nobody said it, you were supposed to know enough.

Of course, K.C. was my friend and, well, Tory's too, sort of. She'd stayed clear of us for a while after Ohio, but then we'd started bumping into each other again, going out. She didn't hang around Freddy so much these days. Now she had one of Richard's best students in tow. A wispy boy named Samuel. He had no chin and so far had stayed mostly with boys.

Pursuing boys who liked boys was K.C.'s current thing. Had been since that thing with Carl, if I thought back through it. She claimed it was sport but she'd let on how she never got anyplace with these guys. They'd lay around touching all night but never really have sex. But then that was about all Tory and I'd been able to manage for these same weeks and months.

So that night in Southampton, Tory and I stood around sipping at drinks we didn't want. We did better with the food— the canapés and cream puffs, the cucumber sandwiches. There was a lot of big food, too. At tables on the other side of the lawn you could get roast beef and lobster, Cornish hens. I swear those tables bowed from the weight, but then we'd smoked some of Tim's hash on the way over—the stuff laced with opium —so that could've been what was making them bend.

We didn't just go into the house, you understand. K.C. invited us. Upstairs, a few of her friends walked around—in and out of doors that led into bedrooms that led into bathrooms. K.C. took us further down the hall to her room. And we stayed there longer than she did, though we weren't much interested in the coke she was offering.

Still, since she'd left us the vial, I pocketed it before we wandered into the hall. We just wanted privacy, Tory and me. That's the only reason we walked further back and found what had to be K.C.'s parents' room.

I was the one who walked around picking up things. Spent a lot of time with the silver-framed pictures on the bedside table. Tory, she stayed single-minded; began right away pulling stuff from her pockets. She was wearing this loose linen suit and had things in her pants and her coat, a packet in her shirt pocket. I was dressed close to the same but my pockets were empty. Except for the vial, that is. I put my hand in my pocket and fingered the thick amber glass while she went into the bathroom. Still held it when she came back with a water glass.

She cooked our stuff in a sterling tablespoon. I hadn't seen her lift it, but I recognized the monogram. That she hadn't even mentioned it made her so much more cheeky and I would've laughed except I worried that for her it wasn't about humor so much as expediency. Lately everything about her had purpose and so anything added seemed mine alone.

She handed me the syringe still in its wrapper. I sat next to her on the bed, which was a dark wood four-poster and massive. Puffy white comforters covered it and the pillows had pillow shams and a lacy canopy dropped light into strange places and shadowed others.

Tory got the stuff cooked and was about to take the syringe, but handed me the spoon instead.

Said "Fucking shit" the whole way to the bathroom.

I'd had the idea by then. Laid the syringe on the bed and took the vial from my pocket. I listened to her moving things around in the bathroom while I tried to get the cap unscrewed with the same hand, since my other one held the spoon.

I heard footsteps from the hall, doors opening and closing. I hadn't before, but somehow when what you're doing looks this bad, you hear everything. Like, I swear, when I tapped some of that coke into the spoon, I heard it dissolve. Then right after, I almost dropped the whole lot of it when Tory called from the bathroom.

"Know what?" she said. "They keep their cotton in a crystal jar with a fucking silver top."

I knew she was on her way back. Could hear her screwing that top back on that fucking jar. Heard this while I was still trying to screw the cap back on the vial.

I'd gotten all jittery and couldn't cover it. And when she got back and took the spoon from me and put the cotton in it, she patted my leg, I thought for comfort until I realized she was wanting the needle; was looking for it.

I found it'd slid under me. Soon as I had it I handed it to her. Then I opened my pants, pushed them down some while she drew the stuff through the cotton and into the barrel.

She was sort of frowning so I stopped looking at her face. Watched the needle instead while she flicked the barrel, pushed a drop out the top.

"This is the new one, right?"

"Yeah," I said. "Why?"

"I don't know," she said. "Nothing."

Then she crouched in front of me and pushed my pants the rest of the way down because she needed to get between my legs. She rested her arms on my knees and I saw she was going for a spot near my groin but a little further south. That's when I leaned back.

I felt her prick me, felt the tug. After that things got funny. She got some of the stuff in, I could feel it, but she'd had to work at it and then it just stayed there. I mean this. It was like it wouldn't move.

That's when I sat up. She didn't look good and her voice sounded hoarser than ever. "Keep still," she said.

She was trying to work the plunger the rest of the way down, but couldn't. She pulled it up again, like to start over, but when she went to slam it, it wouldn't. Before she could bang anything else through, it bunged up completely and she slipped her hold, and that let the plunger come off.

What I felt then could've been the hit or just panic. The fucking barrel spattered blood across the bed, all over the wall-paper, even up to the canopy so it dripped back down on us. Tory was trying to pull the thing out of me. I was useless. Helpless in a way that made it harder for her. I kept wanting to cross my legs and that left her trying to hold me still.

"Darling, you got to help me here," she was saying. "You just got to stay quiet."

It didn't hurt, I don't think. It just scared me, made me want to curl up and so even with her telling me not to, I kept trying to.

She finally got the thing out. There was blood in her hair and some on her face. There was even some on the damn bed-side pictures, splashed across the silver frames and the glass. It was the sort of mess you could never clean up, but I thought at least we should try. Was rubbing one of the pictures with a pillowcase when she said, "What are you doing? Let's get the fuck out of here."

I got my pants on and though my clothes were dark, you could still see these stains even darker. Tory's suit was lighter and so it looked that much worse. The best thing we could do now was find a back way to get out.

I clutched her when we got near the door. She opened it a little and peeked down the hall. I looked back. I probably shouldn't have. It looked about like someone'd been murdered.

Tory had my arm and was dragging me behind her. We left blood on the fucking doorknob even.

We sneaked down the hall to a back staircase, wound up in a pantry that led into another and then into the garage. I stopped dead looking at the bank of cars. There were half a dozen there and berths for a few more.

"You crazy?" Tory said. "Come on."

We ducked out the door, a people-sized one at this end of the row of car-sized ones. Our footsteps sounded loud and crunchy on the gravel. I could hear music wafting over the top of the garage; voices following it and then the ocean. I remembered how I'd thought we'd have our shots then go out on the beach. Roll around outside for a change and that maybe that'd change how we'd been.

We walked the whole way down the driveway, almost, before we found Tory's car. We sure couldn't ask the valets, they were just more people to slink by.

Once she got the car started, Tory backed out the driveway. The other choice was driving up to the house and around and out the other side.

She kept the headlights off until we hit the sleepy little road. Actually, she kept them off for a while even then, which seemed like too much. I guess now we were pretty well safe and away I needed to start making less of this since I figured I'd caused it, though I still wasn't sure how. A minute later she told me.

We'd gotten to where the road met the next bigger one; were stopped at a stop sign and she lit us cigarettes. Handed me mine and said, "You fucking put coke in, didn't you?"

What was I going to do? I said, "Yeah, so?"

"You dumbass. That's what made it gum up."

"Yeah, well, how was I supposed to know?"

"Maybe you didn't have to do it when I wasn't looking. Ever think of that?"

"Yeah, and maybe you don't have to have all those extra boots every night either."

That shut her up, but I wasn't sure I'd wanted it to. It was true she'd started giving herself extra and doing it when she thought I wasn't looking. What mattered about it, I didn't know. It wasn't like her doing it took away from me. Hell, I wasn't sure I wanted to step up there anyway. And I didn't think what I'd done tonight was to get over on her. It more happened by reflex.

We had to cover a pretty long stretch of that nonmoving road called Route 27. We were staying at a Howard Johnson's halfway back to Syosset. That'd been so we could stay in one place for both shows. Right now it seemed stupid.

We edged along and edged along and finally when I thought I'd be the one to start mending it, she said, "You know, you wouldn't like it anyway."

"How do you know?" I said.

She just laughed at me this time. Not mean, just laughing. Then she said, "Because, it gets your heart pumping too hard and you don't like that."

She wasn't laughing now and so I said, "How do you know what I like?"

I said it because I knew what she meant. That she'd noticed the way I acted whenever she came too near me, how I'd veer off. It'd gotten worse since she'd told me that thing in Ohio. I couldn't hide it so well, but I needed to keep pretending she couldn't tell. I had to believe she didn't understand what she could do to me, how bad she could make me feel. Everything depended on this.

I took the cigarettes from the dash and lit one. Tossed the

pack back without getting her hers. She laughed again and got it herself. We drove the whole way sparring lightly like this and I decided she'd leave it alone.

When we got back to the room, she gave us hits of something called Nubain. It came in a bright pink bottle and as far as I was concerned that was the most exciting thing it had going. I knew she still had something left in that packet and maybe I had blown my share, but if she held out on me, got up in the night and banged the whole rest herself, I didn't think I'd be big about it. See, that stuff wasn't brown, it was mostly white.

So, I could tell myself I felt funny because she was maybe holding out on me, for a while I could. We were in bed by now and she had her arms around me and then she went so gentle. This was the thing we'd been doing so much of lately where it never quite got there. And so for me it went instead right to where I was saddest and then I couldn't keep where I needed to be in my head, couldn't keep her where I needed her, which was somewhere further away.

Hydromorphone, Nubain, not even that fucking white shit in her pocket ever seemed to get down under enough to whack this place she managed to hit each and every time she turned tender.

And she knew it. She used it. And so you can see why maybe, these days, I'd be looking for a little something extra myself.

30

Waking up that Sunday was especially cruel. Linda's room adjoined ours and she came in around nine, opened the curtains, ordered coffee. She'd been over and back to the showgrounds already, of course.

Since today was a grand prix day, it meant fewer horses to worry more about. I didn't want to get out of the bed and Tory, she was still pretending to sleep.

A guy came with the coffee. Linda could get room service out of the cheapest motels. All up and down the Northeast and even in the Midwest she'd managed it.

She put the cardboard box on the nightstand by Tory, which meant I had to lean across her. I was trying to cover myself with the sheet, but that seemed so stupid I dropped it.

Linda started tossing clothes from one chair to the other. She sat down with a cigarette, then tossed the pack and the lighter to me. I lit mine and nudged Tory. Handed her one when she finally sat up.

"You cut out too early last night," Linda said. "You really missed it. All kinds of carrying on. The kind you two enjoy."

"Oh yeah?" Tory said.

I crushed out my cigarette; put down the coffee cup. I didn't know if I could listen to this so, for something to do, I bent my knee. Let the sheet fall so Linda could see whatever she wanted, so I could see what I wanted, except I was pretty sure I already knew what that was.

"Yeah," Linda said. "Some kind of screaming coming from K.C.'s mother. The sort you don't hear so often. And then the uproar. Seems someone bled all across her bed."

Linda'd gotten up again while she talked, was neatening our clothes. Holding them up so you could see the stains on them. That's when I got up; walked right by her and into the bathroom. I waited awhile before turning the shower on, but couldn't hear anything they were saying.

I took my time in the shower. Felt too tired to face either one of them. I sat down in the tub so I could look at my leg. This one had bruised different than the others. Like the stuff that wouldn't move was still there. I could feel a bump. And soreness, too much soreness.

When I turned the water off, I sat there a little longer. Then forced myself out, wrapped a towel around my waist, and went back into the room. Linda was back sitting in that chair. Smoke curled around her, moved slowly through the sunlight. Tory sat in her own cloud of it. I started dressing.

After I put my shirt on, Tory got up to take her shower. That left me and Linda.

"That's a nasty-looking one," she said as I started pulling on my breeches.

I didn't answer. There'd been nothing between us since Ohio, since Tory'd come back—nothing much more than looks.

"Come here," she said. "Let me see that."

I did what she told me, stood there in front of her while she poked at me. She said, "We should cut this now, before it gets any worse."

She didn't do anything, though, except touch me and I was

liking the feel of her hands in my breeches, which were the white ones you had to wear for the grand prix classes. Carl'd bought me some in Connecticut when I'd needed them for riding Tory's horses. He'd bought me a red coat, too. The kind they wear fox hunting. I'd felt a little funny about that. Shy. I could've worn a blue coat. People do. Tory still does a lot, for luck.

But he wanted me in red. Maybe he thought I'd raise my game to it. I don't know. I'd gone fox hunting some as a kid, when I first hooked up with Silas. There you have to earn a red coat. I had actually, though as a kid you can't wear one. And women usually just wear red collars on their black coats. They call it getting your colors.

They gave me mine when a horse kicked me in the leg on a particularly cold October morning. They had a kill that day, too, later on. And afterwards what they do to you, if it's your first kill, they put the fox's blood on your face. Brush it on with the end of the paw where they've cut it off. A stripe on each cheek and one on your forehead. It's called blooding.

After that, they dole out the parts. This time, they gave me the mask. That's their name for the head. It's an honor to get it. This woman who was one of the Hunt Masters, she had a soft spot for me, which is why I got it, really, because she felt sad about my hurting my leg and proud I'd finished the hunt anyway. The truth was it just hadn't occurred to me I didn't have to, that I could just ride home early and not see it through.

Anyway, I had no place to put this fox head but my coat pocket. So I rode home with it, back to Silas's barn. When I got off the horse, I felt the thing shift; realized blood had leaked all down my breeches. It'd soaked through my coat. And it'd been a cold day. You wouldn't have thought there could be so much flowing like that.

You're supposed to mount the things. Put them on your wall. You're supposed to have a fireplace for this. A den. What I did was take my coat off. I figured if I could get the thing out of my pocket, I could still wear the coat. That since it was black, you wouldn't see the stain. But when I felt around in there, tried to find something to hold on to that wasn't slippery, I couldn't. I threw the whole thing out, coat and all. Never told anyone. Not even Silas. I mean, I was young then. Eight, maybe nine. I hadn't been with him long enough yet.

So there I was, standing in that motel room dressed completely in white with Linda fingering me, first through my underwear and then pulling it aside so she could get in me. And all I could think about was blood and this made me wobbly and I felt her hand on my hipbone, pulling me further onto her other hand, pulling me onto her lap until I had my arms around her, until I realized what we were doing and where Tory was and when I started to pull away Linda wouldn't let me.

I listened for the shower, still heard it and tried not to think beyond this. Linda took her hand out and started rubbing me, fucked my ass with just her finger. She'd never done me this way, or maybe I'd just never been awake to what she'd done. I kept kissing her until she kissed me back, got lost once she started that, and like she knew where I was, she picked then to bring me off.

After she'd finished me, I stayed in her lap. She was the one who got up from under me and put me back down in the chair. I sat there even once Tory'd come out of the bathroom. Pretty soon after that, Linda said she was leaving. On her way out she told us to be over to the showgrounds by ten.

I watched Tory get dressed, watched her put on all the same clothes as me—the white breeches and shirt. Then she put jeans and a T-shirt on top. You did this to cover your riding clothes, keep yourself clean. I'd forgotten this and seeing her do it got me out of the chair, got me the rest of the way dressed. Then I fussed with getting my other things ready.

Tory didn't say much. She watched me curiously, closely. I felt her looking for a way in, wondered what she'd heard and what she could just feel. We had about enough time for more coffee, some food—a trip to the dining room. I suggested this to start us moving.

To get to the dining room from our room, you had to cross the parking lot. It was late August and as soon as we left the building I felt the heat, especially with all those layers we had on. I'd been okay in the room with the AC but now I began feeling heavy. Almost staggered a little.

"Think anyone else knows?" Tory asked after we'd ordered eggs we wouldn't eat.

"No," I said. "I mean, K.C. maybe, but everyone was there. Didn't have to be us. Not like they know what happened or how."

"They found it."

"Found what?"

"The pump, they found it."

"I thought you took it."

"Oh, right. Like I knew where to look and had time to."

We pushed the eggs around awhile before ordering cinnamon toast and when that came, we pushed it around too, more than we ate. We'd both been getting a little too lean lately.

███ It surprised me how glad I felt to be at the show-grounds, to get back on a horse. Tim gave me Joe Cool first. He was a big one, but not rangy like Bronto. Bronto you had to hold together all the time. He'd barrel around and so you had to watch he didn't flatten out or he'd pull rails just when you thought you'd cinched things.

Joe Cool, he stayed coiled. He'd come along slower than Bronto. Was strung higher, kind of like Frisbee. He popped fences, a real springboarder. He'd get up there so high your worry was losing time in the air. He knew how to make it up on the ground, though. Dash flat out if you let him or slice turns. And always he'd rock back and get up in the air. Just hand things to you, really.

Worked great unless you set him wrong. If you put him in the wrong place, he wouldn't just pull rails, he'd smash through them. You had to stay careful he wasn't carrying you away with him. Sometimes he'd get my juice up where I couldn't see straight. I'd think I was right in there with him and then, too late, I'd see he'd started doing the driving. We'd cracked up in Michigan that way. Took out the Johnny Walker fence, though they got another one made by New Jersey.

Today, I wasn't so much worried about juice as not having any. I tried to siphon some of Joey's, but he just acted edgy; acted like he couldn't be sure of me. I tried to find something to give him, but I just felt tired and sore. Sore on the inside of my thigh where that thing was, that lump.

Tory rode Frisbee first today. Carl'd set us up to go one after the other early in the class. This whole week they'd been setting jump-off slates in reverse order of the original round so if you went early in the class, you'd go late in the jump-off. Looked like Carl wanted to play Tory and me off against each other if he could. Didn't seem like such a great idea to me, especially not today.

I watched Tory while we schooled. Tried to figure how come she had something on tap. Even the biggest fences Carl put us over gave me nothing. I didn't do anything wrong, though.

Tory went into the ring first of the two of us. She had one of those picture-perfect rounds that lull you. But then on the last fence Frisbee dropped his foot. One of those little lazy goofs that come when you're not looking.

"Dammit to hell," Carl said. He started for the in-gate guy before the rail hit the ground. Linda was already there, though, jabbing his clipboard, talking fast in his ear. Then she took Huey from Deb.

I went into the ring as Tory came out. While I made that obligatory circle, I watched them put her on Huey. Saw it was Linda schooling them. That Carl had stayed by the rail for me.

I'd kind of lost sight this was a grand prix, but when I looked at the stands, saw the champagne buckets and picnic baskets, the hats and the dresses and the suits on the men—summer seersuckers mostly—right about then, heading for the first fence, it hit me. Gave me that pump I'd looked for. Of course, it might've just been fear of how bad Carl'd dress me down if I fucked up too.

I didn't fuck up and neither did Joey, and Tory didn't with Huey. They were our only clean ones. Bronto, Lazy Boy, Mr. Clean—every one of them had the last fence down. Sometimes that'll happen in a class, there'll be a jinx fence. Can be a reason for it, like you have to jump toward the crowd, or it's a tough distance. Or sometimes, like today, it just happens.

So Carl got a showdown of sorts, though not how he wanted. Mostly I knew he'd wanted Tory to follow me, not the other way around like it was now. We had three other horses before us and one of them was Ted's.

I hated having to school same time as him. He'd go out of his way to bump me or cut me off. He'd only laid off through Michigan. In New Jersey he started again, but not enough for Carl to stop him. He'd just do this nasty little stuff he did to almost everyone. The way he did it to me was different, though. The look on his face was.

So the five of us left in the jump-off, we all staked space in the schooling ring. Took all the fences we could while the jump crew worked the grand prix ring. Everything everyone did happened fast, but precisely. More than anything you wanted just to keep warm, keep the blood up.

Carl finished us in time to watch Ted. The course wasn't hard, not till the end. That's where the choice was—either make time or play safe. No place else to do it and the only way was to take out a stride. No fancy turns, no touch stuff. You'd just have to gun down there and hope you reeled in in time but not too soon. And the last fence was the same one, the jinxed one. The first two horses on course proved that.

Not Ted, though. He turned in the first clean one. Played it safe like the others, but kept that last fence up. I could see he said something to Tory when they passed. I watched her face change. Then she looked at me. Looked at me funny as she brought Huey around through the timers.

She pressed him right from the start. Kept driving him. They ran through the first part of the course and by the time the last line came, she had him charging. Flat out down to it and asking for more the whole way. It looked like disaster, still you didn't think so since it was them. Didn't think so and then they were off the ground with still another stride left to go.

Huey went into the fence like diving a breaker. His front legs stretched out, shielded his head, then folded over. I think he was trying to tuck them. It was sad, how hard he still tried.

When he hit, he didn't roll, he skidded. On the rails first, then the dirt. Tory bailed. You could see she tried to jump clear. Tumbled into the standard and grabbed on to it like it'd break her fall but it just went down with her, practically on top of her.

She landed on her back, kicking it off. Then staggered up; started walking circles.

Huey got up, too. And then there was this sick moment when his knees buckled and it looked like he'd go down again. He caught himself though. Walked gingerly, but he walked.

Linda got in there. She caught the reins, checked the scrapes on his knees. Led him out. Tory trailed behind them and soon as she came out, Carl grabbed her.

"What the fuck was that? You take yourself down if you want. I don't give a fuck, but that animal's not yours to cripple. Belongs to that man over there."

Carl had her by the arm, was nodding to the stands where, among everyone else standing, one man was sinking back to his chair. He took his glasses off and wiped his forehead. Then started searching for his hat, which had slipped into the ring. One of the jump crew was just now handing it back to him, but he didn't notice. The young boy finally gave up. Set it on the riser beside Mr. Martel's white bucks.

"First time all summer the man comes out to see his horse and this is the show you give him?"

"Tell you what, Carl," she said. "Next time, why don't you do it?"

They'd got the fence fixed by now. I couldn't stall any longer, but I went in there not knowing what to do. Carl'd told me same as Tory. "Chase down to it. Take the stride out. Only way left to win."

Now I didn't know, though. I looked to Carl but he didn't look back; he was still going at Tory and she back at him. And Linda, she was busy with Huey. Only one watching was Tim and so I took what I could from him. He'd gone dead white, which with him was saying something; still he tried to smile.

I went to the first fence figuring I had to try it. By the second fence, I figured since this was Joey, we'd pull it off. Could, anyway. After the third fence I cut the turn to the last line. Stepped on the pedal and tried to find how this was any different than what Tory'd done.

We went a little tight to the next fence. Planned to. It'd maybe give us a little control, enough to last the next three strides. We tore down and I lost count and when we came off the ground we could've been anywhere for all I knew.

I closed my eyes. Really. And so when we hung there, I kept waiting; was sure I'd hear some kind of crash. We thunked the ground and I opened my eyes. Got off his back and galloped him through the timers. Then I looked back to see the fence had stayed up. I'd just won my first grand prix.

31

Tory and I got out of town fast after Southampton. Off the showgrounds, anyway. We sure didn't stay for any parties. Soon enough, though, we were back stuck in traffic—Sunday L.I.E. traffic, which did nothing for Tory's mood. I didn't feel so hot myself. I'd come off the win edgy instead of happy and then, since we had driving to do, we'd taken some speed. Be a long wait for a comedown and already it seemed I'd been waiting for days.

I was sweating from feeling how I did and from the heat, which only turned up hotter the further south we got. We were headed for Philadelphia and it seemed Tory's mood was going to stay bad the whole way. Once we'd hit 95 and the traffic had thinned there was only one thing left to blame it on.

I knew I had to and now I had no reason to put it off, so I just did it, asked her, "What is it Ted said?"

She acted like she hadn't heard me. Did this right up until I thought I'd have to ask it again. Then she said, "Nothing."

I scratched at my leg. At the lump. It itched but was too sore to soothe easily. I waited like this. Didn't want to push unless she truly was going to leave it here.

We'd run out of cigarettes a little while ago and it was

probably stupid to have started this without them. It left me fussing with my leg too much and her twisting the gearshift knob.

"What'd he say, Tory?"

She wiped her hand across her face like it'd help her decide, but then she just started. "He said, 'She sucks good, don't she?' I think he meant you."

"And so what? You think I sucked him?"

"No," she said, "I don't."

The way she said it, I knew she believed me. But this confused me because I didn't believe me. I hadn't done this. Not that way, I hadn't. And not the way she had, though I'd been thinking lately how maybe her way would've been easier. Still, all of this floated around. It mixed in with what she'd told me about her scar, and with what I'd been doing with Linda— this last thing filmy and sticky and making it way too hard to breathe without smoking.

We stopped for cigarettes and then drove the rest of the way straight through. Smoked one after another; had taken to buying separate packs by now.

When we got to Philly, we checked in and then dragged our stuff up to the room. I figured all the motels would be like this now—rooms off hallways instead of off parking lots. I felt much more closed in. Felt this even more because I knew Linda would keep booking the room next to ours.

We didn't unpack. Instead we sprawled on the bed. I more or less fell on it, stayed limp and crumpled up, held on to a pillow. We didn't lie there too much longer before Tory started setting up my shot. I made her put it in my hand and soon as she did I felt hammered by it, more than in a long time. So much so I decided it'd hitched to the tail end of the speed.

When the down came, it spread around. Lumbered through my belly to my limbs. Sunk into them all the way, even dragged on my toes and fingers. I didn't register Tory sticking herself. I do remember her nestling beside me, remember how when she did I was thinking I wanted a look at the bottle so I knew what you called this stuff.

We woke up crunched together. That little bottle was still on the table with the syringe. Guess we hadn't cleaned up. I heard Linda somewhere in the room. Tory did, too, and started putting things away, probably too late.

I smelled the coffee before Linda brought it to us. Smelled her cigarette, too. It hung from her lips, loose in the corner of her mouth, squirming when she talked.

"Party's over, kids. Carl wants you eased off it some."

"Oh, Carl does," Tory said.

"You want to ask him, Tory? Go on and ask him. Made a real impression with that stunt of yours yesterday. Huey's still hobbling from it."

"But you'll fix that, now, won't you?" Tory said.

"Yeah, well, that's my job, right? Fixing the things you break."

Seemed Tory had no answer for this so she got up and started pacing the room. Every now and then she'd stand still, swirl the coffee in her cup, and then sip it. After the third time she started spilling it.

I stayed on the bed. Sipped my coffee and smoked my first cigarette. Linda had lit it for me and right after, she sat down beside me. Having her there next to me, it started first as sweat down my back. I hunched forward and when I leaned back again the damp spread out, clumped instead of trickled. Then I got hot and scratchy in my fingers, had to keep shaking them until I had to put out the cigarette to do it.

Tory finally put down her coffee. Then she went into the

bathroom. I put my coffee down, too. Started to get up but Linda clamped her hand on my leg. I swear she knew just where to grab me, knew exactly where that fucking lump was. She left her hand there. "You're not going to help her," she said. "And you're not going to like how she gets now."

She took her hand off my leg then and I started up again. She caught hold of my wrist and turned it over. Looked at the new bruise on my palm and said, "Look, darling, you're going to need me."

 That night it started. Linda found everything Tory'd stashed and though she didn't even look for the packet I had, I kept it on me. Was hiding it from Tory, I guess. She dosed Tory first, and whatever it was put her out right away. Since this didn't make sense, I tried to convince myself it only meant Tory'd taken something and so what Linda gave her was too much on top.

Linda just said, "Come on, I've got yours in here."

I followed her into her room and even once I had, she left the door ajar like she wanted to keep an eye on Tory. I wanted her to shut it. This was all pretty close already.

At first, I started for a chair but then sat on the bed because there didn't seem any point anymore to pretending about anything. I took off my clothes when she told me to and lay on my back. She poked around at my lump. Said we'd have to take care of it pretty soon.

I told her it didn't bother me, told her this because the idea of cutting it scared me. She laughed at me, then pressed it until I flinched. Then she stuck me and right afterwards she had me turn over.

The stuff didn't come on much, seemed she'd given Tory more and it was me she was taking down. I started breathing too shallow and fast. Was still laying there and her walking around and what scared me was maybe she liked how I'd been the last time—that morning when I'd had nothing and so I could feel her, not the way I usually did but that other way that'd made me hold on to her.

I buried my face into the pillow to see if it'd slow my breathing. Weighed whether I could ask her to give me more, weighed one kind of fear against another. When she sat down with me, she ran her hand down my back and my breathing turned faster before it slowed down. I couldn't decide if the stuff was the kind to come on slow and she'd been waiting or if I'd done this myself, made myself go down.

When she got to my ass, I decided it must've been me because I couldn't maintain it. She wasn't doing anything but stroking me and I couldn't bear this so I asked her could she give me another shot. What I actually said was, "It didn't take, Linda, I didn't get off," and could hear I sounded panicked.

She said to hold on, she said in a little while. "After a little while," she said, "you just take it easy now."

I didn't want to be crying but maybe she wanted me to because when that started she lay down with me. The weight of her body comforted me. It was easier to have her keep me from moving, easier than just not being able.

I turned a little on my side, pulled my leg up under me and she put her hand in my ass. Even once she did that she kept slow. Took me time to see how to fix this, that she wanted me asking her to, and this time when I asked her I meant it.

She fucked me like she had that first time, fucked me until she'd torn me up inside and so much I only cared when I could get her to again. Afterwards, I didn't even care about that. I just lay there with my one leg hitched so far up under me I was hugging it.

She'd gotten up and when she came back she untangled me

from myself. She'd brought me another shot, one I wasn't even sure I wanted, which was maybe the strangest thing I'd felt so far. I was lying on my back the way she'd put me. Had closed my eyes because her hand between my legs lulled me, sent me close to sleeping.

I felt her opening me up and then fucking my cunt in the same lulling, lazy way she'd touched me. I slid down a little towards her even before I heard her asking me to. Her fingers spread out in me and then I felt her stick me there, somewhere in between her fingers. I jerked without meaning to or my hips did, they jerked by themselves and she told me to keep still a minute, keep still a minute longer and I tried to, but I was jerking more, or the stuff and where it was, was jerking me off— that's just how it felt.

I wound up clinging to her. For a long time I stayed that way, not sure what had happened and knowing exactly. Even foundering under this nod, already I craved the next time. She petted me like she knew what I was thinking, petted me like she was promising something, and so when she got me up and took me back to my bed, even once I'd slumped against Tory, I figured somehow we'd work this.

32

After Philadelphia, we went to Rhode Island, to Newport. Now that we'd started hitting cities, the rings were indoor ones and as close and cramped as the motel rooms. I'd never liked riding indoors, not even with hunters, but with jumpers, I hated it. You'd practically land in the spectators' laps. I swear I'd started banking off the fencing, which wasn't fencing really, but walls. Solid things that'd take your leg off, crush you if you hit too hard.

I wasn't doing so good getting used to this and then, here in Newport, they had us schooling outside, on asphalt, underneath a highway overpass. You skidded every time you landed, couldn't help it, and sometimes on takeoffs, too. The horses' shoes slid on the blacktop, making their legs come out from under them. I'd taken to shifting my weight around to someway try and help the balance.

Linda'd been talking to the blacksmith, wanted our horses reshod, but he didn't have this kind of abrasive metal she wanted, was trying to sell her on rubber, which she said wouldn't work. They settled on renailing the shoes with cogged nails, ones with little barbs on the heads. It helped some, but not enough.

Hard to say whether this sliding around bothered Bronto worse or Joey. I guess it just bothered them different. Bronto turned straggly and nervous. He'd dance around trying to keep his feet from touching the pavement and so he liked taking the fences, but didn't like landing. It got to where I'd sort of talk him down. Began cooing before we were off the ground and kept going until we hit it again. Then I had to give him room to slow down because stopping scared him the most.

Joey, he turned ornery. Just wasn't going to do things. He'd duck and stop and, boy, did that set Carl off. None of the rest of us had given Carl enough to be mad about lately and so Joey got the brunt of whatever'd been brewing since Long Island.

This started first with yelling and then went to kicking. Carl'd grab the reins, pull them right through my hands and before I had a chance to get off he'd kick Joey in the belly. Difference in Carl lately was he didn't care who saw him do these things. Got an extra charge, even, from the hush that'd fall. From the way people stepped out of his path. Things he didn't used to notice.

The only advantage to schooling where we did was when you got into the ring it seemed easy. Just feeling the soft footing would settle the horses. And they behaved pretty well. Tory's did, too.

Of course she was an old hand at this indoor stuff and I found myself watching her the way I used to, trying to glean things from her. And from watching her, I started liking her more, liking her the way I hadn't been lately. The stuff Linda'd been giving her maybe smoothed her out. She'd sleep long and deep and wake up nearly normal.

Me, other hand, I wasn't getting much sleep. Hadn't been

since Philly. Every night Linda'd take me so far down I'd get up ragged. Already this week I'd bummed a vial off K.C. Had begun needing a little bump in the mornings to even everything out.

By midweek, it'd got harder still. On Thursday, I was the last to go in the last class of the day, and with Joey. He'd straightened up his act some and if we went clean, that'd put us in a jump-off with Tory and Frisbee.

We started out fine, but then landing after the first line of fences, as we came into the turn, I slipped. One of those times when your foot comes out of the stirrup but you catch yourself. So I caught myself, but when I did, I scraped that lump of mine against the saddle.

The lump had got worse and not better, but I'd found a way round it that'd been working since Philly. I shortened my stirrups a notch and that kept me out of the saddle just that little bit more I needed. When I slipped, though, I guess I had that little bit further to fall and it hurt so bad I thought I might lose my grip altogether and then I pretty much did.

We came out of the turn to a triple bar. Those fences are always so full of air, they're hard to read. They play games with your eyes until you're not sure which rail is where. They play on the horses too, make them nervous, so when I couldn't hold on, when right in front of the thing I dropped Joey, gave him nothing, just left it all in his lap—he did the only thing he could, which was stop.

I knew I should finish the course. That the way things had gone, if we finished clean from here on in we'd still place second. You're faulted less for a refusal than a knockdown and, like I said, Frisbee was the only one so far to go clean. I couldn't do it, though. I had to fight from getting off him.

I walked him back to the gate, which caused some confusion

with the announcers, who finally said we were disqualified and then read the results. Tory shot me a look as we passed. Mouthed something I couldn't make out and then Carl had us. He took Joe by the reins; waited until he got us out under the highway and then started wailing on us.

I hadn't even seen he had Tory's crop. I felt it before I saw it. Carl was mad enough at me and Joey, he didn't care which one of us he hit. And he kept hitting and Joey scuffled; made one attempt to strike back, but that's what took his legs out from under us.

Having a horse fall on you doesn't hurt. Looks like it should, but it doesn't really. They're usually already trying to get back on their feet, so their weight never quite touches you. This time what hurt most was the pavement, and that the weight Joey put on me hit me where I was sore.

That's why even once he'd got up, I didn't. Not until Linda picked me up; walked me away. All the way to her car. I knew what she was up to. Knew there'd be no way to keep her from cutting that abscess this time.

She drove us back to the motel; got her box from the trunk and we went to her room. She pulled off my boots; told me to take off my breeches and my underwear. I did what she said while she washed her hands, got things from her box.

She had me lie on the bed; put a pillow under my good leg and then another on top of it. She sat so she leaned on that top pillow, pulled my bad leg onto her lap. She gave me a stick in my groin and a few minutes later started swabbing the abscess with gauze; applying more pressure than she had to and looking for my reaction. I kept flinching.

"Not numb yet?"

"Uh uh."

She must've given me novocaine or something like it because of all the things I take to fast that's not one of them. Once when I was a kid, a dentist, exasperated by my failure to go numb, gave me a dozen shots of the stuff and then went ahead and drilled, insisting I couldn't feel it. This bolstered an already strong belief that things got to me too much, something I thought I'd outgrow.

Tory came in from our room while Linda was still waiting. She came and sat beside me and when she saw the thing on my leg the question was all over her face, but she didn't ask it. Said only, "When'd . . ." before stopping herself.

She pulled her boots off, crawled back of me, put her arms and legs around me and held on. This probably was good, because when Linda asked me next if I'd gone numb, I said, "Yes." Having her give me twelve shots of that stuff seemed worse than having her go ahead without it.

I bit my tongue while she cut. Watched everything she did. How she followed the blade with the gauze; cut slow and steady. I didn't make a sound, not at first, but Tory's arms felt so solid and tender and so did her lips and her whispering sounded that way, too. It was these things made me cry, not the cutting.

Linda was saying, "Almost there. Just a little bit longer."

I felt the knife go deeper before she stopped. I wasn't looking now. I felt it go deeper and then felt her turn it. After that, just pressure. Her holding the gauze there and then a different piece and then a last piece that had something on it. Something sticky and soft. That one she taped on and then wrapped an elastic bandage over the top.

She got up then and started putting things away. Tory scrunched around behind me until she got the bedspread out from under us, until she'd covered me with it. I'd stopped crying, but I started again. I wanted to turn, put my face in her chest, but I couldn't move well.

A little bit later Linda gave me a different shot and after that Tory's holding only made me feel sweet and drowsy.

When I woke up, I could see light coming through the door they'd left partway open. I heard their voices, could smell their cigarettes, and I guess wanting one of my own got me up. I still had no pants on and couldn't stomach the thought of my breeches. I was about to get a towel when I saw the sweatpants and then the T-shirt and sweatshirt under them.

I pulled the clothes on, went slow and easy with the pants. After, I wandered into the other room. The two of them stopped talking and watched me.

"Don't look too bad, does she?"

"Nope. How you feeling, Cowboy?" Tory said.

"Okay, I guess." Though the truth was I felt woozy and stomach sick and since there wasn't another chair for me anyway, I crawled onto the bed.

"Can I have a cigarette?" I said soon as I saw the pack all the way over by them.

"Sure, darling."

Tory brought one to me and then went back to her chair. I drew on it until my lungs trembled and by the time I exhaled, it'd settled my stomach.

They both sat with me and when Linda ordered the food, she got ice cream for me.

I don't know how the time went, but before she left she said, "Don't get that thing wet," meaning the bandage. "I'll change it tomorrow. Leave it alone until then."

Tory followed her into her room and when she came back I could see she had something in her hand. She wasn't trying to hide it from me. Even the dim light in the room bounced off the stainless steel, made it hard to see, and then she put it down, and next to it she put two ampules that looked like thermometers.

She fitted an ampule to the metal plunger. This really reminded me of the dentist.

"Christ," I said. "That looks nasty."

"It's how she's managing us," Tory said. "Single pops. Guess she got tired of hitting us."

This was the most she'd said about anything and hearing it spill out in this way where I couldn't tell what she knew, it choked me. That and her hand on my throat.

I grabbed at her wrist.

"Hey, come on now," she said. "You'll love this."

I let go of her. She pushed my hair behind my ear and held it there. Had that steel contraption between her teeth and was talking through it.

"Easy," she said, "easy, darling."

By now I knew anytime anyone said that, I was in for it.

I felt her fingers behind my ear and then a little bit under it, smoothing my skin. Then she took the syringe from her mouth. I jolted away from the prick, I couldn't help it. Made her miss so she had to start over.

That next time she made sure I didn't move. Held my head so my face was pressed into the crook of her arm. The worst part was how she put it in. And how once she got it down, she drew more blood up and then sent that in, cleaned the ampule with it.

This was more hydromorphone and so I'd thought it'd take time, but between how long she'd taken and where she'd put it, the blast hit before she had the pin out. I think I pulled it out pulling away, yanking my head from her arm. I needed badly to put my head down and when I did, the stuff made me come. Well, that thing about this that's like coming, but isn't quite.

I turned on my side and crossed my legs, squeezed them together. Did this before I remembered my leg. The hot sort of hurt there felt like the gauze it was wrapped in. Felt good. Hurt in a way I liked. The same dull open ache Linda's hand gave me. The kind of pain that kills pain.

I rolled onto my back and touched myself. Just held my hand between my legs. The pressure had spread out, but wasn't outside of me yet. I wanted to milk the last of it while it was still in there, before it got out and started pressing me down.

I was maybe too late, just a beat or two behind, because now it was holding me down but, well, I liked that too.

Tory'd pitched my ampule and was fitting the syringe with her own. She unbuttoned her jeans, put her shot in her groin. Slid the plunger in slow and drew it out. Did this so many times I got lost watching and then got queasy from following the motion and had to turn my face back into the pillow. I started a little when she tossed the syringe, when it clinked on the table, and then I was out.

33

I didn't ride again until Cleveland. This worked out okay, especially since Joey'd scraped himself bad enough Linda was making him wear his own poultice. We both healed pretty good, and pretty fast, and by Washington we even won some classes and placed third in the grand prix there. Tory and Huey won that one, and those were the points that sent Huey into the National already Horse of the Year.

Tory still hadn't cinched the rider thing, though. There was a woman from Canada right behind her and one of Richard's old students behind her. Even Ted had a shot at it, though not much of one.

Linda was still giving us those single-dose ampules and I'd learned how to stick Tory because she couldn't shoot herself in the neck—or at least didn't like to—and this was about the only way she wanted to get off. She didn't bruise the way I did and so we could do this with her pretty often.

Not me, though. Once or twice and I started to look like I'd been strangled or something. And even though the collars on the riding shirts covered things pretty well, you couldn't wear those all the time. Turtlenecks might've solved it, but I'd started to hate having things round my neck. Had begun tugging my collar a lot. I still wasn't hitting myself, but I guessed I could now. If I had to.

So that's how we went into Manhattan—on single-dose ampules and thinking trouble had passed us. It seemed that way. Seemed like sort of a honeymoon. I mean, we weren't cheating each other and the horses were behaving themselves. Were good even when they had to walk across the sidewalk, down there by Penn Station. Granted, like us, they were pretty doped up.

As usual, we had the best accommodations. For the horses, that is. A lot of people would work off trucks this week, would have to cross that same stretch of sidewalk two or three times a day. Not us. They'd offered us eight stalls right next to the in-gate. But that was too public, so Linda'd arranged for some others further back and out of the fray.

This put us near the vendors. Stores like Miller's and Kauffman would set up booths every year alongside others who traveled the whole circuit selling jewelry and porcelain. That first day in town, Carl bought Tory and me extra pairs of white breeches from the Kauffman guy. At the Garden, they schedule all the jumper classes at night and white breeches and red coats, well, it's sort of like evening wear.

You should see some of the spectators and the owners. They put on ball gowns and slippers, no joke. Especially the ones who're going to present trophies. A red carpet gets rolled out over the dirt and these men in tuxes and ladies in chiffon, they trundle out there hauling silver plates.

The whole week's like that. Soon as you get inside the Garden everything turns that one extra notch up. And you can never hear right. There's always this low white-noise buzz. It runs under everything; muffles all sound so even half-ton horses clomping around sound about like ballet dancers.

So anyway, the horses stayed at the Garden and we stayed at the Wellington. Now, this is not a bad hotel, but it's not the Plaza, which is where people like K.C. stayed; her parents' apartment on the Upper East Side being just that little bit too far away.

The cars and the truck stayed in a parking garage across the street from Penn Station. Let me tell you, that was hard to get used to. Even in the other cities we'd driven everywhere and we would've here, too, if Tory had her way. Having no car meant having no glove box and while we weren't using it quite like we used to, she still wanted the option.

We'd gotten into town Monday morning and Linda'd sent me and Tory to the hotel, told us to check in. Turned out they didn't have the right number of rooms. I lost track of the negotiation, but by the end Tory'd wangled a room for Carl and a suite for us to share with Linda. Tim, he was staying with the horses again.

I didn't think this was smart—staying with Linda—but Tory kept saying it was. Saying so in a way that made me think she still didn't know what had gone on in Philly and Newport. All that had stopped, stopped when Linda gave Tory the rig with the ampules, when I had to rest my leg. I knew I'd been missing it and lately the missing had turned into longing for it.

When we got up to the suite there was a bedroom off a living room. One bedroom with two beds. We took the one by the only window, which didn't look out on anything, but it gave enough light that we drew the curtains. Then we had our hits and lay down. Could keep this reverse schedule all week because, like I said, we had to do the riding at night.

I didn't sleep so good, didn't even come down good, and I

don't think Tory did either. Couldn't fault the stuff, though. It was us. The drive up from Washington hadn't been long enough to absorb all the speed we took. I could see Tory working this into an excuse to get a second ampule from Linda, or maybe try for something else altogether.

I didn't want to wait that long and offered my stash mostly because I couldn't stand how I felt.

"See, I knew it," Tory said.

"Yeah, well, like you wouldn't've."

"No, I wouldn't," she said.

"Yeah, only because you couldn't hold an aspirin for twenty-four hours."

She cooked it in a hotel spoon and then drew it into the syringe. We hadn't used one like that in a while. I mean, I'd come to admire the efficiency of the single-dose rig we had. Even liked how the steel felt in my hand. But still, I'd missed these ones. How small and light they were and the way you could put anything in them; weren't dependent on those ampules, which were sleek and professional and impossible to score.

We did the whole packet and that put us down. That on top of the hydromorph. So when Linda came in and started banging around, she woke us. Of course, that didn't mean we got up and so she came to us.

"You two can't even check into a hotel?"

"Got the best we could," Tory said.

"Yeah, right. Congratulations."

"Hey, come on. There's a whole bar in there, did you see it?"

Linda's face twitched just this littlest bit from pissed off to happy. She wandered out there and we heard ice going into a glass. I could smell the bourbon. I swear I could. A little while later, Tory and I managed to get ourselves out there. Sat on the couch and smoked cigarettes while she had her drinks.

We had to go out that night. If we didn't, we'd fuck ourselves up. Get our sleeping back the wrong way. The bar for this town was Trader Vic's. Not for Linda and Carl, though. They headed for Times Square and while I could see what they'd do there separately, I didn't want to picture them there together.

When we got to the Plaza and down past the Tiki idols, the first person we saw was K.C. She greeted us like we'd walked into her living room and took us back to a long table covered with a white cloth that already had some bad stains. We sat down at the end by the corner. Ordered scorpions and watched.

These were mostly the kids Richard taught. The ones usually instructed to stay clear of K.C. It looked like they'd been let off their chains. At least for this first night.

I still felt good enough from that last bang all the staring didn't bother me. Nothing did. Not even Ted, who came in just after us. He had the Canadian woman on his arm, the one closest to Tory in points. Sometimes I wondered if everything Ted did was to get Tory. If he started every day by thinking of things. And I wondered how many times she even noticed.

She sure didn't act like she noticed tonight, though I'd begun to. Not right off, but when he sent over that drink, a frothy white thing with two straws and an orchid, and then stood across the room toasting us. Well, I couldn't help it.

Tory just picked up the glass and toasted him back. Then she kissed me. Put her tongue down my throat with everyone watching. And then afterwards laughed, while my face burned clear through to my skull. Even the back of my head burned and buzzed. And I knew this was at least partway from liking it. We stayed until the place closed. K.C. walked us out to the curb. Hailed us a cab. Did this as soon as Tory'd mentioned walking.

I watched K.C. wave us away. Watched until Samuel, who

she still had in tow, came out with her stole and her Stoli. He put the fur around her shoulders and the drink in her hand like they'd been married for years. It made me sad, but then that might've been my hit wearing off.

When we got back to the room another one was waiting for us. Linda must've come in and gone out again. She'd put ampules on our pillows, next to the mints. I guess we were all getting a little flashy and reckless.

34

We handled the first day okay. Our trouble started that night, late, when we got back to the hotel. Linda came back with us instead of just giving us ampules and she didn't give them to us once we were in the room either—the living room—and Tory, already she was pacing around from waiting.

I rested against an armrest, then slid sideways into a chair. Linda took over the couch. Had the boxes open on the coffee table and this reminded me of home in Virginia and that tipped me to what was coming, though really I'd understood it before. Had known we'd go back to this, just didn't know when. But then my believing had become so tied to my wanting that I feared I'd made a mirage just to keep myself moving.

I watched Linda draw Tory's shot, a sizable one, and when she started to put the bottle away I held my hand out and she passed it to me. The bottle was one of those ones you have to turn sideways to read. It was something called Numorphan. Oxymorphone it said underneath in parentheses and I thought, that's fitting. The rest of the label was just quantity and contents and though none of it meant much to me I read so intently I didn't realize Tory was watching me, not until she said, "You planning to drink that or something?"

She said this so nasty, I nearly thought she'd caught on to Linda and me. Tory sat on the coffee table now, with her head turned toward me and Linda pressing at her neck. I looked away when Linda stuck her and Tory started to say something about this, about me not looking, but Linda told her to shut up and keep her throat still.

This stuff hit her very fast. Not more than a few minutes before both me and Linda were carting her into the bedroom, getting her out of her clothes, tucking her in. Then we went back into the other room. She gave me a brand name hydromorph, Dilaudid this time. I didn't get even half what she'd given Tory. It came on slower, too, and in those extra minutes she told me to go in and wait for her.

I got undressed and into the other bed. Lay on my side looking at Tory. This part had been bad enough with the rooms next to each other, but having her in the next bed, not six feet away? I started to roll over so I couldn't see her but then heard Linda come in. She went over to Tory, which confused me, got me thinking a minute she might turn things way up, especially I thought this when she put her hand under the covers and I heard some little sound come out of Tory.

But a moment later Linda got up again. She dropped a little piece of gold foil on the nightstand, a wrapper, and then I knew what she'd done was make sure Tory'd stay out. Maybe she'd done this the other times, too, and I just hadn't seen it. I tried to remember something like this but couldn't.

When she came to me, I slid onto my stomach, kept my head turned toward the wall. While it seemed Tory'd had enough to stay dead for days, I couldn't get down where I needed, not with her right there I couldn't. Linda stayed patient with me, with my squirming and tightness. She touched me a lot trying to calm me and then she'd try and get in but I'd still be too tight and not easing up, not a bit.

She took her hand away for a short while and then I felt her fingers near my ass, slipping something small and soft into me and I knew there'd be another one of those wrappers on the table next time I looked.

I went down pretty fast after that. Maybe it was just knowing she'd given me more, or maybe it was where she put it, which seemed to make the rest of it smoother, let her get further easier and let me just let her. So this should've been better but wasn't and I don't think she liked it so much either. And besides, this way I got no second shot, and that's what I'd been craving so hard—that shot being all about where she put it. That next morning, which really was midafternoon, I woke up in bed next to Tory, though I couldn't remember getting there. I didn't hear Linda and didn't see her when I went to the doorway and scanned the living room. I relaxed a little from her not being there. Went back to the bed and gave Tory a shove, she stirred a little but not much. I was feeling pretty groggy myself, so I dug out that coke vial I had and took a couple of bumps from it.

Tory held her hand out and I gave it to her. She started the way I had, with little taps onto the back of her hand, but soon enough she'd dumped all of it onto the night table and tore a piece from the room service menu, rolled it to snort through. Then she got up and took a shower.

We took a cab to the Garden and on the way she told me she'd get us more coke. She kept herself away from me. At least it felt like she did, but this could've been me feeling guilty. I studied her, trying to tell which it was. She still didn't seem quite awake, held her head like it was too heavy for her, and seeing this got me tearing at the seat upholstery, making a little rip in it bigger.

We got through the night. Tory perked up. We both rode fine. Then it was back to the hotel for the same routine as the last night, except when we took Tory to bed, I didn't think she hung on me quite the same way. It made me fidgety, the same as I'd got in the cab from her nodding, and this made it harder for me to go down and so everything hurt more but later on it meant I got that other shot, got to really come off. And now with that to count on, I stopped fidgeting over Tory.

Two nights later I started worrying again when I found her hunched over in Huey's stall banging coke. She didn't see me until she'd finished—was zipping her pants when she looked up. She gave me one of those smiles that just barely still worked, did this while she pocketed the syringe. I just stood there dumb because exactly what could I say? I figured my need for what I got was making her need for this and so I kept quiet about it. I didn't tell Linda.

Back at the room, my knowing and Linda not knowing, this skewed things. I kept edgy. So much so that once we'd put Tory to bed, Linda made my hit bigger than usual and then when she went to give it to me I jumped a little and she said, "You shy of me, Cowboy? After all this time?"

I hadn't been called that name in a long while and her saying it made me miss it. Made me miss everything.

She pressed at my hip until she found a place to hit and then once she'd done it, I folded—let myself sag against her so she was practically carrying me to bed too. Being underneath this felt different, though, like it only muffled my nerves, and so when Linda started in on me, I fought her. Really fought her this time until she began smacking me, until she socked me once pretty good.

We'd made noise doing this and now with the way she fucked me I couldn't help crying out and then just crying, still I don't believe any of this was what woke Tory. I think she'd been awake all along and it was this made her get up. What I noticed first was her pulling on her jeans. We'd left them lying on the bed and somehow I turned and I saw her pulling at them and then, as if in the same motion, she was up and pulling at Linda and then yelling, "Get the fuck off her."

Linda wheeled on her. I felt this as a twist across my legs and then she was off me. I rolled toward them, saw Linda's arm reel back, saw her punch Tory in the mouth. Tory hit back, a blow that glanced Linda's jaw when she dodged it. She hit Tory again, pounded her and then grabbed her by her pants and pulled her onto the bed. She said, "You don't want me to? Then you do it, because she sure wants someone to."

"Maybe you're the one needs fucking," Tory said and when she hit this time it landed, caught Linda in the side of the head. Soon as Linda weaved, Tory started at her pants, had the first few buttons undone and her hand inside before Linda yanked her by the wrist, did this so hard Tory yelped.

I'd stayed right there in the midst of them and now as Linda pushed Tory down, was crouched over her, my face was close to Linda's stomach and I could see that where her pants were open, there was nothing but scars, or one big scar. I started rolling away from them soon as it registered. For the first time I understood they could do things to me I'd never get over.

Linda stopped me from getting off the bed. She held my arm to keep me there and pushed Tory into me and then on me, kept yelling at her to fuck me, to go on and do it, but Tory wouldn't. Wouldn't until Linda left. When Linda went into the living room, that's when she did it, fucked me until I was so busted up I was screaming but couldn't hear it and then couldn't be sure I was screaming at all.

35

We had so little left to do—two classes tonight, a grand prix tomorrow, and with the three of us acting like what happened hadn't, it seemed we might make it. We did make it through the first class, but the next one, well, Tory'd talked about it on and off all year. The Gambler's Choice class—her favorite thing and this the only show left that has it. Every year there's talk of banning it here, too, or at least making it safer somehow. But the bottom line keeps winning. It's a real crowd pleaser, the class that sells tickets.

In this one, they put different dollar amounts on the fences. The harder the fence, the better you get paid for it. And you pick what you jump, make your own course. Can do anything you want in the time allowed, which never seems like enough. Hell, if you can find a way to go back and forth over the top-dollar fence, you can, but Tory said people who did this missed the point. That to win you had to move around more, get a rhythm and see where it took you. She claimed she never went in with a plan. Just knew which fences were where and what they paid. Knew this exactly.

However she did it, it worked. She and Huey won this one year after year. And being good at this class, better than anyone else at it, if anything still mattered to Tory, this did. She said all of show jumping boiled down to this one class. And even if she hadn't said this while she was cooking a stash, I would've gotten the point—distilled and perfect, and a joke on us all. She said they should have a cash register's cha-chunk piped through the PA right as you cleared each fence. Your rising dollar amount on the big board since "that's all this is ever about." That's how she put it.

So after that first class, Gambler's Choice was all we had left. I was on Joey, my only one for this class, and Tory was on Frisbee, always saved Huey for last.

While we schooled them, I noticed it. She'd shot herself right past her timing, was rushing everything. She'd get Frisbee under the fences mostly, pulled up in front of way too many. She kept wanting to start over.

I saw the looks going back and forth. Not just between Linda and Carl but between just about everyone else standing around. I looked at Tim. He came over and rubbed his towel across my boots. Said, "What is it with her?"

"Nerves?" I asked.

Neither one of us took our eyes off her. I didn't know about him; I was afraid to.

Finally, Carl grabbed the reins. Got Frisbee standing still and then talked very softly to Tory. He had his hand on her leg. Was soothing her with it.

I couldn't hear a word he said and was trying so hard to, I didn't notice Linda'd come up beside Tim.

She had me bend down close to her. Said, "What's she been doing?"

"Shooting coke," I told her.

"How long?"

"Two, maybe three days."

Linda patted my leg the way Carl was patting Tory's and it worried me more than anything else she could've done.

Then she went to Carl, then the guy at the in-gate. When she came back she told me she'd moved my horse ahead of Tory's. I told her fine, I didn't care, whatever.

Carl had Tory working a king-size cross rail. One way, then the other, then back again. Linda kept me working Joey. This schooling ring was as crowded as any place in Manhattan. You'd bump and bash around and every time anyone hit me, I had to keep from hitting back. I was okay, though. A little jumpy, but okay. Okay enough.

I tried to keep my mind on Joey, on what Linda was having me do. But I kept looking at Tory and Carl. Didn't notice then that the next person to bump me was Ted, bumped me and Joe hard and into a corner.

"Bugged, huh," he said. "Or buggered maybe." And he was looking at her, too.

"Shut up, Ted" was all I could come up with.

I got Joey turned round; took him back the other way to the oxer Linda had raised. I buried him to it, but he struggled over. I calmed myself down after that. Tried to. Next time I came to the fence I found a better place to it, but when we landed we nearly ran head-on into someone coming at it from the other side. That's how it was in that pit, and worse tonight with everyone steering clear of Carl and Tory.

I saw Ted go into the ring and was glad for it, both to be rid of him and because Linda said I went after him. I wanted badly to get this over with. Linda had me watch Ted, though really I was watching Tory. Tim'd brought Huey and Carl had her on him now.

I saw her bury him to three fences. Saw him trying to sort it out, take over even, but she wouldn't let him. And then Ted cruised by me and I went in; realized I'd no idea what was where so I walked Joey around. I didn't pay attention to the dollars. Wasn't like I could register amounts and start counting. Instead I paid attention to what looked hard and I could see how that'd work, too. The top-dollar fence was easy to pick out—a huge blue-and-white vertical by itself in the middle of nowhere. An invite to someone to try and dash back and forth.

I kept looking until I realized I could get nabbed for showing Joey the fences and right about then they blew the horn, which meant I only had so long to get through the timers.

Once I'd done that I forgot everything else. I hit that blue-and-white vertical first and Joey didn't blink. Then I jerked him left to a liverpool and back right to the Johnny Walker fence. After that, I gunned him around the turn to the blue-and-white again. That's when I felt it getting away from me, realized I could do whatever I wanted and the pumping started, got going to where I thought it'd split my eardrums.

I wasn't over the blue-and-white before I was planning how to get back to it. This time I did the jerking in the air and too soon. Joey couldn't help but drop his back foot.

The damn thing crashed down and it's not like they stop the clock and reset it. So Joey got left dodging poles and me, I was trying to get to the next best big-buck fence—an oxer near the in-gate.

Once we got over it, we had nothing else to get to, not fast. So I whipped him around and back to it. Did this before I saw it was only set for one way. On this side, there was just air, nothing else between the ground and the top rail. Joey put on the brakes before I did and by then we'd lost too much time to recover. The horn blew before we could get another fence in.

It'd felt so fast and furious, but when they announced my total I realized how slow I'd been, how cautious.

I didn't know Tory was going right after me. Not till we

passed at the in-gate. She looked at me like she didn't know
who I was, like maybe she didn't know who she was.

I jumped off Joey. Threw the reins to Tim and ran after Carl.
Said, "You can't let her."

"Come on," he said. "She's fine, now."

I could hear the jump crew fixing the fence me and Joey'd
clobbered. I turned to watch, watch Tory, made Carl watch her.
She acted composed, but not like herself. Something about her
this way bothered me more than if she'd been rattled.

"Don't you see, she doesn't look right," I said and though I
didn't mean to I started walking toward the ring. Carl grabbed
me around the waist. Stopped me about when the horn blew.
Right when the gate swung closed.

The gate at the Garden is a solid wall—like a hockey rink's,
only taller. You can't see over it. I followed Carl up a metal
staircase to a catwalk. Got there just in time to see Tory head for
that oxer that'd finished me.

She headed for it that same way—backwards. But she'd done
it on purpose. Right away you could see why. It gave her a
straight line, practically, to the vertical. Using that oxer backwards was the only way you could use it, but she'd been the only
one so far to realize it or at least risk it.

I wanted this to make me feel easy. Wanted to believe it
meant she knew what she was doing. Problem was, I could see it
starting. The same thing I'd felt. The thing she never let happen.

You could tell by the third fence, anyone could. She was
already across the ring in her head, but she still had to land the
fence she was jumping. She managed to, it was the liverpool,
and where I'd gone right, she went left back to the vertical, then
the oxer—first one way, then the other, and then the vertical
again.

This time she got him under it. Huey heaved over, though,
and while she knew to go to the liverpool, even started fading

out to it, all of a sudden she cut back again, made a dash for the vertical, but with her eyes fixed somewhere up in the blue seats. Two strides out and aimed for the standard, that's when she asked him to jump.

Huey hurled himself into the air. By the time they reached the fence, he'd dropped into the downside of his arc. I think I heard something first, heard Huey squealing as his knees rammed the standard. His chin hooked over it as the whole fence began falling forward and carrying him with it.

The weight of the thing somersaulted him. He tried to toss his head to get loose, then tucked it more as he flipped the rest of the way over. The fence crashed before he did, a clattering and then this huge dead thud. The only thing worse than that sound was the silence that followed. A collective intake of breath from the crowd and then nothing. This was as bad as it gets. He'd landed flat on his back, his body stayed just like that before rolling over.

Tory'd gone to the far side of him. Had gone off him that way so I couldn't see her. I started over the barricade and first Carl tried to stop me, then he followed me.

Somehow Linda got out there before either of us. The three of us were running, but then she stopped, and we saw why, and we stopped. It was the angle Huey's head was turned. And then there was Tory, sitting in the dirt beside him. I couldn't hear what she was saying and I made myself walk closer until I knelt down beside her.

"Huey, come on and get up," she was saying. And she kept saying it. And the worst thing about being that close was you could tell he was breathing.

"Tory," I said, but it was Carl who got her out of there. There was no way else to do it. He picked her up and carried her. I started to follow them, but Linda said, "I need you here."

"What for?" was what I wanted to say, but I crouched beside

her. Her hands trembled. She didn't know where to touch him, what to do. Somebody needed to know what to do.

Finally they sent a vet out to us. And then, because there was no choice, they brought out the forklift. One they used for moving the fences, and the tractor with the flatbed trailer came behind it. Linda was asking the vet if it was okay to move him. Her face had never looked so young to me before.

All the vet said was it wouldn't hurt him and so she and I held his head when they hoisted him and just about every guy on the jump crew helped get him onto the flatbed. We rode with him out of the ring. They couldn't get that tractor back very far and so Richard, who'd wound up with the stabling near the schooling ring, gave us the closest stall.

Getting Huey in there wasn't easy, but Linda insisted. Her and me and all those guys, we somehow managed. Then she had everyone get out, even the vet. Me, she sent to get her box. When I got back there, to our stalls, I found Carl and Tory and Tim, too.

I didn't wait, I just picked up the box and started back, but Tory's voice stopped me.

"Wait, I'm coming with you," she said.

Carl stopped her. Said, "No, darling, you stay here with me." Then he told Tim to go get a cab and hold it for him.

I looked at him. You understand—I couldn't look at her.

"I'll take care of her," he said. "You go on."

It wasn't until then I knew I wanted it the other way around, but I brought the box to Linda, the black one. I knew it was the one she'd meant. Her hands fumbled the combination. She had to do it three times before she got it open.

All this time I held Huey's head. He was very quiet. Linda said twice she didn't think he could feel anything, that she was sure he couldn't feel anything.

I kept petting him and tugging his forelock. Then I remembered to pull on his tongue. He always liked that. He liked you to pull on his tongue.

I didn't see Linda set up the shot. I didn't see anything she did, not until she held the syringe up to clear it.

"You have to do it right now?" I asked and when I saw her face I felt real bad for having said it.

She said, "It can't be soon enough for him."

I pulled his tongue while she did it, I watched his eyes, but they didn't change. The thing that changed was his breath. I felt it a little while longer, but not by the time she took the needle out.

I didn't let go of him, though. Didn't want to, not yet. And I didn't think Tory'd want me to. She wouldn't want me to just get up and go, not right after.

I don't know how long Linda let me stay there, but I know she stayed with me the whole time. She sat across the stall, her legs flat out in front of her and the box still open and not very far away.

Finally, I heard her close it. Then she came over and took my hands off him. She got me up on my feet, and then she held on to me. She said, "Look, Tim'll go back with you."

"I stayed this long, I can stay," I said.

I felt her hands in my hair and then I was holding her, too. And she said, "Sure you can, okay, sure you can."

36

We had things to do before we went back to the hotel. Things that had to be done right away. People helped us and we held together. Well, I did until they dismantled that stall and started wrapping Huey in some big green-black tarp. The people from the city did this before they carted him away.

I couldn't watch it. Neither could Tim and so he and I went back to the stalls and waited for Linda. He took out his pipe and we started smoking it right there and then and the opium in it settled my stomach.

When Linda came, all three of us went out to the street. No one was going to make Tim spend the night there, that was sure. So we all got in a cab and rode the twenty blocks or so quiet. The cabby could tell to leave us alone.

When we got up to the room, Carl met us at the door like he'd heard us coming.

"I didn't know what to do with her," he said. "She keeps crying."

"Shit," Linda said. "I forgot my boxes. I got to go back for my boxes."

"I'll do it," Tim said. "Let me do it."

You could tell by how close he'd stayed to the door that he didn't want to be here. Not right now, anyway.

"You can manage it?" Linda asked, but she was already stuffing cab fare into his hand.

I didn't want him to leave, but I couldn't go with him. Didn't want to do that either. I kept looking at the door to the bedroom, it was cracked a little ways open but you couldn't hear anything, couldn't see anything.

Carl made Linda and me drinks and made another for himself. I could see a glass that must've been Tory's because it was in pieces beside the baseboard and wet streaks stained the wall above it.

Linda saw what I was looking at, said to Carl, "I think we better get moving as early as we can. Get her back home. I'll find someone to drive the truck. Tim can take her car. You think her and Lee should go with you or with me?"

"I don't know. You do better with her when she's like this than I do."

"Carl, honey," she said, "it's never been like this."

I started edging around the room. I knew I should go to her, I just couldn't yet. I told myself when Tim came back with the boxes, that's when I would, but being in here with Carl and Linda, that was bad, too. I wouldn't have thought anything could wreck them and now that it had, they were hard to be with.

I didn't know why I hadn't got wrecked yet. Guess it was why I wanted to stay away from Tory. I kept seeing her sitting there and telling Huey to get up. And thinking about this made me want Tim to get back here. Wanted his pipe because without it I thought I'd get sick.

I went into the bedroom, thinking I was heading for the bathroom. I heard Carl and Linda stop talking, felt them watching me. There was no light on in there and I didn't turn one on. I just went over to the bed. I sat down on the side by the window because that's the way she was facing.

She wasn't sleeping and she wasn't crying, though you could tell that she had been. Crying, I mean. You could tell by her breathing. The long ones shook and the short ones were raspy.

I found her hand and I held it and I patted her and after a while she said, "Linda took care of him?"

"Uh huh," I said, "she took good care of him, honey."

"You, too?"

"Uh huh."

Seeing her still dressed in her riding clothes, with her boots even, I didn't like that. I pulled her boots off for her, loosened her collar. She still had her fucking coat on and it was hard to get her out of it.

I still had mine on, too. Had the whole time and only yanked it off now, and my boots. Then I got in the bed with her. Got behind her and put my arms and legs around her; held her tight as I could.

Soon I heard voices from the other room. Heard Tim. Heard him put down the boxes. Linda came in a little after. She had the needle set up already and I couldn't seem to take my eyes off her, not until she went for Tory's throat, began kneading a big vein there.

Turning away, I caught sight of Tim. Saw him standing in the doorway just before he walked away from looking. Saw on his face how this looked to him. Realized I cared how it looked to him, though that wasn't why I said no when Linda offered me mine. I said no because of last night and tonight. Because between the two I could barely keep hold and I needed to, and if I let that stuff succor me just this once more, I wouldn't be able.

37

I knew I'd go with them because it wasn't finished. The very next day, they packed up fast.

Linda'd decided we should all drive together so I was in the back of Carl's Thunderbird, holding Tory's head in my lap, and both Linda and Carl were in the front seat, with Linda driving.

See, I couldn't walk out on them. Not right this minute. I needed to see she got home all right. After that I was turning around. Planned on staying awhile with K.C. I knew she'd be roaming her parent's apartment and figured she'd put me up, decided this because I couldn't think of another way.

I hadn't called to ask her, though. I needed to wait until I got back up to New York again. I was afraid if she someway answered no, then I wouldn't leave them and I knew I couldn't take chances with that. I'd already tried to get a flight back from Virginia. Found out the Visa card had been reported stolen way back in March. They hadn't told me right out, of course, but they'd sure said enough.

I admit this surprised me. And it kind of stung until I thought about it and then I considered myself lucky I hadn't found out in person; hadn't gone to some ticket counter and had one of those little red buttons pushed on me.

I kept the credit card, though, sort of as a reminder. I had it right in my pocket, and as we drove I stuck my hand in to feel it. Kept running my finger along the edge until it hurt, until it cut a little, until I'd finally cut my finger. In this way I made sure I knew why it was there. Knew it the same way I'd learned everything else and was still learning. Learning mostly things I already knew. And how to use them.

About the Author

Heather Lewis started riding horses at the age of four and showing them at six, and continued riding through high school. While she attended Sarah Lawrence College, her writing caught the attention of Allan Gurganus, with whom she subsequently studied creative writing. A recipient of the New Voice Award from the Writer's Voice Project, she has supported her writing by working as a bookseller, a freelance copy editor, and an advertising copywriter. She lives in New York City, where she is working on a new novel.